Ruby Hands

Winner of the Eludia Award

Hidden River Arts offers the Eludia Award for a first book-length unpublished novel or collection of stories by a woman writer, age 40 or above. The Eludia Award provides $1000 and publication by Hidden River Publishing on its Sowilo Press imprint. The purpose of the prize is to support the many women writers who meet with delays and obstacles in discovering their creative selves.

Hidden River Arts is an interdisciplinary arts organization dedicated to supporting and celebrating the unserved artists among us, particularly those outside the artistic and academic mainstream.

Ruby Hands

A NOVEL

Cheryl Romo

SOWILO PRESS

Philadelphia   2017

Author's Note: This is a work of fiction. Other than the mention of historical figures, the characters and events in this book are a product of the author's imagination. Any similarity to real people, living or dead, is coincidental and unintentional.

Cover design by Miriam Seidel
Interior design and typography by P. M. Gordon Associates

Library of Congress Control Number: 2017956327
ISBN 978-0-9994915-0-8

SOWILO PRESS
An imprint of Hidden River Publishing
Philadelphia, Pennsylvania

For Charley Roberts,
who has always stood by me,
and my parents,
who honored me with their love.

Part I

Summer 2005

JUDY GARLAND WASN'T supposed to be here. Rather than Nirvana or the Stones, the morning drive-time jocks on San Bernardino's golden oldies station had inexplicably gone mushy and were playing "Over the Rainbow."

The song reminded Daisy of when Judy Garland belonged to Easter and family—grandparents, uncles, aunts, assorted cousins—who would arrive at the green house next door to Grandma's for Sunday ham, mashed potatoes and boysenberry pie. Cocktails in hand, the guests would laugh and sing until Dorothy found black-and-white Kansas again. Once her parents were in bed, Daisy and Kevin would sneak outside in their pajamas to count the few stars bright enough to shine through L.A.'s smog cover.

Daisy didn't need reminders of the past. She punched the CD button and heard Nat King Cole crooning "I'm Lost." But Cole was her mother's favorite singer. She could almost see her long-dead parents gracefully dancing barefoot across the living room floor. They were beautiful then, like movie stars.

She turned off the music and glanced at the medallion of Jizo, the Buddhist god of compassion, hanging on the mirror in front of the strawberry air freshener that had lost its scent months ago.

Kevin, a sailor, had sent Jizo, the god who was supposed to help people in trouble, from Japan a few weeks before he disappeared on his way home. The Navy insisted her little brother must have fallen overboard or committed suicide. Daisy knew better.

On this morning, nothing felt right. The medallion swung from side to side. "Damn it, Jizo," Daisy said. "I could use a little help here. I'm trying to focus on the positive."

Positive: The monsoon season, which brought flash floods to the northern Arizona desert, was late this year. There hadn't been any electrical storms to knock the power out or bring down trees. The sky was clear, with just a scattering of cumulus clouds. Los Angeles–bound water in the Colorado River, just beyond the ridge, sparkled. The last of the spring flowers, white desert lilies, were in bloom—and the rattlesnakes were in hibernation, making it safe for her children to play outside. Plus, there was a pound of hamburger in the refrigerator and a box of macaroni-and-cheese in the cupboard. Gabriel and Dora wouldn't go hungry tonight.

But Daisy was driving with the windows down because the air conditioner in her Ford Escort didn't work. The desert temperature would hit 110 degrees before the day was out, and she didn't look forward to driving home feeling like fried bacon. Already nauseated and dehydrated, she brushed stray wisps of hair away from her eyes, used the back of her hand to wipe rivulets of sweat off her forehead, and pushed the gas pedal down. For two weeks, she'd felt like shit. Last night her hands had been so shaky that she painted her toes, instead of her toenails, ruby red.

She was late for work—again. But this time it wasn't because one of the children couldn't find a homework assignment or the dogs had gotten out through the broken gate or Harlan, her ex-husband, drunk as usual, had broken into the house. This time she was late because of a headache, a monster headache that had kept her up most of the night with shooting pains that ran behind her eyes and made her head feel like it was going to explode. Always a careful driver, Daisy clutched the wheel with both hands and eased up on the pedal until another shooting pain, this one so intense she could barely keep her eyes open, forced her to swerve.

One phone call. Just one phone call to the boss and she could hang a U-turn and drive home. Gabriel and Dora had already left for school and wouldn't be back until the afternoon. If she could keep her eyes open long enough, she planned to collapse on the king-sized bed with the faux leopard-print spread, the unmade bed with the fancy French ironwork headboard in the master bedroom where she and Harlan, who once loved each other, had made love until they didn't.

Now the bedroom was where Daisy slept alone. It was the sanctuary where she kept the Compaq Presario computer Aunt Kate had sent from New York for her thirtieth birthday. The computer had become Daisy's window to a world outside of a decaying town. Lately she'd been plugging into chat groups and talking to strangers, people who didn't know she was being pummeled and harassed.

In the beginning, Daisy thought it was her fault that Harlan didn't love her anymore. She began wearing makeup and lost ten pounds, even bought a pair of red bikini panties. None of it mattered. When Harlan fractured her wrist and blackened her eyes, three women from the domestic violence center came to visit Daisy in the emergency room at the hospital. They said no one had a right to hurt her. She wanted to believe them. Even her ex was scared after she called the cops, at least for a couple of minutes. But the cops never did anything. From then on, Harlan hit her where no one could see the marks.

Next to Daisy's bed sat the wooden desk her father, Philip Prout, had built in the garage one summer from wood he'd salvaged after the bowling alley fire. When Daisy was twelve, her father died. That's when Daisy's already high-strung mother really flipped out. Mad at the world, Celeste Prout sold the green house and severed ties with the rest of the family. She cashed in Philip's insurance money, boxed up her bowling trophies and dragged Daisy and Kevin to the outskirts of nowhere.

Mesquite was five miles outside Parker, Arizona. The community—a modest housing development with a clubhouse, boat docks and beach access on the river—was rumored to have been financed by a Las Vegas–based organized crime family looking for a quick way to diversify some business interests. At first, the community seemed a going concern until the developers pulled out and filed for bankruptcy. That's how the tribal council ended up, without much success, trying to run a half-built resort.

By the time Celeste and her children moved to Mesquite, it had become a run-down fly speck in the desert populated by drifters, loners and retirees overwhelmed by the stresses of urban life. Once situated in her new environment, Celeste began painting landscapes and took up semi-permanent residence on a barstool at the American Legion Hall, the white tilt-up building with the giant "Bud" sign in the middle of town. Daisy and Kevin largely fended for themselves in a three-bedroom tract house on reservation land leased from the Colorado River Indian Tribes. It wasn't a tough life. While the children missed their family and friends, they grew to love the desert and the people who thought the purple mountain range and the land below it sacred. Daisy, whose brown hair turned gold in the sunlight, had her father's dimpled chin and a sweet smile. She was a curious, bright child who laughed easily. Kevin, on the other hand, was mischievous. Small for his age, he had his mother's red hair, freckles and blue eyes.

On weekends, Daisy and Kevin roamed the desert roads on fat-tired bicycles. They liked to spend time with the Grannys, two dark-skinned tribal women who lived in a wood-frame home that had once been used for an Army barracks and later for housing forcibly relocated Japanese Americans during the war. The Grannys, Mabel and Tillie, raised goats and chickens and taught their "little white Indians" to garden, care for the animals and do beadwork. When supervised, the children's small fingers were particularly adept at creating beaded necklaces and earrings sold as "genuine Indian handicrafts" at tourist shops and the local bus station.

Thanks to encouragement by her school teachers, Daisy developed a passion for books and, as an adult, kept her latest favorites—Sue Monk Kidd's *The Secret Life of Bees*, Betty Louise Bell's *Faces in the Moon*, and Robert Hellenga's *The Fall of a Sparrow*—on her father's desk next to neatly stacked college textbooks. After Daisy's divorce, she had qualified for Pell Grants for low-income students, and now she was scheduled to graduate in September with a bachelor's degree in education from a University of Arizona satellite program. She'd applied for, and been offered, a full scholarship to attend graduate school in Phoenix.

Even in hard times Daisy had accomplished more than just being the battered ex-spouse of Harlan, a defrocked Pentecostal preacher, who'd lately been working as a drug dealer. These days only Gabriel and Dora made sense to Daisy—and, to a certain extent, the little kids she taught each weekday, mostly dark-eyed children at the reservation preschool who were eager to learn to read and write. They liked their teacher (called her "Miss Daisy") and brought her gifts of drawings and macaroni necklaces that she displayed on a bulletin board covered in red construction paper. But Daisy couldn't earn enough on a teacher's salary to support her family, and Harlan hadn't bothered to pay child support.

Things might have been different if Harlan had recognized the divorce granted by the family court in Parker. According to him, the *Bible* says men are the only ones who can divorce their "harlot spouses." So, when he was served with divorce papers at one of his girlfriends' homes, he got drunk and beat Daisy. Over the next two years, six restraining orders were issued by a judge. Harlan didn't recognize those either. He continued to stalk and harass her while law enforcement looked the other way. Most of these violent episodes, as later itemized in police reports, were described as "family beefs."

Daisy tried to tough it out. Neighbors, aware of the family's precarious financial situation, sometimes rang the doorbell and anonymously left food on the porch. Every Christmas Eve, Daisy went shopping at the Dollar Store with money she earned recycling bottles and cans collected in the desert on weekends. Daisy had inherited her mother's house in Mesquite and lived there with her children. But Harlan told everyone that it was his, bought and paid for. Of course, everyone knew it was a lie—just as everyone knew it was dangerous to cross the town bully.

One phone call, just one phone call. Daisy reached for the faded turquoise backpack on the passenger seat, but the strap caught on the gearshift handle, spilling the contents onto the floorboard in a heap: cell phone, lip gloss, wallet, loose change, nail polish, help-wanted ads, chewing gum . . . Her head was throbbing; black spots were floating in front of her eyes. She leaned down to retrieve the phone and felt the car veer to the right before the front tire sank.

It was a roller coaster ride: sliding, twisting, smashing, and tumbling down a steep embankment toward the dry riverbed. Upside down, right side up, upside down, right side up. Falling, jolting, rolling . . . The sound of branches snapping as the vehicle screeched and crashed through sagebrush. Daisy screamed. Her forehead smashed against the windshield and she heard the glass crack. The airbag slugged her in the chest and propelled her backwards as it inflated. The vehicle's metal groaned—before the carcass became a dead heap in a cloud of swirling dust.

Everything stopped until Nat King Cole began singing again.

Daisy was terrified. Realizing the cell phone was still in her hand, she elbowed the airbag out of the way and managed to lift the phone to eye level. She squinted in the dust to read the lighted dial. Hell, the worst they could do was fire her, right? One phone call would do it. She punched speed dial and told the answering machine: "Sorry. This is Daisy Sandoval. I'm going to be late for work. I've been in an accident."

The phone dropped from limp fingers as her eyes closed. Daisy was spinning, floating, surrounded by lavender flakes that looked like butterflies. Everything went white . . . She saw Kevin smiling at her. *Kevin, why are you here?* She heard other voices. *Am I dead?* Blood rushed to her head and she knew she was upside down. Hands were reaching for her, pulling at her arms. Her legs were pinned by something. She was in the middle of a tug-o-war. She felt no pain, nothing.

"Oh my God." It was a man's voice followed by another. "Is she all right? Get her out of there, quick. This thing could explode." More pushing, pulling, shouting. "Daisy, you okay? Open your eyes. Look at me."

She blinked and saw black eyes and a long nose. She could see pores, almost count them, in a mass of leathery wrinkles surrounded by straight black hair covered with dandruff flakes. *Wait a minute. I know this guy.*

. . .

Tommy Mesa, a tribal handyman who moonlighted as a bill collector for the utility company, was driving with a coworker when he noticed a cloud of dust in the ravine and realized there must have been an accident. Tommy, a full-blooded Mohave called "Big Nose" by friends, pulled his silver Chevy pickup to a stop and ran down the hill. Right away, he recognized the car, a battered Ford Escort. Only last week, Tommy had seen the car in the driveway when he knocked on a door to demand a $43 past-due payment to keep the electricity on. Daisy Sandoval had managed to back him off by lying that the check was in the mail. Tommy wasn't going to push it. The woman was penniless. He saw the bikes outside and knew she had children and, without air conditioning in the desert, people die. Next month, he expected to come knocking again.

"Guess I don't have to worry about paying my electric bill anymore," Daisy said.

It was a joke. Tommy didn't understand. "I don't know nothin' about your problems, lady," he said. "The firemen are coming. They'll get you out. Don't try to move."

Sirens wailed. A fire truck and an ambulance arrived. Firemen pried open the door and two paramedics lifted Daisy out of the car and onto a stretcher. She was struggling to speak: "I have the worst headache of my life." It was the last thing she said before passing out. The paramedics examined her and determined she had a severe head injury. They called for support. Within fifteen minutes, a helicopter landed on the rural road. Daisy, now hooked to IVs and monitors, was going to a Phoenix hospital with a trauma unit that specialized in head injuries.

Tommy watched the pretty woman fly away. "*Hooro aly'ii=m*," he said. "I am sorry for you."

An hour later, the tribal police deputy who'd been busy on another call rolled in. By then, the Ford Escort had already been towed. The deputy noted in the accident report that there wasn't much to investigate. It was a clear day, no other vehicles involved, single driver, no evidence of alcohol or drugs, straight road, no skid marks. Everything that might indicate there had even been an accident, other than a scraped guard rail and flattened bushes, looked normal. There was just a mark in the dirt where the Escort had cascaded down into the drainage ditch. No witnesses, no statements to take, nothing at all . . .

Lifting his cap to wipe beads of sweat from his forehead, one of the paramedics glanced out the helicopter's window and observed that the shadow on the desert floor looked like a giant dragonfly zigzagging toward home. After less than thirty minutes, the aircraft was approaching its destination and, in moments, would land on the helipad marked with a cross. On the roof of the four-story hospital, two nurses and a doctor waited for Daisy Sandoval. St. Andrew's Hospital, endowed by the Goldwater family and others belonging to Arizona's ruling elite, was one of the best trauma care facilities in the country, famed for its neurological institute and Ian McPherson, the chief brain surgeon.

"She's not going to make it," the paramedic said.

"Don't say that," his partner replied. "It's bad luck. Besides, she might be able to hear you."

"I don't think she's hearing anything. My God, she's young. Good-looking woman. I think I've seen her somewhere. What was the name?"

"Daisy Sandoval."

"Sounds familiar. What a waste. One of the guys at the scene said she has kids."

The other paramedic frowned and looked closely at the woman's face. "Tribal member?"

"Could be, considering the hair style. That's it. I remember her. She used to date that Mohave dude who became famous. Big war hero who died a while ago. You know the one. Someone's going to be sad tonight. At least we don't have to see it."

A rush of wind caught the chopper's tail and the aircraft swayed. Daisy groaned and tried to move her arms, but she was bound, strapped in. Her eyelids felt like they were glued shut. *What were those noises?* She could hear a voice. It sounded like her father—and *that* was impossible.

Part II

THE PLANE FROM LONDON had been delayed three hours at Heathrow—and Kate Thorsen was bleary-eyed and jet-lagged after spending a sleepless night squeezed into a United Airlines economy seat between a woman with a head cold and a college student with shoulders like a football player.

Sitting in the bright sunlight, Kate wore sunglasses and rumpled clothing. Beside her was a battered carry-on bag full of dirty clothes. She was having lunch on the patio of a trendy sidewalk café on 14th Street in Washington, D.C., with George Small, a senior editor at *National Geographic*. It had been twelve hours since her last meal and she polished off a tuna melt on wheat and drained the last of a sixteen-ounce bottle of diet peach Snapple. She was about to attack the potato chips when she absentmindedly rummaged through her purse and took out a rail-thin cigarette and lighter. "Last one. Do you mind?"

Aghast, George lowered his aviator glasses and looked at her. "You don't smoke," he said. "And how in the hell did you get that lighter through airport security?"

"I tend not to follow rules," she replied. "Give me a break."

"That's insane. That stuff will kill you."

"Tell me something I don't know," she said as she lit the cigarette and took a deep drag. "Sorry, it's been a long day." She savored the taste before she stood up, turned her head away and exhaled against a wall. "Ah, much better."

It took only a moment for the nicotine to clear her head. She had a late afternoon meeting scheduled with a State Department official for a new story she was working on for *National Geographic*. While she still took assignments from other publications, *National Geographic* was her main client. George had been her editor and mentor for a decade and she respected his judgment. Over the years, they'd become friends. Still, she didn't like sharing personal problems and lately she'd been feeling closed in, as if her life wasn't her own any longer.

The problems began when she wrote a story for the *International Herald Tribune* in Paris because George thought the subject matter (*xenoglossy*, the ability of an individual to spontaneously speak a language previously unknown to him) too loopy for *National Geographic*'s readership. While in France, Kate had witnessed events that she didn't want to think about, including the death of a colleague. As fate would have it, the wires had picked up her reporting for the *Herald Tribune*. It was then that she'd been approached and offered a lucrative contract by a major New York publishing house to write a book about her experiences. Of course, the publisher wanted every gritty detail. She signed the contract—and felt like a whore.

"Kate, you okay? What's going on?"

"I'm burnt out."

"It's a common experience." George, at sixty-five, was closing in on retirement and planned to leave *National Geographic* at the end of the year to run a bed-and-breakfast in Maine with Catherine, his wife of forty years. Some days he felt his life was ending. Maybe it wasn't, but it felt like it. Yet he was concerned about the future of the freelance journalist he'd groomed after she'd left the *Christian Science Monitor*. Kate had done excellent work for his magazine until she'd become involved in what he called "that mess in France."

It was time for a sales pitch. "I'd like you to consider working for us as a staff editor," he said. "I want you to be ready to take over my job when I retire. You'd be a good fit. The rest of the staff likes you. Hell, you can even drag Terry around with you."

"I'm not with Terry," she said. "He's just a friend and lives in Paris, remember?"

So that was it. After ten years of living out of a suitcase, chasing dreams of independence, Kate Thorsen, award-winning journalist, was being offered the glorious opportunity to become a drone tethered to a cubicle in a drab D.C. office. And, worst of all, her boss was now trying to orchestrate her love life.

"Come on, you know I care," George said. "Terry would follow you to the moon if you asked him. Look at it this way: It's ugly out there. Newspapers and magazines are folding all over the country and damn good journalists are out of work. How long do you think you can float out there as an independent contractor?"

He didn't get it. Kate put her elbows on the table and leaned forward. "I *don't* know how long I can last," she said. "Cut me some slack for trying."

"Honey, come in from the cold. I'm offering you a steady paycheck and health insurance. For god's sake, how long has it been since you've seen a doctor or a dentist?"

Kate wanted to vomit. "I'm flattered, really I am. You've always been good to me, but I've spent much of my life working for lousy bosses in organizations that ended up being not worth my time. I'm sick of politics and bullshit. I want to write stories I care about. Maybe, with luck and distance, this book thing will work out and I can keep on doing what I want to do."

"Even if your book sells, and I hope it does, it's not going to give you the security you need. You're not getting any younger and there's no shame in having a day job and continuing to write."

"Enough already," she said. "Change the subject."

But George wouldn't let up. "Don't get me wrong. You look terrific, but you've lost weight and now you're puffing those goddamned coffin nails. I'm concerned."

Kate defiantly re-lit the spent stub in the ashtray, took another drag and extinguished the butt. "I'm just trying to get through the day here."

George patted her hand. "Point taken. But I want you to think about my offer."

Kate groaned. "When do you need an answer?"

"Soon," he said. "I want to personally train my replacement."

By this time, Kate wished she'd skipped the Snapple and ordered a beer, maybe two. "Sorry, I'm tired from the flight and spending six months writing in a miserable Cornish cottage in a village where it never stopped raining."

"Okay, new subject." George raised his arms in surrender. "What do you want to talk about?"

"Well, I've been thinking about getting a puppy."

"A puppy? What would you do with a dog? You're never home. Listen to me, there's an offer on the table. Think about it."

"I'll consider it," she said.

"Where do you go from here?"

"After I meet with Wayne Wilson at State and get a good night's sleep, I'm going home to New York to eat Snickers bars in my own bed in my own apartment. I'm meeting my agent and editor next week to polish the book."

Kate's cell phone rang; she picked it up.

"Is this Kate Thorsen?"

The caller had an accent she couldn't place. "Who's this?"

"Not important. If you're Kate Thorsen, Daisy Sandoval needs help. She's in the hospital. Not much else to say."

Kate stood up. "What? Is this a joke? If it is, it's not funny."

There was a pause at the other end. "No joking. Daisy's my friend. If you care about her, call St. Andrew's Hospital in Phoenix. Tell them you're a relative. They're looking for a relative. It's an emergency."

The caller hung up. Kate turned to George. "Daisy, my niece, has been hurt."

"I didn't know you had a niece," he said. "You've never mentioned any family."

"You thought my mother was the Virgin Mary?"

George blushed. "What happened?"

"Well, the guy who called didn't give me much to work with. Just said contact the hospital. I haven't seen Daisy in a while.

She lives with her children on a reservation a few hours outside Phoenix."

"You're Native American?"

"I'm a mutt," she said. "Listen, I've got to make this call." Kate dialed information and got the number for St. Andrew's. Her heart raced while waiting for someone to answer. She was supposed to have gotten together with Daisy the last two Christmases, but her niece had bowed out at the last minute, saying the kids were sick. They had kept in touch by letters and e-mail until about two months ago when communication stopped. Secluded in Cornwall, Kate was immersed in her book and barely noticed. But she'd promised to be at Daisy's graduation from the University of Arizona in September.

"St. Andrew's Hospital. How may we help you?"

"I'm looking for a patient," Kate said. "Her name is Daisy Sandoval."

There was static in the background before the operator returned. "Just a moment, I'll transfer you." Kate expected Daisy to pick up the phone.

"Intensive care, nursing station. This is Jeannie." Kate explained that she was Daisy's aunt and had just learned she was in the hospital. "We've been looking for adult next of kin for three days," Jeannie said. "We're doing everything we can. Your niece has suffered a ruptured brain aneurysm. She's critical but stable, in a chemically induced coma. What we need from you is authorization for brain surgery. You don't need to be here. At this point, there's nothing you can do. All we need is a signed release form. Do you have a fax machine?"

"Listen, I'm not signing a release until I know what's going on. I want to speak to someone in charge about my niece's condition. I want to see her. Is she stable enough to wait until I get there?"

There was a pause. "Where are you?"

"Washington, D.C.," Kate replied. "I can be there in about six hours."

"She's stable enough," the nurse said. "I wouldn't delay. We'll see you when you get here."

George had overheard Kate's end of the conversation. "You want me to drive you back to the airport?"

"Would you please? They want permission to do brain surgery. I hate to ask this, but will you call the Marriott and cancel my reservation?" He nodded.

Minutes became precious. While George navigated through heavy lunch-time traffic to Reagan National, Kate called the State Department and postponed her meeting. Then she e-mailed her literary agent to let her know she wouldn't be arriving in New York due to a family emergency. Although there were long lines at the airport because of the Fourth of July weekend, not many vacationers were heading to the desert in the height of summer and she was able to purchase a ticket to Phoenix for the next flight. While waiting to board, she felt numb. She drank two cups of black coffee until her stomach burned and her head ached. While rummaging for aspirin, she noticed that the only thing she had to read in her carry-on was a copy of *The Tibetan Book of the Dead*, which she'd picked up in London. Considering present circumstances, the book took on new meaning.

Though she didn't consider herself religious, Kate did believe in moments of grace. On the flight to Phoenix, she looked out the window at the clouds and the endless stretches of brown dotted with green below. She wondered how her future might change because of Daisy. She would take the job George had offered. Perhaps she could persuade her niece and the children to come stay with her in New York until she went to D.C. Then maybe they could rent one of those old brick homes in Virginia, the ones with the big backyards. They could plant a vegetable garden. She'd always wanted to cultivate a garden. By then, they would have a puppy, maybe a cocker spaniel or a shepherd.

Kate lacked courage to face the alternative. Daisy *had* to survive. Something had gone wrong after Daisy's divorce. Kate didn't know what it was, but she knew. When she was in France, she'd called her niece and offered up her apartment and three roundtrip plane tickets. "I'm traveling constantly," she said. "Why don't you and the kids get out of the heat and stay for the summer? It's fun in the city. Who knows? Maybe I can figure out a way to come home sooner."

But Daisy wouldn't budge. "Right now, some things are going

on," she said. "Besides Gabriel and Dora wouldn't be happy in the city, and their dad wouldn't allow them to travel." Wouldn't allow them to travel? It didn't make sense. As far as Kate knew, Harlan rarely saw his children.

BLACK SABBATH'S "HEAVEN AND HELL" pumped through the speakers full blast in the smoke-filled living room, and the neighbors in the apartment next door were banging on the wall. "Turn that goddamn music down," a woman yelled.

On the couches, six adults, four men and two women, sat glassy-eyed smoking cigarettes and drinking vodka mixed with tropical fruit punch out of 32-ounce Big Gulp cups. At the kitchen table sat remnants of dinner: empty Carl's Jr. Six-Dollar Burger wrappers and French fry boxes. When Uncle Frank raised a plastic straw and offered a hit to Harlan, he passed. "I'm cool," he said. "Goin' to bed in a minute."

Patrice, Harlan's acquaintance since a love-at-first-sight encounter outside Carl's Jr. earlier in the evening, was passed out on the bed in the guest bedroom of Uncle Frank's Phoenix apartment. Gabriel and Dora were lying awake on the floor on the other side of the darkened room. They were inside red-and-blue sleeping bags once used for school and church camping trips.

Dora looked discouraged. "We've been here three days. How long do you think we have to stay? Who's taking care of the dogs?"

"Don't ask me," Gabriel said. "I don't know what's going on."

"Did Dad say anything about Mom?"

"Nah. He just said the hospital would let us know if anything changes."

"Is she going to get better?"

"Sure," Gabriel said. "She's probably going to have to go to rehab like Uncle Frank after he got shot. Couple of months and she'll be home good as new."

"Why won't they let us see her?"

"Dad said we're too young. The hospital has rules."

"I don't get it. I'm old enough."

"You're only eight. Now just go to sleep," Gabriel said, turning his back to her. "I'm tired. Maybe we can talk to Dad tomorrow when he's sober."

"Do you think he's ever sober? You know he's not supposed to drive anymore."

"I heard about it. Wait a minute. I have an idea," he said. "We could talk Uncle Frank into taking us to the hospital. We could just walk in there like we own the place. They'd have to let us in."

Dora snuggled up next to her big brother. In the morning, the eight-year-old planned to ask Patrice if she could borrow some makeup to make herself look older. "Wait, don't go to sleep," she said. "I have another question. Why isn't Aunt Kate here?"

AFTER THE PLANE LANDED, Kate rented a car and arrived at St. Andrew's, seven hours after she'd received a call from the stranger who wouldn't leave his name. It was still daylight, the sky cloudless, the heat oppressive, crickets were chirping, and steam rose off the sidewalk. She found a parking spot and speed-walked into the sprawling hospital complex, rolling her carry-on bag behind her. The hospital receptionist directed her to an elevator that went to a fourth-floor wing that housed the acute care facility. Stepping out, she passed an older couple and noticed the woman quietly sobbing on the man's arm.

There were no sounds on the ward other than the soft beeping of machines. The smell of chemicals that Kate always associated with hospitals was curiously missing in this ward, a place that seemed lifeless. It was the kind of sterility Kate had observed in coroner's offices where the clients were beyond caring. Passing through the long hallway, she saw motionless patients lying in beds in semi-darkened rooms with the only sound that of the sucking in and out of ventilators. A bright light at the end of the dim corridor beckoned. "Excuse me," she told the heavyset woman at the nurses' station. "I'm Kate Thorsen. I've come to see my niece, Daisy Sandoval."

The nurse looked up. "We've been expecting you," she said. "You're late."

"What? I just flew in. Did we have an exact time we were scheduled to meet?"

"I'm sorry, Dr. Almirante, your niece's physician, expected you earlier. He's gone for the day. I can set up an appointment for you tomorrow."

It was like talking to an automaton. "That's fine. But I'm here now and I've come a long way. I'd like to see Daisy."

"We're trying to deal with the most serious issues," the nurse said. "We're not looking at injuries she might have sustained in the auto accident."

"What accident? I don't know what you're talking about. What happened?"

"I'd like to see some identification before I continue."

The woman had to have worked for the DMV before she went to nursing school. "Fine. Here's my passport and driver's license. I spoke to someone named Jeannie earlier today. My late sister, Celeste Prout, was Daisy's mother. I'm Daisy's only living adult relative. She's divorced and has full custody of two minor children. What else do you need to know?"

The nurse handed back the identification. Then she wrote something in a chart and directed Kate to a semi-private room halfway down the hall. "Don't touch her," she warned.

"Why? I thought you said she was in a coma."

"We're having problems keeping her calm. She gets, uh, agitated. Her blood pressure rises. We don't want that."

"Okay, I won't touch her."

The nurse went back to her clipboard. Kate took a deep breath and entered Daisy's dimly lit room. It was a small, functional room. There were no chairs for visitors and barely enough space to stand because of all the equipment. There was an empty bed on the other side of the room. For a moment, Kate felt faint and held the bed rail unaware that tears were rolling down her cheeks. Nothing, absolutely *nothing*, had prepared her for seeing Daisy connected to tubes, machines and monitors. With her long eyelashes and perfectly shaped brows, Daisy didn't look injured. She looked more like Sleeping Beauty with tubes up her nostrils and an ugly hose taped and shoved down her throat.

"Oh, my sweet little girl," Kate said softly. "What happened? I'm so sorry." She lightly touched the tip of Daisy's forefinger. It felt warm. She sensed a response and leaned over and whispered in her ear: "I love you." Then she moved to the end of the bed and noticed that the hospital sheet didn't cover Daisy's feet. Exposed, they were dainty feet—and she had done a lousy job of painting her toenails red; polish was smeared onto her toes.

"Sweetheart, I promise you free manicures and pedicures for the rest of your life," Kate said. "We're going to get you well and get you out of here. I'm not going to leave you. And we'll take care of Gabriel and Dora together."

There was a soft tapping at the window. Kate turned to see two brown sparrows balanced on the window ledge pecking at the glass. "Hello, there," she said. "Daisy, we've got some friends." When a nurse entered the room, the birds flew away.

"Hi. I'm Ron," he said. "I'm taking care of Daisy this evening. And you are?"

"I'm Kate Thorsen, her aunt. I just heard about the accident."

"Yeah," Ron said, clucking his tongue as he checked a monitor. "Sorry. You'll have to leave. She's getting excited. I'm going to have to sedate her some more."

"Can I stand in the back of the room for a moment? I just got here and I've come a long way."

"Sure," Ron said. "You can't stay long though. There's a cafeteria on the third floor. Why don't you go down and get a cup of coffee? I'll be done here in about fifteen, twenty minutes."

Kate took a deep breath. Then she asked the question: "Is she going to make it?"

Ron leaned forward and lifted Daisy's eyelids. "She's very sick," he said. "You do understand that, don't you?"

"No, I don't." Kate burst into tears and pulled a tissue from her purse and blew her nose. "She's young. She's a mom with little kids. She's graduating from college in September. This can't be happening."

Ron didn't try to console Kate; he let her babble on. "You're talking to the doctor tomorrow, right?" She nodded. "You should ask him before you sign the authorization for surgery. He may have answers for you."

As Kate was about to leave the room, she noticed a bulletin

board with Daisy's name on it where previous visitors had written get-well messages and left contact numbers for hospital personnel. She pulled out her notebook and jotted down all the names and numbers. One message was from a Pastor Williams; Kate recalled hearing Daisy talk about him as if he were a close friend. Another was from Daisy's boss at the preschool. She didn't recognize the other names and saw no messages from Harlan or the children.

Kate took the elevator downstairs to the cafeteria. She drank coffee in a quiet corner and began placing calls. She needed to find someone who could tell her how to get in touch with Gabriel and Dora. She started with Pastor Williams, but he wasn't answering. She left a message. Ditto for Daisy's boss. She would try the others later. When she returned to Daisy's room another nurse had joined Ron. Whatever they were doing, it looked intense. They asked her to come back in the morning. She protested and then caved when it was obvious they didn't want her there.

It was dark outside when Kate, exhausted, drove down the nearest major street and found the Wingate Inn, a business motel whose advertising hailed it as "highest in guest satisfaction among mid-scale hotel chains with limited service." She didn't know what "limited service" meant and checked in. She placed a wakeup call for 6 a.m., ate a Snickers bar from the hallway vending machine and fell asleep in her rumpled clothes.

At midnight, she awoke hearing a voice say, "I'm very, very sick." It sounded like Daisy. The curtains in the room were fluttering erratically like labored breath. Kate felt the voice was telling her that her niece was straddling the fence between life and death. *Stay with me . . . Daisy, stay with me . . . Don't let go . . .*

THE NEXT MORNING, Kate dismissed the voice she'd heard as a symptom of her exhaustion. She took a long shower and washed her hair and put on different dirty clothes, using a washrag to blot spots off her shirt. She sprayed herself with cologne and tied her hair back in a ponytail. Not her best look, but she doubted anyone would notice or care. On the way downstairs, she made a mental note to check at the front desk after breakfast to see if the motel had laundry facilities. After a cup of coffee and an apple pastry, she learned from Dave Huntley, the Wingate Inn counterman, that there was indeed a laundromat downstairs for guests because "We're built for business."

She planned to wash clothes when she returned from the hospital and asked Dave to book her room for two more nights. "I don't know how long I'll be in Phoenix," she said. "My niece is in the hospital in critical condition."

Dave shrugged and smiled. "No problem. This time of year we don't have that many guests anyway."

Kate returned to her room to check phone messages. No calls back from the minister or Daisy's boss. There was a message from George wondering if she'd arrived safely. She left him a message saying she'd call later, she was on her way to talk to Daisy's doctor. When she opened the motel door to walk to her car, she was assaulted by a blast that felt like the inside of a furnace. It was eight a.m. and the weather service was predicting a high of 114 degrees. She cranked up the air conditioner in her rental car.

Dr. Joseph Almirante was standing at the nursing station when Kate arrived, and he led her into a sparsely furnished office with his medical degrees on the wall. The first thing he did was to explain how the hospital staff had performed an emergency procedure to save Daisy's life within hours of her arrival at the hospital. "We had to drain fluid and stop the bleeding," he said. "We didn't need anyone's permission to do that."

"But you need my permission to do brain surgery, right?"

"Yes," he said. "We're concerned that if we don't relieve the underlying pressure your niece is going to have a stroke."

"You're just treating the aneurysm? Is that correct?" He nodded. "Do you have any idea what caused it?"

"We can't be sure," he said. "Aneurysms are cowardly killers. They're balloon-like bulges that can slowly grow in the walls of brain arteries. They can go undetected because they present no symptoms until the bulge explodes, damaging the brain."

"Was the head injury from the accident?" He shook his head. "Could this have been caused by an injury sustained earlier?"

"At this point, we don't know—and it doesn't matter. We're trying to save Daisy's life. Dr. McPherson specializes in aneurysms and has evaluated your niece. He recommends operating as soon as possible. But we need your permission for the operation. And a word of caution is necessary. There's always an element of risk."

"What happens if you don't operate?"

"Complications are setting in," he said. "Without the operation, she won't survive."

Kate signed the document that Dr. Almirante passed to her. "I'd like a copy."

"Of course. Dr. McPherson will schedule the surgery, most likely tomorrow morning. We'll let you know. You can talk to him or his assistant, Dr. Bass, if you like."

"Good. I'd like to arrange to bring her children in to see her before the operation."

"How old are they?"

"Ten and eight."

"Under the circumstances, yes."

"One last thing, can I see Daisy now?"

Daisy, her breathing labored, was in a fresh hospital gown. The one yesterday had had pink flowers; this one was pastel yellow. Kate forced herself to be cheerful. "Hello, Daisy. How's my sweet girl today? I see they finally put a chair in here for your visitors. I'm going to sit down right here next to you and we can talk about stuff. I called Pastor Williams and your boss and I just talked to Dr. Almirante. Seems like a nice guy. He tells me they need to do one more procedure, so we can get you well. I'm going to find Gabriel and Dora today to see how they're doing. Maybe I can bring them here tonight. You'd like that, wouldn't you? I knew you would."

What was left of Kate's family had imploded when her brother-in-law, Philip Prout, died suddenly. At the time, Philip's children were about the same age as Gabriel and Dora. Within months, Kate's older sister moved with her children to the Mojave Desert where she eventually became what the locals called the "Georgia O'Keefe of Mesquite." When Celeste wasn't painting landscapes and portraits, she was off wandering in the hills. She became a leather-skinned recluse who collected colored rocks and created garden sculptures that looked like abstract paintings. After her rock creations were prominently featured in an issue of *Arizona Highways*, people drove from out of state to see them, so Celeste put a "Rainbow House" sign out front.

As the years passed, Celeste's fame as a painter and garden sculptress grew. She earned a comfortable living with outside commissions and began bringing home pickup trucks filled with rocks, which were then hefted into place at her direction by an ever-changing assortment of young protégés in tight Levis and cowboy boots. When she wasn't rock hunting or painting, the artist could generally be found in one of the neighborhood taverns, her favorite being the American Legion Hall where a country rock band played on weekends. She paid scant attention to her children.

Meanwhile, Kate, fifteen years younger than Celeste, worried about Daisy and Kevin. There wasn't much she could do for her niece and nephew, other than to spend as much time in Mesquite as possible. Back then, she was just starting out in journalism—or "paying her dues," as it's called in the trade. As a young reporter, she moved around the country from newspaper job to newspaper job covering every beat from city hall to cops. During her visits to Mesquite, however, Kate grew close to both children. Daisy and Kevin were bright and inquisitive—and seemed well-adjusted and happy, though Kevin struck her as a bit of a rebel.

After high school graduation, Kevin got out of the desert as fast as he could by joining the U.S. Navy. It was easy for Kate to understand his desire to experience more than land-locked wilderness. When Kevin was lost at sea two years later, Celeste fell apart and took off. She abandoned everything, including Daisy, then a senior in high school. Kate felt inadequate and overcome by sadness. In a desperate search for meaning, she took a job covering religion for a national newspaper in Boston and asked Daisy to come live with her. But the girl wouldn't budge. "This is my home," she said. Yet she wanted advice from her aunt about everything—from putting on makeup to boys to what books to read. Kate rarely wore makeup and her love life was nonexistent, but she could recommend books and sent them like clockwork to her niece. They would also talk by phone until Kate pleaded "red ear," their signal for sign-off.

At the same time, other threads were being woven. Daisy finished high school early and was attending college to become a teacher; she was dating a Mohave boy and working weekends at a snack bar. Pretty soon brown-wrapped care packages began periodically arriving at Kate's Boston home filled with handmade earrings in shimmering colors that spoke of rainbows and waterfalls. It turned out that Daisy was apprenticing with the Mohave grandmas whom she had turned to for love as a child. "Granny Mabel told me I have *sumach a'hot*, a gift for making beautiful things," Daisy wrote, adding that both grandmas had invited her to meet Nopah, their nephew. "He's a spirit dreamer and he might be able to tell me about Kevin and my dad."

Relieved of constant worry, Kate threw herself into her job and also began accepting freelance assignments from other publications, firmly and incorrectly believing that work could make up for the lack of a personal life. Then tragedy struck again. One year after Kevin disappeared, hikers found Celeste dead at the bottom of a remote canyon in Skull Valley. The Phoenix and Tucson papers ran obituaries on the well-known artist and her mysterious end. No one knew whether she'd fallen or jumped.

Shattered, Kate took a leave of absence from her job at the *Christian Science Monitor* and went to Mesquite to comfort Daisy. They arranged to have Celeste cremated and buried in Pioneer Cemetery on the outskirts of town—next to a marker that had been placed for Kevin, though his body had never been found. There was no funeral or memorial service for Celeste, but after the burial of her ashes, Kate and Daisy decorated both graves with American flags and used colored stones from Rainbow House's gardens as a border around the plot. They glued iridescent blue plastic hearts that lit up in the dark on tiny white trellises they planted in the ground. They then let go a bouquet of helium balloons decorated with hearts and sang Nat King Cole's "I'm Lost," Celeste's favorite song. That night they returned to the cemetery to watch the blue hearts light up—and discovered the trellises had been stolen. "Grave robbers," Daisy said. "Just my luck."

Emotional desolation is palpable. As the days passed, it became clear that mourning cannot be rushed. So Kate ended up staying with Daisy for a month and nearly lost her job in the process. "We need you back at work," the editor replied when Kate called asking for more time. She ignored her boss and somehow kept her job.

Rainbow House hadn't changed much and it looked as if Celeste had never left. The living room was still full of oversized furniture, antique tables and homemade lamps that didn't match. The wood-paneled walls were adorned with Celeste's watercolor portraits of Native Americans and abstracts of the mountains around the reservation. At some point, Daisy had moved into her mother's room with the bedroom set that had belonged to her parents. Kevin's bedroom had become a shrine. High school pennants and baseball trophies were everywhere—along with rock posters of Nirvana, U2 and Smashing Pumpkins. It was a time capsule for a boy who wasn't coming home.

Work began afresh each morning. The closets, garage and attic were packed with cardboard boxes that appeared to have been unopened since the family moved from Los Angeles a decade earlier. Something had to go. Little by little, they attacked the garage and began bringing boxes inside. They put them in the dining room around the big round table. The more boxes they opened, the more apparent it became that the house wasn't a house at all. It was a museum. "There's no way I'd ever get rid of any of this," Daisy said. "I love having our ghosts around."

While sorting through Celeste's things, Kate and Daisy grew closer. They swapped family stories about growing up in Los Angeles. Kate was amazed at how much Daisy could remember about her early life—and always blown away by how smart she was. The women went through gallons of iced green tea, chips and salsa, and fruit popsicles. They made salads and big pots of vegetable soup and served it in Grandma Ingrid's Depression-era ice cream bowls. They used the old family silver, china and crystal for elaborate candlelight dinners. Each evening, they strolled along the river. One morning, as they sat at the breakfast table drinking coffee in Celeste's psychedelic-colored mugs, Daisy asked if Kate wanted to see the family jewelry.

"Of course," she replied. "I didn't know there was any." They went to the master bedroom and Daisy crawled into the closet behind her clothes. She came out with a box covered in faded brown velvet. It was a music box that played "Clair de Lune" when the lid opened. Inside were vintage rings, brooches, gold watch fobs and necklaces. It was a kaleidoscope of color: blue sapphires, red rubies, yellow diamonds, green emeralds, white pearls . . .

"Oh, honey," Kate said, her heart sinking. "This is heirloom jewelry. It might be worth a fortune. For your safety, don't wear it anywhere or show it to anyone. There are a lot of creeps out there. Why don't we go to town tomorrow and put all this in a safe-deposit box at the bank?"

Daisy pouted like a stubborn child.

Frustrated, Kate asked: "Why not? You could sell some of it, couldn't you? At the very least, we could have the pieces appraised and insured. This shouldn't be sitting around your house. I'm going to be a nervous wreck worrying about some burglar breaking in when you're home alone."

"Listen, I'm not selling anything," she said. "I like to have the things I care about close by. Nothing bad is going to happen. The worst has already happened. Except for you, my family's gone. This jewelry is for my kids, the ones I'm going to have someday. I want to be able to tell them stories about our family."

O child of noble family, listen with undistracted mind.

A year later, Daisy called to say that she'd broken off with Leon Blue, her longtime boyfriend, and was marrying Harlan Sandoval, a Pentecostal preacher. She asked her aunt to be the maid of honor. Kate was confused. She'd met Leon and liked him. He was older, worked for the tribal council, and had served time in the military. He had an incredible smile. "You sure you're not moving too fast?"

"I know what I want and this is it," Daisy said. It was the same stubborn tone she'd used when they'd talked about Celeste's jewelry. "Harlan's an amazing guy and we're in love. We're going to have lots of babies."

The wedding was a simple ceremony with a handful of guests. Daisy wore a long white cotton dress and carried a bouquet of sunflowers tied with pastel ribbons—and the groom wore a white tuxedo. Kate had to agree that Harlan Sandoval was good-looking and charming, almost too charming. Six months later, Gabriel was born and two years after that Dora arrived.

. . .

A nurse entered the hospital room. "You look like you need a break," she said. "Daisy has other visitors waiting outside. Why don't you go get something to eat? It's lunchtime. She'll be fine and she'll have plenty of company. Her friends are just down the hall."

Two women and a man were standing by the elevator. "You must be Aunt Kate," one of the women said. "I'm Abby, Abby Nelson. This is Dan Martin and his wife, Maria. We went to high school with Daisy. She was always talking about you. When did you get here?"

Kate recognized the names from the hospital bulletin board, but her niece had never mentioned these friends to her. "I arrived last night," she said.

"How's she doing?"

Abby's question sounded reasonable. But Kate wasn't sure who was asking, as if it mattered. "She's alive. The doctors want to operate tomorrow. Do you know where Gabriel and Dora are? I want to bring them to the hospital."

"They're with Harlan," Abby said. "I think they're staying with one of his uncles in Phoenix. I'm sure Pastor Williams knows how to get in touch with them. He's been at the hospital. Did he call you?"

"No."

"Did the hospital call you?"

"No."

"How did you find out?"

"Some guy who wouldn't leave his name called me," Kate said. "Sorry, I'm feeling a little shaky right now. I need something to eat."

"Listen, why don't you call Harlan's mother? Mama Lou knows where the kids are staying. I've got her number right here if you need it."

Kate flinched at the memory of Harlan's mother at Daisy's wedding. Who could forget the loud woman with the big red hat?

Lou Sandoval put Kate in touch with Harlan. Kate arranged to pick up Gabriel and Dora that evening. Back at the motel, she looked in the bathroom mirror and saw a stranger. She was falling apart. The lines in her face looked deeper, her eyes were swollen and red. Tomorrow Daisy would live or die—and Kate Thorsen, the reporter who thought she could fix anything, could do nothing.

The building where Harlan's Uncle Frank lived was on the outskirts of Phoenix. Sweating in the heat, Kate walked in circles trying to find the right apartment number. When she'd talked to him earlier, Harlan didn't seem to have a clue about where he lived. One of his friends came on the line with bizarre instructions for how to twist and turn through the complex: "You go past the carport with the old green Oldsmobile with two flat tires. Turn left. Then go two buildings to the right past the brown dumpster with graffiti on it. Go down the alley to the right and around the corner to the first apartment, the one with the blue door."

Once she finally found the place, she was assaulted by blaring music. Harlan was drunk, bare-chested, barefoot, and wore gray shorts. He had a malt-sized can of Budweiser in one hand and a lit Marlboro in the other. Gabriel and Dora, in oversized T-shirts, jeans and sneakers, were standing behind him. They'd grown since she'd seen them last. Kate noticed that Gabriel, wearing a Yankees baseball cap over a buzz cut, had ruddy cheeks. He was a dead ringer for Philip, his grandfather. With her turned-up button nose, Dora was adorable, little red-and-blue barrettes holding back unruly dark hair. She was a miniature version of her mother, except for big eyes that floated like black olives on marshmallows.

"Auntie Kate!" The children yelled in unison, rushing forward with hugs and kisses. They clung to her like lost puppies. "We missed you!"

The man Daisy referred to as the "Sperm Donor" after her divorce just smiled. "Hello there, Auntie," Harlan said, smacking his lips and slurring his words. "You're looking mighty fine, mighty fine."

Resisting the urge to deck him, Kate smiled and hustled the children away from their father. "We have to hurry," she said. As they were leaving, Harlan said he was sorry he was too busy to go to the hospital with them. "No problem," she said with clenched teeth, as she left holding Dora's hand and with her arm about Gabriel's shoulders. They walked in unison to the car.

"Auntie Kate, how's Mommy?" It was Dora. She was curled up in the backseat biting her fingernails. "Daddy says he doesn't know anything."

"She's pretty sick, honey, and they're going to operate on her tomorrow."

Gabriel, his hands folded in his lap, looked tense. "Was this caused by the accident? I'd like to get the facts straight."

Kate took a deep breath and spoke slowly. "The doctors aren't sure," she said. "Was your mom sick before the accident?"

"The night before," Dora said. "She had this awful headache and couldn't sleep. She was going to stay home, but she wouldn't get paid. So Mommy went to work. We heard the ambulance. Then Dad came to take us to Phoenix. We've been at Uncle Frank's ever since."

Kate was about to ask if they needed anything, when Gabriel spoke: "Is our car totaled?"

"I don't know," Kate said. "I called the police today, but they don't have the report yet. I just got here last night."

"Why did it take you so long?" Gabriel turned his head to look at her. He was angry. "Why weren't you here in the beginning? Where were you?"

Kate was taken aback. "I didn't know anything about it," she said. "A man called me after I got off the plane from England."

"Who was it? Was it my dad?"

"I don't know who it was. He just said he was your mom's friend."

"I wonder who it was," Dora said. "Maybe it was Mom's boyfriend."

"I don't think she has a boyfriend," Gabriel said. "It was probably somebody from work." The boy again put his hands in his lap and lowered the visor on his baseball cap.

"What's up with the Yankees cap?" Kate asked, trying to lighten the mood.

"Derek Jeter," Gabriel mumbled.

"What's special about Derek Jeter?"

"He's like me."

She was confused. "You're a shortstop?"

"Nah. He's mixed like me."

"Hey, Gabriel, I'm a mutt too."

"Not like me."

There was an awkward silence before Dora broke in. "Auntie Kate, do you know who's taking care of our dogs?"

"I didn't know you had dogs, sweetheart."

"Yes, we do. Mommy gave them to us for Christmas," she said. "They're pound puppies. Mitzi, the little black girl dog, is mine. Gabe has the boy dog."

Kate turned to Gabriel. "What's your dog's name?"

"Fred," he said. "He's a watchdog and he keeps the burros and coyotes away from our house at night. Mom says Fred's better than a pit bull because he's not mean. He knows how to fetch too."

"Don't worry, I'll find out about the dogs," Kate said. "Tonight we'll focus on letting your mom know how much we love her. After we see her, you guys can tell me how to contact your neighbors. I'll call and make sure someone's caring for Fred and Mitzi."

Dora let out a huge sigh of relief. "Phew," she said. "Thanks. My dad said he didn't know anything about the dogs and he wouldn't let us call anyone."

Kate squeezed the steering wheel so hard her thumbs ached. When she leaned to glance in the rearview mirror, bloodshot eyes looked back at her. She was becoming someone she didn't recognize. As they drove into the hospital parking lot, she gently tried to prepare the children for what they were about to see and explained that their mother would appear to be sleeping, but was probably aware of what was going on around her.

"I had a sense she knew it was me when I visited," Kate said.

"So, she's like Snow White or Sleeping Beauty?" Dora asked.

"Sort of . . . The doctors gave her medicine to keep her relaxed, so she can heal. When they do the operation in the morning, the doctors are going to try to remove a lump in her brain that's making her sick."

"What does Mom look like?" Gabriel asked. "Is she all banged up from the accident?"

Kate turned her head, not sure what to say, begging for seconds to translate her thoughts. "It's hard for me to explain, but your mom looks kind of normal. She has a tube in her throat and a couple of tiny ones in her nostrils to help her breathe. They had to remove a little hair on the back of her head, but you won't even notice it."

Gabriel exhaled, making a loud "whoosh" sound.

Kate continued. "There's something else—and this is important. We have to be soft and sweet when we talk to her. We don't want her to feel excited. The nurses are worried about getting her too excited. Can you handle that?"

Dora's marshmallow eyes opened wider—and Gabriel, fighting back tears, lowered his head and bit his lip. Both children said they could handle it, but admitted they were scared. As they got out of the elevator and entered the coma ward, Kate stepped between the children and held their hands tightly. They walked down the long corridor, passed all the quiet people and tiptoed into the room where Daisy waited.

The sparrows were gone. "Mommy, Mommy, Mommy!" The cry was repeated like a mantra until only muffled sobs were heard in the soft light. Kate wished she could compel Daisy to open her eyes to relieve this suffering.

O child of noble family, possessing the power of miracles resulting from karma means that now you have miraculous powers . . .

Less than an hour later, Gabriel and Dora were emotionally spent and couldn't speak. It was time to go. They drove out of the hospital complex and straight to a nearby Denny's, where they ordered cheeseburgers and fries and strawberry malts and chocolate chip cookies for dessert. The Denny's waitress put the children's leftovers into Styrofoam containers to take home. Gabriel and Dora solemnly carried the stacked white boxes to the rental car like priests transporting sacred communion vials on silver platters. Concerned about their safety, Kate didn't want to return her niece and nephew to Harlan. She suggested they stay at the motel with her. "I have two big beds and there's a swimming pool," she said.

"We want to go home to Dad," Gabriel replied. "He needs us to take care of him."

Dora nodded, smiled and rubbed her weary eyes.

This time Kate went deep inside the apartment with the blue door and snooped around like a county social worker looking for health and safety violations. She turned on lights. She opened the refrigerator and saw milk and bread and beer inside. She went into the bathrooms and opened medicine cabinets. In one bedroom, she saw the children's sleeping bags on the floor. The apartment was relatively clean. Harlan was alone, but drunker than he had been earlier in the evening. She ignored him. "You sure you kids don't want to camp out at the motel with me?"

"Nah. We'll be fine," Gabriel assured her. "We know how to handle Dad."

Still concerned, Kate gave them each business cards with the motel and her cell numbers on the back. "Call me anytime for any reason," she said. "I'll check to see how Fred and Mitzi are doing and let you know as soon as I find out. You were very brave at the hospital tonight. I'm proud of you and I know your mom is proud of you too. Say a prayer for her tonight. Prayers help."

Back at the motel, Kate called Diane, the mother of one of Dora's friends, and learned that the dogs were being kept in the yard at another neighbor's home. Kate let the children know. Just as she was about to hang up, Dora came back on the line to tell her that her father's friend came over and ate all the leftovers from Denny's. "That big jerk," Dora said. "He spilled my fries on the floor."

Kate would have used a stronger term. "I'm sorry, honey. Some grownups are inconsiderate. Stay away from the creep. How about Denny's again tomorrow? We'll get even better food and eat the whole thing. Deal?"

"Deal," Dora said. "Love you, Auntie Kate."

It was late. Kate was exhausted and sleep came easily. Two hours later, she abruptly awoke after having a dream about a little girl with a rainbow halo holding hands with a boy whose head was shrouded in dull, smoke-colored fog. She heard movement in the room and switched on a lamp. The bulb blinked and pinged. She got out of bed and turned on more lights. There was no one there, but she saw a disturbance, like heat rising in the air, behind the reading chair. Wide awake and trembling, Kate looked at the clock: 2 a.m. Then she checked to see if the hospital had called. No messages. She called the nursing station and learned Daisy was stable and surgery was still scheduled for the morning.

WHEN THE SUN ROSE, Kate awoke and did deep-breathing exercises to calm herself. She drank decaffeinated tea, instead of coffee, and had strawberry yogurt for breakfast. When she went back upstairs, she glanced at an e-mail from George. It was a copy of the article she vaguely remembered writing about the Mohave tribe. Because of the odd dreams she'd been experiencing, one paragraph caught her attention:

In the old days, the Mohave believed they were different from other people. They believed each member of the tribe had a predetermined role to play and the creators set these roles. They were fatalists. The Mohave also believed in the power of dreams. In their world, everything was derived from dreams, including knowledge and foretelling the future. A dream could be nocturnal or through a flash of insight—and important dreams, called "power dreams" or "great dreams," always came to an individual involuntarily. In some situations, the Mohave believed, the dreamer was allowed to freely meet with spirits, sometimes in the form of a bird or other animal, on a different plane. They had highly trained specialists called "spirit dreamers." Spirit dreamers were said to be capable of bringing a soul back from the other world and, sometimes, they could induce the soul to return to its body. When the spirit dreamers themselves were near death, they were obligated to give all their knowledge away to a close relative, generally a son.

All elegance and angles, Ian McPherson looked like Liam Neeson. The tall, slim surgeon reminded Kate of a dashing matador when he swooped into the hallway practically wearing two adoring male assistants on each arm, like a cape. "We'll do the best we can." McPherson didn't say anything else before he whirled around and left with his acolytes.

While attendants wheeled Daisy out of the room, Nurse Ron squeezed Kate sympathetically on the shoulder. "She's in the best hands," he said. "Why don't you go down the hall to the waiting room? There's a television and some brain-dead magazines. Whoops. Sorry, inside joke."

"No offense taken," she said. "I'm a reporter. I'm used to it."

Ron laughed. "Well, it's going to be a while. We'll come get you as soon as we know anything. Oh, if you need one, there's a chapel on the ground floor by the gift shop."

Kate thanked him and headed down the hall. Not ready for a chapel just yet, she went to the waiting room and nestled in with the Tibetans. She was leafing through the book, trying to find out the symbolic meaning of dull lights and fog, when a chipper African American woman with salt-and-pepper hair walked in. She was dressed completely in white, down to her shoes. Though she wore no hospital identification, Kate thought she might be a chaplain.

"Are you Daisy Sandoval's aunt?"

"Yes," Kate said, sitting on the edge of the chair. "Is something wrong?"

"No," she replied. "Pastor Williams sent me."

"Is he here?"

"No," she repeated. "He sent me instead. Sister Eileen will be here in a moment."

The conversation didn't appear to be going anywhere, so Kate went on the offensive: "Excuse me, just who are you?"

"I'm Sister Sarah."

Just as Kate was about to ask Sister Sarah what her job was, a Native American family quietly filed in and sat down. The old man with clear blue eyes didn't speak, but was clearly in charge. His ears were pierced and his long white braids were tied and woven with red flannel bands. Under the collar of his blue work shirt was a leather bolo held by an elaborate silver clip studded with turquoise and coral. He wore a turquoise and silver belt buckle and his jeans had faded almost white. The worn heels of his leather cowboy boots suggested a horseman. Accompanying the man was a statuesque, curvy woman with lush dark hair wrapped on top of her head in a bun. She was chewing gum and wearing a loose-fitting Hawaiian print top, black Capri pants and rubber flip-flops. Two dark-haired children—a girl of about five in a blue-and-white sundress, and a boy about seven in a T-shirt and jeans—sat down and stared intently at Kate. They didn't say anything and didn't stop staring.

"Nopah," the old man finally said. She thought it was his name. "Nopah," he said again, smiling at her as if she was odd.

"Hello to you too," Kate said, trying to figure out what was going on.

The Native Americans were followed in by a bouncy woman dressed in a frilly white cotton dress with ruffles on the skirt. She introduced herself as Sister Eileen and sat down in the last vacant chair, opened her purse, pulled out a bottle and began rubbing hand lotion on her legs. Soon the room smelled of coconut. "Dry skin," Sister Eileen said. "Want some?"

Kate shook her head.

No one spoke again. Kate returned to her reading, the women in white were sharing a leather-bound Bible, the adult Native Americans sat expressionless, and the children watched cartoons on a television set mounted on the wall. Two hours passed this way before Nurse Ron entered the room. "The surgery went well," he said. "Daisy's in the recovery room. You should go get some lunch. You must be starving."

Instead, Kate went outside to call Gabriel and Dora.

"Mommy survived the surgery!" Dora was cheering.

"I'll call as soon as I know anything else."

After she hung up, Kate returned to the waiting room because she'd forgotten to collect the Tibetans. The book was on a table where she'd left it, but the room was empty, except for the lingering smell of coconut. When she was allowed back into her niece's room, her heart sank. Daisy's coloring was wrong: she was yellow. On her head she wore a crown of hideous black wires. Was it wise to let Gabriel and Dora see their mother this way? She called Harlan, saying she would pick up the children in the morning because Daisy was still in recovery. As lies go, it was a small one. Better that she maintain a solitary vigil.

O child of noble family . . .

That night Kate dreamed of a blue butterfly. At first she thought it was a playful, happy dream. The butterfly flew gracefully through an open window of a tall, white building. It flew around the room fluttering its wings before it alighted on a lovely piece of polished rosewood in the shape of a rectangle. The blue butterfly stopped briefly before flying up and out the window. When she awoke, Kate understood the dream: Daisy was leaving.

At first light, the hospital called to inform Kate that her niece had had a massive stroke and complications were quickly setting in. Daisy's condition was now categorized as "extremely critical." Kate threw on clothes and ran out the door. When she arrived at the hospital, a surgeon she hadn't met before was waiting for her.

"The stroke was an eight on a scale of ten," he said. "The person you knew is gone and will never come back. Another emergency surgery has been scheduled for this afternoon. We want to remove portions of the damaged brain. If she survives the operation, which is a small percent, she will be permanently paralyzed and could be institutionalized for the rest of her life."

Kate's voice faltered as she measured her words carefully: "What happens if you don't operate? Daisy wouldn't want to live like that. Why not leave her be?"

Hell hath no fury like a doctor questioned by a layperson. "Why . . . Why you, *you* can't decide that," he said, glaring at her. "You'll have to speak to Dr. McPherson first. This is not *your* decision to make." The physician left in a huff.

Entering Daisy's room was the hardest thing she'd ever done. A sobbing Kate was stroking her niece's forehead when, five minutes later, the resplendent Dr. McPherson and his entourage arrived. The surgeon went to Daisy's bed and lifted her eyelids and checked the monitors. He pinched her cheek.

"Ms. Thorsen," he said. "May I call you Kate?"

"Of course."

"I'm sure you have your niece's best interests at heart," he said.

"But you really need to trust me. Another surgery is necessary to keep her alive. In my experience, it's always best to let the medical professionals make these decisions. I'm sure you're aware of the risks, but whatever happens to your niece during surgery could, ultimately, help other patients."

Kate paused before replying: "I'm sure you're a fine doctor, but you don't have to live with the consequences. I've been told that Daisy, the Daisy we know and love, is already gone. Believe me, this isn't easy. But I'm the adult family member here and I'm the one who will have to face Daisy's children. I'm also the person who knows what Daisy would say if she could speak. There will be no further surgery. I'm sorry."

Then, with a dramatic and unexpected gesture, the chief surgeon extended a slim, elegant hand. She took it. "I would have done the same thing if this were my mother or daughter," he said, glancing briefly at his patient before he swept out of the room.

Almost like magic, the women in white reappeared in the hallway before entering Daisy's room. Sister Sarah and Sister Eileen greeted Kate warmly. Then they went outside to talk to one of the nurses. The vigil was nearly over, and some of the nurses had begun giving a guilt-ridden Kate the thousand-yard stare. Nurse Ron was the exception. He glided into the room to gently explain that once the machines were disconnected it would take only minutes for Daisy to stop breathing. Kate lobbied for enough time to have the children brought to their mother's bedside. "Of course," he said.

Frantically, she called Harlan and asked him to bring Gabriel and Dora to the hospital. "Give me thirty minutes," he said. It was the first time she thought she heard a hint of compassion in his voice.

The Tibetans believe everything is transitory. They pray to the goddess of compassion: *om mani padme hum*. Kate found herself repeating the ancient mantra again and again . . . In the waning light, she thought she saw a miracle. Daisy's coloring was returning to normal. Even with the crown of wires, her face was transforming. She looked rosy, peaceful. A few minutes later, Nurse Ron, fingers nervously fluttering, returned and said there was a problem. He was pressing buttons and straightening tubes. In the midst of hope for a miracle came the patient's reply. "The IV tubes have stopped working," Nurse Ron said. "Nothing like this has ever happened. I'm not sure what to say. I believe she's telling us she's ready."

Within the hour, Gabriel, Dora and Harlan arrived. Kate tried to explain what was happening—and asked Nurse Ron if the hospital chaplain could come to be of comfort to the children. "Already on his way," he said. The grief in the room was unbearable. Standing by their mother, the children kept repeating, "Mama, don't go. Mama, wake up." When the time came to unplug the equipment, the children were taken by a nurse to speak to the chaplain in another room.

Kate stayed behind as Nurse Ron calmly asked what she wanted disconnected first. "My God, I don't know," she replied in horror. "I've never done this before." He proceeded to unplug tubes and wires and turn switches. It was then that the miracle happened. Daisy wasn't supposed to be able to take a breath without the machines, yet after they were disconnected, she didn't die.

The sobbing children returned and held their mother's hands when, out of nowhere, another nightmare unfolded. "I'm not going to watch this," Harlan said, stalking out of the room before returning to order his children to leave. "Gabriel and Dora, you come with me. Right now! We're going home."

Gabriel refused to budge. "Mama wouldn't leave me alone to die and I'm not leaving her," he said. "You go. Leave me here. I'm staying."

When Harlan raised a hand to strike the boy, Nurse Ron intervened. "You'll have to get out. I'm so sorry," he said, in a gentle but firm voice. Harlan bristled. When Kate reached out for Gabriel and Dora, Harlan shoved her away and dragged the hysterical children out of the room. Kate felt nauseated and dizzy, but she remained at the bedside. Nurse Ron was in and out as the hours passed. Time was spinning and Kate began to sense that the hallway outside was filling with people who spoke in whispers. The women in white lingered and Daisy's high school friends arrived. Other people came and went. Daisy breathed in and out, in and out . . .

In time, the miracle became an embarrassment—and hospital administrators decided to move their lingering patient to a hospice room with a spectacular view of the Phoenix skyline. Daisy breathed on . . . In and out, in and out . . . At midnight, a nurse came into the room and told an ashen-faced Kate to go home and get some rest. Daisy's other friends wanted to spend time at the bedside.

Kate reluctantly returned to the motel and entered a dream world filled with monsters. Before dawn, she heard Daisy's voice call out, "Mommy!" *Why Mommy?* Kate staggered to the bathroom and threw up. She hugged the toilet bowl and felt violently ill. Fifteen minutes later, she arrived at the hospital barely able to walk the final steps to the hospice room. Another miracle: Daisy was alive and breathing. She was radiant. Kate brightened and smiled and kissed her and held her tight in the morning light. She stroked her forehead and noticed a brown-colored tear rolling down Daisy's cheek. The labored, shallow breathing continued while the sun rose. Nurses arrived, but Kate didn't look at them. It was a private vigil. Her entire focus was sending love: *om mani padme hum*. In and out . . . In an out . . . *om mani padme hum* . . . Then a peaceful, deep breath arrived. The next one didn't come . . .

It was over. Kate held Daisy until her body grew cold. There had been no miracles, just respites.

GABRIEL AND DORA had to be told their mother was gone. When Kate arrived at the blue door, the apartment was crowded with strangers laughing and talking. There was food on a table, cans of soda, open bottles of liquor. In an adjacent room, adults and children were dancing together to soft jazz. Others were crowded in the living room on chairs, couches and the stairs. Daisy had just died. How did they know?

Harlan, well groomed but smelling of bourbon, was the perfect host and grieving spouse. In a twist of the absurd, he led Kate by the arm, as though she was a feeble old woman, to a seat instantly vacated by a heavyset guy who looked like a gangbanger. Harlan offered her a drink, which she declined. "Tell everyone what happened," he said. It was an order, not a request, and all eyes turned in Kate's direction. It felt like an ambush.

"There's nothing to say. Daisy died," she said. When she finished, Kate looked up and saw Gabriel and Dora, their heads peeking over a second-story balcony rail. It was surreal. She stood up to comfort them, but three burly men drinking beer on the staircase blocked her path. They didn't budge.

"Sit. Come sit, Auntie." Harlan ordered her back to the couch. "We have questions and need answers."

These people knew something Kate didn't. The atmosphere was icy. There seemed to be an understanding among them that the female relatives would speak and the men would keep their mouths shut. "You're not going to try to take our kids are you?" The almost-shouted question came from a brassy, rawboned woman sitting on the other end of the couch.

Kate was caught off guard, especially with Dora and Gabriel within earshot. "Let me make this clear. I don't know who you are or why you care. I'm here because Daisy died this morning," she said. "I came to comfort my niece's children. That's all."

Standing in the middle of the room, Harlan put his arm around a woman Kate vaguely recalled had once been a friend of Daisy's. They both smiled at her. "We'll take the children," the woman said.

The situation was insane. "And who is we?" Kate moved closer to Harlan's friend.

Before the woman could answer, a slovenly woman with coal-black eyes stepped forward. "You're taking care of the funeral arrangements, right? They'll probably let you take it out of the life insurance from her job."

"I don't know anything about Daisy's life insurance," Kate replied. "I assume that whatever she had will be put away for the children's education. If you're asking whether I'm going to pay for the burial expenses, then yes, I'm prepared to do that. I'm on my way to Mesquite to see what needs to be done," Kate said. "Harlan, do you have Daisy's purse? The hospital didn't have it. I need her keys to get inside the house."

"Shit," he mumbled.

At the same time, Kate looked up and saw Gabriel disappear

from the landing. The men on the staircase moved as the boy pushed his way down holding out a backpack with a bunch of keys dangling from the strap. He handed it to her. "This is all we have," he said. "One of the neighbors gave it to us after the accident. I think Mom's cell phone's still in there, but since we've been here somebody broke it. The house key is the one with the pink fingernail polish on it." Gabriel fell crying into Kate's arms. She held him tight and looked up. Dora hadn't moved and stood frozen on the landing.

Kate called out to her. "Dora, do you and Gabriel want to go to your house with me? We can check on your dogs and you can show me where your mom keeps her documents." The little girl didn't respond.

Gabriel took the lead: "We love you, Auntie. But we have to stay here. Dad needs us. We're supposed to see our grandma this afternoon and more people are coming over."

Kate kissed the boy's cheek and ran her fingers through his soft hair. "Okay, do what you think is right. We'll have other times. I'm sorry. I don't want you to do anything you don't want to do. Your mom was . . . Well, as you can see, I'm pretty upset right now. Just know that she loved you both more than anything. It looks like I'll be sticking around for a while to straighten up the loose ends. I can come back whenever you need me. You still have the card with my numbers, right?"

Gabriel blinked—twice. It was like a code. There was something else going on. Kate didn't want to leave, but sensed the situation would become volatile if she didn't get out of there. She half expected one of Harlan's goons to insist on escorting her to her car. No one moved. With the exception of Gabriel and Dora, Kate couldn't imagine Daisy being in the same room with any of these people. But, as the philosopher-poet Robert Graves said, no good could come of offering common sense to the insane.

By the time she got to the front door, Gabriel was hovering by her side. He whispered in her ear where she should look in the house for his mother's documents and valuables. "Mom wanted to be cremated and buried in the old cemetery with Grandma and Uncle Kevin. She told us she might die."

It felt like the air had been sucked out of the room. The boy must have misspoken. "I didn't quite hear you. What did you say?"

Gabriel spoke up. "Mom thought she might die."

Kate was visibly shaken. "What do you mean your mother *knew* she might die? Please tell me. She wasn't even sick. What's this about?" Right then and there, she wanted to sit Gabriel down to talk to him, but the adults were craning their necks to look at her before they turned their gazes in Harlan's direction.

It was a setback for the perfectly groomed grieving spouse. "Fuck you," he said, as he slammed his fist into a wall and marched out of the apartment, slamming a door behind him.

All attention returned to Kate, who didn't know if the "fuck you" was for her or her nephew. It had been only hours since all her concern was directed toward Daisy. Now the children's welfare became paramount. Kate was strident: "Gabriel and Dora, come with me. I need to talk to both of you. Let's get out of here."

"We can't," the boy said. "We have to stay."

"Why?"

"I'll explain later. It's complicated."

At that, Dora silently drifted downstairs and moved to the room where people were slow-dancing. Kate cringed as she watched the third grader begin dancing with a thick-shouldered, grown man with a mustache. Dora's pretty face was blank, lost in cloudy preoccupation. So Kate walked up to her, tapped her on the shoulder, but was ignored. It was hopeless, at least for now. When Kate hugged Gabriel at the front door, the hair on her arms stood on end. The child named for an angel was cold as ice.

THE THREE-HOUR DRIVE from Phoenix to Mesquite was insane—and she was certain that Interstate 10 had become the Highway to Hell. Kate was doing sixty while other drivers were flying past at ninety, tossing beer cans out their windows. It was 115 degrees outside and, luckily, the air conditioner in the rental car worked. She turned it up full blast and tried to forget the idiots zipping past until great gut-wrenching sobs overtook her. She felt completely alone. Emotions spent and nothing left to give, she let the silence stretch.

The Tibetans believe the dead don't know they're dead and linger around loved ones for a period of time. The Tibetans also believe the sound of truth reverberates like a thousand thunders. Kate demanded truth. In the emptiness, questions formed themselves. *What happened to Daisy? What would happen to Gabriel and Dora?* The rolling reverberation continued . . .

In Quartzsite, a winter oasis for rock hounds and tacky weekend garage sales, she stopped for gas and used the restroom. She bought a pack of cheese-and-crackers and a Diet Coke. Absentmindedly, she reached out for a pack of cigarettes and, realizing it was foolish, bought a package of Sour Rainbow Rattlers, a children's candy, instead. At least sugar wouldn't kill her.

On her way out of town, she noticed a ragtag, open-air store that sold rocks by the pound. She thought of Celeste's love of rocks and decided to stop. As Kate wandered up and down the aisles looking at dusty bins of green malachite and quartz crystal and rocks she couldn't name, she came across a basket of marbles, the kind she'd played with as a child. She picked up a white cat's eye and liked the feel of it. She looked for a shopkeeper but couldn't find one. At the back of the lot was a small mobile home and she knocked on the door. No one answered. She put a dollar on the door mat. Then she noticed a Nazi flag flying from the roof, took the dollar back and pocketed the marble. On this day, becoming a thief made as much sense as anything else.

The land was desolate but beautiful. Open skies, jagged vistas and memories of vision quests. Dirt roads on the horizon crossed the mountains. The asphalt shimmered with specks of quartz as the sun rose to its zenith. It had been years since Kate had taken this road bordered by lava rock plopped in clumps like chocolate ice cream. Maybe God, whoever he or she was, had a sense of humor. What was it about this desert that made Kate feel both dangerous and elated? It was as if the black-and-purple mountain range forming a gateway to the reservation beckoned like a rowdy old friend who would only get you into trouble, lots of trouble. Yet she was being sucked in, talking to Daisy as if she were a passenger in the car:

O child of noble family, where are you?

Soon Whipple Mountain's fickle finger beckoned. Kate knew the mountain was considered sacred by the Mohave tribe. She carefully followed the white-line beacon of the main road through the town of Parker. Founded in 1908, Parker is a bump in the road near the Arizona-California border that began as a railroad stop. At first, the trusting and resourceful Mohave, farmers and guardians of the Colorado River, welcomed the railroad to their land. They thought it would improve the marketing of their farm products, not become another encroachment on their way of life. Eventually Parker became the heart of the Colorado River Indian Tribes' reservation. The plural "tribes" is a surprise to most people. It was to the Mohave as well, after the U.S. Government ordered them to accept displaced members from other tribes onto their ancestral homeland.

Kate drove through Parker to the Colorado River, turned left and soon came upon a familiar sign: Mesquite, Population 1,200. The community was almost an afterthought, built on land the Mohave considered unlucky and unsuitable for farming. When Celeste and her children moved to Mesquite, tribal leaders were leasing the acreage through a private development company of non–Native Americans in hopes of bringing in much-needed revenue. In turn, the settlers agreed to build custom homes on tribal land in exchange for ninety-nine-year leases. The plan was that Mesquite would morph from being a wasteland into a vacation paradise. Then the outside developers abruptly left the reservation. Tribal leaders, with no experience in this line of work, tried hard to become property managers. It was one of the reasons the battered Mesquite sign on the main road had never been replaced or repainted.

Most of the homes were built close to the highway and clustered around a tacky strip mall. The mall featured a budget motel, coffee shop, corner market (that doubled as the post office), the American Legion Hall and a snack bar. At one time, there had been a fancy real estate office and a hotel on the riverfront, but the windows were boarded up and the wood trim was rotting away. However, the community changed the closer you moved toward the Colorado River. That's where newer waterfront homes with private boat docks, recreational vehicles, privacy walls and security company signs warning of "armed response" could be seen.

Kate planned to stop by Daisy's house, halfway between down-and-out and luxurious, to look for documents before going to the mortuary. From what Gabriel had said, it seemed likely that Daisy had a will, or that she'd left written instructions for burial arrangements. Kate didn't expect anyone to be at the home, so it was a surprise to see a man with chiseled cheekbones sitting alone out front in a faded gray Toyota pickup truck. Kate pulled into Daisy's driveway, got out of the car and approached him.

"Can I help you with something?" she asked.

The man got out of the truck and slowly walked toward her. He was about six feet tall and had long dark hair that hung halfway to his waist. Native American, Mohave, probably. "I came to say I'm sorry for your troubles," he said. "She's in another place, not here."

Kate recognized the accent. "Wait a minute . . . Are you a friend of Daisy?"

"I was a friend."

"Are you the person who called me?"

"I did call."

"You're a tribal member?"

He nodded.

"Thank you for calling me."

He said nothing in return, but pointed toward the yard. "How about that dog over there? I don't like the looks of that dog in this heat. I put water in the bowl for him."

Kate turned around and noticed a white dog tied to a fence post in front of the house. "That must be Gabriel's dog. I'm sure he'll appreciate your kindness when he comes home."

"Are you going to care for the children?"

"I don't know," she said. "They have a father."

"He's not a good man."

"I know what he is," she said. "Will you tell me your name?"

"Edward Van Fleet."

"It's nice to meet you, Edward Van Fleet. I'm Kate Thorsen, Daisy's aunt. Would you like to come inside with me? I'm here to collect some things before I go to the funeral home."

Edward turned his head and gazed toward the mountains. "Not right now," he said, taking a deep breath. "I have things to do. Maybe later on . . . Don't worry about the dog. I'll care for him."

"I appreciate that," she said. "How can I reach you?"

"I live close," he said. "If trouble comes, call the Bluebird Café where I work."

The response caught her off-guard. Kate had been to the Bluebird many times with Daisy, but didn't understand the use of the word "trouble." What trouble? Edward shrugged and said nothing else. Puzzled, she stood and watched the pickup drive away. How did this man know she'd be coming here this afternoon? She needed more information. Before going inside, she called Diane, the neighbor who'd told her the children's dogs were being cared for by another neighbor. There was only one dog at the house.

"I live across the street," Diane said. "I'll be right over."

The empty house beckoned. Kate unlocked the front door and entered a shadow world. The utilities had been turned off and there was no electricity or water. She had an overwhelming sense that something dreadful had happened in this place. The curtains in the living room, dining room and kitchen were wide open. There was no logical explanation for her unease. It was a mundane scene of interrupted domestic normality. There were dirty dinner dishes in the kitchen sink, two half-eaten bowls of Cheerios on the table, and a pile of decaying dog shit on the carpet. The house smelled awful from being closed up in the heat—and she saw a new air conditioner in an unopened box in the living room.

The windowless hallway to the bedrooms was dark. Mindful of scorpions and rats, she felt her way toward the bedrooms. She opened doors. The children's rooms—other than the usual kid clutter of toys, dirty clothes and unmade beds—appeared normal. But as she drew nearer to Daisy's room, Kate began clutching her hand to her heart.

O child of noble family . . . What's going on?

Holes were punched in walls and the door of a linen closet, which contained family photo albums, had been unhinged. The hallway floor directly in front of the master bedroom was littered with broken glass. The white door to the bedroom was covered in what looked like scratch and kick marks. She thought of Daisy hiding in her room. What kind of terror had happened in this place? The door's heavy security lock had been pried open. The bedroom had been vandalized. Laundry baskets once full of children's clothing and towels were toppled and the contents scattered. Torn drapes hung limp in front of a broken bay window. Drawers had been ripped from a bureau, the contents ransacked and strewn about. Daisy's computer, the one that had been in the corner of the room when Kate last visited, was gone. Electrical cords had been ripped from wall sockets. Reaching behind Philip's old desk, Kate found the document box Gabriel had told her about. It was empty. When she crawled to the back of the closet, the door to Celeste's secret hiding place swung open to her touch. The brown-velvet box that had held the family's heirloom jewelry was gone.

There was a loud banging at the front door. Kate froze and then looked for something she could use as a weapon. Prepared to do whatever was necessary, she crept down the hallway clenching a wooden coat rack like a spear and peered through a side window. Standing outside was a mousy-looking, dark-haired woman in sweats. She must be Diane, the neighbor from across the street. When she opened the door, Diane immediately reached out to hug her. Kate recoiled, then set the coat rack down and realized she was covered with ants. "Excuse me," she said, brushing ants from her clothes. "There's a problem in the house."

The woman didn't take notice, as if ants in the desert were an everyday occurrence and no explanation was necessary. "I'm sorry about Daisy," she said. "We heard this morning. My kids are taking it hard. She was like a second mom to them."

"Thank you. I'm going to miss her too." Kate continued scratching and brushing ants from her arms and legs. She felt ridiculous, like a contortionist on steroids. "I came by to get some documents of Daisy's before going to the funeral home. We've got a serious problem inside, it looks like someone broke in. Have you seen anyone hanging around? I'm about to call 911."

"Oh . . . Well, I've seen that big Indian hanging around."

"What Indian?"

"I think his name is Edward. From what I understand, he had a thing for Daisy. There was actually a break-in the day of her accident," Diane said. "The tribal police came out and talked to Marlene Stone, one of the other neighbors. I know they went through the house together, but I don't know what happened after that. Everything's been crazy around here lately. We can see if Marlene's home. You should talk to her about it."

Kate couldn't put her finger on it, but there was something about Diane she didn't like—and something about Edward she did. It was a gut instinct and the feeling was pronounced. "Can I get Marlene's number from you?" Diane nodded. "Thanks. I'll give her a call. I'll probably be around for a few days trying to get things sorted out."

"Let me know if you need any help."

"I appreciate it," Kate said. "By the way, what's up with that neighbor you told me was taking care of the kids' dogs? The white dog is out front in the heat."

"Oh, um . . . I think those neighbors went on vacation and took the little dog to the pound. They were afraid to touch the big one because he's mean," Diane said, stumbling over her words. "It, uh . . . just didn't work out. Tell the kids we're sorry."

It was a bullshit response. Kate figured Diane probably was the "other" neighbor. She let it go. Right now, more important questions needed answering. "Do you know what was going on with Daisy and Harlan? Had he been causing problems for her or the kids? I'm just curious."

The question appeared to hit a nerve. Diane winced and stumbled over a response. "Well, uh . . . no, I can't . . . You do know the Sandovals are a big deal around here, right? So, uh . . . if I were you, I wouldn't be asking too many questions about Harlan or, well . . . It's just not a good idea."

"It's my job to ask questions."

"You're, uh, not writing this down, are you? Daisy told me you're a reporter. I'm not going to talk to you if you're writing some kind of story about this."

"Don't worry. I'm only asking questions because I have a responsibility to Gabriel and Dora to find out what happened to their mother. Tell me what you know about the accident."

"Not much . . . As far as I know, she was driving to work and ran off the road. Happens all the time around here. I don't know anything else."

She obviously knew more and Kate attempted to draw her out. "What business would the Sandoval family be in?"

"Lots of things, uh, I'm not sure," Diane replied. "I think I better be getting back to my kids now."

It was hopeless. "If you think of anything else, I'll be staying at Motel 6," Kate said. "Do you know where the Mesquite Funeral Home is located?"

"It's just down the road over there." Diane pointed to a street near the river. "Sorry about Daisy. I'll, uh, see you around."

Before Kate left the house, she took photographs of the damage done to Daisy's room and hoisted the king-sized mattress against the broken bedroom window as a temporary barrier. Once she talked to Marlene and law enforcement, she'd determine her next move. She took the empty document box, locked the front door, and went over to Fred and petted him. He was a friendly dog, just sad and lonely. "Don't worry, boy," she said. "We'll think of something."

THE MESQUITE FUNERAL HOME was a tidy, squat building sitting alone in a field of dirt and rocks. It had a sign out front saying the office was closed for a funeral until 3 p.m., so Kate drove to the Motel 6 and took a room that made the Wingate Inn look and smell like the Waldorf Astoria. Kate noticed fat, fluffy cats hanging out around the manager's office—and when she saw a flock of pigeons on the motel roof (and an abundance of feathers in the parking lot), she figured it out. Still itching from the ant attack, she took a shower, washed her hair and put on semi-clean clothes. She briefly thought of putting her dirty clothes in the parking lot dumpster, and then reconsidered. There had to be a laundromat around. While she contemplated that, she sent an e-mail update to George, letting him know her niece Daisy had died.

Kate's stomach then rumbled. The Bluebird Café, a coffee shop favored by locals, was located in the strip mall. It was named after Bluebird, a Mohave singer and holy man who was interviewed and photographed by anthropologist Alfred Louis Kroeber. He had begun studying the Mohave tribe at the beginning of the twentieth century. In Kroeber's photo in the café's entryway, Bluebird's face was clean-shaven and his multicolored hair cascaded beyond his shoulders. Kate thought he resembled Abraham Lincoln.

The waitress, Shirley, looked to be in her mid-forties and wore her heavy eyeliner Cleopatra style. Her black hair was stacked high and gel-styled in an Elvis pompadour that towered at least three inches above her head. Kate asked if Edward Van Fleet was working. "Why yes, doll, I believe he is," Shirley said. "Edward's our chef."

"Can I talk to him?"

"Sure. Just go stand by the counter," she said. "I'll let him know you're here. What's the name, doll?"

A few minutes later Edward came out of the kitchen wearing a white apron over his clothes and wiping his hands on a towel. His long hair was tied in a ponytail with red yarn and he wore a hairnet that nearly touched the tops of his dark eyebrows. He seemed irritated. "What do you want?"

"I've a favor to ask."

"I'm working. This is our busy time. What is it?"

Kate was embarrassed. "Would you please take care of Gabriel's dog, Fred? I don't want him staying alone out front of that empty house." She took out her wallet. "I can pay you."

"I know his name. I don't need money. I just feed him scraps."

"Please," she said. "I won't feel right if I don't pay you." She handed him a twenty-dollar bill. Embarrassed, Edward tucked the bill in the back pocket of his jeans. "This is temporary about caring for the dog. I need to work things out with the children. By the way, there's a problem at the house."

"What problem?"

"Someone broke in and took some things."

"There are people here you don't want to know." He took a deep breath and smiled. "Don't worry. I'll get the dog and care for him. Fred can stay at my place as long as he needs."

Edward's offer made her feel better. When Shirley brought the food, Kate decided it was the most delicious tuna melt she'd ever had. She even ordered apple pie and coffee for dessert. When Shirley brought the check, she said, "We have the best breakfasts in town, doll. You come back and see us. We'll take good care of you while you're here. Sorry about your niece."

"You knew Daisy?"

"Oh, yes," Shirley said. "Everyone loved Daisy."

FUNERAL HOMES GENERALLY smell like fresh flowers, but this one reeked of Pine-Sol. Mrs. Jensen, the mortuary director, helped Kate make Daisy's cremation and burial arrangements—and Kate, running low on cash, used a credit card to pay the tab. Her book advance was almost gone and she didn't know when she'd be paid for her next writing assignment. Freelancing was a financial roller coaster; she'd known that going in, but it was tough letting go of the only dream of independence she'd ever had.

"The other arrangements have already been made," she said. "Services are Saturday morning at ten at the Holiness Church of God."

"How could that be?" Kate was incredulous. "Daisy just died this morning."

"News travels fast," Mrs. Jensen replied. "Just so you know, the church is the Sandoval family's place of worship. They generally get what they want around here. Between you and me, a wedding at the church was scheduled for Saturday, but it got bumped over to next week. Pastor Williams will officiate at the funeral. He may want to talk to you beforehand. I'd give him a call, just to make sure everything's kosher." Kate knew Daisy had stopped going to the church after the divorce. Why was the funeral being held there?

It was late afternoon when she left Mrs. Jensen and stopped at the hardware store in Parker to buy two pots of red geraniums, a trowel and a gallon of water. The blast of scorching heat, which arrives just before twilight in the desolate valley, was brutal. She drove across the old railroad tracks, ignoring a stop sign, and passed through the black wrought-iron gates of Pioneer Cemetery. Navigating the single-lane internal road, she looked for newer graves, where the inhabitants were honored, and ignored the dirt-covered sections where sagging wooden crosses spelled forgotten. The cemetery was almost deserted, save for one man who appeared to be mine-sweeping the graves. She parked the car on a dirt shoulder and carried the brown paper bag and the jug of water. As she paced the rows decorated with photos, empty beer cans, American flags and plastic flowers, she noticed that fire ants had built mounds over new gravesites covered by decayed flowers.

A dozen years had passed since her last visit to this worn cemetery, but Celeste's grave wasn't hard to find. Everything was flat and there were no fancy twists or turns or the kind of shade trees you'd expect to find in lush urban cemeteries. People were buried in simple straight rows, like streets in a housing tract, based upon their chronological, and often premature, dates of death. In this part of the world, life was hard, swift and unpredictable. Down the road at the old Indian cemetery, the dead died younger.

The "Loving Mother" marker for Celeste was next to a marker for Kevin as "Loving Son and Brother." The local masons had done a lousy job because there were sloppy crumbles of cement around the markers. The crumbles looked like bits of hardened Play-Doh. When Kate unsuccessfully tried to brush them aside, she scratched her hand, drawing blood. Upon closer inspection, she realized the patches of green grass here and there were a mirage. Under the thin and isolated blades, the ground was petrified. She used the plastic jug to pour fresh water over the markers, washing away accumulated filth. When she was done, the green-gold marble stones almost sparkled. It was her only real accomplishment on a day pockmarked in defeat. Then she sat down, closed her eyes and tried to talk to her sister and nephew.

"Hi, Celeste. I'm not very good at this kind of stuff, but I wanted to tell you Daisy will be here in a few days. You probably already know, right? Well, if you're floating around somewhere, I hope you'll take care of her. I think she's going to be confused about what happened earlier today."

She pulled the *Book of the Dead* from her purse. "This book says Daisy could be wandering around for forty-nine days and what she sees could scare her because she won't know she's dead. I don't want her to be frightened. Tell her the kids are going to be fine and I'll take care of everything. But I was thinking that, maybe, you could help her. And, if you can, I could use a little assistance here myself. I know Gabriel and Dora love their father and he deserves a chance to be a good dad, but I don't know if they're going to be safe with him. Frankly, I'm worried. Well, that's about it. I love and miss you."

That said, Kate lifted the trowel high to stab the petrified earth—and failed to crack dust. She pulled the white cat's-eye marble from her pocket and held it like a talisman. She poured the rest of the water over the potted plants and put them on Celeste and Kevin's markers. Then she put the marble on her sister's name. "Sorry, sweethearts," she whispered. "I'm not going to be able to plant your flowers." By morning, she expected the red geraniums to be decorating a grave robber's front porch.

WHEN SHE CRUISED by Daisy's house, Fred was gone. Kate hoped he liked Edward's place. When she got back to the motel, she called Marlene Stone. A husky Kim Carnes voice answered. "My little girl died today," Marlene said, stretching her words between puffs on a cigarette. "I loved her with all my heart. This is horrible, just horrible."

They arranged to meet at the American Legion Hall, which looked like a post office from the outside. Kate remembered the saloon from the nights when she'd had to escort Celeste home after she'd had too much to drink. It was a bar-restaurant with a country and western feel, a hangout for locals who drank, line danced and threw darts. During the winter months, the Snow Birds, retirees and veterans from across the country, appeared in Mesquite with their motor homes and speedboats trailing behind. While aging bones craved dry desert heat, the retirees waxed nostalgic for the old days. "Good people," they called themselves, and after a couple of beers, the retirees often moved in tandem out to the parking lot to salute the oversized American flag.

On this evening, the parking lot was filled with pickups. The place hadn't changed much, except for the four flat screens flickering in the dimness of the smoky, air-conditioned saloon. The stools around the horseshoe-shaped bar were filled. Kate thought she might recognize Marlene from Daisy's descriptive e-mails and letters, which were full of stories about "my gorgeous best friend, the ex-Vegas showgirl who used to date Frank Sinatra." No one in the bar matched that portrayal, but as soon as Kate took a table Marlene arrived.

Now in her mid-seventies, Marlene still possessed a lithe dancer's body, and she sauntered into the Legion Hall wearing a floral blouse, tight white pants and gold stilettos, with her flaming red hair held back on one side by an elegant silver clip. A pair of Daisy's beaded earrings dangled from her earlobes. Every male eye in the place turned as Marlene glided like a cat across the room. Up close, she had on the most extraordinary set of false eyelashes that Kate, who couldn't even apply mascara without smearing it, had ever seen—and layers of soft-muted shadow in various brown and gray hues on her lids that went up and up and trumpeted in pearl-white beneath perfectly shaped and penciled eyebrows. Kate waved, though she felt like a shriveled prune before this obvious master of face painting. How Marlene managed to look good in wilting heat was a feat of magic.

The waitress, a sun-kissed young woman with camel lips protruding from her skin-tight jeans, was at their table in a matter of seconds. "What'll it be, ladies?" They ordered iced tea and shrimp salads. Marlene dabbed at one eye with the paper napkin and a speck of mascara fell on a perfectly rouged cheek.

"I feel I know you," she said to Kate. "My little girl talked about you all the time. She called you 'the world traveler.' She was proud of you. I don't know what I'm going to do without Daisy. We had so much fun together."

It seemed a curious introductory conversation and Kate wasn't quite sure how to respond. "Daisy talked about you too. Said you were her best friend. You'll have to excuse me. This has been a long, hard day."

Kate felt vulnerable. She needed to put into words what she'd seen and experienced in the last few days. She told Marlene about the hospital equipment that stopped working and how Daisy kept breathing, even after the respirator was disconnected. She told her about how brave Gabriel and Dora had been at the hospital—and what a complete shit Harlan was. She told her about the women in white who claimed to have been sent by Pastor Williams and about the Native American who introduced himself as Nopah.

The color drained from Marlene's face. "Nopah Round? Nopah Round came to see Daisy at the hospital?"

"I don't know if his last name was Round. He just said Nopah." Kate couldn't figure out what the big deal was. "He was old and he came in with a young woman and two small children. He was in the waiting room with me during Daisy's surgery. I didn't see him or his family after that. I guess they left."

"There's only one Nopah. He's a Mohave holy man. The Mohave believe in destiny and they don't believe in interfering in other people's lives. Nopah's a spirit dreamer. He never mixes with the outside world—and he absolutely doesn't go to hospitals. He doesn't even drive. His daughter must have driven him to Phoenix. For him to have come all that way for Daisy means something. I'm just not sure what." Marlene was fingering the beadwork on her earrings like she was working a rosary. "Daisy grew up with the Mohave. You knew that, didn't you?"

"Yes, I know."

They ate their salads in silence and, unbidden, the waitress brought them another round of iced tea. Once finished, Kate pushed the salad plate aside and asked Marlene to tell her about Daisy and Harlan's relationship. The older woman's face shifted and her voice became a low snarl as she mimicked spitting on the floor and squashing a bug under her spiked heel. "That guy's a real bastard. He thinks he's a major player but he's nothing but a smart-mouthed punk. There were several times in the last couple of years when I've wished I still had the connections I had when I was working in Vegas. Harlan didn't deserve Daisy—or any woman, for that matter. I pray he doesn't live to see another sunrise."

The lady had a flair for words. "I don't get it," Kate said. "When I first met him, I thought he was okay, or at least had potential. Daisy certainly thought so. I don't understand what happened, but he comes across now as an inept drunk."

"Don't let him fool you. He's sly as a fox and he's politically connected. I don't know what he has on people, but they jump when he orders them. After the divorce, Harlan was always around, harassing, breaking into the house when Daisy wasn't home. He'd follow her and call her at work. She couldn't even go out to dinner without that creep showing up. In public, he puts on this big pious act and talks about being a former preacher and bringing his family back to the Lord."

This time, Marlene actually spat on the floor—and then pulled out a green-and-white pack of ultra-slim menthols and offered one to Kate. She took it. They both lit up.

"What happened with him being a preacher?"

"Right before she divorced him, Daisy told me Harlan was leaving the ministry. She didn't say why. I felt sorry for her and the kids, but I didn't want to push it. I'm not that nosy. But the gossip around here was that Harlan knocked up one of the deacons' daughters."

Kate groaned.

"Oh, it gets worse," Marlene said. "Let me tell you something about a certain kind of man. If he hits you, get out. Run if you have to. I don't care if the guy boo-hoos and slobbers and apologizes all over the place, he'll smack you again. Harlan beat Daisy every chance he got. Any excuse would set him off. My God, he sent her to the emergency room twice that I know of. One time he broke her nose and messed her up so bad she couldn't go to work for a week. And the goddamn cops, pardon my French, wouldn't do a thing about it."

Incensed, Kate crushed and twisted the spent cigarette on her empty salad plate until the shards of tobacco looked like ground pepper. "Why wouldn't the police do anything? Domestic violence is a serious crime. There are state and federal laws to protect victims. Why didn't I know any of this? Why in the world didn't Daisy get a restraining order?"

"Honey, she had a restraining order. I think she had more than one—and it never stopped Harlan. You don't understand how it is in a small community with oversight from three different, but overlapping, law enforcement agencies. The tribes have their reservation police, the county sheriff patrols the unincorporated areas, and Parker has a police department. As I said before, Harlan is connected. He grew up here. Some of the cops are his buddies."

Marlene lit another cigarette. "This isn't the kind of community where women, especially intelligent women, are taken seriously. Daisy's divorce was through the family court in Parker and the judge there issued the restraining orders. But the trick is that law enforcement has to enforce the orders. Otherwise, it's just a piece of paper. Around here, Harlan can do no wrong."

Adrenaline pumping, Kate moved to the edge of her seat. "Daisy never said a word to me," she said. "I could have helped her. Why wouldn't she let me?"

The former showgirl looked weary, as if she was trying to explain carnal life to a cloistered nun. "Honey, women who are abused are ashamed. They blame themselves. They don't want anyone to know what's happening to them, especially if they have children. There were people here who tried to protect Daisy, but, well, you can see how far that got."

The implication was clear. "Did Harlan do something?"

Marlene surveyed the dimly lit room. "I think we need to meet again in a private place. How about tomorrow morning at my house? I can already hear tongues wagging all over town."

They stood to leave. Several couples were slow-dancing and, in the shadows behind their table, Kate noticed a guy with shaggy blond hair sitting alone. He looked familiar and out of place among the graybeards with the big belt buckles and cowboy hats. When she turned to look more closely, he tipped his beer mug to her. Was he one of the people she'd seen at the Phoenix apartment? Kate felt cold. After she stood to hug Marlene, she looked back at the table. Blondie was gone.

"This has been hard. I'll see you tomorrow after I run a few errands. You do know the funeral is Saturday morning, right?" Marlene nodded. "Good. Then if it's convenient, I'll stop by your house before noon. Oh, one more thing: What about the break-in? I was at the house today. It's a wreck. Diane told me there was a break-in the day of Daisy's accident. She said you came over and talked to the police officer. Is that correct?"

"Yes, that was a dreadful day," Marlene said. "First, we heard sirens and next thing the helicopter came. My phone was ringing off the hook. I got a call from another neighbor telling me that a tribal police deputy was snooping around Daisy's house. I drove right over there and told the deputy I was a friend of the family. They'd received an anonymous call saying there had been a burglary. I had a house key and he let me come inside with him. Well, as you saw, Daisy's room was a disaster. Someone had broken a window and her things were all over the place."

"I saw it too," Kate said. "So, what did the deputy do?"

As she spoke, Marlene began rhythmically tapping fingernails on her tea glass. "It was like that old Joey Bishop routine where his wife catches him in bed with another woman. He dresses, makes the bed and pretends nothing's happened. The deputy said it was obvious that Mrs. Sandoval was a rotten housekeeper. He said he was going to call the health department and get the house condemned. It was beyond bizarre. In effect, he told me there was no break-in."

THE MOTEL ROOM was hot and stuffy. It was 95 degrees outside and probably topped the century mark in Kate's second-story room. The antiquated box air conditioner croaked and groaned when she turned it on. Within seconds, the machine hummed and clanked and everything smelled like Freon as the air ruffled the drapes and blew directly across the lumpy double bed like a wind demon from the Arctic. There were only two AC settings: full blast and off, but she didn't dare open the window because the roar of motorcycles in the parking lot was deafening. Must be a bikers' convention in town for the weekend, she guessed, and the overflow came to stay at the motel where they always left the light on.

She grabbed a wad of toilet paper from the roll in the squalid bathroom with the leaky faucet and rusted pipes and put it on the nightstand covered with cigarette burns. She drank cloudy water from a clear plastic cup and vowed never to smoke again. Blowing her nose repeatedly, she knew she was coming down with a miserable head cold, a whopper. Except for aspirin, she didn't have anything to relieve the symptoms or the congestion. Hell, she didn't even have a summer dress to wear to the funeral, although she could probably wear the black wool sheath she wore in England. As she pulled the covers up around her to buffer the air blast, she stared at the cracks in the ceiling. The drone of the motorcycles could still be heard outside, but in time her mind began to drift.

The Tibetans believe that chanting day and night helps the spirit of the deceased reach paradise, whatever that was. Kate didn't have enough voice left to chant for Daisy, so she turned off the lamp. *Nopah . . . She needed to find Nopah.* In the morning she would ask Edward to help her.

At four a.m. the phone rang. Kate was startled awake and then remembered her cell phone was on the sink outside the bathroom. As she stumbled across the darkened room, she stubbed her big toe on the edge of the bed. "Goddamn it," she said, as she hopped around on one leg. Despite the throbbing pain, she managed to reach the phone on the fourth ring. The caller was George Small's wife, Catherine, who immediately apologized for forgetting that she was two time zones away. She sounded frantic.

"I wanted to let you know that George had a heart attack yesterday and they did an emergency bypass. He's at Bethesda. The doctors say he's doing well and may be able to come home soon. The reason I'm calling is he's been worried about you being alone with everything going on. He wanted me to send you an advance for work you're doing with Terry right away. But I don't know where you are or where to send it."

"Oh, Catherine, I'm sorry. This is a shock. I had lunch with George last week and he looked fine. I don't know what to say. Please give him my love and tell him I hope he feels better. Is he able to receive calls or visitors?"

"Not yet, just family," Catherine said. "He's in intensive care."

"How are you holding up?"

"I'm doing all right," she said. "The kids came down from Vermont, so I'm not alone."

"Good," Kate said. "No one should be alone."

"That's the truth—and I'm very sorry to hear about the death of your niece. I understand she had young children. That's awful."

There was a pause. "I have to go . . . I've got to get back to the hospital. The kids are waiting. Before I forget, where do I send this mail? George wanted me to overnight it."

Why George was sending her an advance was a mystery. Perhaps Catherine was hysterical and had misunderstood the urgency? Meanwhile, Kate felt the most important thing she could do was to contact their mutual friend. Terry Ryan, a linguist and sometime translator, lived in Paris, where he taught at a university. Kate knew the time zones would hinder her ability to reach him, but she tried. She left a message about George's heart attack and asked Terry to call her.

WHEN THE BLUEBIRD OPENED, Kate stood in line with a dozen bikers and their girlfriends. She admired their colorful tattoos and enjoyed listening to their animated conversations about upcoming hog rallies. Because of the size of the crowd, it was thirty minutes before she was seated. She ordered the Cowgirl Special—scrambled eggs, sausage, toast, orange juice and coffee—from Shirley, whose black pompadour was now sprayed pink and blue. "Love your hair," she said.

"Thanks, doll," Shirley said. "I went to a party last night. Needed something a little special. Hoping to get some action. Been a while, if you know what I mean."

"Yeah, I do." Shirley's honesty was refreshing in a world where few people bothered to speak the truth. "Is Edward working today?"

"Edward should be here soon," she said. "He goes up to 'P' Mountain every Friday morning to greet the sun. I'll let him know you're here when he comes in. But with this crowd, I can't guarantee he'll have time to chat today."

"That's fine. I don't want to bother him when he's busy. I'll be here for a few days and I can stop in again. Just let him know I'm staying at Motel 6. He's taking care of my nephew's dog. I want to make sure he's still okay with that."

"Are you kidding me? Edward is head over heels for that dog. You're probably going to have to fight to get the pup back from him. Your nephew's Gabriel, right?" Kate nodded. "He's a great kid. He used to come in here for dinner with his mom and sister on Friday nights. It was their big night on the town. I think Daisy got paid on Fridays," Shirley said. "That little boy took good care of his mama. A real gentleman—used to hold the chair out for her and everything. His little sister was a dickens, though. We were always shooing her out of the kitchen. Nice family. I'm going miss seeing them around."

Kate winced. "I'm trying to persuade the kids to come back east to live with me. I don't seem to be having much luck."

The waitress gave her a curious look and lowered her voice. "Those kids are Sandovals. You be careful now. Their daddy isn't someone to mess with." Then she surveyed the room. "I best be getting back to work now."

"Do you know Daisy's service is tomorrow?"

"Oh, sure. They ran it on the cable access calendar this morning. Die around here and everybody knows. No such thing as privacy in a small town. Should be a big crowd at the church. Daisy was real popular."

"Is there a florist nearby?"

"Just one. It's inside the funeral home. Always reminds me of a big fish tank because of the glass walls. Except for funerals and weddings, people don't spend a lot of money on flowers. They wilt pretty fast in the heat."

. . .

Kate ordered a large stand of pink roses in the shape of a heart and told the florist to affix a white satin banner with "Mother" in gold letters across the front. It was a magnificent arrangement, at least in the FTD Flowers catalogue, where prices weren't included. The clerk looked like she'd just hit a jackpot, leaving Kate positive she'd been charged three hundred dollars only because of her outsider status. At the moment, cost wasn't important. She signed the gift card: "To Mommy, We will never forget you. Love always, Gabriel and Dora."

The Holiness Church of God, a little storefront next door to the main post office, was where the funeral organized by the Sandoval family would be held. When Kate tried the door of the church, it was locked. She knocked. When no one came, she knocked again, this time louder. Then she heard movement inside followed by the slow shuffle of steps on a creaky wood floor. When the steps grew louder and abruptly stopped, the door opened a crack. An elderly man with bifocals, milky-white eyes and thin tufts of eroding salt-and-pepper hair peered out. He ushered her inside. The man took halting steps as he escorted her through the chapel.

He wore a too-large dark suit that hung limp on his thin frame like an oversized tent. He had a pronounced stoop in his back that made him pitch forward—and Kate guessed he was younger than he appeared. This was not the fiery and charismatic jokester Daisy had described in her letters. "Pastor Williams?"

"Call me Elias," he said with a wan smile, his false teeth too big for his face. "You must be Daisy's Aunt Kate. Come with me." He led her through a double door and down a long hallway to a dank, cluttered room with an old gray metal desk and a banker's lamp. The desk was covered with papers and prescription bottles. It was obviously an office, but there was a couch with folded blankets and a pillow in the corner. On a TV tray in front of the couch was a half-eaten turkey sandwich, an apple cut into small bites, and a full glass of milk.

Kate looked around. "Do you live here?"

"Yes," he said. "We're a busy congregation and I'm always on call. I've been sick the last few months and it's been easier for me to stay here. Sisters Eileen and Sarah look in on me and do the cooking and cleaning. I'm sure you met them at the hospital." Kate nodded. "Since Mrs. Williams was called home last year, my life's become quite simple. But I prefer it this way."

"You obviously have things to do. I'll be on my way, but Mrs. Jensen at the funeral home thought you might want to talk to me before the service. The cremation and burial at Pioneer Cemetery have been arranged. Daisy wanted to be buried next to her mother and brother. I've ordered the grave marker and flowers from the children. The ashes will arrive here early tomorrow morning. I'm not sure what else to say . . ."

He looked amused. "You've been busy."

"I'd rather be doing something else," she said. "I was told you needed to talk to me and don't know what you need. I'm willing to help in any way. Just tell me what to do."

Instead, Elias decided to talk about his religion. "The Pentecostal Christian Church is a worldwide, conservative evangelical movement that began in 1901 as a multiracial denomination in Kansas. It really took root in Los Angeles," he said. "Today, it's one of the fastest-growing religions in the world."

The only things she knew about the church were that services were supposed to be full of enthusiasm and loud gospel music— and the followers believed "baptism of the Spirit" was accompanied by speaking in tongues and spiritual healings. Whatever Pentecostals did at funerals, she hadn't a clue.

"At this point, what we need from you is a tribute, about a page in length," Elias said. "We want you to write about Daisy and her family before she came out to the desert. Tell us a little about her parents and her brother. We can have one of the sisters or deacons read it tomorrow, unless you would like to do it. Everything else is being taken care of by the Sandoval family. They've indicated what they want and a special offering has been lifted. Of course, there will be food and fellowship afterward. Do you have other questions?"

Elias's businesslike response came as a surprise. Kate went blank, took a deep breath and sneezed. "Sorry, I've caught a cold. I'm not used to the climate. How soon do you need the statement?"

"God Bless. Don't worry. You'll adjust to our climate, eventually. As for the statement, later this afternoon would be best. We'll probably include it in the celebration-of-life booklet. Mrs. Sandoval, the children's grandmother, is doing a little something. The children may be writing a poem. There is one thing: If you have any family photographs, especially of Daisy as a child, we'd like to see them. I'm working on the sermon. This calling home was so unexpected."

Pastor Williams's voice was beginning to crack and his cough was raspy, guttural. His hands trembled, but he continued speaking. "In the last few years, Daisy had stepped away from the faith. I assumed it was because of the Sandoval family. Not long ago,

Daisy told me she was thinking of coming back to the flock," he said, shaking his head.

"She didn't say anything about it to me," Kate said.

"Neither here nor there," he said. "Anyway, I hear Harlan Sandoval is planning to move into your sister's old house with his children. I don't think Daisy would have approved. Just so you know, we're not asking him to speak at the service tomorrow. I'm sure you're aware he's had, well, a difficult history with us and is no longer a pastor in our congregation. We thought it best to exclude him to some degree. He will be in attendance, however. Be aware that we understand this is a difficult situation for you and the children. We're going to pray for a solution. Would you like to bow your head with me?"

"Sorry," she said. There were more important things to worry about than praying for things that weren't going to change. *Harlan was moving in with Gabriel and Dora?* This was news to Kate. It wasn't his house; it belonged to the children. "I'll see if I can find photos for you," she said. "And the statement will be ready later this afternoon. I'm staying at Motel 6 in Mesquite. You may already have my cell phone number. I left messages when I was with Daisy at the hospital." Elias nodded. "Do Sarah and Eileen need help with the program?"

"I doubt it. They're very efficient," he said, reaching for a container of water and a pill bottle. "I will want to talk to you privately after the service. I have some concerns about Harlan raising the children. Of course, I'm sure his family will be there to help out."

IT WAS ALREADY ELEVEN and Kate had promised Marlene she'd be over before noon. There was barely enough time to run by Rainbow House to get the photo albums she'd seen in the linen closet. Daisy's giant key ring was the kind a teacher would need to unlock classroom doors and equipment sheds filled with balls and playground toys—and, standing in the sun, Kate fumbled with the ring trying to get the front door unlocked.

Since her previous visit, nothing appeared to have been disturbed, but Kate couldn't bring herself to enter Daisy's room. She made a mental note to call a locksmith to change the locks and a repairman to fix the bedroom window and repair the splintered interior door. The idea that Gabriel and Dora would come home, even with their father, and see their home vandalized was too ugly to think about. Fortunately, she recognized two photo albums at the top of the linen closet and pulled them out. She knew Daisy's family and childhood memories were reflected inside.

Marlene's home overlooking the banks of the Colorado River was spectacular—a white stucco and glass multistory contemporary, obviously custom built, that looked like a series of ice cubes cascading toward the water. The curved driveway was bordered by rows of fifty-foot queen palms, and parked in front of the garage was a shiny black 1994 Mercedes-Benz S320 sedan. It was a classic, the kind of tank Stuttgart doesn't make anymore.

The doorbell sounded like wind chimes—and Marlene, surprisingly pretty without makeup, came to the door wearing a black leotard and matching tights with her auburn hair pulled back into a ponytail. "Sorry, I was in the middle of my routine," she said. "Please come in."

The climate-controlled home with solar panels on the roof smelled vaguely of mesquite—and the floor-to-ceiling blue-tinted windows brought the beauty of the river setting inside. Scented candles were burning on glass and chrome tables. Most of the other furnishings were southwestern and the floors were polished Spanish tile. "Your home is amazing," Kate said.

"I like it. My husband, Don, and I moved here after he retired from Southern California Edison," she said. "We enjoyed the desert, and the dry heat was good for our arthritis. Plus, living on the river gave us something pretty to look at."

"Tell me about the painting over the fireplace."

"Oh, that's my mother. Her Anglo name, because everyone was required to have one, was Naomi Jones. Her tribal name was Red Feather. In the Mohave culture, wearing a red feather means you're going to war—and my mama was always at war with someone. She enjoyed a good fight."

Marlene stepped in front of the fireplace and gazed at the painting. Red Feather was wearing a hint of a smile and a light-blue high-necked blouse with a brooch made of white seashells and beads. Delicate vertical lines had been tattooed on her chin and her dark hair was braided and tied on top of her head with red ribbons. "I think Red Feather's about fifteen in this likeness. I had a portrait painter copy it from an old black-and-white photograph. He added the color. At first I didn't think it worked. Now I do. She was an interesting woman who never gave hard times an inch. She was a kick."

Kate was intrigued. "Tell me more about her," she said.

"Mother grew up on the reservation, and when she was old enough, the authorities forced her to go to the reservation boarding school where they tried to beat the Indian out of you. Wouldn't let you speak your native language or follow tribal customs. Back then, we dumb Indians were forced to assimilate into the white man's superior culture. What a crock! We weren't accepted and didn't belong anywhere. One foot here and one foot there, as they say."

It was the stereotypical story of most indigenous people. "Horrible things were done in the name of progress," Kate said. "Was your father Mohave too?"

Marlene grinned, started to laugh and lit a cigarette. "Gosh no. I'm what the Mohave call a 'cross breed.' Cross breeds are supposed to grow up to make peace between warring cultures. Fat chance . . . Anyway, my dad was black. Back then they called them Negroes or coloreds or, you know, worse. His parents came to the desert from Los Angeles with a group of African Americans who wanted to establish their own community in Lanfair Valley. That's not far from here, just down the road near Joshua Tree. The U.S. government had opened up the territory for homesteaders. Well, my father's folks dreamed of creating a paradise where they could live freely without racial discrimination. But the grand enterprise failed and less than twenty of the original families stuck it out and got homestead deeds to their property. The others turned tail and went back to L.A."

"Your dad stayed?"

At some memory, Marlene chuckled. "Sort of . . . Thomas Lincoln Taylor was a tough buzzard, a wanderer—and he wasn't crawling back to Los Angeles, no sir. My dad went to work for the Santa Fe Railroad."

Kate grinned and shook her head when Marlene offered a cigarette. "So, how did your parents meet?"

"Right here in Parker. Dad was a railroad porter and Mother was selling Indian jewelry at the train station. They sparked right off. Never married, but it was a good match. They had four kids and were together, on and off, for about thirty years. Sadly, I'm the only one left." Marlene got up and began dancing barefoot across the living room. "My Indian name is Star Feather. Isn't that pretty?" Kate smiled. "I grew up and went to school here on the reservation. I couldn't wait to leave. When I was eighteen, I bought a train ticket to Los Angeles and never looked back."

"How did you end up in Las Vegas?"

"Can't you see the stars in my eyes?" Marlene said. "I didn't want to be Star Feather. I wanted to be the next Rita Hayworth or Lana Turner, but after months of that Hollywood-casting-couch bullshit I was sick of it. One night a girlfriend introduced me to a guy who hired me for the chorus line in Vegas. I was there when the Flamingo opened."

"You must have some great stories to tell."

"You bet I do. But I gave up the glitter to marry and have a family. My husband was terrific. Then it ended."

"What happened?"

"Don died five years ago," Marlene said. "Let's talk about Daisy."

"I'm sorry," Kate said. "I didn't come here to bring up sad memories."

"Don't be sorry. After Don passed, that's when Daisy and I became close."

Kate's hands trembled. "The truth is I'm still in shock. After talking to you last night and seeing what was done to the house, I'm having trouble dealing with the idea of walking into that church tomorrow and seeing Harlan."

"You're missing the point," Marlene said. "The ceremony is to honor Daisy's memory. It has nothing to do with Harlan. Rise above it. Mark my words: Harlan will end up rotting in jail before he burns in hell. After the funeral, you can find out what needs to be done to protect those kids and the property Daisy left them.

"After Daisy's divorce, she helped me around the house for a little extra money. When I hurt my back last year, she took care of me and did the grocery shopping and laundry and everything. Daisy became like a daughter to me. Gabriel and Dora used to come over with her. They played pirates in Don's boat in the garage. It was their playhouse. We had some good times."

"Nice to hear something was going right."

Marlene sipped her tea. "What happens to the kids? Will you take them?"

"I'm trying to put the pieces together," Kate replied. "I don't know if I have any legal standing. I need to talk to an attorney—and the theft of Daisy's computer and her mother's jewelry needs to be reported to the police."

Marlene frowned. "Let's examine this. Who had the motive for the jewel theft? Harlan. Who would have taken the computer? Harlan. But I doubt the cops will ever pin anything on him. Every time someone tries to nail him, he skates, lawyers up or disappears."

"What do you mean?"

"Arizona's criminal records are on the Internet. Look him up. Every charge that's ever been made against him has been dropped. He's never spent more than a night in jail. Oh, dear, I almost forgot. You need to find Daisy's car. She told me she was carrying documents about Harlan's illegal activities in the trunk. Find out where they towed that car. It's a place to start."

Kate felt her pulse quicken. "What are you talking about?"

"You heard me. Supposedly, Harlan is in business with some bigwigs around here. Right before the accident, Daisy told me she'd gotten hold of some documents and was going to turn them over to the feds."

"Oh, my God."

"That's what she said. It could have been an exaggeration, I don't know." Marlene raised one eyebrow. "The papers were supposedly hidden in the car because she was afraid to leave them at the house because Harlan kept finding ways to get inside."

"Anything else I should know?"

"This may be nothing, but I've heard the Sandovals have this thing about gathering up their 'blood' children. They supposedly raise them together in what they call 'clan' houses. I'm pretty sure that's why Daisy told me she wanted you to take Gabriel and Dora if anything happened to her. She said she was going to make you the beneficiary of her life insurance. You better check on that policy. Oh, shit . . . Go to the preschool and see if you can get her last paycheck. Then close her checking account before Harlan gets there."

Kate felt numb. "I don't have any standing other than a piece of paper from the hospital saying I'm the adult next of kin. And I'm not sure the children want to be with me. If Daisy had a will, it's gone. Gabriel told me to look in her document box. I found it in her room. It was empty."

"Honey, I don't know what happened. All I'm saying is that two weeks ago, Daisy told me that she didn't think she would live much longer. She was scared. She couldn't sleep. It just broke my heart."

"She told Gabriel the same thing."

KATE WAS GOING to have to scramble on the funeral tribute. She got out of the rental car carrying Daisy's photo albums and noticed two men sitting in a sedan in the motel parking lot. They stared at her. Looked like cops. As she climbed the staircase, she could feel eyes burning into her neck.

At the top of the landing, sitting on his haunches, was Edward, his black hair flowing unfettered, in front of the door to her room. Fred was curled up next to him, wagging his tail. A black guitar case stood propped against the wall. Edward stood and brushed his hair behind his ears. "You wanted to talk to me?"

Kate leaned down and petted Fred's head. The dog began licking her hand. "Good boy, good boy. You look happy," she said, rubbing Fred's ears. "Edward, do you play the guitar?"

"Some."

"What kinds of songs?"

"Little bit of everything." He looked confused. "Why did you want to talk to me?"

"When I was at St. Andrew's Hospital in Phoenix, I met a man called Nopah. I think he was Daisy's friend. I was hoping you could help me find him."

Edward put his hands in his pockets, leaned forward and lowered his head until they were both at eye level. He frowned and looked down at the sedan in the parking lot. "Someone's watching you. You're in trouble already. I can see it. What's wrong?"

"Nothing's wrong," she said with irritation. "Do you know who those men are down there?"

"Look like cops to me."

"Me too. What are they doing here?"

His voice was flat. "You didn't break the law, did you?"

She shrugged her shoulders and mopped sweat from her brow. "I've been obeying all laws, as far as I know." Then she noticed Edward didn't sweat. Maybe that's what Pastor Williams meant when he'd told her she'd get used to the heat. She wasn't planning to hang around that long.

Removing his hands from his pockets, Edward bent over to pick up the guitar case. "Nopah doesn't talk to outsiders. I'm surprised you know his name. I'll see what I can do."

Impulsively, Kate reached out to hug him and was startled when his dark eyes warned her away. "Sorry," she said. "I didn't mean to be forward."

"You know how to find me. Come, dog, let's go."

There was a red light blinking on the phone with a message from the front desk saying a package had been delivered, addressed to her. She went downstairs to retrieve it and was relieved to see the men in the sedan had left the parking lot. Myra, the motel manager, lived in an apartment behind the office with her too-thin daughter and three cute grandchildren. Myra was a bubbly, heavyset woman with a friendly smile and millions of freckles.

"Good to see you again," Myra said. "This FedEx envelope came for you this morning. How's the room? Do you need anything?"

Kate smiled as she took the envelope. She wasn't about to tell Myra her motel was one of the worst she'd ever been in, the tired carpets stunk, the Freon was making her sick, or that she could see mildew growing in the shower tile. "Thanks, I'm fine with everything. No problems. Is there a laundromat in town?"

"Why, we can take care of that for you."

"That's the best news I've heard today."

"Just put your things in the white plastic bag, the one that's on the shelf in the closet. I'll send one of the maids up for it—or, never mind, you can just bring it down here," Myra said. "I'll wash it myself."

"Thanks. I'll bring the bag down in a minute," Kate said. "By the way, I'll need the room for a few more days. I'm here on family business and things are taking longer than I thought."

"No problem," Myra said. "We're happy you chose Motel 6."

"Is there a supermarket or a shopping center nearby?"

"You betcha. Just go down that road over there toward Parker. The market's right before the Blue Water Casino. The shopping center has a Safeway, a Dollar Store, a Walmart and a women's shop. You can find anything you want. We're almost like the big city these days. We even have a movie theater right outside the casino. We're growing so fast that people are saying we're a new boomtown."

Myra was right. Some things had changed on the reservation since Kate had last visited. She tossed the FedEx envelope into the backseat and drove to Safeway, the first real supermarket she'd been to since London, and bought supplies. Then she headed toward Mohave Mama Boutique, a store painted bright pink and lime green with curvy suntanned mannequins in bikinis displayed in the window. She bought a lightweight navy-blue dress for the funeral, two flowered sundresses and a pair of sandals.

Back at the motel room, Kate filled the plastic bag with dirty clothes and took it down to Myra before returning to check messages. One was from Terry saying he was boarding a plane from Boston to Phoenix and would meet her at Daisy's service. She called and left him a message saying he didn't need to come, but looked forward to seeing him. She opened the FedEx envelope from George and found a cashier's check. She took a long, warm bubble bath and shaved her legs and armpits for the first time in a week. Then she washed her hair and brushed her teeth. She put on the new yellow sundress, pulled out her laptop and began composing a tribute to her niece using *The Tibetan Book of the Dead* as inspiration:

O child of noble family, Daisy Marie Prout Sandoval, let your mind rest. Do not be afraid. You are loved by so many that your journey will be pleasant and without reproach. Look to the pure white radiance where you will encounter the joyous souls who tread the rainbow path before you. Honor thy family. They will come to greet you and fill you with love in a light-filled cathedral with many rooms. Others you have known and loved will greet your radiance as well. There will be much joy at your homecoming.

It was kind of a loopy tribute. But Kate was too tired and angry to care what other people thought. So what if they said Daisy's aunt was some kind of New Age fruitcake? The point was to say Daisy was more than the limits imposed on her by Sandovals or anyone else. Daisy would have laughed.

Hair nearly dry, Kate took a deep breath before opening the photo albums where all the smiling faces never changed: Celeste, Philip, Kevin and Daisy camping in Yosemite, birthday parties, feeding animals at the zoo, weddings, graduations, funerals. She finally selected a family photo that had been made into a Christmas card. Philip, Celeste, Daisy and Kevin were all wearing Santa hats. She found another of her niece looking shy on her first day of kindergarten. The last she chose was of Daisy and Kevin, wearing toy soldier helmets, flexing their biceps for the camera.

When Myra brought the laundry up, Kate was crouched at the table by the window wiping away tears. "Honey, are you getting ready for your niece's funeral?" Kate nodded and blew her nose. "Well, come on down to the office. You can have a cup of coffee and use our computer to print out copies of everything. We have one of those Photosmart gizmos. Makes nice copies. You don't want to lose any of those original pictures, especially now."

"Did you . . . Did you know Daisy?"

Myra looked at her. "It was impossible *not* to know Daisy. She was my grandchildren's preschool teacher, one of the sweetest people I've ever met. She used to make cookies for all the kids during Christmas and colored eggs for Easter. And what a laugh she had! That girl was one hell of a fighter too, a real tiger mama. She went to tribal council meetings and demanded old playground equipment be replaced and that they fill the gopher holes in the yard where the children played. Daisy was the one who wrote a grant request that allowed the school to finally provide adequate art supplies. Let me tell you, she will be missed around here. No one stood up for the kids like Daisy Sandoval."

Kate blew her nose again. "Oh, Myra, you have no idea how much I needed to hear that. Since I arrived, everything has been confusing. People have said things. Did you hear that Daisy's house was vandalized?"

"That's horrible," Myra said. "Most folks around here loved and respected Daisy. Those who didn't, well, you might want to ask *them* why. There are a lot of strange ones in that Sandoval family. This is just my opinion, you understand, but all they care about is getting what they want. They're Ruby Hands."

"What does that mean?"

"It's kind of hard to explain, but you know how most people support each other for the common good?" Kate said she understood. "Well, in any community, it seems to me, there are always a few who take advantage of others. They're the Ruby Hands."

THE HOLINESS CHURCH OF GOD'S Sister Sarah answered the door. When she read Kate's Tibetan-influenced eulogy, her eyes bulged. "You want me to read *this*? This is not the kind of statement we make in this church. This is Jesus' church, not some pagan devil's house."

"I don't think Jesus will mind," Kate said. This woman was starting to get on her nerves. "We're an unconventional family. Get used to it. And don't worry, I plan to read the eulogy myself."

"It's your funeral," Sarah said.

Kate refused to dignify the remark. "I'll be here early tomorrow."

"There's one more thing," Sarah said. "The funeral home called this afternoon. Daisy's body is still in Phoenix. It hasn't been cremated yet. The coroner has delayed his investigation because of some question about the cause of death."

"Considering the circumstances, I'm with the coroner on this one."

It was a fitful night. Naked under damp sheets with Freon blasting, Kate felt overwhelmed. Once the funeral was over, the real work would begin. Before she went to bed, Kate had called the apartment in Phoenix where Harlan was staying with the children. No one answered. She figured they were probably on their way back to Mesquite—and she had no idea how to contact anyone else in the family, except Mama Lou Sandoval. Over the years, Kate had heard enough about Mama Lou to make her wary. "She's a dragon lady," Daisy once said. "She comes across as this fluffy kitty, but be careful of those claws."

At four a.m. Kate's cell phone rang. It was Gabriel and he sounded like he'd been crying. "Where . . . Where are you, Aunt Kate?"

"I'm at the Motel 6," she said. "What's wrong?"

"I ran away," he said.

"Why? What's going on?"

"It's my dad. It's all of them. I don't want to be a Sandoval any more."

"Where are you? I'll come get you right now."

Kate threw on clothes and rushed to her car. She met Gabriel at a payphone in front of Tony's, an all-night gas station. The boy fell into her arms muttering something about his father, but Kate couldn't understand what he was saying. "Where's Dora?"

"Dora's fine," the boy said. "She's with Grandma Lou."

Once Gabriel composed himself, he clenched his jaw and wouldn't say anything else, except that the Sandoval family was staying in adjoining rooms at the Best Western in Parker. Kate felt she had to let Harlan know Gabriel was safe and with her. It was nearly dawn when she called. After a brief conversation with Mama Lou, Harlan grabbed the phone. "You get my son back here or I'm calling the police," he yelled.

Under the circumstances, Kate felt she had no choice but to take the boy to the Best Western. Harlan was waiting for them in the parking lot. Gabriel opened the passenger door, threw his aunt a kiss and sulked off, with his father pushing him from behind.

A LARGE PART of the community had come to the Holiness Church of God on a day when the air hung like a limp rag and the temperature was expected to hit one hundred twenty degrees. Mourners quietly filed into the lobby for Daisy Sandoval's send-off, but it became clear that some of them had never been inside the church before when they turned the wrong way and ended up in the community room filled with long tables covered with butcher paper where a feast had been prepared. The misguided mourners quickly left the wafting aromas in the feast room and found their way back to the flower-bedecked chapel, where industrial fans had been cranked up to reduce the incoming heat.

Sisters Sarah and Eileen, wearing shiny white choir robes with blue trim, were beaming. "The Holy Ghost is moving," Sarah said. "The Lord will have his way and the demons will be cast out and spiritual prayer will spread through this sanctuary like wildfire!" No one attending Daisy's "celebration of life" ceremony could know that the sisters had excluded Kate's eulogy from the program. They had talked it over the previous evening and deemed the city woman's words blasphemous. What the mourners would see presented to them was sanitized family harmony reflected in smiling photos of Harlan, Daisy and the children, a tribute to "my daughter" from Mama Lou Sandoval, and a poem called "My Mother the Angel" by little Dora. Daisy's divorce from Harlan wasn't mentioned, as if it had never happened.

Kate sat back and quietly surveyed the crowd. She was looking for allies and was touched by the number of people who'd turned out to pay their last respects. She didn't give a damn what the church sisters thought or did with their program. But she wondered how she would react when she had to face Harlan and his extended family. After everyone found a seat or a place to stand, the pianist made an entrance. He bowed and sat down. Other musicians followed and soon keys were tinkling, guitars strumming, drums beating, a bass thumping and flutes lilting. The vibration in the room was being raised by a blend of rhythms—and the drums were particularly moving. Scattered coughs were heard and throats were cleared when the music abruptly stopped—and

Sisters Sarah and Eileen began draping white sheets on the floor in front of and around the altar.

Reeking of whiskey, Harlan Sandoval arrived late with an entourage of hip-looking, well-dressed friends worthy of a rap star. Gabriel and Dora followed with their grandmother. The children kept their heads bowed and eyes down. Kate couldn't figure out if the downcast eyes represented mourning, modesty or fear. She wanted to talk to them, but was nudged aside by Harlan's friends. In a show of nobility worthy of her status as a clan matriarch, Mama Lou dabbed at her eyes with a white lace hankie and blew air kisses to friends and family. She was followed by two other sons, their wives and close to a dozen children under the age of twelve. As the Sandovals neared the front of the church, Sisters Eileen and Sarah escorted them to reserved seats in the first two rows of pews.

Kate sat in the fourth row with Marlene and Terry Ryan, who'd arrived on the gambler's special tour bus from Phoenix. "I think I'm in a little trouble with the church sisters," Kate whispered to Marlene.

"Those nitwits," the older woman replied. "I wouldn't give them a second thought."

Funerals bring out the best and the worst in people. Kate hoped for the best for the children's sake—and looked down the row and saw Daisy's three high school friends, the ones she'd met at the hospital, sitting with other thirty-something friends. Two rows behind her was Edward, his black hair tied back at the nape of his neck with a piece of red yarn, and next to him was another man with his hair tied back in the same red yarn. All became quiet when Pastor Elias Williams, in flowing black robes, entered the room. He took a seat in an elaborate wood-carved chair on a pedestal. Other pastors in long black robes sat behind him at lower levels in less ornate chairs. The program began with prayer and scripture readings. A choir began singing a gospel hymn. People were holding their hands high and clapping. When the music stopped, there were words of consolation from a church elder followed by another gospel hymn. It was then announced that it was time for brief "expressions" by friends and family. Harlan did not stand, nor did anyone else in his family or entourage.

Kate seized the moment. Her voice trembling, she stood and recited her Tibetan-influenced eulogy. Then Marlene stood and cleared her throat. She walked over to the pianist and said something. In a voice filled with emotion, the one-time showgirl told the mourners that Daisy was her best friend and "adopted daughter." She took a deep breath and began singing "Over the Rainbow."

The next to speak was the man sitting with Edward. He walked to the front of the church. "My name is Tommy Mesa," he said. "Some people call me Big Nose. I wasn't a friend of the woman who died. But I knew who she was. I found her after the accident. I want to tell her children that they had a good mother. She was brave. I will never forget her."

At that, Elias Williams seemed to gather his strength. He was helped up from his chair by two other pastors. Once his hands touched the pulpit, Pastor Williams, eyes flashing, began a tirade, a soul-fried sermon. He chastised the community for racism and sexism and spoke of his personal pain when Daisy fell away from the church. "She was comin' back, yeah," he said, glaring at Harlan.

People responded with "amens" and "you know she was."

It was fire and brimstone. Williams began prancing and dancing. He was Mick Jagger on a catwalk. It was pure theater—and the drummer behind him set the beat.

Boom . . . Boom . . . Boom . . .

There were cries of "Hallelujah!" and "Praise the Lord!"

Boom . . . Boom . . . Boom . . .

Sweat blooming on his face, Pastor Williams suddenly stopped directly in front of Harlan. The old man looked like the Grand Inquisitor. "You are headed for the Devil's hell," he hissed, voice blazing with outrage. Clenching his fists, Harlan turned his head to ignore the attention, but the old man was in hot pursuit. He moved closer until he was eye to eye, waving his hands and expelling breath on Harlan's face. Then Pastor Williams began jumping from side to side.

Boom . . . Boom . . . Boom . . .

It looked like a confrontation was about to happen when Harlan raised his fist and clenched his jaw. He puffed out his chest and stood to confront his accuser. "Back off!" he growled. "Back off me, old man!"

In a rage, Pastor Williams moved in closer until the two men were almost touching, standing puffed chest to puffed chest, with the old man shouting: "You are headed for the Devil's hell! The Devil has your soul in his claws!"

Boom . . . Boom . . . Boom . . .

When Gabriel and Dora began crying, Harlan looked at them briefly and appeared to surrender. He bowed his head and got down on his knees as if begging forgiveness. Pastor Williams was still dancing and began vigorously moving his hands back and forth on Harlan's scalp. "You are headed for the Devil's hell," Williams yelled. Again and again he hurled accusations while the drum continued beating. The supplicant didn't budge.

When Williams finished what looked to Kate like a public exorcism, he began doing the same thing to Gabriel and Dora. Alarmed, she stood up to protect the children and moved to the front of the church. Marlene squeezed in behind her. The old man extended an arm to ward Kate off and winked at her. Only then did she realize he was performing a religious ritual—and the children, rather than being afraid, were familiar with the game. Cries of "Hallelujah! Praise the Lord! Amen! That's right!" echoed from all parts of the room. Every action was beyond the pale of anything Kate had ever experienced.

The rabid preaching was followed by comforting, extolling, touching. People began coming to the front of the church; they were hugging and dancing in the aisles. The drums grew louder and louder and louder until the scene was one of deafening chaos. Middle-aged women were babbling in tongues that sounded nonsensical. Irritated, Kate decided they were exhibitionists or—worse yet—professional mourners, when they began dramatically swooning and falling to the floor. They were wriggling on the strategically placed white bedsheets and looked as if they were having grand mal seizures. A heavyset woman was groaning and moaning. One of the mumbo-jumbo babblers was on top of Kate's foot.

"What should I do?" she whispered to Marlene.

"Honey, just kick the bitch with your other foot."

By now, multiple ministers were putting their hands on other people's bowed heads, ruffling their hair, symbolically drawing out whatever impurities lurked inside their sinful brains. It resembled mass paranoia. There were cries of "Amen!" People were chanting in unison, "Amen, that's right!" Then, as quickly as it began, Pastor Williams fell silent. Drained of energy, he seemed on the verge of collapse and was helped to his throne by the other pastors. When he sat down, Kate approached him. "I did it," he muttered, clasping her hand tight. "I publicly defied the Sandovals. I'm my own man again."

The music stopped when the drummer hit a cymbal. It sounded like the clang of a dinner bell. Immediately, the women stopped speaking in tongues, got up off the floor, straightened their dresses, dusted themselves off and smoothed their hair. Mourners were quietly filing out of the chapel, headed toward the big room where matrons were serving lunch in long white aprons.

Not sure what to say, Kate approached Gabriel and Dora and embraced them. "You both look so nice," she said. "Hey, kids, I need to talk to you. Can we go sit down somewhere quiet?" Out of nowhere, a crowd of children formed a circle around them. Kate couldn't figure out what was going on. *Who were all these children?* Her niece and nephew averted their eyes.

Finally, Gabriel, his face flushing, spoke. "Aunt Kate, we've decided to stay with Dad," he said. "We'd like to see you as often as possible. But we're staying in Mesquite with our family. We're going to fix up the house."

"We want to be with our cousins," Dora said, turning to the children circling, pressing closer.

There was something odd about these kids. Kate felt ears, big ears that listened, surrounding her. It was a claustrophobic feeling, as if Stephen King's Children of the Corn had come out to play. In her entire life, she had never felt a negative reaction toward children before—until now. *What was happening?* It was as if she was an intruder, an outsider, a pariah.

"You can change your minds, you know?" she said to Gabriel and Dora. "I'll always be here for you, no matter what."

Expressing no emotion, her nephew and niece simply walked away and hugged their father. At the same time the Children of the Corn pushed to the front of the church and began dismantling the stand of flowers with the "Loving Mother" banner. Electric fans whirred like wasps in accompaniment to the thrashing and ripping sounds of little nibbling fingers as they destroyed the fresh roses. Wincing, Kate watched in disbelief as petals and ribbon littered the floor of the sanctuary. Then Sister Eileen, smelling like coconuts and carrying a batch of white sheets, walked up to Kate with a packet of gift cards from all the floral arrangements. "Here, you take care of these," she said, ignoring the frenzied children as if they were invisible.

On the other side of the church, Mama Lou, dabbing her eyes with the lace-bordered hankie, held court as people stood in line to express their condolences. Among them, Kate saw the blond man she'd seen at the American Legion Hall. Harlan's three brothers huddled in a corner snickering. *Were Gabriel and Dora really making this decision to stay? Or was someone making it for them?* Kate shook her head in disbelief.

When she turned, Edward bumped into her. There was sadness in his face and anger in his eyes. "I need to talk to you in private," he said. "It's important."

They went outside and stood in the parking lot in the sweltering heat. "What's up?"

"The dog is dead," he said.

"Gabriel's dog?"

"Yes."

"My God, what happened?"

"Someone slit his throat." Edward's voice was flat. "I found him on the porch when I came home from work last night."

Unnerved, Kate was having trouble processing what he'd said. "Why would someone kill an innocent dog? I don't understand."

"It was a warning," he said. "That I should stay away and not help you."

"But why?"

"More trouble is coming. Don't worry . . . I won't stop being your friend. But I think you should let things settle. Go away for a while. Let me know when you come back. I will help you. We will deal with this and finish it."

Kate physically jumped when she felt hands touch both her shoulders. She swiveled and faced Terry. He'd overheard the conversation with Edward. "We're going back to Washington," he said. "Then I'll come back here with you. Edward's right. You don't have to handle this by yourself anymore. This is a bunch of crap."

Edward walked away. When he got to his truck, Tommy Mesa, his friend, was waiting for him.

FROM TIME IMMEMORIAL, the *Pipa aha macav*, or people by the water, believed they had emerged from the shadows of Spirit Mountain. They traced their myth of origin to *Akaka*, the raven bird messenger of The Great Creator, who led them to their home and told them to care for the land along the Colorado River because it was the source of all things. Their personal god was Mastamho, the deity who taught them how to live.

The Mohave believed in destiny, spirits and omens. Dogs were thought to be equal to humans, so it was considered unacceptable for an animal to be harmed or killed, especially at the hands of an enemy. After Daisy's memorial service, Edward and Tommy were taking Fred's body to a sacred place in the black mountains.

When a human dies, the Mohave hold what they call "a cry." Friends and family gather to mourn and the deceased is cremated with all his or her possessions. Bird songs are sung. Edward and Tommy decided that Fred, a good dog, deserved a cry. Before they left the parking lot of the Holiness Church of God, the men took two eagle feathers from the glove compartment and tucked them into the red yarn at the napes of their necks. Evening or sunrise would have been the best time for a cry. On this day, however, the afternoon would have to do. Fred's body and his belongings— collar, leash, tennis ball, water and food bowls—were wrapped together in a black plastic bag in the back of Edward's truck. On the other side of the truck bed were a shovel, container of gasoline, dog food and fresh water.

In the Mohave way, the two friends were openly emotional and shared feelings of loss with tears and polite conversation. "You take things hard," Tommy said to his friend.

"I know, I know," Edward replied. "You're a good person, Big Nose. I'm glad you spoke at the church. It was the right thing to do. The children should understand the value of what they've lost."

Tommy was circumspect. "She was a decent woman. There was no ridicule in her. When I saw her, she was making jokes at death. Did you see the husband bragging and having fun in that church? He is no good, I tell you. Worthless even . . . I heard from a woman I know that he is sex-crazed."

"What's bad about that?"

"Nothing, really. But I've heard he forces himself on women. You could see the old priest knew the man's no good. The aunt knew it too. We must hope the kids learn. They will have no decent life if they go their father's way."

The road ahead was clear and the clouds were thin and wispy. "It's too bad," Edward said. "Those kids are just learning to fly."

"Are you going to help the auntie?"

"I will try. She has a good heart. Did you hear she wants to talk to Nopah?"

"No shit?" Tommy spat the toothpick out of his mouth and began laughing. "Do you think he will speak to her? No . . ." He laughed again harder. "That's pretty funny. Such a thing couldn't happen. Could it?"

Normally it wouldn't. Nopah was a Mohave medicine man, an *ahwe sumach*. He was an important tribal elder who consulted omens, healed people and worked magic against the Mohave's enemies—and he protected the tribe from those who brought in sickness and disease. As a spirit dreamer, *xelyetsxa'm cama*, or one able to travel to another realm to meet with the dead, who often took the form of birds or animals, Nopah had the power to induce them to return to their bodies—or so it was widely believed. Nopah wasn't a witch—and that, Edward and Tommy agreed, was a good thing.

"You understand how Nopah feels about outsiders. But what do I know? I heard he went to the hospital in Phoenix to see the dying woman," Edward said. "The aunt told me she talked to him there."

Tommy straightened up in the passenger seat. "Is that so? Nopah went to Phoenix?" The situation was more confusing than he'd thought. "Do you think the dead woman was part Mohave? No . . . That couldn't be. I did hear stories about how she spent her girlhood with Nopah's aunties. Do you think the aunties might have adopted her?"

"Stranger stories have been told," Edward said, shaking his head. "Consider that Oatman woman in the old days. The Apache stole her and her sister from a wagon train and then sold them to the Mohave. The little sister got sick and died. But I heard our tribe treated the older one with kindness and loyalty. She adopted our ways. When the white soldiers came to take her from us, she didn't want to leave. She was proud to be like a Mohave. Maybe the woman who just died was like a Mohave too?"

"You need to stop playing your guitar and read more. The Oatman girl was just a slave," Tommy said. "I find it hard to believe she liked being a slave better than she liked being with her own people."

"Maybe . . . But I think the woman who lived in Mesquite was different. She had a strong face and a real shadow. Her ghost walks among us."

"If you can prove it, that might change my view," Tommy said, slapping his thigh for emphasis. "Have you had dreams about this woman? Has her spirit spoken to you? Would you consider her a valuable person?"

Edward paused to think about this. "Yes, I have seen her in dreams. I think she was a valuable person. Remember, I knew her a long time. She was once in love with my uncle."

"Oh, yeah?" Tommy slapped his thigh again. "Your uncle the warrior? The one who performed great deeds in battle?"

Edward paused to recall how much he'd looked up to Uncle Leon, the soldier who came back from the Gulf War with bad dreams; the warrior who fell in love with the young white woman; the broken man who got drunk and died of love sickness. "Yes, that one," he said. "But there was more to this woman than her relationship with my uncle. She stood up for Mohave children— and I don't think the school leaders liked her for that. Her husband was a big troublemaker, a crazy man. She tried to stand up to him."

The two men locked eyes and felt a current of sorrow engulf them. They'd reached the end of the road and were nearing the cave on the side of the mountain where the ancestors used to hide food and water. They parked the truck near the volcanic rocks and together gently lifted the dog out of the truck bed. They would return for the shovel and the other things once the proper place was found.

"I saw the dog in a dream," Edward said, looking down at the bag. "He was running fast with the boy Gabriel. I think something was chasing them."

Tommy listened carefully to what his childhood friend had to say. "What tribe is this man Sandoval? Where did he come from?"

Edward considered this question long and hard. "I don't know," he said. "I'm told his family just showed up here after most of the white people in Mesquite began leaving their homes. I hear they came from Texas."

Out of respect for the dog, Tommy and Edward followed the old ways. In silence, they dug a hole and lowered Fred's body face down into the grave with his possessions. They put dry dog food and water over him as nourishment for his journey to the land of the dead. They covered the funeral pyre with mesquite kindling and poured in a small amount of gasoline. They lit the fire, threw their eagle feathers into the flames, and sprinkled tobacco from a broken cigarette at the four corners of the smoldering grave. As the sun fell into the shadow of the mountains, they sang the mourning songs their fathers had taught them.

That evening they returned to the Colorado River and purified their bodies in the water. A blue dragonfly, a symbol of protection, flew round their heads. They would remain chaste for the next four days. When Fred's ghost came to visit their dreams, they didn't want to go insane.

ON THEIR WAY out of town, Kate stopped at Pioneer Cemetery to tell her older sister that Daisy's arrival had been delayed. As they drove through the iron gates, she again saw the man with the long pole sweeping in and around graves. "Terry, what's that guy doing?" she asked.

"Looks to me like he's engaging in the ancient art of witching."

"Oh, God, please. My family's buried here." Kate looked crushed and Terry rolled his eyes in vague bafflement. "Is he a witch?"

"Let's check the sucker out."

They parked the rental car off the road and marched toward the man, who seemed startled at their approach. "Hello there," he said, tugging off a blue baseball cap to wipe his brow. "Don't see too many visitors around here on a hot afternoon."

"We're curious," Kate said. "What are you doing? Are you a grave robber? If you are, just get the hell out of here. I'm prepared to call the police right now."

"Listen, lady, calm down. I'm a volunteer with the Arizona Pioneer & Cemetery Research Project. We're trying to find and identify pioneer graves. This is one of the oldest cemeteries in the state." He handed Kate a business card with the group's name and website. "My name's Ned Dickens. You don't look like you're from around these parts."

"I have family buried here," Kate said.

Terry upped the ante. "So ye be a witcher with a business card, eh? In my country, we'd hang ya up by the balls for desecrating respectable family graves. Don't ya know ya can go to hell for somethin' like this? You lookin' for wedding rings, watches, what?"

"I'm not desecrating anything. We're trying to find and honor our pioneers. We don't disturb anything."

The man sounded sincere. Realizing they'd jumped to conclusions, Kate tried to make amends: "I'm sorry, Ned. My friend here is Irish and, you may have heard, the Irish have a foul sense of humor. Pay him no mind. I'm Kate and this big lug here is Terry. We're a bit touchy at the moment. We just came from my niece's funeral. So, what's the sweeper thing for?"

"First things first: I'm *not* a witcher," he said adamantly. "I'm a retired librarian. In America, we call what I'm doing grave dowsing. It's a lot like water dowsing—and you've probably heard of that." They both nodded. "It's the same principle. To be honest, we don't know exactly how it works. We just know it does. The rods detect the magnetic field between the living and the dead. Every living thing has electricity or magnetism. When we die, the magnetism remains in our bones. Strange as it might sound, the field remains even if there was a cremation."

It sounded fishy. Why come to a cemetery where most of the graves are recent and marked? When Kate asked, Ned said Pioneer Cemetery was believed to be much older than the records that had been passed down. "We think it originally was a Boot Hill where markers were probably wood that has since rotted away. All we're trying to do is give dignity back to the dead. We have historians working with us, going through old documents—and we're trying to mark all the graves we can find."

How did they know if a body was buried in a certain spot? "In an established cemetery, we pace the rows. For some reason, the rods will cross if the grave is a male and open when the grave is a female," he said. "I'm not sure I can explain it. You have to try it for yourself."

It sounded delusional to Kate, but Terry seemed familiar with the process. "Do you do any talking to the dead?" he asked.

Ned hesitated. "Sure, if I have a name. You said you have family here. Give me a name and let's see what happens."

Kate accepted the challenge. "Celeste Prout."

"Show me where you are, Celeste," he said. Ned's rods appeared to lift and pull as he slowly made his way like a stumbling drunk across the cemetery grounds. Then he whistled and motioned for them to follow. The rods were open and they were standing square in front of Celeste's grave. "She's here," he said.

Coincidence? Good guess? A skeptical Kate wasn't convinced. "How about Kevin Prout?"

This time the rods didn't budge. Ned looked puzzled. Kevin's marker was right next to Celeste's. "I don't know how to explain this," he said. "But Kevin Prout's not buried here. He's somewhere else. Are you sure he's supposed to be here?"

Kate felt goose bumps up and down her spine. "You're right, Ned. Kevin's not here. His body wasn't recovered." Looking nervous, the grave dowser excused himself, saying he had to get back to work.

The July sun poured down as Terry wrapped a comforting arm around Kate's shoulder. "It's going to be okay," he said. "Someone else is here. Just thought you might want to know. Not buried . . . She's visiting. Daisy wants to thank you for everything you're trying to do."

Under normal circumstances, Terry's message would have seemed bizarre. But this kind of thing had happened before. Kate had seen it firsthand in Central France when her *National Geographic* colleague, Evangeline Girard, was dying. It was then that Kate realized Terry Ryan, her Irish-Gypsy friend, had a special gift for communicating with the unseen. Even so, Terry's announcement created a tangle in Kate's heart.

Part III

HARLAN WAS HAPPY. It was a Monday morning in July, two days after the best funeral ever. Everybody said so, even though Daisy Sandoval's body wasn't there because the medical examiner still had some questions about how she died. Head trauma or some such . . .

There was supposed to be a graveside service after the funeral, but Pastor Williams announced they would "skip that part" and simply sing songs and hear more testimony about the pretty woman with shiny brown hair that hung down to her shoulders. Harlan, wearing a new black suit, sat in the front row with Gabriel and Dora. Both children were on their best behavior, as expected. People came forward to praise Daisy as a wonderful mother, friend, coworker and neighbor.

So, even without her body, the funeral was a big deal. Nearly the entire population of Mesquite showed up to pay their respects to Oak Hill School's only preschool teacher. There was plenty of gospel music, testimony, and sweat-soaked mourners swooning in the aisles fluttering their white hankies. Afterward, Pastor Williams was jubilant when he counted seven souls saved and declared the fried chicken, green beans and biscuits served by the apron-wearing church ladies the tastiest funeral food in memory. "Hungry souls," he said, "need food."

But Williams had stepped out of line during the service—and he would pay for his mistake. No one pushes Harlan Sandoval around, especially in public.

Daisy was dead. And Monday was a day for the living. Wasn't much sense in grieving about the dead—and the living, well, they just had to up and do. The good Lord, everyone knows, gives bounty to the desert dwellers when times are hard. Times were always hard in Mesquite, a place where the rattlesnake population rivaled the number of humans in the frying-pan days of summer. Times were particularly hard for the Sandoval Clan, ever since Papa Vernon ran off to Mexico six years ago with a young woman in a string bikini he met down at the American Legion Hall. Since then, Mama Lou, a matriarch of mammoth proportions, and her four strapping sons had had to make their own way.

As long as you didn't get caught looting a house, death meant opportunity, and the Sandoval Clan enjoyed a good scavenger hunt almost as much as they enjoyed selling drugs to fools with cash. "Hell," Mama said, "there wouldn't even be any scavenger hunts if desert people didn't croak regularly."

Scavenging was easier, though, when dealing with a departed family member. The Sandovals, while not technically blood kin to Daisy, believed they had first dibs on whatever property she left behind. After all, she had once been married to Harlan, the oldest male in the clan, and he was the father of her two children. The divorce was a technicality, Mama said. While Daisy may have thought she got rid of her husband, the church said a woman wasn't allowed to divorce a man without his permission.

The Sandoval boys, in work clothes and construction boots, rode in an orderly caravan along the dusty two-lane road near the river outside town. At the rear of the procession, Mama—in a sleeveless, polka-dot dress and a floppy hat—was wiping tears from her milky eyes. On this day, Harlan, lost in thought, drove and Mama rode shotgun in the air-conditioned, shiny red Cadillac with perfect white upholstery that had been paid for in cash.

Mama, dangling flesh hung low, maintained appearances. Every morning, regardless of the heat, she put on full-volume black mascara and frosted-blue eye shadow and painted her lips with ruby-red lipstick. Harlan sat at the Cadillac's wheel smoking a Marlboro, daydreaming about buying a pearl-white Escalade.

"Praise the Lord for what we are about to receive," Mama said, bowing her head before raising her eyes to look at the fine profile of a man she had created. "Son, I believe this will be a blessed day. You know, I always admired some of those items Daisy's family left her, especially that deep fryer and those diamond rings. I would like to take the ice cream bowls home. You remember the ones I'm talking about?"

Harlan tossed the cigarette butt out the window and patted the soft plump of his mother's hand. "Yeah, I remember. They were her grandmother's bowls. That house was a museum. I could never get Daisy to get rid of anything. You get first pick on everything. This is your day."

By the time the caravan arrived, it was one hundred five degrees in the shade, so hot the crows sought shelter in the cottonwoods and tarantulas were taking the sun on the sticky blacktop. They arrived at the beige ranch-style home, surrounded by palm trees and rock gardens, and parked the two pickups in a dirt strip by the garage and the Cadillac in the driveway. They moved the children's bikes off the sun porch to make room for the blue-and-white cooler filled with beer for the men and orange sodas for Mama.

Harlan, suffering a pounding headache after last night's celebration with tequila shots at La Posada, was sweating through his shirt. It wasn't a hangover—yet. He was still half drunk and could barely contain his excitement. Finally he had come into money, a nice house, a little nest egg that could be sold for cold cash. And the local real estate speculators were already courting him like the refined gentleman he believed himself to be.

Daisy had been a fool, Harlan thought, and should have known that he would never recognize a divorce or acknowledge that a judge had the right to give her the house and full custody of *his* two children. Everything was simple: there was no divorce. His wife just didn't get it—and his blood simmered when he remembered how she waved those ridiculous restraining orders. Pissed him off royally. No one dared piss off Harlan Sandoval. Those flimsy pieces of paper that said he couldn't threaten, assault or trespass, that he couldn't go near his home or be within two hundred feet of his own wife, were a joke. A man wasn't supposed to talk to the woman who bore his children? Didn't Daisy realize that no judge or court order could keep him away from what was his? And didn't she understand that those dykes at the domestic violence center were losers spewing garbage, telling Daisy that Harlan was going to kill her and send flowers to her funeral?

Harlan never bought flowers for anyone.

Gabriel and Dora weren't in the caravan. After the funeral, they were taken to visit relatives in Texas. This freed Harlan and the rest of the clan to do what they always did without hysterical kids mucking things up. But games needed to be played. Pretending he had no house key, Harlan kicked in the front door. Once inside, he switched on the air conditioner and discovered that it no longer worked—and a new unit, sitting in a cardboard box in the corner of the living room, hadn't been installed. The house felt like an oven. Saying he was concerned about the impact of the heat on Mama, Harlan and his brother Andrew carried the sofa from the living room and placed it on the covered front porch. That way Mama could sit in shaded comfort next to the cooler while her boys went to work.

She fanned herself with one of Daisy's magazines. "This is nice of you, son."

Harlan shrugged. "It's a pigpen in there. That woman never did know how to clean a house."

Every culture has customs and taboos regarding death and burial. Some cultures claim that not following proper etiquette after a death can lead to contamination, bad luck and supernatural haunting by restless, angry ghosts. Some feel it imperative that bodies and possessions be immediately burned and destroyed, while others dutifully tend to remains, treasure belongings and pass on family heirlooms from generation to generation. Some Native Americans, for example, believe that when a person dies in a home, the home itself should be destroyed, while in Namibia, it is customary that when a man dies his family descends on his home and takes everything of value. His widow, even if she has children, is not allowed to protest. Once the paternal relatives have finished looting, the woman and her children are thrown out of their home.

Much like the Namibians, the Sandovals had customs and traditions regarding death. Under clan rules, the house was Harlan's property. And, as the father of Daisy's minor children, he had the right to take anything that could be sold, pawned, traded or used. His children had no rights. Tributes would be paid, of course, and Mama was first in line. Harlan, who would personally dole out the booty, planned to give his mother the jewelry Daisy had inherited from her mother.

Since he'd gone through the house less than an hour after Daisy's accident, he knew where everything had been hidden. No one was home when Harlan entered through a back door with a duplicate key he'd stolen a couple of weeks earlier from Daisy's dresser. He knew what he was after. First he collected the important things, like the information he'd heard Daisy was preparing to turn over to the cops about his drug-dealing business. While there, he found the lock box where she'd hidden everything. He destroyed the divorce papers and a handwritten will. The stupid broad had left everything to her Aunt Kate, assuming she would raise *his* children. Only natural that something happened to the bitch.

That day, Harlan inhaled deeply as he smoked Marlboro after Marlboro and watched pieces of the last testament flush down the toilet before he filled the bowl with sand. *No more flushing, he thought, from now on I will piss on your sweet baby-blue carpet.* Before he left, Harlan broke the window in the master bedroom and locked the back door on the way out. A few minutes later, he spoke in a high-pitched voice when he called police from a payphone at the corner market to report a break-in at the house. Then he stood in the shade and watched while the deputy in his khaki uniform checked on the home with one of the neighbors, a red-haired busybody in a pink bathrobe and slippers. The deputy didn't hang around for long. Those guys never did.

Now the payoff. "Here you are," Harlan said, handing the jewelry box to his mother. "This is for you."

Mama, her fingers raised to her chubby cheeks, blushed like a girl being courted. "Why, son," she said as she opened the box. "Oh, my . . . Dear Lord on high. Why, thank you." She put a small diamond ring on her left pinky and it stuck halfway down. "Oh, my, my, my . . . These are lovely. I'll have to have them resized, of course. Daisy was a tiny thing. You *sure* these are for me? These are real, aren't they?" Harlan nodded. Rubbing her thumb and forefinger together, she asked: "You saying this is my cut?"

Harlan kissed her cheek. "Yes, Mama, you deserve fine things. And there's more," he said. "Don't you worry, I got you taken care of."

There is no greater joy than the rare moments when a son is able to make his mother happy. Harlan, seeing tiny rivers of mascara rolling down Mama's blushed cheeks, nearly burst with pride. At last he was earning respect from the woman who had brought him into the world and taught him the ethical lessons he put into practice every day. Truth to tell, Mama had recently had a heart attack and probably wasn't going to be around that much longer. Once she was gone, the pieces of jewelry would be returned and Harlan would explain to the rest of the family that he needed to put them in a safe-deposit box for his children. Not that he would. Harlan had already hawked the largest of Daisy's heirloom rings to bankroll an upcoming weekend in Vegas with one of his girlfriends.

Compared to burglary, an occasional occupation for the Sandoval boys, scavenging was cinch work. The brothers moved fast, opening drawers, cupboards, rummaging for anything that might have value and spilling everything else onto the floor. They were drinking beer, swapping stories and having a great time.

"Whatcha got there?"

"I got me a nice pocketknife."

"Whatcha got there?"

"Looks like a decent CD player."

As far as Harlan was concerned, if his children got out of line they knew what to expect. Fact was, he beat them as regularly as he'd ever beat his wife. *Don't want kids growing up soft, no sir.* And he was pretty good with a leather belt, rarely left marks. Jeez, he'd even had to knock some sense into his son the night before Daisy's funeral. The kid wouldn't stop crying. Harlan cut his pretty daughter some slack, at least for now. The things a father does for his children. At ten and eight, they were pretty near grown anyway and would be parceled out to Harlan's "blood" relatives once they started receiving Daisy's Social Security checks.

Mama always said blood was everything—and Mama was the maker of the rules. Didn't matter if there was a formal marriage ceremony with a woman because, once you were Sandoval property, you were always Sandoval property. The bitches that bore clan children sometimes had a hard time understanding. But they either got the rules straight or they ended up, well, like Daisy.

Harlan, good-looking in a shopworn Bruce Willis way, planned to continue living as he'd been doing, with whom he pleased, and his two children by Daisy would see him when he felt like it. He'd had other children by other women and didn't see them much either. No matter. Busy men don't have time. Harlan wasn't some fool with one of those regular jobs. He was a manipulator, a con man, a smooth operator who dabbled in various enterprises— and there were plenty of women hungry to trade for things they wanted, like the drugs he sold or could get for them. Fancy ladies, parties, drinking, drugging, smoking, gambling, fine clothes . . . that was the life. Harlan, the ex-preacher, now saw himself as an entrepreneur and businessman.

It took two days to go through everything. The Sandoval brothers ended up ripping the garage door off its hinges to get better access to the sealed boxes stacked on shelves and rafters. They opened every box and spilled the contents onto the concrete floor. Whatever they didn't want was thrown into piles, and it wasn't long before the house and garage were littered with debris. On Wednesday afternoon the ritual was finalized. The leftovers (books, children's toys, family photos) were thrown in the trash. Mama said it was for the best because the quicker the children forgot who their mother was, the better. "No sense them being down about what can't be changed."

Harlan's brother Ronald took the new air conditioner, a lawn mower, and antique tools that had belonged to Daisy's grandfather. Because Harlan owed him money, Andrew carted off two television sets, a stereo, and the computer and printer. Michael didn't want anything but cash that would come when Harlan sold the house.

Clan wives and cousins, who arrived each day with bags of food for lunch, stuck around long enough to cherry-pick Daisy's personal things. They took cosmetics and perfumes and whatever caught their fancy in the kitchen. No one could figure out why Harlan wouldn't let anyone touch Daisy's clothes hanging in the closet. They just figured the clothes spooked him for some reason when he shooed them away from the closet and out of the master bedroom. "Off limits," he said.

Family heirlooms—the antique silver, cut crystal, jewelry— were all given to Mama. As they were loading boxes into the trunk of the Cadillac, Mama asked for Daisy's refrigerator. "It's a fine one, a real nice piece of machinery."

"We can pick it up later," Harlan told her. "We don't have room."

"How about the washing machine and dryer? They still work, don't they?"

"Don't worry. I'll come back."

On the way out, Harlan propped the front door open with a patio chair. With the garage door ripped off, this left the house exposed so neighbors could come in and take what they wanted from the piles of refuse. From the outside, it looked like an act of kindness, sort of like donating to the desert dwellers' Salvation Army thrift store. It was not altruistic, however. It was a calculated move. The Sandovals wanted to leave everything open so no one could prove they'd taken anything. It was part of the game.

As Mama was getting into the passenger seat of the Cadillac, she noticed a white-faced owl peering down at them from a high branch of a scrub oak. She had heard the Mohave stories about ghosts taking the form of owls—and Mama sensed this was no ordinary owl.

"That bird's been out there every day since we've been coming here," she said. "I don't like the looks of it. Owls are supposed to sleep during the day. Isn't that right?"

Harlan shaded his eyes with a hand and looked up. The owl

spotted him and flew out of the tree screeching: *kuit, kuit*. It headed toward him, straight for his face. As it landed, Harlan tried to hit the bird with his fist. He missed and the scraggly predator brushed him, scratching the right side of his cheek. Instinctively he turned away to avoid another blow while Andrew grabbed a rake leaning on the side of the house and ran to Harlan's aid. Andrew struck and the bird, momentarily stunned, took off screeching. Blood slowly trickled down Harlan's face and rolled past his neck and onto his shirt.

THEY WERE GOOD-HEARTED suckers at the American Legion Hall, and they passed the hat around to help Daisy's kids. At the local market, they put coins in a jar on the counter. Practically the entire community stepped forward to help, even though most people understood it was a scam, another Sandoval "cash-raising sale." But they wondered where little Gabriel and Dora had gone.

One morning, Marlene called Kate in Washington. "Harlan's trying to sell the house to real estate speculators," she said. "You've got to protect the children's inheritance."

Three thousand miles away, Kate, staying at George and Catherine's home on the Potomac River, was frustrated. "What can I do?"

"Get a lawyer. That's my advice," Marlene said. "There's a pretty good one here. He's a retired prosecutor from Los Angeles. Damn nice guy. At least talk to him."

"We don't need criminal counsel yet. But I may want to talk to him. I found a decent probate attorney," Kate said. "Because there's no will we can locate, we're going to have to go to probate court to pay the medical bills. It could take a month for the court to decide if I have any legal standing."

But Marlene wouldn't let go. "You've got to try to get guardianship of Gabriel and Dora. People are worried. No one's seen them since the funeral."

"There's nothing I can do. The children don't want to be with me," Kate said. "They want to be with their father and his family. They told me flat-out at the funeral. Listen, I'll come back as soon as I can. I've got work to finish up here."

She could hear Marlene's crest fall on the other end of the line. But Kate hadn't given up. Since leaving Arizona, she'd been using the hospital's adult next-of-kin document to cut her way through the legal maze. Her gut told her that the most important thing was to find out what had happened to Daisy. At night she fell asleep listening to the croaking frogs and chirping cicadas while plotting her next moves. She had never felt quite so angry before.

Following double bypass surgery, George was recuperating and expected to make a full recovery. Catherine and a private nurse tended to his every need. For a man who had just beaten death, he was in good spirits and insisted he would be back to work in a week or so. "I canceled my retirement," he said. "Almost losing my job made me realize how much I miss it."

"I can't keep this," Kate said when she handed him back the cashier's check he'd sent her in Mesquite. "I don't need it." All she wanted was to return to Arizona—and, though she tried not to think about it, she was worried about Gabriel and Dora. If Harlan or one of his brothers could slit a gentle dog's throat, what might they do to a child?

Before leaving Daisy's funeral, she'd picked up the guest book that gave her names of Sandoval family members and Daisy's friends and colleagues. She was able to track down a number of addresses and phone numbers. Besides Marlene, Daisy's school friends were the most helpful. Kate had been trying, unsuccessfully, to reach the Sandoval family.

Elias Williams, sounding frail again, said he hadn't heard from any members of the Sandoval family since the funeral. "They haven't paid the offering they promised the church, so I guess we'll stand in line on this one," he said. "When you come back, let's go to the cemetery together. We'll pray for Daisy and the children."

It took a while, but Mesquite Funeral Home officials finally notified Kate that the coroner had released Daisy's body for cremation and burial. The medical examiner had deemed the cause of death "inconclusive." Daisy's car, which could shed light on what had happened to her, had been towed to a lot on a dry lakebed in the middle of the Mojave Desert. It was going to be auctioned off within a month because, Kate was told, law enforcement had decided not to pursue an investigation. Hospital reports provided disturbing new information. Amphetamines had been found in Daisy's system. Kate knew her niece, who had high blood pressure, would never have played Russian roulette with amphetamines.

The probate attorney managed to fax Kate certified copies of Daisy's divorce documents, which indicated she'd been granted the house and its furnishings, the Ford Escort, and child support payments of $500 a month, which she never received. She'd also been given full custody of Gabriel and Dora. A family court judge, to keep Harlan away from his ex-wife and their former home, had issued six restraining orders. Even with this information, Kate found herself running into stone walls. No one connected to the Sandovals would speak to her. And the women who ran the local domestic violence shelter said they were prohibited from speaking due to client confidentiality. Kate had to get back to the reservation.

IN A MOTEL ROOM near the casino, where Harlan was temporarily staying, the nightmares began. It was always the same dream, regardless of how much liquor he'd consumed before he passed out. He was in a canyon and blocked from leaving by boulders and a black tree with an owl in it. The owl flew toward him and, as it did, it became a warrior with a skullcap of owl feathers and a white-painted face with black and red swirls. The warrior's long claws gouged out Harlan's eyes before breaking through his skin, ripping organs and intestines.

In desperation, Harlan paid a visit a few days later to a Mohave fortune teller, the aunt of one of his girlfriends, who lived in a wood-frame house on the reservation. She may have been a witch, but it didn't matter. Harlan gave her five dollars, a carton of American Spirit cigarettes and a six-pack of Bud before asking her to interpret the dream. After snapping open one of the beers and drinking it in three gulps, the fortune teller smoked a cigarette. She blew a healthy stream of smoke across Harlan's face. Then she closed her eyes and held his hand.

"Dreams tell the future. They're omens. What I see is that Daisy's house is protected by a brave, a warrior friend of your former wife. Darkness breeds there," she said. "You have disturbed the sleep of the dead. If you don't stop violating Daisy's memory, the dream means you are going to die."

Harlan refused to put stock in a prediction made by a withered Indian hag who swilled beer like a man. Later that day, he tucked a snub-nosed revolver into his waistband. He was going to take out the owl, but the bird was gone.

Each afternoon when he returned to the dank house, drunk or near drunk, he continued smashing and destroying—breaking windows, kicking in walls, ripping off cupboard doors, tossing furniture out of broken windows and spreading glass shards throughout the home. Photo albums, scrapbooks, children's toys, family bibles, food from the refrigerator—it didn't matter what—all ended up in a heap as rat food. It didn't take long for the place to stink like a sewer.

Meanwhile, the real estate speculators who'd been courting Harlan to buy the house expressed alarm about its rapid deterioration. Ever the diplomat, Harlan blamed his dead wife for the condition of the property, saying she had been a poor housekeeper and that neighborhood vandals must have come in and trashed the place. The speculators dangled fifteen thousand in cash, though the property was worth ten times that before the cleansing ritual began, and said they'd take the house "as is" if no further destruction occurred.

Harlan was about to close the deal when something odd happened. He was nervous and called his lady friend to postpone the Vegas trip. For several days, he remained alone in his motel room watching cartoons because he was hearing voices in his head telling him he was "passing away." Though he didn't realize it, Harlan, his brain frying on speed and booze, began hallucinating in broad daylight. He imagined he saw a black-faced Mohave warrior, with white owl feathers on his head, coming toward him. At the same time, Harlan's bones ached, the pain in his gut was intense, and each morning he woke up to discover fresh scratch marks on his face.

One morning after three beers and a tequila chaser, Harlan summoned the courage to return to Rainbow House. He headed straight for the master bedroom where, despite the heat, the air felt chilly. But he was relieved to see Daisy's clothes, the ones that spooked him, hanging neatly in the closet with the mirrored doors pushed to one side. He could see her wedding dress underneath the protection of a plastic garment bag.

Harlan recalled the day he'd met Daisy. It was spring. She was working at the riverfront snack bar. He'd ordered a hamburger. "I think you're cute," she said. Daisy wasn't like the women he'd known before. It wasn't her hair or the way she smelled of lilacs or the alabaster skin dotted by freckles or the button nose that turned up at the end. It was something else—and he wanted a piece of it. He asked her out. On their first date at Nick's Pizza Parlor, Daisy talked on and on about her father who'd died when she was twelve.

"My dad was honest," she said. "He told me that our family tradition was always to stand up for one another. No matter what. It was us against the world. Daddy said, 'You take on one of us and you take on all of us.'"

Harlan was glad he didn't have to tangle with the man.

. . .

The smell of lilacs, Daisy's favorite scent, brought him back. Where was that smell coming from in a room filled with human and rat shit, broken glass, empty beer cans and garbage? Harlan moved closer to the clothing. A lingering scent in the fabric? It was possible. It felt like the closet itself had formed a barrier that protected the costumes of life from the chaos around it. There were no rat droppings inside, spider webs, dust, nothing . . . Nothing had touched Daisy's clothes. Everything was clean and fresh.

Harlan felt a rush and picked up his sledgehammer. He began breaking down drawers that had been in Daisy's hand-crafted oak desk. Harlan kept swinging. Sweating waterfalls, he pitched the pieces of splintered wood out the broken window into the yard. The main frame of the desk looked formidable. Harlan swung the sledgehammer and moved his arms in a quick overhead motion before thrusting his full weight toward the desktop. It was a strong blow that managed to crack the wood.

Now we're cooking.

Die, motherfucker.

Then Harlan took four steps back and arched his spine and delivered a running blow with all his might. There was a snapping sound. A projectile whizzed toward him and a flash of black blasted toward his eye. The piece of wood entered his body like a bullet and Harlan vaguely felt himself falling, spinning, incapable of knowing if he was screaming or silent. A few seconds passed before he began slowly, ever so slowly, trying to pull out the piece of wood, as sharp as an arrowhead, from beside his right eye.

Cognizant that he was on the floor and bleeding profusely, Harlan wondered if he was dying. Somewhere in the fog of his brain, he could hear a voice whispering the word "tradition." He couldn't figure out what it meant, but was relieved when it stopped.

MAMA LOU WAS in a foul mood. She'd been nagging her sons about Daisy's refrigerator for two days until they couldn't stand it any longer. Finally, Michael and Andrew got up from the couch, slammed the front door, jumped in the pickup and peeled rubber for half a block. Mama Lou went back to watching an Oprah rerun and eating Hershey's kisses.

Five minutes later, the boys drove into Parker and stopped at Red Eye Liquor for a six-pack and cigarettes. They ogled Luanne, the dark-eyed clerk with legs up to here, and arranged to hook up at the casino later that night. Then they went to Ace Hardware, borrowed a dolly from the manager, and drove, with speakers blasting Peter Frampton, along the dusty road toward Rainbow House.

"I don't know why she wants another refrigerator," Michael said. "She already has one that works."

"Fuck, don't ask me why," Andrew said. "I don't understand women. They want this, they want that. Mama says she wants to put it in the garage for storing stuff. What kind of stuff? I wish Pa was still around. Maybe he could talk sense into her. That house is full of crap and now we're getting all of this Daisy shit. You can barely walk around without tripping on something."

Michael didn't like to think about what had happened since

Papa Vernon took off. It was easier if he didn't. Some days, he wasn't so sure that Papa had really left. The old man had never said anything, not a hint, and there'd never been as much as a postcard. After Papa retired from the utility company, he was a homebody who sat on the front porch reading the Bible and smoking his pipe. The old man had never laid a hand on anyone—and it didn't make sense that some young tramp in a bikini had turned his head. Hell, the old man probably couldn't even get it up—and Michael found it curious that Pa's wallet was in a shoebox in Mama's closet.

Regardless of the dignified lady air she put on in front of people, Mama was the family enforcer, the one with the big wooden paddles and leather straps. Michael had scars on his back and legs to prove it. All she ever talked about was "Sandoval blood" and how the clan had to stick together. In truth, she didn't really mean Sandoval blood at all. Most of Pa's family had come to Arizona from Mexico. What Mama really meant was "Maugh blood," poor Southerners who'd left Mississippi for the Southwest after her daddy came home from what they called the "big war." Mama was nobody's fool. She figured there was a long-term political advantage if people thought the Sandovals were Hispanic or Indian.

At sixty-six, Mama Lou already had a dozen grandchildren and four great-grandchildren. Most of them were mixed bloods—and Mama promised her boys it would someday bring them gold. When Harlan, Andrew, Michael and Ronald hit puberty, Mama had encouraged them to get out and "sow their seed." In other words, make lots of babies. It wasn't hard because the Sandoval brothers attracted women of all colors. And, just like that, Mama was proven right. When uranium and other rare metals were discovered on tribal land, anyone who could prove they had some Indian blood got a piece of the action. And when the casino finally came to the reservation, tribal leaders voted to share the wealth. It was gravy time—and, no matter what, Mama always got a fifteen percent cut of everything. When the Sandoval Clan finally connected with the Mexican drug suppliers, life got pretty sweet. In some ways, Michael thought his mother could have taught Warren Buffett a thing or two.

Of course, there were some people who whispered behind Mama's back that she was trying to use Harlan as a respectability card with his pretty white wife, nice house and cute kids. They missed the point. Back when Harlan decided to become a preacher, that's when Mama first began envisioning a different type of life for herself. Finally, she was on her way to being a *real* respectable lady, a pillar of the community even. So it was hard for her when Harlan washed out of the church. That's when Papa disappeared and Mama went nuts for a while.

With Harlan's divorce from Daisy and whatnot, the timing couldn't have been better. Harlan no longer felt the need to be a respected member of the community. Methamphetamine was a new enterprise on the reservation. And Harlan was a natural salesman with excellent connections. Plus, having all those cousins scattered around came in handy for the distribution. So Mama sent her boys out in the world and waited for her cut. At times it was a bit much for Michael, who had always wanted to play professional baseball. But Andrew, who hadn't been sober since sixth grade, was a hothead, always had been, and he loved, really loved, dealing drugs and living fast. Everybody said Andrew was just like Harlan, only meaner. Ronald was slow and, mostly, he did what his older brothers told him to do. Ronald, who could barely read and write, turned himself into the family jewel. He could get women pregnant faster than anyone around. By the time he was thirty, Ronald had six kids by three women—and the good part, Mama said, was that his children tended to have unusual learning disabilities, which meant more federal government checks coming in every month.

. . .

"If I was you, I wouldn't be mocking Mama," Michael, eyes narrowing to slits, said. "She's getting up there. It isn't polite."

"Okay, okay."

"Remember when she used to tell Pa she was going to poison him? Or hit him with a baseball bat in his sleep? Do you think she meant it?"

"Yeah, she probably would have done it too," Andrew said, opening another beer. "How about some Grateful Dead? I'm sick of this Frampton pretty-boy stuff."

"Frampton is the king. How can you be so stupid? You don't recognize musical genius? If you don't shut up, I'll put on Wayne Newton."

"I knew it. You're gay, a real little sissy boy," Andrew said laughing. "Who else in their right mind listens to Peter Frampton? Think about it. If you drove down the streets of L.A. blasting this fluff, someone would pull out a gun and shoot you dead just for having bad taste. Do you hear me? This is embarrassing. Turn that shit off."

Michael gave his brother a grin before hitting him up the side of the head. "Is that so? Don't you think the L.A. gangsters would shoot you for listening to the Grateful Dead? It's coma music. Think about *that* for a minute."

"Just drop it," said Andrew, laughing so hard snot came out of his nose. "That's enough. Got any Kleenex?"

As they neared Rainbow House, they were surprised to see a 1971 Chevy with chrome rims parked in the driveway. Andrew slammed his hand on the dash. "Hey, that's Danny's taco wagon. What's he doin' here? Isn't he supposed to be in Bullhead City picking up a load? How are we supposed to make a living if he's not doin' his job? Friggin' lazy asshole. He's probably got a chick in there."

"Look, let's just get in and get out. Real quick. This place gives me the creeps," Michael said. "Some of the girls think the house is haunted."

"I wouldn't be surprised if it was haunted," Andrew said. "Probably Daisy or her mother—or both. Harlan really knows how to pick women. Pretty soon all he's going to have is a harem of ghosts dancing round him. He should have stayed a preacher. Then Mama wouldn't be on our backs all the time. Besides, I heard preachers get more pussy than rock stars."

"Interesting," Michael said. "Maybe that's why Harlan was so pissed when they kicked him out of the church. He liked the fringe benefits."

"Hey, if Danny's inside, he can help us load the refrigerator.

We'll be out of here in five minutes." When they got to the porch, the front door was open and they went in. "Hey, Danny," Andrew called. "We know you're in here."

They were greeted by silence. The house was filthy, ratty, broken down, darker than when they'd last been there. It stunk like a dead animal and there were dirty socks and underwear on the floor. Cigarette butts, empty beer cans and a couple of withered condoms were scattered around the living room. Cockroaches were skittering for cover across the carpet and black graffiti letters had been spray-painted across the sliding glass door leading to the patio. The writing was indecipherable.

"What the hell? This used to be a nice place," Michael said. "Remember that Christmas morning when we built the swing set for the kids? And Daisy sure could fix a pea salad and fried chicken like no one else in the world. What the fuck happened? I mean, we left it a little messy, but not like *this*. Danny, get your ass out here before we drag you out!"

There was no response. Andrew lit a cigarette. "Jesus, it looks like a bomb went off. What do you think? Neighborhood kids? Who else would do this? Call Harlan and tell him to come quick. Maybe we should help him burn this place down. That's what the Mohave used to do when people died. They used to burn everything the person owned because they didn't want ghosts hanging around."

Putting his index finger in the air, Michael shushed his brother. "Quiet, I think I hear something."

"Not me," Andrew said. "I'm booking."

"No, listen . . . I heard something in the back." It was a soft sound, like shuffling cards or wings flapping—and that couldn't be right. "It must be Danny," Michael whispered. "Let's give him some privacy."

"Fuck that," Andrew said, pumping up his chest before he began yelling. "Hey, Danny! It's Michael and Andrew. Just pickin' somethin' up. What's goin' on? Come on out here and show your ugly face."

The whirring sound again. "Damn," Michael said, as they tiptoed down the hallway toward the master bedroom. The hallway was littered with broken glass and the bedroom door covered with scratch marks. Michael took a deep breath and gently pushed the door open. Harlan, covered in blood, was lying on the floor. "Omigod! Call for help!"

While the brothers waited for an ambulance, the mystery of what had happened to Cousin Danny was solved. He came running shirtless and barefoot from Diane's house when he heard the siren. "What happened?"

"Looks like Harlan had an accident," Andrew said.

"Yeah, I see that. Jesus. That's a lot of blood."

"You forgot to zip," Michael said, pointing at Danny's pants.

The paramedics arrived and began tending to Harlan. "He'll be okay," one of them said. "We'll get him to the hospital. What was he doing here anyway?"

"His wife died," Michael said. "He's was trying to fix up the place to sell it."

The guy looked around the disheveled room. "Fixing up the place? Whatever," he said, "y'all can follow us to the hospital."

When Danny said he had to go get his shirt and shoes, Andrew snorted. "You better watch yourself, cousin. That lady's old man is a long-haul trucker—and he's one mean son of a bitch."

Danny's face turned purple. "I was just doing a favor. Harlan needed a ride to the house. I went to Bullhead City this morning and then had to make a delivery to Diane. It seemed like perfect timing."

"Looks like you delivered more than speed." Andrew nudged his cousin in the ribs. "Go get your stuff and meet us at the hospital."

"You know how it is," Danny said. "Woman home alone all day . . . Along comes a kindhearted stud—and nature takes its course . . ."

"Save your excuses for your wife," Andrew said. "How long you been diddling Diane?"

"Since ninth grade."

The paramedics wheeled Harlan out on a gurney; most of his head was covered in gauze. When the cousins followed, they saw a police car had pulled up as well.

"So what's the story?" Michael demanded of Danny. "What was he doing over here anyway?"

Danny scratched his head. "It was weird. I picked him up at the motel, just like I've been doing every day for a week, brought him over here. According to him, he was cleaning up the place. Said he didn't want my help, so I left him alone, told him I'd be back in a couple of hours when I finished my business. I left my car in the driveway because the neighbors might start talking if it was parked out front of Diane's place. What is that word? I can almost visualize it. Oh, yeah, discreet. I was being discreet."

"Okay," Andrew said. "So you know a five-dollar word. B-F-D . . . You were being discreet while plugging a mousy housewife. What else?"

"Well, you guys know your brother better than me, but it's my opinion that Harlan's been acting crazy lately. Driving over today he was mumbling something about curses and ghosts. I don't think he's been getting enough sleep. Maybe he's flipping out. I was thinking a family intervention might help. He could get treatment or something."

"A family intervention, huh? You been watchin' Dr. Phil again, Danny?" Andrew said. "When we want your advice, we'll ask for it. Now where's the fuckin' delivery?"

"In the trunk of my car," Danny said, eyes bulging. "Oh, shit."

Andrew lowered his voice. "So, we're standing around just shooting the breeze, leaning on your taco wagon, while the cops and paramedics are crawling all over this place. Danny, am I correct in understanding that you're telling me that you've got our goods in this trunk, right here on the *fucking* driveway of a dead woman's house?"

"Sorry, I didn't think."

"You never think. That's the problem," Michael said, under his breath. "One of the cops is watching us."

"This is what we're going to do," Andrew whispered back. "Danny, you and Michael are going to get in your car because you need to go tell Mama that Harlan had an accident."

Danny didn't get it. "You want us to rush?"

"No, goddammit. Don't peel rubber and don't speed. Don't

draw attention. I'll stay here and deal with the cop in case he has questions. Go back to Mama's and wait for me. She'll want to go to the hospital, but I don't want you using your car for *anything* until I get there and we move the goods. No screw-ups. Got that?"

THE PRESSURIZED AIR in the cabin wasn't helping her clogged sinuses. "I'd like a Bloody Mary," Kate, still fighting a head cold, told the flight attendant taking drink orders and handing out mini-bags of pretzels. Terry, whose long limbs were slowly being crushed by the pigmy leg space afforded in economy class, ordered two glasses of whatever red wine was available. Then he pulled a twenty out of his wallet and handed it to the blue-eyed woman with curly auburn hair before she pushed her bulky cart on to the next row.

Never one to appreciate airplane etiquette, Terry didn't bother with the plastic cup. Unscrewing the cap, he drank directly from one of the miniature bottles. Once he'd drained it, he unscrewed the second. "Medicinal qualities," he said. "Ah, much better."

"You smell like a wino," Kate joked.

"Not French, but California vino isn't bad." Red juice dribbled onto his salt-and-pepper beard and he dabbed his ripe lips with the undersized cocktail napkin. "You know, this seat is killing my butt."

Sitting in the window seat, Kate set down Theodora Kroeber's *The Inland Whale*, a book about California Indian legends, on the tray table and leaned toward her companion's ear. "Would you like to switch?"

"Thanks, but it wouldn't help. My body is simply too impressive for steerage. I'm a first-class sort of gentleman. I'll survive. It's a short flight. Thank God we're not going to New Zealand." Terry picked up the airline magazine and pretended to be reading before elbowing Kate in the ribs. "Have you ever thought about walking away from this?"

"Walking away from what?" she laughed. "The plane?"

"That's not what I meant. I'm asking a serious question. How about coming back to Paris with me after we finish this business? There's plenty of room in my apartment. We're good together, we've always been. It doesn't feel right anymore without you around. Think of it: croissants and me for breakfast, wine and cheese for dinner, staying up all night watching the city lights and dirty—no filthy—French movies and . . . Let's become lovers. You and me. Together."

"You are the sweetest man I've ever known." Kate looked at him with desperation and patted his cheek. "Why are you saying this? You're acting like a fruit loop. You know I care about you, but it's not time for this discussion. I've a head cold and I'm trying to stay focused on Gabriel and Dora and what I need to do for Daisy. I'm in crisis mode."

Terry leaned close and whispered in her ear. "Those kids *aren't* your responsibility." Kate shot a dagger at him. "No, come on, wonder woman . . . Listen to me for a second. You need to hear this. You're wasting your time worrying about Daisy's children. Whatever she could do for them, she's already done. She completed her job and she's gone. These kids have a father and they chose to be with him. They have their own destinies to fulfill—and you're not a part of that."

The flight attendant returned to ask if they wanted drink refills—and they both shook their heads. "I understand what you're saying," Kate said. "I really do. The shit of it is that I don't know if the children actually made the decision to stay with Harlan. They're too young. There's something else going on. I got the feeling the children were under a lot of pressure. They weren't the same kids I knew in the past or saw when Daisy was in the hospital."

"Okay. So, Dad's a bad guy, a complete asshole, but maybe that's what these children want. They're mixed-race kids. Believe me, I understand a little about how that can screw up your self-esteem. Still, they have the right to choose their own identity, whatever that identity is, and it may not be what you want for them. Kate, they've just lost their mom—and they're probably scared to death of losing their dad too."

The plane hit turbulence and began shaking. The red "fasten seat belt" sign lit up. "Whoa," Kate said, fanning herself when the shaking stopped. "I hate that."

"Just like riding a roller coaster. Breathe slowly . . . We'll be on the ground soon." Terry was eating pretzels like he would never see another meal in his lifetime. How he could eat with the plane shaking was a wonder in itself. Kate handed him her unopened pretzel bag—and he inhaled the contents. "Look at it this way: What's the worst that could happen if you do nothing more to try and help Daisy's children?"

It was a question she didn't want to hear. Kate's throat felt like sandpaper, a sinus headache was blurring her vision, her stomach rumbled, and her mouth tasted like rotten tomatoes from the Bloody Mary. She popped a Halls honey-and-lemon cough drop under her tongue and immediately thought of being at her grandmother's house drinking Earl Grey breakfast tea in delicate white cups with saucers. She imagined sitting in the yellow kitchen with the big window overlooking the camellias in the backyard. Tea with honey was Grandma's remedy for everything. Why did those you love always die? Gabriel and Dora were the only family Kate had left.

"Terry, I understand what you're saying. I'm trying hard to be an adult here. I want to be fair. If there's any way I can help Harlan become a better father, I'll do it. Heck, I'll even back off and never bother any of them again. However, and this is important, I need to find out more before I can determine which way to go. Daisy's estate is a modest first step. The court's going to insist her medical and other bills are paid. Until this legal issue is resolved, everything's in limbo. We don't even know if Daisy had life insurance. I need to talk to people to find out what led up to Daisy's death. You wouldn't be asking me this question if Harlan killed my niece, would you?"

"No, of course not."

"I thought you'd say that," she said. "We don't know and we owe it to the children to try and find out."

The fasten seat belt sign switched off. Terry pressed his seat to the recline position and stretched his legs into the aisle. A little girl, hair tied with pink ribbons and dressed in a Dora the Explorer T-shirt, came bounding down the aisle. She giggled as she hopped over his feet. "Cute kid," he said, turning to Kate. "You've been dreaming again, haven't you? I know you too well. You always get these little worry lines around your eyes when you've been dreaming too much. It's not healthy. What's going on?"

As usual, he was right. Kate sniffled, blew her nose, and blurted it out. "I've been having terrible dreams that the kids are in danger. They're on a mountain or trapped in a dark room with a guard in a uniform. There's a forest. I see Daisy asking me to help. She's with someone. I see him in shadows. It's not Harlan. Then I have creepy dreams of these creatures that look like owls. I don't know . . . Maybe I'm going nuts."

"You're not going nuts," Terry said, kissing her cheek. "Your dreams have been right before. But this is going to be rough. The reservation is a closed society. There are exceptions like Marlene and Edward. But most of the locals don't want people from the outside snooping around and asking questions. No one is going to help you. And this Sandoval family is something else. It'll be like facing down the Sicilian mob. I'm with you all the way, but are you sure you're ready for what's going to happen?"

"I don't see that I have a choice."

The plane dropped and rocked. The pilot came on over the speaker system and told everyone to return to their seats. "Buckle up and put your seats in an upright position," he said. Terry reluctantly moved his legs out of the aisle and sat up straight. Twenty minutes later, they were approaching the Phoenix airport and descending fast, a little too fast. The plane was shaking. Kate held her breath and pulled out her pocketbook copy of *The Tibetan Book of the Dead*. She didn't open it, just held it tight. Terry looked at her and chuckled. But she noticed the big guy was sweating.

They touched down with a squeal of brakes and a thumping sound before slowly rolling toward the terminal. Kate had always thought it odd when passengers clapped at touchdown just because the captain had landed safely. All around her, people were putting their hands together. When she looked out the window and saw a fire truck and two ambulances with lights ablaze awaiting their arrival, she realized something was wrong with the plane. "Had a little problem with the landing gear," the pilot said in a monotone.

THE PLAN WAS to pick up a rental car and drive out to the salvage yard in the desert halfway between Phoenix and the reservation before going to Mesquite to check on Rainbow House. Kate was carrying Daisy's keys and the backpack with her wallet and identification. She planned to use the hospital's next-of-kin document to get inside the wrecked car. If that failed, she had Terry, a persuasive diplomat with a gift of blarney. Failing that, she would pretend to be Daisy.

While they waited to pick up luggage, Kate checked her messages. There was a garbled message from Marlene saying something about an accident. Her hands shook as she punched in the number. After three rings, the gravelly voice answered. "Marlene, we just got to Phoenix. We're going to check on Daisy's car. You said something happened? The message wasn't clear. Are the kids okay?"

"I hope so," she said. "No one has seen the kids. And Harlan's in the hospital."

Kate's first instinct was to feel relief. Then she felt guilty. After all, Harlan was Gabriel and Dora's father. "What's wrong?"

"Well, honey, I hear he's an *ii do ilak=k*."

"A what?"

"It's what the Mohave call someone who's lost an eye."

"Harlan lost an eye?"

"Well, around here losing an eye means his family has to hold a ceremony to reintroduce him to society. Most folks are nervous about being around an *ii do ilak=k*."

"For heaven's sake, why?"

"Don't ask me to explain. It's an old Indian superstition, probably about evil eye. I hear he's going to be fine, but I don't know what the hell he was doing over at Daisy's house when it happened. Some of the neighbors think an evil spirit attacked him. Everyone is saying Rainbow House is haunted. I think it's a lot of hooey, but some of Harlan's buddies are talking about burning it down."

"You can't be serious," Kate said. "The house belongs to the children. It's not Harlan's house to do anything with."

"Well, you weren't here and neither were they. The Sandovals have been trashing the place. I hear Harlan's pretty mad about the accident. Christ, one eye isn't the end of the world. He could have lost his balls and that would have been a blessing."

"Marlene, don't talk like that," Kate scolded. "It just puts you on his level. You're better than that."

There was a long silence on the other end of the line. "Okay, okay. By the way, there's no need for you and Terry to stay in that crappy motel. There's plenty of extra room here. We need to talk and work out a plan. Tribal members are telling me Harlan's been around trying to find out if Daisy had a life insurance policy through her job."

"He can't do that. The estate is in probate. Everything's frozen until the court makes a decision. Harlan doesn't have legal custody of the children or any right to Daisy's money or possessions. They were divorced. She had full custody. I'll call my attorney. Maybe we can stop him."

"Now you're talking," she said.

Kate felt she was being outmaneuvered in every direction. She liked Marlene's no-nonsense approach, but staying at the ice-cube home didn't feel right. She'd been looking forward to returning to see Myra at Motel 6 and having Edward cook her meals at the Bluebird. She'd already reserved adjacent rooms. "Let me check with Terry and see what his plans are." Terry said he didn't care where he slept, but Kate politely declined Marlene's offer anyway. "Look, we should be there in maybe two, three hours. Can we bring something?"

"Just bring your sweet selves," Marlene said. "Oh, one more thing. Don't go over to Rainbow House. It'll be a shock. Let's go together. The cops are supposed to be patrolling. They don't know you—and I've told you how it is around here."

TUMBLEWEEDS BLEW across the road. It was a clear, hot day with enough wind to stir up the dust devils. The landscape grew starker. Terry drove the rented Toyota Camry with the windows up and the air conditioning blasting along the endless stretch of highway. He was steering erratically and weaving from side to side to avoid potholes, mountains of beer cans, cardboard boxes and broken bottles. "Don't you Americans have any pride?" he said with disgust.

Kate, lost in thought, ignored his tirade. Along the way, she saw forests of dying cacti and a collapsed wooden structure that someone had once called home, another reminder that the desert eventually reclaims everything. The desolation of the landscape choked her breath. When Terry slowed down as they passed the neo-Nazi rock shop in Quartzsite, she told him about the stolen white marble for Celeste's grave. "That's my girl," he said, bopping her arm. They stopped for gas, bottled water, chips, and used the restrooms before resuming speed.

Taylor Swift was crooning some bubblegum song about losing her man. Swift was a kid. What did she know about lost love? Kate hadn't had sex since she'd fantasized the act after falling hard for a married Frenchman. She'd stopped herself just in time, reasoning it would be wrong to betray another woman. Still, it had been a long time. So many lovers had come and gone over the years—some good, some not—but Terry, the incredible Romany Irishman, had remained only a friend and loyal supporter. She depended on him, but they'd never made love—mostly because she thought it might destroy their friendship.

The car swerved wide and she automatically braced herself by putting a hand against the glove compartment. "Sorry, Kate. These people drive like maniacs out here," Terry said, after being nearly driven off the road by a couple of yahoos in a pickup with a Confederate flag decal in the rear window. Though the other drivers couldn't see it, Kate gave the pickup a piece of her middle digit. Terry laughed and said, "Remind me never to pick a fight with you."

Instead of taking a left at the intersection toward the reservation, they turned right and followed a road sign pocked with bullet holes that said "Pete's." The rest of the letters had been obliterated. They rode straight into the bowels of the desert on a two-lane, barely paved highway full of ruts and more potholes. No other cars passed them in either direction. Five miles out, they came to a large black-and-white metal sign for Pete's Salvage Yard.

It was a dusty, desolate-looking place with an aluminum Quonset hut for an office surrounded by a chain-link fence. There were two tow trucks and a flatbed in the dirt lot. Snarling guard dogs announced their approach. With relief, Kate noticed the fang-baring German shepherds were attached to heavy chains.

It looked as if every wreck in Arizona had ended up in this surreal graveyard of twisted steel. Some vehicles were stacked atop one another like a slum apartment building Kate had once visited in Rio. There were wrecks that imitated buckled accordions, while others resembled flattened, gnarled carcasses. It was like something out of Dante's *Inferno*. As they walked to the office, they passed clusters of mangled jet skis and motorcycles. How many people had had to die to get all these modern-day relics towed to this hell? Kate was in no mood to speculate. She wanted to get in and get out. The place gave her the creeps. "Lovely place, simply lovely," Terry quipped.

Inside the Quonset hut, industrial-size fans were blowing hot air, ruffling the crude posters tacked on the wall, posters of naked women with breasts that Mother Nature didn't provide. The man behind the counter introduced himself and asked if they were looking for salvage parts. They shook their heads. Pete Linthicum, sun-weathered and rail-thin, was sucking on a Tootsie Pop, but there was a still-smoldering cigar in the too-full ashtray near a phone. Linthicum was one of the filthiest people Kate had ever seen—and she'd seen a lot of dirty people in her travels. The shirtless man stunk and was covered in black smudge marks and grease. His face, chest and arms were smeared with dried mud. He looked crusty and unaccustomed to visitors, particularly women. Linthicum wiped his blackened right hand on a rag without removing his eyes from Kate's chest.

"Whatcha lookin' for?"

"We need to pick up a few things from inside a car," she said. "The police told me it was towed to this lot after an accident in Mesquite three weeks ago." Kate pulled out Daisy's keys, driver's license and auto insurance card.

Linthicum picked up the driver's license and examined it. He handed it back with a questioning look and pulled out a logbook.

"You're lucky," he said. "Car's still on the lot. It's totaled, but not as bad as some. We're about to auction it off. Who are you? That's not your picture on this license."

"No, it isn't. It's my niece's car. I'm her next of kin."

"How do I know that?"

"I've got this notarized document from the hospital." Kate pulled out a copy of the statement she'd signed for St. Andrew's and her New York driver's license. "My niece died in Phoenix a week after the accident."

Linthicum grimaced. "Well then, I've got to notify the investigating officer. You can't be messing around with a car if there's a police investigation going on. No one let me know this was a fatal. I should have been notified. We have rules to follow."

"I've already contacted the police," Kate said. "There's no investigation. It's closed. My niece had an aneurysm while driving. There were no other cars involved. All I need to see is if she left some papers in the car. It's for the insurance company for her children. We're also trying to find her will."

It wasn't quite the truth but would have to do.

Linthicum wasn't buying it.

Terry, who'd been examining hubcaps hung floor-to-ceiling along the back walls, stepped up to the counter next to Kate. "My friend, it's a simple matter," he said, using his best awe-shucks brogue. "The little lady here just needs to check inside for some family papers. We're not looking for any other valuables. It's a mission of mercy for the wee ones." That said, Terry put a fifty-dollar bill on the counter next to Linthicum's ledger. The lot owner glanced at the bill, didn't say anything and didn't pick it up.

"Please," Kate said. "There are two small children involved and we're running out of time. We've come all the way across the country. We need your help, sir."

Without missing a beat, Linthicum looked across the counter at Terry and tapped his grimy index finger twice on the bill. Terry pulled out his money clip and peeled off another fifty. "Well, I might be able to help you. For the children's sake . . . I'll have to have one of my boys go out there with you. I want a witness if you take anything but papers," he warned. "I've got the cops on speed dial. They can be here in five minutes. I don't want any trouble. You hear what I'm saying?"

It was impossible not to.

A scruffy young man in a sleeveless white T-shirt with a picture of Kurt Cobain on the front appeared in the open doorway. He wore a holstered gun like an old Western outlaw—and Kate noticed with dread that his knuckles were tattooed with two simple words: "fuck" and "you." The rest of his body looked like a canvas for a schizophrenic tattoo artist. When he turned, Kate noticed the back of his shirt had lyrics from Nirvana's "All Apologies": *I wish I was like you. Easily amused.*

"What do you want, Pete?"

"Kenny, will you take these folks on down to see the red Escort parked at Cold Corner? They got keys. They're looking for papers in the car. *Papers only.* If they try to take anything else, buzz me, you hear?"

"No problem, boss. Follow me," Kenny said, motioning to Terry and Kate. "We'll take the cart. It's easier to get up the hill. You'd never make it in that rental car out there. Don't mind the dogs. They bark a lot but they haven't killed anyone lately."

It was an interesting ride. Kate and Terry were squashed into the back of a souped-up golf cart with oversized tires and a green-fringe top. They were soon bouncing along in the dirt at fifteen miles per hour eating dust and sand kicked up by the electric vehicle's front wheels. "Kenny, what's the gun for?" Kate called out.

"Security. We get dimwits up here looking for a new set of wheels," he said. "Then we get airheads from Phoenix searching for UFOs. Some idiots think the place is haunted and come out to do voodoo rituals or whatever. Makes you wonder about people. Couple years ago, we found a German tourist's body in a trunk. The cops missed her. She was almost mummified, but what a stink! I'll tell ya . . . Can't stand to think about it to this day."

They were approaching a slope. Kate nudged Terry's leg. Kenny turned back to look at them as he slowed to a stop. "Right up there," he said. "It looks bad, but at least there's no blood and guts all over it. I hate the ones where the brain parts are dried up. You can't get that shit off."

"Yeah, I always find that part hard too," Terry said.

"Oh, God, Terry, stop it. This is it?" Kate held her breath and felt her eyes fill with tears. She looked away when she saw Daisy's car.

"I'll unlock it," Terry said, patting her hand as he took the keys from her trembling fingers. Kenny hung back, watching them. "We'll check the trunk first."

"Be careful," Kenny warned. "Rattlers crawl in sometimes to get out of the heat."

"How about you stand behind me with the gun drawn then?"

"Don't mind if I do."

It had become a slippery situation; Kate was terrified, and too many crime novels and *CSI* reruns had nourished her imagination. The first thought that popped into her head was that Terry was about to be robbed and killed by a psycho with "fuck you" tattooed on his knuckles. Of course, she would be killed as well. Perhaps even raped, tortured and robbed. Then both of their bodies would be stuffed into a trunk until they became stinking corpses or were smashed by one of those car crushers. Who would ever find them? Who would care?

It didn't happen that way. When Terry popped the trunk, there was nothing inside but a spare tire. Kate moved closer and peered through the windows. The air bag had deployed, the windshield was shattered, and part of the roof was crushed. It was obvious the car had rolled and that Daisy's rescuers had had to remove the driver's door to get her out. Kate felt sick. Seeing papers on the floor in the backseat, she took the keys from Terry and opened the rear passenger door. As she leaned in, she noticed Kenny standing close behind her with the gun. "Careful now," he said. "You don't know what's under those papers."

It was too much. A tiny statue of Jizo—the Buddha who protects children, mothers, firemen and travelers—was hanging on a golden cord on the rearview mirror. There was a child's library book on the backseat, coupons for half-price dinners at Taco Bell, and a Barbie doll in a cheerleader costume. Kate used Daisy's umbrella to lift a small stack of papers. No snakes underneath. She picked up the papers, the book and the doll. She removed Jizo from the mirror. Under the front passenger seat, she found small things she guessed had come out of Daisy's purse a lip gloss, cologne, loose change, clear nail polish, help-wanted ads, chewing gum and a prescription bottle.

"Hey," Kenny said. "You're only supposed to take papers."

"Kenny, the woman who died in this crash had two small children. Do you think your boss will mind if we take a little girl's doll home to her? Come on. This is a child's library book. These tiny items are all they have left of their mom. Now put your damn gun away and let's get out of here."

Kenny complied like a recalcitrant child, but the search was a disappointment. There didn't seem to be anything unusual in the car, just an overwhelming feeling of sadness. "Kenny, do you guys clear out stuff before you park the cars?" Kate asked. "This one seems so clean."

"Only if it looks like we need to. Ever since we found the trunk lady, we always check the trunks. We wash away blood and body gunk too."

Terry handed Kenny a twenty and the boy tipped his cap. "We appreciate your help. We'll get out of your hair now."

As they drove away from Pete's Salvage Yard, Linthicum picked up the phone. "Yes 'um. They were here and they're gone," he said. "No, they didn't find anything. Nothin' to find. See you at the Rez."

THE MOON OUTSIDE the window was full—and Dora and Gabriel pressed their noses against the glass and spoke in hushed tones. "Do you think Aunt Kate's mad at us?" she said.

Gabriel scratched his head. "She's a smart woman. I think she understands," he said. "We'll make it up to her when we see her. We didn't have much choice."

"That's true. So, when will we see her? I don't like it here. I want to go home."

"Me too."

"How come they're keeping us here? We don't even know these people."

After a brief trip to San Antonio, Texas, to meet Grandma Lou's elderly relatives, the children had been returned to Phoenix, where they were confined to a small room in a house in a run-down neighborhood near the public housing projects. They felt like prisoners because they were staying with an aunt and uncle they were sure didn't like them. Gabriel tried to calm his sister: "If we're not good, they said they'll call child services to come and take us."

"What are child services?"

"It's like going to kid jail," he said. "They'd probably split us up and we'd never see each other again."

"Yikes," Dora said, sucking her thumb. "That's scary."

"Yeah, it is," he said. "We need to be cool until we figure out how to get home."

"What's wrong with Daddy? I heard them talking about him after dinner."

"They told me he had an accident and he'll be in the hospital for a few days. They say he's going to be fine, just different."

"Is he in rehab?"

"No. They said he hurt his eye."

"That doesn't sound so bad."

"No, it doesn't."

"Can we go see him? Please, please! I want to cheer him up."

"We're in Phoenix," he said. "It's too far."

"Well, I don't see what that has to do with anything," she said. "There are cars and planes and buses and trains that can take us home. Maybe we could call a cab."

"We don't have any money. We're stuck. For some reason, they're keeping us hidden. They won't say why."

"That's stupid."

"I agree."

"Guess what?"

"What?"

"I had a dream about Mommy."

"What about?"

"Well, she said she's alive in a different place."

"Yeah, a dead place."

Dora was pouting. "She didn't say that. And I believe her."

"Let's go to sleep now," he said. "If they find out we're still up, we'll be in big trouble."

"Gabriel, who's taking care of our dogs?"

AS THEY DROVE, Kate began sorting through the papers found in Daisy's car. There was a handwritten list filled with names and dates that didn't make sense. It was in Daisy's handwriting, sure enough, but it was going to take time to decode what the list meant. As she thumbed through the pages of an address book, she saw a few familiar names and phone numbers. Most of the names she didn't recognize. She decided to compare them to the guest book from the funeral. She needed to talk to people. She wanted to sit down with Elias and Edward. She wanted to ask Nopah Round why he'd been at the hospital. He knew something; she was certain of it. And, regardless of Marlene's warning, she was going to spend time alone at Rainbow House.

"Terry, I've got Daisy's cell phone, but it's an old one, it doesn't seem to have a list of outgoing calls. Is there any way to find out who she's been calling?"

"Sure, we can do that. Shouldn't be hard. I've got resources. If we had her computer we could find out a lot more. Once we're able to get a time frame and get a few things figured out, we'll turn the screws on the Sandovals. Our attorney should be able to help. I'm sure Harlan knows where the computer is."

Our attorney? He was thinking as a team. There were a million things Kate could have said, but nothing came out of her mouth.

"I've got a favor to ask," Terry said. "While we're here I'd like to go to the Mohave cemetery and pay respects to my old professor. He's buried there."

"Of course," she replied. "You don't need to ask me. I think we have to request permission from the tribe, but I can't imagine there would be a problem. I went to the cemetery with Daisy to visit her former lover's grave. I don't think she ever got over him. He was a nice guy. I met him a few times. Who was your professor?"

"George Devereux."

"Get out of here!" She was incredulous. "The anthropologist-psychiatrist who studied the Mohave and wrote the seminal books on the tribe?"

"Yes, one and the same. Devereux was the father of ethnopsychiatry. I studied with him at the University of Paris and then did some fieldwork on my own with a Romany tribe in Central France. I became a linguist because the pay was better, but my heart was in anthropology. I didn't want to become a psychiatrist. I'm not quite sure why he did either, except that his brother committed suicide. People who go into mental health often come from dysfunctional families."

"I honestly never thought about it."

"Anyway, what impressed me most about Devereux was that he didn't look down on or judge people who were different. He respected intelligence. And he considered it an honor to learn about indigenous cultures and belief systems. Like Claude Lévi-Strauss, Devereux transformed the way we understand primitive people. By the way, I'm told by my colleagues at the university that Devereux is the only non-Mohave buried in the reservation cemetery."

"Wasn't Lévi-Strauss the anthropologist who said Amazon cannibals prefer their friends boiled and their enemies roasted?" Terry chuckled, and Kate went on, "It must be a huge honor for Devereux to be buried in the tribal cemetery. Was he French? I think I heard Daisy talk about a Frenchman that the Mohave shamans liked so much they told him all their secrets and took him around to their sacred places. She thought it was scandalous."

"From what I understand, he had carte blanche with the Mohave. The funny part is Devereux wasn't French. He was born in Transylvania and changed his name from György Dobó. His mother was notoriously anti-French. So, maybe he was getting back at Mom with the name change. I don't know, really. But I always suspected that he might be Romany. You know how we Gypsies are about hiding ourselves in plain sight. Devereux wouldn't talk about it. Still, there were little things."

"Has anyone written a biography on him?"

"Not really. There's a lot there if you can get hold of the material. I know he started out as a poet and hung out with famous writers in Paris. Then he crossed the ocean and became a disciple of Alfred Kroeber, the anthropologist who studied California

Indian tribes. Of course you know who he was, you're reading his wife's book. Well, Kroeber persuaded Devereux to take another look at the Mohave. And that was it. The pretend Frenchman was hooked. Oh, he studied other cultures, but all he ever talked about was the Mohave. They were his soul brothers."

"You make me feel like an idiot for not knowing about Devereux," Kate said.

"No one can make you feel anything," he chided. "Eleanor Roosevelt said 'no one can make you feel inferior without your consent.'"

"Well, damn. I thought I knew a bit about the Mohave. Now I find out you know more than I do. Why didn't you say anything? Do you enjoy indulging me?"

"Call me a gentleman. Anyway, Devereux was past his prime when I knew him," Terry said. "Nevertheless, my first wife had a big crush on him. One of those European habits I doubt you'd understand. She thought him the sexiest and most charming geezer alive. Had I not been there to stop it, she would have consummated the relationship and probably killed my teacher in the process."

Kate put down Daisy's papers and stared hard at her friend. Terry never talked about his past. She knew he'd been married before but had no idea he'd been married more than once. "Your first wife? I didn't know you had more than one."

Clearly struggling to find the right words, Terry stumbled. "Mazeppa was a poet, a good one. We were . . . just . . . just . . . students when we met, too young to know what we were . . . ah . . . doing. We married and . . . um . . . drifted apart. She started running around with a radical crowd . . . a grubby bunch of anarchists. After we . . . uh . . . split up, she went to the Soviet Union with her friends." Kate watched his fingers clench and unclench from the steering wheel. "Mazeppa died. She . . . a . . . was trying to cross the border out of East Germany. I was in Paris teaching. Her . . . ah . . . friends told me a border guard shot her in the back. When I heard, I wanted to believe she was trying to come back to me."

Kate reached out and put her hands over his. She didn't say

anything. "For a long time, I was a wreck," Terry said. "My second wife, Elsa, was a dancer, a ballerina. We met in Prague, one of those summer-of-love things. It didn't last long. How could it? I was still in love with Mazeppa. Elsa and I were together until she wisely found someone else." He took a deep breath and smiled. "And, Ms. Thorsen, I've been footloose and fancy-free ever since."

"Life sucks, doesn't it?"

Terry let out a belly laugh, pinched her cheek until it hurt, and she pinched him back. "And now I've got you to worry about. Look what you've done to me! My manhood is being compromised. When are you going to succumb to my charm? Is there no romance in that black heart of yours? Can't you feel my secret love potion oozing out your nostrils?"

"What?"

"There's more where that came from," he quipped. "Watch your mouth or I'll put it to good use."

"Is that right?" Kate began to wonder if she'd been wrong, downright stupid even. Terry was a fascinating man and she'd barely paid him any attention. The banter continued. "Are you hinting there might be more to us than just working together?"

They were near the intersection where the salvage yard sign was pocked with bullet holes. Terry immediately pulled over and stopped the car. He removed his seat belt and unsnapped Kate's. He took her in his arms and kissed her hard on the mouth before he kissed her again with his tongue. It was liked being plugged into an electric wall socket. No words were spoken; they tempted each other with their eyes until Terry started the car again and gunned the engine. "Why don't we stop at a real hotel?" he said. "Give Marlene a call and let her know we've changed our plans. We'll meet her later for dinner at the River Willow. It's inside the casino."

How did he know what the restaurant inside the casino was called? "Yes sir," she snapped back. Driving with one hand, Terry drove back toward Parker. His other hand was firmly on Kate's inner thigh and moving upward when she called Marlene and then canceled her reservations at Motel 6.

THE BLUE WATER RESORT & CASINO was a gleaming white oasis on the Colorado River just outside Mesquite with a golf course, a 164-slip marina and a sandy beach. The towering four-star hotel, built in 1995, was—without exception—the most impressive resort hotel this side of Vegas. "You want me to check and see if they have a room first?" Terry asked.

At least he didn't know everything. Kate was nervously twisting and untwisting her fingers while she waited in the car watching Terry stride across the parking lot, the breeze ruffling his soft-brown, curly hair. She'd known him nearly five years. She'd depended on him and he'd never let her down. How could she have missed it? She knew so little about him. Had she become so career-driven she'd forgotten the joy of abandoning herself? If this was a mistake, it was going to be a big one. But it felt right. She had to take that chance.

After he booked the room, they walked through the marble-floored casino, past the restaurants and the white-haired retirees bent over computerized slot machines. They rode up in the brass elevator holding hands. When Terry opened the door to the room, Kate gasped. One wall of the suite was floor-to-ceiling tinted glass overlooking a private patio on the turquoise-blue river. The view was spectacular. There was a raised king-sized bed in the middle of the room, ceiling mirrors over the bed, and a fireplace in the corner. The suite was decorated in plush whites and muted grays; a bottle of champagne chilled in a bucket on the coffee table. Two crystal goblets stood gleaming next to a tray of cheese and crackers and a bowl of Godiva chocolates. She waited for his next move.

"Let's take a shower together," he said, confidently leading her toward the bathroom where white terry-cloth robes were neatly folded on a table. They undressed quickly and entered the large, glass-enclosed shower stall and let the steaming water run all over them. The soap smelled like lemons. Kate wasn't surprised that Terry was an experienced lover, but she hadn't expected the pleasure she felt when he began softly washing her body and shampooing her hair. They hadn't kissed since they sat by the bullet-riddled sign on the side of the highway. When she reached for him, he pushed her back. "Don't touch me yet," he said. "Let's wait." They moved from the bathroom filled with steam and out into the light of the master suite. Standing naked before her, Terry poured two glasses of champagne. They toasted. It was beyond sensual; Kate was in heat. "For what we are about to do," he said as they clinked glasses. "We'll always be friends, right?"

She'd barely taken a sip when he led her over to the bed and pulled down the white comforter. He took her glass and set it on the nightstand beside his. She looked up at the ceiling mirror and watched as he deftly positioned her on the bed. Terry was hovering over her and looking into her eyes. Then he leaned down and began exploring her mouth with his tongue. He licked her ears, her eyelids, caressed her breasts, spread her legs, and pulled her up to a standing position. He grabbed her buttocks, kissed them, and began gently manipulating her into a state of frenzy. When he lay down beside her, she felt the tickle of his beard during a rhythmic stroking manipulation that drove her to abandon. And, for the first time, Kate understood why women treasure lovers with facial hair. When Terry finally entered her, Kate thought it felt like what the British call "joyous carnality"—or maybe it was just wanton lust. Hours passed without notice as the lovemaking grew more intense. Kate felt like a moron for waiting so damn long . . .

THE SHINY RED CADILLAC was parked in the shade under the aluminum carport. Next to it was a small mobile home that sat to one side of the concrete driveway by the clothesline where Mama hung sheets to dry. Toward the back of the quarter-acre lot was a padlocked garage and a cactus garden. In the center of the yard was the towering eucalyptus tree where the Sandoval boys had built forts and played soldier when they were little.

Deliberately plain, except for the New England–style screened front porch with two wooden rocking chairs, the outside of the home on Rattlesnake Lane resembled every other hardscrabble place near the highway—except for the five-foot cinder-block wall and iron gates surrounding the property. The house was larger than it appeared. Inside, the décor was a comfortable mix of rich colors, family photographs, and athletic trophies lined up at the top of a built-in bookcase. Mama's pride and joy, though, was the antique china cabinet filled with porcelain tea cups and delicate crystal figurines.

A large soup pot was simmering on the range in the kitchen, filling the air with the smell of chicken, celery, Ortega chilies and onions. Mama—hair in big plastic purple curlers, wearing a flowered housedress and her newly resized diamond rings—was barefoot and humming along with Elvis: *Love me tender, love me sweet . . .* She had genuine feelings for that man.

She pulled the broom out of the closet and swept loose crumbs under the green leather couch in the living room before she began swiping fresh cobwebs off two crystal chandeliers. The gleaming fixtures hadn't been hooked up yet, but they were hanging nicely on gold hooks that Michael, her dutiful son, had screwed into the ceiling. The chandeliers were newly acquired accent pieces to the maple dining table that was surrounded by six Shaker chairs that an old lady had brought with her when she moved to Mesquite from upstate New York. Mama was glad the lady was considerate enough to leave her front door unlocked when she died. Mama never did learn where the boys found the maple table or the chandeliers. But they looked mighty nice, didn't they?

The boys were always surprising her with gifts. It was a source of constant amazement to her how much could be salvaged from people who no longer had material needs. Mama had one of those fancy marble chess sets from Mexico, a jewelry box full of antique gold watches, a stamp collection (thanks to the late Mr. Harvey) and a near-new refrigerator in the kitchen. Every room in the house was crammed with treasures: a complete set of English china in the Elizabeth blue-rose pattern by Johnson Brothers (Mr. Harvey again), antique clocks, radios, books, television sets and an air conditioner (courtesy of Daisy and still in its original container). Plus, all those cardboard boxes stacked in the back bedroom filled with stuff she hadn't had time to sort through.

James Taylor began singing "You've Got a Friend" and Mama smiled as she stirred the chicken soup and then set the ice cream bowls and silver spoons on the maple dining table. She put out linen napkins, the ones with pretty flowers embroidered in the hemlines, and a cube of real butter on a silver serving tray next to her salt and pepper shakers, little statues of Elvis and Priscilla. She sang along: *Lord, I'll be there, yes I will. You've got a friend, you've got a friend, Ain't it good to know you've got a friend?*

This was going to be a day for celebration. Harlan was coming home from the hospital after nearly losing an eye over at that witch's house. Mama never did like Daisy or her mother. Didn't like those two snooty grandchildren much either. From now on, Mama was going to see to it that Harlan got whatever he needed. She owed him that much. None of the good life she was enjoying would have been possible if Vernon, that Bible thumper, was still around. Mama, wiping her brow from another of those dang hot flashes, was grateful that she had one son who knew how to take care of the family business and was smart enough to keep his mouth shut.

Before she went to take out her curlers and change clothes, Mama quickly surveyed the house. There were fresh red carnations in a cut-glass vase in the living room and the faux-leopard print bedspread was draped just-so over the back of the couch. The bathrooms were spotless and she'd put fresh white sheets on the bed in Harlan's old room. Amazing what a little spit and polish will do.

$\bullet\ \bullet\ \bullet$

After Harlan's three days in the hospital, Michael and Andrew wheeled him, still wobbly from pain medication, to the parking lot in a wheelchair. They loaded him into the backseat of Danny's taco wagon and returned the wheelchair to a nurse. She handed them a bag of gauze bandages and two prescription bottles of Vicodin.

"Remember, no more than one pill every four hours," the nurse said. "Absolutely no alcohol with this medication. Oh, and Harlan has an appointment with the eye specialist on Tuesday. Here's the appointment card."

They rumbled toward home listening to Carlos Santana. "Did you notice that everyone who works at that hospital smells like disinfectant? It's nauseating," Andrew said. "I hate hospitals."

"I think they try to keep things clean," Michael replied. "You wouldn't want to end up in a filthy hospital where they've got bugs crawling up the walls."

"I see your point," Andrew said. "But I still don't like that smell."

Head drooping to one side, Harlan was pale and silent. His right eye and cheek were bandaged in white gauze. He looked and felt like hell. During the two-hour surgery, doctors said, they'd removed a good-sized wood chip from close to the eyeball. It was a miracle, they said, that he didn't lose his sight. A cut and multiple abrasions on the side of his head resulted in six stitches that would leave a permanent, crescent-shaped scar from the corner of his eye to his cheekbone.

Mama was waiting out in front of the house wearing one of her gauzy white church dresses and gold high heels. "Good to see you home, son," she said, leading Harlan into the house and pointing toward the sofa. "I'm fixing some chicken soup and your old bed is waiting for you. Come on in. This way, boys. Easy now."

Michael and Andrew walked on either side of their older brother, supporting his limp body as they eased him in and set him down on the couch with a thud. Danny, still on top of the shit list for leaving Harlan and their shipment unguarded, stood outside kicking dirt clods. "Danny, get your ass in here," Mama barked. "I didn't go to all this trouble to have you standing out there like some retarded child. We've got work to do. Wipe your feet before you come in."

Mama moved the Glade cinnamon candle to the center of the dining table and everyone came in and sat down, except Harlan, who was having his meal on a TV tray in the living room. As always, Mama bowed her head and everyone held hands as she began to say grace: "Lord, thank you for this meal we are about to receive. Thank you for protecting Harlan and bringing him home to us. Give us the strength to deal with our enemies in such a way that they will never again be a problem for our family. Amen."

The ice cream bowls were filled with homemade soup. Hot cornmeal biscuits were passed around and lathered in butter. Mama poured milk in everyone's glass and sat down again to eat.

"Ma, I want a beer with a tequila chaser," Harlan yelled.

"Don't have any tequila, son," she replied.

"Ma, I'm waiting," Harlan yelled again. "Dammit, I'm hurting here."

Scrunching her face up in exasperation, Mama got up and went to the refrigerator. When she arrived in the living room, she tenderly kissed Harlan's bandages and handed him two cans of Budweiser. "We're out of hard stuff. Here, baby," she said. "Just a little something for the pain."

THE FORMER SHOWGIRL asked if something had changed when they walked into the River Willow Restaurant. "You two look like newlyweds," she said.

Was it that obvious? Kate blushed and told Marlene they'd found nothing in Daisy's vehicle that would help solve the mystery of her death. "The big excitement was having a loaded gun pointed at our backs when we tried to search the car."

"Jesus, what happened?" Marlene asked. "Where the hell were you?"

"Pete's Salvage Yard."

"Pete Linthicum?"

Kate nodded. "This Pete jerk sent us out into the middle of the desert with a little goon wearing a gun strapped on his belt. The kid pointed the gun at our backs the whole time we were looking around, said he was protecting us from snakes. I don't think that was why. It was pretty clear the trunk had been cleaned out before we got there. All we got were a few scraps of paper, a library book and Dora's Barbie doll from inside the car. No last will and testament and no drug documents."

Marlene was silent for a moment. "I shouldn't be telling you this, but I know Pete Linthicum. I've know him a long time and I've heard rumors he's in business with the Sandovals," she said. "I didn't realize he would be the one to have Daisy's car. There are plenty of other junkyards around here."

Kate and Terry stared at their companion in disbelief. "What kind of business?" Terry asked.

Marlene leaned toward them and lowered her voice to a conspiratorial whisper. "From what I hear, you name it. I've heard rumors the shipments come across the border to the reservation before being distributed through a pipeline across the country. There are domestic sources too. There's a physician in town everyone calls 'Dr. Happy.' We shouldn't be discussing this here. No telling who's listening."

The waitress, a trim woman in a white shirt and black pencil skirt, returned to take their orders. They each ordered the house special: trout almandine, fresh asparagus, garlic mashed potatoes and orange-and-walnut salad. Terry ordered two bottles of Beringer Private Reserve Chardonnay. While they waited for dinner, Kate asked Marlene what it was like growing up on the reservation.

The former showgirl batted her eyelashes and crossed her hands demurely across her chest. "It was another world," she said. "When I was a kid, we believed the land and its creatures were to be respected. The river was the center of the universe. People depended on the land. Most of our parents were farmers who grew beans, squash, wheat, alfalfa and pumpkins. We kids collected berries and, of course, ate a lot of raw fish that we caught with sharpened sticks. I learned to weave baskets before I was five years old. It wasn't like it is now."

The waitress uncorked the wine and set down a basket of warm bread and a small butter dish. "How were women treated on the reservation?" Kate continued the conversation. "I've always wondered. You hear all these stories about women being abused and walking behind their men."

"In my time, it was different. I'm not saying women didn't work hard or they didn't have problems. On the whole, women were treated fairly, a heck of a lot better than the starlets in Hollywood. We weren't pieces of meat, that's for sure. I can't speak for the other tribes, but Mohave women were equal partners. They had a say in everything. Marriage ceremonies were informal and couples lived together until they didn't want to be together anymore. As I mentioned before, my parents never made their marriage legal, at least not in white man's terms, but they were together thirty years. Getting a divorce just meant moving on."

"I like the sound of that," Kate said, kicking Terry's leg. "I've always heard the Mohave liked to fight, that they enjoyed warfare with other tribes. Is that true?"

"Sure," Marlene said. "In the old days, Mohave braves were fierce warriors. It was sport. People got killed, but it was more like a football game. From what I understand, they thought war was the only way to regain lost honor. You can't tell me the same thing doesn't apply in modern times. Look at all the wars the United States has waged in the name of honor."

"You're absolutely correct," Terry said.

"Of course I am. In the old days, when Mohave warriors went to war, they fired a volley of arrow shots into the enemy camp as a warning. If the enemy shot back, the fighting started and all hell broke loose. But the enemy had a choice to fight or not fight."

The waitress brought the salads. "One more question and I'll leave you alone," Kate said. "What's the big deal about the Colorado River? People talk about it like Catholics talk about the Pope or the Holy Grail."

"That's an easy one," Marlene said. "The river is the center of the universe. The Mohave, the first people to live on this land, believe the dead—humans and animals—live under the Colorado River. Special souls go to Spirit Mountain where Mastambo, a god, resides. They believe the spirits of the dead are alive in another world, a place called the Land of the Dead."

"Do any of them become ghosts?" Kate asked.

"If they choose to, spirits can connect with the living. That's not necessarily a good thing. I wasn't going to mention this, but Edward told me about what happened to Gabriel's dog. Whoever killed that helpless animal will reap a bitter harvest."

STARTLED AWAKE by sunlight in a room with clean white sheets and a view of the river, Kate nearly forgot where she was. She rolled over and found Terry, wearing a white robe, sitting beside her with a silver service tray that held steaming plates of mushroom-and-cheese omelets and warm blueberry muffins. There were two glasses of orange juice and a pot of coffee. On the bread plate was a wrapped Snickers bar. "Where shall we start?" he asked. "Shall I ravish you before breakfast or after?"

Nothing worse than morning mouth. Embarrassed, Kate got up and ran toward the bathroom. "I'll be right back—and you'd better not touch that Snickers bar. It's mine." He gave her one of those "whatever you command, you shall have" looks, so after breakfast and a shower, she had him.

An hour later they picked up Marlene, wearing a nicotine patch on her cheek, at the ice-cube house. "Nice digs," Terry said, as he took in the pristine waterfront home and the modern furnishings. "I could get used to this."

"Bet you could. I told you to stay with me. Living too long in a Parisian garret turns your soul gray," Marlene said, patting Terry's cheeks with the tips of her manicured fingernails. "My word, you two look radiant this morning," she said. "It's either that love nest you're staying at or you must be drinking lots of our water."

"It's the water. I see you're giving up smoking," Kate said, changing the subject. "Good for you."

"No, honey, I do this periodically to dry out," she said. "Then I return to my naughty little habits. At my age, life would be a waste without vices."

"I agree. Winston Churchill said that success is going from failure to failure without loss of enthusiasm," Terry said. "And Churchill drank like a fish, chain-smoked cigars, saved the British Empire and lived to a ripe old age."

It was a short trip, three minutes tops, to Rainbow House, where the royal palms looked like Tim Burton grotesques guarding the aftermath of a tornado. "Whoa," Terry said in disbelief. "Your niece and her children *lived* here? I wasn't expecting anything like this."

Kate couldn't speak. The front door was wide open and the garage door had been ripped from its hinges. Crushed cardboard boxes had been pushed into a side yard and their contents mingled with a mountain of unrecognizable detritus. Empty plastic bags were hanging from trees like weird fruit. Children's clothing had been scattered about the front yard. Jackets and jeans had been blown by the wind and were tangled on low-hanging branches and cactus needles. Aluminum beer cans dotted the yard, creating curious reflections in the sunlight. Dark-blue paint had, inexplicably, been splattered against the beige house. Someone had opened a bag of concrete, wet it, then let it spill and dry in a mound in front of the garage. The Rainbow House sign had been ripped off and the fence post where it once hung had been demolished. Mattresses were stacked outside against a wall.

In the midst of the chaos, a pretty young woman with dishwater-blonde hair and a freckle-faced girl about Dora's age were sweeping the walkway with a worn-out broom and a rake missing most of its spokes. A rusted black van, sliding door open, was parked in the driveway filled with what looked like cleaning supplies. "Who in the hell is that?" Marlene said. "I've never seen those people before."

The child smiled broadly and ran toward their car. "Hi," she said. "Who are you?"

"I'm Kate. This is Terry and Marlene. And who are you?"

"My name's Leslie and that's my mommy over there. We're cleaning the house because we're going to live here," she said. "We're so excited."

At that point, Leslie's mother stepped up behind her. "Hi," she said. "I'm Lori. Who are you?"

"I'm Daisy Sandoval's aunt," Kate said. "This is Daisy's house. I'm afraid you're going to have to leave."

"But Harlan Sandoval told us this was his house. He said if we cleaned everything up, he'd give us a discount on the rent."

"When did he say that?"

"After Daisy's funeral."

Kate could see the confusion in Lori's eyes. This was obviously a poor woman trying to care for her family who'd been conned. Behind her drop-dead smile, Lori's discolored teeth were badly in need of a dentist. "You knew Daisy?"

"Oh, sure. Everyone knew Daisy," she said. "Her daughter went to school with Leslie. I didn't really know Harlan or his son. One of Harlan's brothers, Andrew, told him we were looking for a place and Harlan came into the market where I work. Andrew's a regular customer. He stops by every morning to buy a bottle of Jim Beam."

Over the years, Kate had learned to detach in order to retain objectivity. But the veil of separation she wore as a journalist crumbled. "Harlan had no right to say this was his house," she said. "I'm sorry he lied to you. The house belongs to Daisy's children. The estate is going through probate. The only people who can live here are Daisy's children. Harlan has no legal standing. He wasn't Daisy's husband. They were divorced."

"I didn't know," Lori said.

At that point, Leslie, bubbling over with excitement, reappeared and grabbed Kate's hand. "Do you want to see the stuff in the backyard? There's pictures and everything. Come . . . Come with me." The child led her to the rear of the house and opened a gate to the backyard. It was a nightmare. It looked like the entire contents of the house, except for the scattered items and the mattresses stacked out front, had been dumped in heaps three to four feet high across the patio and yard. Nothing had been spared—and nothing breakable was unbroken.

"Who did this?" An edge in her voice, Kate turned to Lori. "Why would anyone do this?"

Lori shrugged her shoulders. "Harlan did most of it. Andrew probably helped," she said. "Harlan told me everything in the house was junk. He said he was going to rent a dumpster and have it all hauled away. That's when he told me all I had to do was clean the inside of the place and it was ours. But it's hard to clean because the water and electricity have been turned off. Then I heard he had an accident and was in the hospital. Leslie and I just kept cleaning because we need a place to stay."

Kate tried to get a grip on her emotions. She pulled out her camera and began taking pictures of everything. There were three-legged chairs because someone had sawed the fourth leg off. Children's stuffed animals, clothing, towels, linen, photo albums, books and an old family Bible had been thrown in twisted heaps upon twisted heaps like the stacked dead of Jonestown. Most of the items had been gnawed on by rats. There were dolls with no heads and sports trophies with Gabriel's name scratched out. Food from the refrigerator—celery, broken eggs, cheese—sat rotting atop Daisy's ancestor pictures, and the glass in the frames had been smashed. Craftsman lamps had been cut in two, the lampshades shredded like confetti; the last of Celeste's watercolors had been slashed with a knife. Antique tools that had once belonged to Kate's grandfather were gone and Grandpa Mac's toolboxes sat open, like half-buried caskets, in the dirt. Generations of heirloom needlework created by grandmothers and great-grandmothers had been ripped apart. Handmade bedspreads, throws, and infant baptismal clothing were covered in urine stains and rat excrement.

It was sick, sadistic. Harlan had tried to wipe out Gabriel and Dora's mother; he'd tried to destroy their past, their home and their heritage. And for what? What kind of father destroys his children's toys and school mementos? Kate leaned down and picked up a nibbled photo of Daisy and Kevin and another, ripped in half, of Kate's parents taken on their wedding day. The sight of these defaced memories felt like a rape. These were the faces Kate had grown up with, the people she loved.

O child of noble family . . .

She couldn't take anymore. "Lori, why don't you and Leslie go home now? We've got work to do here," Kate said, handing the young woman a business card with her cell number. "I'm staying at the Blue Water and you can always reach me through Myra at Motel 6. Call if you think of anything, anything at all. I'd like to stay in touch. I'm sorry. Harlan had no right to do this to you."

After the mother and child left, Terry put his arms around Kate and hugged her. "Don't touch anything else," he said. "We'll come back tomorrow with gloves and disinfectant and see if we can save something for the kids. Let's get out of this madness."

Fury swirled in Kate's green eyes. "I want to go inside," she said. "Marlene, why don't you wait outside with Terry? I need to do this alone. I won't be long."

"Honey, I feel badly for you, but you don't know what's in there. We're coming in," Marlene said.

The house was dark. Kate could see Lori and Leslie had been trying to tidy up and had stacked some items in cardboard boxes. The refrigerator and larger furnishings were gone. The acrid smell of stale beer and discarded cigarettes lingered. One of the kitchen cabinets had been partially ripped from the wall and dangled precariously over the sink. The toilet in the main bathroom had been removed and the toilet in the master bath was filled with sand. The master bedroom was in worse shape than it had been before. The bed and end tables were missing, but Daisy's clothes were curiously still hanging in the closet.

Daisy's desk, splintered and scarred, was in the middle of the room. On the floor next to it was an ax. A puddle of what looked like dried blood was visible on the filthy bedroom carpet. It had to be Harlan's—and, for the first time since they'd arrived at Rainbow House, Kate smiled. Then rage kicked in, the kind of rage journalists can't afford to have. "Where does Lou Sandoval live?"

"Oh, honey, no," Marlene replied. "You don't want to mess with those people. I don't think you understand who they are. Let's call the police." Kate shook her head. "Don't do what I think you're going to do."

"We'll call the police later," Kate said. "I'm going to find Harlan. This won't stand. You don't need to come. Terry, you don't have to come either. This one I can do alone."

"Forget it," he said. "I'm with you, remember?"

"Me too," Marlene said. "Lou's house is less than a mile from here. It won't take but a couple of minutes. Got any weapons on you?"

Terry picked up a screwdriver from the bedroom floor and stuck it in his pocket. "I'm armed," he said. "Let's go rumble."

THREE VEHICLES WERE PARKED on the street and the front gate was open. They entered the enclosure and Kate asked Terry and Marlene to wait outside on the porch. Kate knocked on the door. No one answered. She knocked harder. She heard movement inside and the door opened. Standing behind it was the blond man she'd seen at the American Legion Hall, the one who'd tipped his beer mug at her. "Yeah," he said. "What do you want?"

"Is Lou Sandoval home?"

"Who's asking?"

"Kate Thorsen, Gabriel and Dora's aunt. Who are you?"

"I'm Cousin Danny," he said with a smirk. "Mama Lou! Auntie Kate's here to see you," he yelled before he disappeared, leaving the door ajar. Determined to confront Harlan, Kate pushed the door open and walked into the living room. An episode of *Cops* was on the flat-screen TV and a Tampa cop was putting cuffs on a spread-eagled guy in boxer shorts.

Gabriel and Dora's father was lying on the sofa in black silk pajamas with a bandage over one eye. Two other men, probably his brothers, were sitting on the floor. Kate saw her mother's hand-painted bowls half full of tortilla chips and bean dip on the coffee table next to empty Budweiser cans and an ashtray filled with Marlboro remnants, just like the cans and butts scattered all over Rainbow House. She scanned the room and did a double take when she saw Daisy's new air conditioner, still in the box, sitting in a corner behind the dining-room table. Then Blondie went into the kitchen, came back cracking open a fresh can of beer, and sat down on Philip Prout's green leather recliner. *Don't sweat the small stuff,* she told herself.

"Danny, bring me one of those—and, hey, look who's here, bring one for Auntie too," Harlan said, turning his attention to the visitor. "Hey, Auntie, how you doin'? I've been meaning to call you. I'm going to need some money to buy the kids' school clothes. As you can see, I'm laid up. I can't work for a while and it's going to take time for the children's Social Security checks to begin arriving. We could use a little help. A couple hundred should do it. What do you say?"

How did this pig look at himself in the mirror? A few seconds went by as Kate evaluated the situation. She was outnumbered four to one and didn't want to involve Terry and Marlene. This was her fight. Moving in front of the couch, she stood above Harlan and felt an odd tightness at the back of her throat. She was coiled and ready to strike. Even so, she spoke in a clear, calm voice. "I want to know where the children are," she said. "I want to see them."

Harlan's one good eye darkened as he extended an arm and wrapped his hand firmly around the back of Kate's knee and pulled her suggestively toward him. "Get your hands off me," she growled.

"Touchy, touchy," he said releasing his fingers. "My goodness, you need to get out more. Auntie Kate has a nasty temper."

"Where are Gabriel and Dora?" No response. "And who gave you the right to trash Daisy's home?"

Harlan listened, clenched his jaw and replied: "Hey, boys, can you believe this shit?" They ignored him, kept their eyes riveted on the television. "That's my house, lady. I can do whatever I want with it. By the way, who are those people on my mother's porch? Tell them to get their asses out of here. In case you haven't noticed, this is private property."

If she could have strangled him, she would have. "Let's be clear about one thing, Harlan. It's not *your* house. It was Daisy's house. Gabriel and Dora will inherit it. Right now, the house and everything that belonged to Daisy are under court protection. The estate's in probate and, as next of kin, I'm the executor. You can be prosecuted for destroying or taking property."

"My goodness, Auntie, you're cute when you're mad," he said. "Isn't she cute, boys?" Ears open, three pair of eyes remained fixed on the flat screen.

Kate felt a rush of blood pumping. "You haven't answered my question." She raised her voice. "Where are the children?"

Harlan lit a cigarette, blew a puff of smoke in her direction and flipped his ash on the carpet. "Safe and sound in the bosom of their blood family," he said. "They're visiting relatives while I recover from my unfortunate accident. It's none of your fucking business, bitch. They don't want to be with you. I've got witnesses who heard them tell you that. They're my children and that's my house. Unless, of course, you would like to buy it. Maybe we can work out a deal. Did you bring your checkbook?"

The guy was a piece of work. "I've read the divorce documents," Kate said, nearly spitting at him. "I have certified copies of everything. You got nothing! Nothing except child support payments you never made. You owe your kids for back payments. Did you know that they could sue you? Put you in jail for nonsupport? Listen, I know you physically abused my niece."

Harlan took another puff, but she noticed his hand trembled slightly. "The court gave Daisy full custody of the children. We can prove you rarely saw them," she continued. "You're not a father. You're a leech."

"Bullshit!"

Kate raised her voice again. "I saw what you did to Rainbow House. And I know what you did to that poor dog."

Andrew was chugging his beer, stifling laughter. "You can't prove anything," Harlan said. "It's my word against yours."

"Sorry to tell you this, but people *saw* you," she said. "There were witnesses and they're ready to come forward." It was a bit of a stretch, but worth it. From the look on Harlan's face, she knew she'd scored a point.

The kitchen door swung open. With a flurry, Mama Lou walked into the room as if she hadn't been listening from the other room. She was wearing a pink floral Hawaiian dress and heavy makeup. Her hair was pulled back into a tidy bun. Around the overhang of her neck folds, there was a silver heart pendant studded with malachite poking out, the necklace Kate had sent Daisy last year from France. Waving her hands in the air, Lou's fingers sparkled with the heirloom rings last seen in the jewelry box at Rainbow House. *Don't sweat the small stuff*, Kate told herself again.

"Well, look who's here. What a wonderful surprise," Mama said, drawing out each word like she was pouring maple syrup. "Why didn't you boys tell me Kate was here? Can I fix you something? Tea? Coffee? Lemonade?"

Kate shook her head.

Mama Lou walked to the screen door and shaded her eyes with her hands to look outside. "My goodness, is that someone sitting out on my front porch? Why, if it isn't Marlene Stone and your friend. Terry, isn't it? Good grief, invite them in."

No one moved. So Mama zeroed in on her oldest son: "Harlan, what kind of manners you been picking up lately? You and the boys go somewhere else and watch that nonsense. Kate and I have some catching up to do."

Harlan lifted himself from the couch and pitched an unopened beer can at the screen door. Then he picked up one of the ice cream bowls and threw it at Kate, barely missing her but splattering her shirt with red salsa. "What the hell's going on?" Mama said.

The screen door opened abruptly. Terry, brandishing the screwdriver, marched in like a rogue elephant with Marlene right behind him. Harlan ignored them and focused his attention on Kate. "Listen to me, bitch," he said. "If you know what's good for you, you'll take your scrawny ass and go back to wherever it is you came from. You're not welcome here or anywhere else on the Rez. Is that clear? Get the fuck out!"

In a blur, Terry moved in front of Kate. "Wanna step outside, Harlan?"

"Sure, as soon as I get my crutches. Hey, Andrew, Michael, Danny, why don't you take Fat Boy outside?" Andrew and Danny stood up, but Michael remained seated. Then Harlan began cackling. "You see, Kate, there's a lot more of me than just me. You want to take us all on? You ready to die?"

A wide crack had been revealed in Mama Lou's carefully constructed mask of civility. "What's gotten into you, Harlan? This is no way to treat guests."

"Fuck it, Mama," he said. "They weren't invited."

Wiping away the dripping salsa, Kate moved in front of Terry until she stood nose to nose with Harlan. "Let me make this clear: you lay one finger on those children and you're a dead man. Got it? You touch Daisy's house again and I'll put you behind bars."

"Oh, I'm so scared," Harlan said. "Auntie's going to hurt me if I'm a bad boy."

"That's enough," Terry said, grabbing Kate's arm and leading her out the door. Marlene curtly said goodbye to Lou and slammed the screen door closed. Face flushed, Terry got into the rental car, turned on the ignition and hit the gas. They sped down the highway. "Dammit, dammit," he said as he pounded a fist on the steering wheel. "Kate, don't ever tell me to wait outside again."

• • •

Once their uninvited guests had driven off, Mama Lou asked Harlan to come into her bedroom. It was an unusual request, something she hadn't done since the night when she asked him to help her out with Papa. Like a meek child, he sat on the pink satin bedspread and waited for her to talk. She stared at him for a long time, not saying anything. "What?" he finally asked. "What do you want from me?"

"Son, it seems to me that something's getting stirred up around here," she said, handing him a cigar box from the top drawer of her dressing table. "It disturbs me no end. I don't like the tone. It's time you pay Pastor Williams a little visit. Remind him of how things are supposed to be. We need to get this attitude thing turned around before it becomes a problem."

LOST IN ROCK AND ROLL, Kate was singing along with Mick Jagger on the radio. "You sound like a foghorn." Terry said, as they drove toward the Bluebird for lunch. "We need to work on those pipes."

In the backseat, Marlene was ripping off her nicotine patch. "Those damn Sandovals. Now I'm hungry as hell. I don't want to go to the Bluebird. They don't serve alcohol. Let's go to the Legion and order a pitcher and sandwiches. I'll get drunk, dance and blow smoke rings at the dart board."

"Down, lady, down . . . I need to see if Edward's working," Kate said. "I've got to talk to him. We can go to the Legion later." Marlene slunk down into her seat. Terry rolled his eyes and kept on driving. The Bluebird's parking lot was nearly full, but they squeezed into a spot between a Hummer and a Ford Bronco. Once she extracted herself one bent leg at a time, Kate's step quickened as she approached the café.

Shirley, hair sprayed lime-green and grape-purple, was holding the front door open, waving them inside. "Welcome back, girl-friend," she said. "We missed you." The two women hugged. "We've got a turkey dinner special today. Only $7.99. How about it?"

"Sounds good to me," Kate replied. "But Terry and Marlene may want something else. I need to talk to Edward. Is he working?"

"You bet he is. He's been asking after you. I'll let him know you're here. Y'all want coffee?"

While Marlene and Terry were seated, Kate went toward the kitchen. Edward turned, saw her and pulled off his apron. "Mario, can you take over for a minute?" They sat at the back of the restaurant at a corner table for two.

"I can't stay long," Kate said. "My friends are with me. But I wanted to talk to you about the Sandovals. They're causing problems. And after what they did to Fred, I'm worried about you."

Edward met her gaze. "I'm not concerned about them. This is my home. I worry for you. You shouldn't be alone."

"Terry's with me," she said. "So, I'm not really alone."

"Oh." Edward looked across the room and smiled when Terry waved at him. "I see what you mean. Good. You need friends. I wanted to let you know that Big Nose and I took care of the boy's dog. He was given a proper burial. When you see Gabriel, tell him I'll take him to visit the grave. The dog is safe now."

"Thank you," she said. "You've been very kind to our family. I'm beginning to think you're an angel."

"No, I'm a fry cook. Oh . . . I also wanted to tell you that I've been at Pioneer Cemetery to tell the woman you'd be back. They placed the stone. She hears me when I sing to her. She's worried about her children."

The fry cook continued to surprise her. Was this just an example of the Mohave politeness she'd read about? "Have you spoken to Nopah?"

"Yes, I have," Edward said. "Nopah says he will see you."

Kate beamed. "When?"

"There are some rules," he said. "I will take you. No one else may come. When do you want to go?"

"How about tomorrow when you get off work?"

Edward smiled and returned to the kitchen.

After turkey specials at the Bluebird, the trio was off to buy cleaning supplies at the hardware store. Before they dropped Marlene off at her house, Terry arranged for her to escort him to the Mohave cemetery the next day. While Terry was paying respects to his former teacher, Kate would be meeting with Nopah, the Mohave holy man. As the car passed the Colorado River, a shimmering light reflected above the water line. Kate thought it a good sign.

Part IV

ONE NIGHT SIX YEARS EARLIER, Mama had called Harlan. She spoke calmly, no emotion, her voice a monotone: "Son, do you mind coming over? I've got me a little problem." It was out of character for Mama to call so late and then not explain why she was calling, especially on a Saturday night when he had to preach in the morning.

Irritated, Harlan bolted out of bed, dressed, and left Daisy and the children asleep in their beds. He drove quickly to the house where he'd grown up and was disturbed when he got there and saw lights blazing, like a party was going on. When he opened the unlocked front door, there was Vernon Sandoval, as peaceable a man as ever lived, sprawled flat on the floor of the living room. Papa was wearing a thin cotton nightshirt and there was blood all over him, seeping into a thick pool around the back of his head.

"Oh, my God," Harlan yelled. "Wha— What happened?"

Mama was whistling, not a tune. Just whistling, long and low . . . Harlan could see she was in one of those moods she got stuck in occasionally. She was standing over Vernon in a pink nightgown holding a little pistol in her hand. She held it like it was nothing more than an eggbeater and she was about to bake a chocolate cake.

"Is he dead? Can you tell? I've got more bullets if we need them."

Her eyes were blurry, out of focus. It was the same look Harlan remembered Mama had had that Christmas Eve when she cracked the newborn baby's head against a rock because she didn't want any daughters. Instead of opening presents the next morning, Papa and Harlan, just a boy himself then, buried the unnamed baby girl in a red beach towel under the big tree in the yard. They didn't talk as they dug. And Papa never spoke of what happened to that girl again. Harlan was relieved when Mama's next two babies were male.

"Son, I asked you a question and you didn't answer me." Mama said it matter-of-factly, like if Vernon wasn't dead, she didn't have any qualms about finishing the job. "Is he alive or not?"

Harlan got down on the floor and felt for a pulse, lifted his father's eyelids and pressed his ear against the old man's chest. "Mama, he's gone. Why did you do this? Have you lost your mind? You want me to call the police?"

"Oh, Lord, no," she said. "Don't call anybody. I just want you to help me get rid of him."

Wiping away tears, Harlan didn't know what to do. "Tell me the truth. Did you have a fight tonight? Is anyone else in the house?"

Mama, who generally wielded a frying pan when she wanted to smack her husband around, shook her head. An icy silence passed as Harlan's mind raced. He'd never expected this. "We'll bury him next to the baby," she said. "Hurry up before it gets light. Go get the shovel and a flashlight. We'll wrap the old bastard in a shower curtain and pour bleach on him to cut down the smell. We'll need some rocks. I don't want coyotes coming in my yard digging up your daddy."

"Why did you do this? Papa never hurt you or anyone. Mama, why?"

"He was getting on my nerves," she said. "He disgusted me."

"Give me the gun," Harlan said gently, slowly extending his hand.

"Don't you touch me," she said, brushing his hand aside and pointing the pistol at her son's chest. "It would be no big thing to knock you off. Double the pleasure and double the fun."

The ground was solid. It took Harlan more than an hour to dig a hole big enough for Papa, even though he was a small man. After they lowered the body, wrapped in a plastic shower curtain, Mama emptied two gallons of bleach into the hole. Then she went into the garage and dragged back a forty-pound bag of cement and poured it in before turning on the outdoor water spigot. "Wet it down real good," she ordered, handing Harlan the garden hose.

"How are you going to explain this? People are going to ask after Papa."

"I'll just say the old prick met some young hussy down at the American Legion Hall and took off with her," she said. "Who's not going to believe that?"

After the grave was filled with dirt, cement and rocks from the cactus garden, a lawn chair was strategically placed over what was left visible of the freshly turned earth. Then Mama yawned, announced she was tired and was going to bed. While she slept, her dutiful son scrubbed blood off the living-room floor before he rushed home, showered and tried to get his head around the sudden dramatic turn of events. The assistant pastor and respectable family man couldn't tell his wife. He couldn't tell anyone.

The next morning at church, there was Mama in her Sunday best pretending to be upset, wiping her eyes and telling friends the story about how her rotten husband ran off with a young thing in one of those Brazilian bikinis. Though it sickened him, Harlan helped spread the lie. Even his brothers believed it—or pretended to. It ate at him, though. After a while, Harlan didn't care much about anything or anyone. Eventually he lost his job, his wife and his children. He drifted, got drunk, started fights and lived in a hell of his own making. No trace of Vernon Sandoval was ever found, and Mama continued to forge his signature and cash his Social Security checks every month. It wasn't long before Harlan was reborn as a man to be feared. Now he was working for Mama again.

THE FILTH AND STENCH were overwhelming. Because there was no electricity, they were forced to work during daylight hours when the heat was oppressive. Kate had made arrangements to have a carpenter meet them at Rainbow House to board up the windows and the garage door. A locksmith would be there before noon to change all the locks and repair the doors.

She'd purchased "No Trespassing" signs, a hammer, nails, work gloves, plastic bags, rat killer, bug spray, heavy-duty storage crates, duct tape, cleaning supplies, gallons of purified water, brooms, dustpans, a shovel, flashlights and a first-aid kit. She'd also come across party decorations at the hardware store, wire strings decorated with metallic blue hearts. The decorations reminded her of when she and Daisy put blue hearts around Celeste's grave. On impulse, Kate bought four six-foot-long strings to hang along the front porch on hooks that had once held up Christmas lights. Up close, the hearts sparkled, but from a distance they looked like barbed wire.

"What's that for?" Terry, mildly amused, asked her as she strung the hearts. "Are you doing some kind of wicked Hoodoo?"

"Voodoo," she said, "to keep Sandovals away." When Kate stood back to admire her handiwork, she wasn't satisfied. "I wish we had sage to burn. We really should smoke the entire house, every room. It's supposed to purify and protect."

"You can ask the soothsayer when you see him," he said. "The Mohave surely have a purification ceremony. If you want, I'll do a Gypsy ritual. Of course, you'll have to pay me—and I don't come cheap, though I'll consider taking it in trade."

"I'll think about it," she said, stifling a laugh. "Considering what we're doing, when did you have your last tetanus shot?"

"Before I left Paris," he said. "I told the doctor I was traveling to a Third World country to save a damsel in distress."

"You're funny," she said, "and perceptive in a desperate way. Listen, Big Guy, we've got a lot of work to do and if you're not up to it, that's okay. This is my problem and I can handle it. You can go sit by the hotel pool and come back for me in a couple of hours."

"You're not doing this without me," he said. "I thought I made that clear."

Earlier, Kate had called the tribal utility company to get the power and water turned back on, but the customer service rep wanted proof that she had a legal right to be in the house. A next-of-kin document from a hospital wasn't good enough. So Kate called her attorney, who said he'd just received confirmation from the probate court that she'd been named executor of the estate. He faxed a copy to the hotel and she faxed a copy of the copy to the skeptical customer service rep. She paced the hotel lobby and waited an hour before calling the utility again. This time, she was told it would take two or three days for the utilities to be restored and she'd need to personally come to the office that morning to make a deposit and pay for the arrears, plus interest, on Daisy's delinquent bill.

While at tribal headquarters, Kate requested that a dumpster be delivered for the excess trash. For that, she had to visit another department. Harlan had already ordered a dumpster, the clerk said. "Well, cancel that order," Kate said. "Mr. Sandoval is out of the picture. The house belongs to Daisy Sandoval's children and I'm the executor of the estate." The clerk said there would be a five-day wait while the matter was investigated. "Tribal bureaucracy," Kate said to Terry as they walked out. "Don't you love it?"

To make room for the promised dumpster, they needed to clear space in the side yard where a mountain of debris awaited. In the wilting heat, Terry and Kate were covered head to toe. They wore heavy rubber gloves, caps, tall work boots, long pants and long-sleeved shirts because of the ever-present possibility of snakes, scorpions, rats, spiders, fire ants and other unidentified creatures. "Let's leave the garage till the end," Terry said. "I'm not ready to tackle what's probably in there."

She harbored the same sentiment but decided to play with him. "I thought you wanted to be an archeologist?"

"I said I thought about being an *anthropologist*," he replied. "I wanted to study people, not their garbage."

Securing the perimeter was the logical place to start. They posted the "No Trespassing" signs, hanging the first where the "Rainbow House" sign had been ripped off. They swept the porch and cleared the front yard of debris, raking it into piles. Inside, Terry cleared the broken glass in the hallway while Kate poured bleach on Harlan's bloodstain. The logic was to create one clean room for storage, assuming they found anything worth saving. "This reminds me of Cormac McCarthy's *The Road*," Terry said.

"Good description," she said. "At least the father and son kept walking."

"There is that . . . Hey, maybe that's why people keep moving from place to place. They don't like cleaning up their messes."

"You, Big Guy, are my mess," she said. "I'm going outside to see if I can salvage any of the family photos."

"I'll come with you."

They worked side by side. An hour later, Terry went back into the house. Kate was sifting through toys in the side yard when he returned looking frantic. "I forgot that there's no toilet in one bathroom and the other one is filled with sand," he said. "What are we going to do?"

Harlan's depravity knew no limits. "I don't know," she said. "How about the bathtub? If that doesn't work, maybe we can find a bucket somewhere. We can't go outside. Anyone can see us and I'm not baring my butt to the wildlife around here."

"I'm going across the street to the market," he said. "Maybe they'll let me use their bathroom. This is an emergency."

"Bring me a Coke and a bag of ice for my head," she begged. "Please?"

After Terry half-ran toward the market, Butch Gibson, the carpenter, and his teenage son arrived. Their truck was filled with plywood boards and they wore tool belts around their waists. "If you don't mind my asking, what happened to this place?" Butch asked.

"Ex-husband happened," Kate replied.

"Was he drunk or just pissed off?"

"Insane." It was as good a term as any, and she couldn't think of a more apt description for a low-life bully who spent his days smashing children's toys and dismantling furniture.

"I remember the family that first lived here. Celeste . . . Celeste Prout. Yes, that was her name. Nice lady. She was well known around these parts. I did some work in the kitchen for her. Custom cabinetry, that's my specialty. She had two kids. Something happened to the boy. After she left town, didn't her daughter, a pretty little thing, live here with her family?"

"You mean Daisy?"

"That was it," Butch said. "Was it Daisy's husband who did this?"

"I'm afraid it was."

"What does she say about it?"

"Daisy died. The ex did this afterward."

"This was recent?" Kate nodded. "Was he all torn up or something?"

"I guess so."

"God Almighty. I didn't know. Sorry, I don't read the papers anymore. Didn't Daisy have children?" He looked at the toys strewn around the yard. "Where are they?"

"Their father took them," she said. "We're trying to find them."

Butch turned to look at his son. The boy didn't say anything. Then Butch turned back to face Kate. "I'm real sorry for your troubles," he said, his voice a whisper. "We'll get you fixed up as best we can." While he was measuring the windows for boards, Kate asked if he could repair the toilets and fix the broken cabinet in the kitchen. He knitted his eyebrows and said he couldn't promise anything, but he'd give it a try.

She continued shoveling trash into piles. It irritated her to no end that someone had stolen Daisy's trash barrels. Lovely neighborhood . . . The ground was littered with school pictures of Gabriel and Dora. She carefully put the photos that hadn't been nibbled by rats in a cardboard box and the rest went into a big plastic trash bag. Then she noticed a packet of letters tied with a black ribbon. The return address indicated they were from Kevin while he was aboard the ship where he disappeared. What a kid. He was so full of life, the last person she'd expected to die young. Kevin was curious, fun, athletic—and his red hair and freckles always reminded her of Britain's Prince Harry. She slid an envelope out of the stack and opened it:

Dear Sis:

How are you doing? How's Mom? I can't wait to get home. I'm sorry I haven't written for a while. There's just been a bunch of stuff going on. Some of the guys on this ship think they're gangbangers. They're pathetic. I never expected to see the kinds of things they're doing and getting away with. It's like they run the ship and the officers pretend they don't see . . .

It was too much. Kate put the letter back in the packet. This wasn't the place to get sidetracked. Later, she'd carefully sift through everything. Right now, she was in a race with rats. *Sorry, Kevin.* Terry was across the street returning from the market carrying a six-pack of sodas and a bag of ice when a white Ford pickup stopped and parked in front of the house. The driver was a leathery man with graying hair and a handlebar mustache, a Harrison Ford in cowboy boots. He got out and approached her.

"What's going on here?" he said. "Who are you and what do you think you're doing? This is my property."

Kate fired back. "I might ask you the same question." She was in no mood to put up with impertinent strangers. "Who are you?"

"I'm a friend of the Sandovals. Known 'em for years," he said. "I've been talking to Harlan about buying this place. My partner and I are real estate developers and we made a deal. We own most of the houses around here. I suggest you get moving."

"How interesting . . . Sorry, this place isn't for sale," she said. "It's under the jurisdiction of the probate court. I'm Kate Thorsen, executor of the estate."

"Comes as news to me." The man spat on the ground and then wiped his mouth with the back of his hand. "I'll be talking to Harlan this afternoon. As far as I know, he's the legal owner of the property. If his wife died, then he owns it straight out."

"In case you didn't know, they were divorced years ago. Harlan Sandoval isn't the owner of this house and neither are you. See that sign over there? It says 'No Trespassing.' Please leave before I call the police."

By the time Terry reached Kate, he was out of breath and his eyes darted from the stranger back to Kate, who stood grim-faced with the shovel turned sideways in her hands. "Is there a problem here?"

"Terry, I asked this gentleman to leave. He claims to be a close friend of Harlan Sandoval. But the funny thing is he hasn't moved a foot. Would you escort him back to his vehicle? Or shall I take care of it?"

"You made your point, lady," the real estate developer said. "I'll be talkin' to Harlan to get this straightened out. My understanding is the house is for sale and we're buying it. You hear me good, now. We own sixteen houses in Mesquite and we want this one." With that, he walked to his truck and created a cloud of dust as he made a U-turn toward the Sandoval house.

"That bastard," Kate said putting down the shovel. "'Well, we own sixteen houses and we want this one.' The jerk didn't even tell me his name. Asshole . . . He's probably a slumlord running a housing scam for registered sex offenders."

"Your charming vocabulary continues to amaze me," Terry said. "By the time we leave here, people will be calling you Kate Shoots Mouth First."

. . .

Marlene showed up with a nicotine patch on her ear and an old straw hat covering her head. "What are you two doing?" she said cheerfully. She handed Kate an empty cardboard box. "Just put things in here and we'll clean it all up later. I brought some food too. Go eat it before the flies do."

Kate said she'd lost her appetite. "It's been an awful day."

Terry tried to lighten the mood. "Hey, sexy lady, I don't think you're supposed to put nicotine patches on your ear," he joked. "You'll get a red mark."

"This is just temporary. Besides, I'd rather have a red mark on my ear than on my ass," she said, patting her butt. "This baby's still worth money in some circles."

Terry circled her for a better look. "I bet it is," he said. "I think Kate and I had better stay at that hotel. You and I might get along too well at your place."

"We could be the talk of the town," she quipped.

In spite of herself, Kate burst out laughing. "Will you two children behave?"

Part V

It was a lazy Saturday morning, and Elias Williams awoke with a sense of peace. He was an old man with the good fortune of knowing his time was short. Elias had known it even before the doctor told him about the cancer. Last night, he'd dreamed of a flock of golden angels, heard them singing, and seen his mother and father smiling at him. But where was his wife? The only son who'd died fighting in Vietnam? Would they come in the next round of dreams?

Patience, he told himself, *patience*.

Elias turned on the radio and tuned it to the San Bernardino golden-oldies station, the one he liked the best. Rock and roll had always been his secret vice. "It sure feels nice," Fleetwood Mac crooned. "You can take me anytime you like." Good words. There was something invigorating about the music that lifted him. It was pure poetry.

As a Pentecostal preacher, Elias had spent most of his adult life trying to alleviate the pain and grief of parishioners. While his weekly sermons promised forgiveness and a new day in heaven, was his message of salvation but a hollow promise? Elias wasn't sure anymore. A smudge of doubt had been creeping in for years, especially since Christian, his son, died so far from home. How could a man of the cloth make sense of that? And what kind of God took the innocents and left the wicked?

In a way, the cancer was a blessing. It made it difficult to eat, and Elias's frame was wasting away. He was disappearing and soon someone else would stand up and jive at the podium every Sunday morning. Someone else could raise vibrations and save souls. The pain was hard, though. Now it was even getting difficult to get the childproof caps off the tops of all those bottles of pills the doctor insisted he take. Elias's fingers, the ones that used to dance over piano keys, didn't quite work right anymore. He washed a handful of pills down with water and struggled to swallow them.

Sisters Eileen and Sarah had put a nice bowl of Cheerios in milk with a cup of fresh apple juice on his desk. Apple juice always made him think of the red apples on the tree in the yard of the washboard cottage in Louisiana where he'd grown up. Apples were so round and beautiful. The sisters had left him a note saying they'd gone to run errands. Flowers needed to be purchased for the Sunday service and, thanks to recent donations, the church could finally afford a new coffeemaker and an extra electric fan.

Besides eating Cheerios, all he had to do today was write the sermon for tomorrow. What would he write about? Hell, damnation, waste? All the hate festering inside people until they exploded? He'd buried a fifteen-year-old boy yesterday, a child he'd known since birth. Teddy Mitchell had died joyriding in his mother's car; died because he lost control and the car rolled over; died because he wasn't wearing a seat belt. Life was cheap in the desert, good for at least a funeral a week. Why did desert dwellers refuse to wear seat belts? Why did they drink and drive? Take drugs? Kill each other? Commit suicide? Senseless deaths . . .

A little plastic statue of Bart Simpson with elongated face and high-top hair looked at Elias from across the desk. Daisy Sandoval entered his mind's eye and he heard the words, "The longer we love, the stronger we love." He felt her next to him, still bound to walk the Earth. A smile flashed across his face, the first of the day. He'd loved Daisy and would never understand why the young woman's burden had been so heavy, why her life was cut short.

He would never forget how she bounced into the church every Saturday morning carrying plastic bags of used comic books, magazines and her children's outgrown clothes and toys for other kids, kids who needed more. Always full of mischief, Daisy claimed it was her job to make the old man laugh before he had to put on his black robes and become what she called "the pious preacher creature."

"Lighten up, preacher creature," she'd say. "Laugh with me."

And laugh he did when Daisy told him silly stories about her children, her latest projects, the owl family that came to live on her porch—and lots of funny, funny tales about her mother's addiction to barstools and young cowboys with tight butts. "Our family cornered the market on nuts," she'd say. Yet she never spoke about Harlan—and Elias thought it wise not to ask about his one-time protégé. For some reason, Leon Blue, her first love, became a topic of many conversations as Daisy struggled to understand the emotional impact of combat on soldiers and the depression that followed. Leon, she said, was gone before he died. Elias didn't understand.

The last time he saw her, Daisy, looking more radiant than ever, said she was going to write a book called *Saturdays with Elias* and tell everyone in town that the goody-two-shoes Pastor Williams of the Holiness Church of God listened to rock and roll, lusted after Salma Hayek and smoked Cuban cigars in the church rectory. Her parting words: "Who's going to love you as good as me?"

It seemed only right that Elias didn't share his feelings of loss. Reaching for his pen, he made a note on the desk calendar to visit the cemetery. The past was being erased, and he made notes for everything these days. Surely the sisters wouldn't begrudge a few flowers from the Sunday display? Daisies, yes, white daisies would be nice.

THE NEXT VISITOR to the house-that-wasn't-for-sale was Sally McDowell. She was a frumpy old woman in a pink-flowered, snap-up nightgown. Sally shuffled rather than walked, and Kate wondered if she'd just been dropped her off from the nearest mental hospital.

Sally said she'd been stopping by to visit Rainbow House every day since someone left the front door open—and wondered if the water heater worked, could she have it. "I'm also looking for a nice set of salt and pepper shakers," she said. "Have you seen any inside?" It was nuts. Kate repeated that the house was under the protection of the court and nothing could be taken from it. "I just want to look around," Sally said, purring in a childish voice. "It's interesting, isn't it?"

"Sorry," Kate replied, as she went back to work on a mountain of rubbish. "Please leave and don't come back. See the 'No Trespassing' signs? The police are patrolling and we have private security."

But the old woman wouldn't budge. Sally stood there as if she had no place else to go. That's when Terry, always the gentleman, stepped in and sweet-talked her. "You must be thirsty," he said, handing her a can of soda. "Why don't you go home now? We'll see you later. We'll be here tomorrow and we can talk more then."

After Sally walked away carrying her unopened soda, Terry turned to Kate: "We need to brush up on your diplomatic skills. That was just a poor lady looking for company. She probably lives alone and has no one to talk to."

"Are you kidding me?" she said. "Remember, I'm Kate Shoots Mouth First. Sally probably stole the trash cans and god knows what else. Did you smell her breath? She was plastered."

"Okay, okay . . . But you're still a hard-hearted woman."

Meanwhile, Butch and his son were replacing the garage door. Kate had no idea how the two men were able to lift the heavy boards or how they managed to screw them securely into the stucco. "Nice work," she said.

After Sally's departure, another pickup arrived and parked in the driveway blocking Butch's vehicle. Kate approached and asked what the driver wanted. She didn't feel like dealing with another interloper. "I'm James, Harlan's cousin," he said, not bothering to introduce the woman sitting next to him. "We live in the neighborhood and wondered what you're doing at the house. Does Harlan know you're here? He told me he'd meet us here this morning.

I know he's been fixing the place up so he and the kids can move back in."

Incredulous, Kate snorted: "Fixing it up? Is *that* what he calls what he's done?"

"That's what Harlan told us. Anyway, we're thinking about buying the house. Nice place. Or at least it used to be. We're supposed to do a walk-through with him."

Enraged, Kate didn't even try to be polite. She pulled out a copy of the court order and shoved in Cousin James's face. "The house isn't for sale," she said. "Harlan doesn't own it and has no right to step foot on the property. You can give him that message. I'm Daisy's aunt and this house belongs to her children. That's it. Move your truck. You're blocking the driveway and my carpenter's vehicle."

James gave her a cold stare, as if she didn't fully understand the situation. "I'll let Harlan know what you said. He should be by here anytime now. Good luck with whatever it is you think you're doing. You'll probably need it."

"Tell him I said to drop dead. We've got protection." Kate turned her back on Cousin James and returned to sorting while he backed out of the driveway.

"What protection do we have?" Terry looked at her like she'd lost it. "Is there something you haven't told me?"

"We've got shovels, hammers, brooms, nails if we need them . . ."

By this time Kate had filled three cardboard boxes with potentially salvageable material. She stacked broken furniture and garbage for the dumpster near a tree on the far side of the property. The locksmith was due any moment. Now it was her turn to go to the market. "Terry, you want anything? I'm going to see if they'll let me use the restroom."

"They will. I told them what Harlan did to the house and the two women who run the place weren't surprised. They remembered you talking at the funeral. I don't need anything. But we should break for lunch in about an hour. We can run over to the American Legion. It's the closest place. Oh, while you're at the market, check with Mrs. Hunter. They have a little post office at the back of the store. She runs it. That's where Daisy's mail would've been delivered. Show her your court appointment and see if she'll let you pick up the mail. That might help us reconstruct what's been going on, seeing as how Harlan and the rats shredded nearly every piece of paper."

"Sounds like a rock group, Harlan and the Rats. I like it."

Ten minutes later, Kate returned with a small stack of mail and a brown paper bag full of Snickers bars. "You want one before they melt?"

"I don't like to take a lady's stash, but I could use a sugar rush right now. What time is Edward picking you up?"

"He said half past three. Can you still get into the cemetery that late?"

"No problem. Marlene said it stays open until sundown. Should give us plenty of time to visit my friend. I see you got the mail."

"There wasn't much. Mrs. Hunter said Harlan has been dropping by to pick it up. Apparently the scum sucker's got Daisy's post office box key. Mrs. Hunter didn't know about the probate court and apologized. She thought Harlan was moving into the house with the children. You were right. She's a nice lady. From now on, she's going to hold the mail at the counter for me. That way Harlan can't get his grubby hands on anything. I wonder what he's looking for."

"Could be one of the keys to the mystery. My friend is still working on Daisy's cell phone records. The land line at the house has been disconnected. I wish we could find her computer."

"I'm positive Harlan made sure no one will ever find it."

While they ate melting Snickers bars, the locksmith arrived. It would only be a matter of time until Rainbow House was boarded up, secure—ready for a hurricane or whatever else was about to hit.

IN A MOMENT OF INSPIRATION, Elias decided that a good topic for his Sunday sermon was forgiveness. He thought broadening the theme, using examples from the lives of heroic leaders, might give his congregants something they could identify with and aspire to in their daily lives. It was tragic that so many people were unable to move on because they didn't know how to forgive.

Of course, Jesus immediately came to mind. But Elias wanted

to tell the story of someone on a smaller scale, an ordinary person who changed his or her life with the courage to move on. He was wracking his brain, trying to think of an appropriate illustration, when he began scanning the bookcase for ideas. This might work, he thought, and pulled out a book called *Azim's Bardo*. He remembered meeting the author, Azim Khamisa, at a church conference in San Diego where Khamisa spoke movingly on redemption. The book was the story of Khamisa's son, Tariq, a college student working part-time delivering pizzas. Tariq was senselessly murdered for the money in his wallet while trying to deliver a pizza. After much grieving, Khamisa swallowed his pride and approached the gang member who killed his son. He forgave him. It was a powerful message.

Elias had just begun writing the sermon, which he titled "Victims at Both Ends," when he heard knocking at the front door of the church. One of the sisters probably forgot her key, he thought, or they've just too much to carry to unlock the door. "Just a minute," he yelled, as he padded slowly down the hallway in his bathrobe and bedroom slippers.

When he opened the door, he saw a familiar face, a young man he'd known since his visitor was a boy who regularly came to church with his mother. "Why, come on in," Elias said. "It's been a long time. What can I do for you?"

BY THE TIME Edward arrived, Rainbow House's porch sparkled with metallic blue hearts, the windows and garage were boarded up, locks had been changed, "No Trespassing" signs had been posted, boxes were stacked in a neat row against the far wall of Daisy's bedroom, and carpenters were working in the bathrooms. Edward looked amused when Kate, her face covered with dirt, smiled at him.

It had been a productive day, even if the backyard remained littered with debris. Kate and Terry had fended off poachers, made friends with the women who ran the market, picked up the mail, and begun the tedious process of restoration. If and when they found the children, Kate hoped for the best. Physically, she felt like a train wreck: dead-tired, sweating and covered in grime. She needed a shower, but the best she could do was wipe her face with a hand sanitizer, spray musk cologne on the offending parts of her body, suck on a throat lozenge and brush the tangles out of her matted hair. "Where are we going?"

"Not far," Edward replied. "I'm not sure how to say this, but it would be best if you don't touch Nopah. He's old-fashioned and believes non-Mohave blood is contaminated. It's nothing against you personally."

"Don't worry." Kate, pouting, gestured at her filth. "What if he touches me first?"

"Then you don't have to worry."

Wiping his brow, Terry looked like a West Virginia coal miner coming off a double shift. His face was black and his clothes, well, they reeked. "I'm going back to the hotel for a shower before I pick up Marlene," he said. "You may wish to inflict your grime on others. However, I refuse to offend a lady, especially one of a ripe age."

"Are you trying to make me jealous?" He laughed when she put her arms around his waist. It was the first time Kate had been away from Terry since Daisy's funeral. She was beginning to like being part of a couple.

"You take care," he said. "Tell that Nopah dude not to spit on you too much and, whatever you do, don't smoke any peace pipes or suck on rocks."

THE SHOCKS IN EDWARD'S TRUCK must have died in the last century. Kate could feel the redistribution of her pelvic bones each time they hit a bump. Soon the truck was winding its way into the black mountains above Mesquite and the sky was darkening. There were occasional rumbles of faraway thunder and the air smelled of horse manure and burning wood.

They rounded a bend and saw a stand-alone souvenir shop on the left-hand side of the road with a plume of smoke rising from a chimney. The sign outside said "Angelica Trading Post," and colored Christmas lights illuminated the front windows. The exterior of the building was run-down, in need of a new coat of white paint—and a brown horse was tied to a hitching post.

Into this scenic picture of yesteryear, Edward pulled the truck, stopping in the dirt parking lot. "This is it," he said. "Nopah lives in the back of the shop. His daughter, Mary, runs the store."

In the shadow of the mountains, a cool breeze had risen and there was now a feeling of static electricity in the air and frequent flashes of light. The storm was escalating, moving closer. Shivering, Kate was glad to be wearing sturdy clothing and wished she'd brought a jacket. "Where does the name 'Angelica' come from?"

"*Angelica archangelica.* It's a magical herb. Mohave shamans use it for healing."

It wasn't the first time Kate had heard of angelica, a plant employed by healers in cultures around the globe for purification, healing and exorcism. In the United States, some Native Americans used it as witchcraft medicine to remove ghosts and evil spirits; and she'd heard that African American folk magicians utilized the herb in Hoodoo rituals and placed it in mojo bags for protection. "I'm familiar with the plant," she said, betraying excitement in her voice. "Healers in parts of Europe and Scandinavia use it for various ailments. I didn't know the Mohave used it."

Edward looked bemused. "I guess it works," he said. "Some of the old people say it helps the aches in their bones. I'm Mohave, but I don't know a lot about the old ways. I've learned small things from Nopah and Mary."

A bell tinkled when they entered the shop, startling a fat gray cat that had been asleep. Annoyed, the cat lumbered across the floor in front of them and collapsed into a large basket. The aromatic smell of sage was burning in a blue ceramic dish and Anima's "Ancient Voices" was playing softly in the background. Handcrafted pottery, jewelry and baskets were displayed for sale—along with uncut quartz crystal, children's toys and tobacco products. A refrigerator in the corner offered a variety of soft drinks and flavored Arizona Tea for one dollar a bottle.

Inhaling the incense, Kate felt at home and made a mental note to buy a bundle of sage to burn at Rainbow House. She looked closely at the items on display and gravitated toward a bookshelf filled with maps and tourist books. She picked up a copy of *Massacre on the Gila* by Clifton B. Kroeber and Bernard L. Fontana. She knew it well. It was the story of the last known incident of intertribal warfare in the area, an account of the 1857 offensive by Mohave and Quechan warriors against the Maricopa. What made the book fascinating was that Kroeber, a historian and the son of anthropologist Alfred Kroeber, and Fontana, a historian-anthropologist, wrote about Mohave military strategy and the underlying causes of war.

When Kate looked up, a striking woman with thick, dark hair and ice-pick eyes was gesturing with a sweeping arm toward the back of the store. Hers was a familiar face. She was the woman she'd seen with Nopah at the hospital—and Kate wondered where her children were.

"Mary, this is the friend I told you about," Edward said. "When Mary isn't running this place, she makes the best tacos on the reservation."

"It's good to meet you," Kate said, as she returned the book to the shelf and turned to Mary, who had colored feathers woven into her French-braided hair. "I like your shop. It has a good feel about it. Plus, this is one of my favorite books."

"Not one of mine. We lost that battle." It was obvious Mary was irritated. "You wanted to see my father? He's waiting for you."

"Yes, I do have some questions."

Mary pointed to a doorway covered by a sheer drapery panel. A pale yellow light seeped past the thin curtain. Edward moved forward and pulled the curtain back. He stepped inside and beckoned. "Good evening, Father," he said. "This is my friend. She is the aunt of the woman who died. I understand you have met before. I'll leave you alone to talk."

Looking leaner than he had when she'd seen him at the hospital, Nopah Round was sitting barefoot on the cold floor in a room filled with golden light. He had a blanket around his shoulders. The shaman didn't acknowledge her presence and continued staring fixedly into space. Kate had seen this kind of behavior in Native Americans before and knew it didn't matter whether she was in the room or not. Nopah would continue staring into the void until he felt like talking. She waited for him to make a move.

Minutes passed until Nopah extended a bony arm and pointed to the floor, indicating she should sit down across from him. Then, while she sat, he smoked three consecutive cigarettes. When he finished smoking and was ready to communicate, he reached for Kate's right hand and studied her palm. "Long life line," he said, pushing her hand away. *So much for not touching.* Then he raised his left hand and made circular motions in the air as if he were a cowboy twirling an invisible rope.

When he stopped twirling, he held both her hands. "Heh," he said, examining her fingernails. "Heh, heh . . . You eat too much sugar."

It was a struggle not to giggle. The shaman's pronouncement was made with all the solemnity of a doctor diagnosing terminal cancer. *Too much sugar?* It was ludicrous. "Sorry, uh, did you say I eat too much sugar?"

"I did. Why you want to see me? You got troubles?" Nopah slapped his knee and belly-laughed. "I got my own. My people have big troubles. We have too little hope and not enough to feed our children. These are bad days."

Because it was her first experience with a Mohave healer, Kate wasn't sure what she was supposed to do or say. She tried to be sympathetic. "It is a hard world," she said, reaching for her wallet before Nopah brushed her hand away. What would come next, she had no idea. Thanks to Terry, she knew there could be some spitting involved—and she wasn't looking forward to it.

A shaman in any primitive culture must undergo a long, unbidden apprenticeship under the guidance of a spirit—usually in the form of a bird or animal, considered a god in disguise—before the power to cure or divine is received. If Nopah had such a gift, as Marlene insisted he did, then Kate decided it was time to cut to the chase. "Excuse me, sir. I didn't come to see you to talk about myself," she said. "I came to ask about my niece, Daisy Sandoval." Nopah narrowed his eyes and glared at her. "I saw you and your daughter at the hospital when my niece was dying. Do you remember?"

"It was a dark time," Nopah said, as he waved his hand over his head. "I came to that place to see if the mother would survive because of the boy. It was not to be. My concern is for the boy."

Kate was confused. "You mean Gabriel?"

"That is his name."

"Why would you care about Gabriel?"

Nopah stared at her in puzzlement, as if the question made no sense because the answer was obvious. "He is my grandson."

This news came as a complete shock to Kate, who sat back and ran her hands nervously through her dirty hair. "You're Harlan Sandoval's father?"

There was a long silence while the shaman smoked another cigarette. "That man is not the father," he said between puffs.

Another twist. "I don't, don't understand," Kate said, fumbling for words.

"I thought you knew about this," he said, extinguishing the cigarette. "The boy is the last seed of my only son."

Kate took a leap: "Are you talking about Leon Blue?"

"We do not speak the names of the dead," Nopah said in a scolding voice before putting a hand across her mouth. "It is forbidden. My son is dead, but the child . . ." The shaman's voice drifted, he closed his eyes, and he seemed to be somewhere else, listening to other voices. "Ah, yes . . . I see . . . The boy has a role to play. Like me, he is a spirit dreamer. The mother understood. She promised me she would allow him to prepare. The time has come for his teachings. I want you to bring the boy to me."

Trembling, she attempted to hide her rising anxiety. "How could Leon Blue have been your son? He has a different last name."

"Our women are free to keep their names."

"Where is your wife?"

"Under the river."

Perplexed, she chose her words carefully and spoke deliberately. "I don't want to offend a tribal leader, but I have trouble with what you've just said. My niece would have told me. We were very close. Besides, I don't know where Gabriel is because Harlan Sandoval has taken both his children away."

"You must find the boy," Nopah said. "Face south."

"Excuse me?"

"Face south and take off your shoes." Nopah pointed to the floor, tapped it and motioned her to lie down. Though it made as much sense as walking on hot coals or wearing a pyramid hat,

Kate obeyed. She was trying to be culturally sensitive, but this was a new one. As she lay on the floor, the room grew darker. She wondered if the shaman had a dimmer switch attached to a hidden string on his finger. At the moment she thought it, Nopah announced that he didn't need light to see.

He began stroking the sweaty palms of her hands. Black eyes gleaming, he hovered over her, blowing into her ears and kneading the muscles in her neck, shoulders and feet until she felt drowsy and closed her eyes. Disgusting tobacco breath and spittle followed and she tried not to gag or squirm. Where was the chanting coming from? Nopah was singing. Squinting her eyelids, she could see the shaman reaching into a leather pouch. He began sprinkling crushed tobacco leaves on the carpet all around her. "I am cleansing the spirit and energy," he explained. "Do not be alarmed. You have nothing to fear. I am not a witch."

Good to know. Though Kate struggled to remain alert, her eyes drooped and closed. She felt she was floating and no longer knew if they were alone. The blowing sounds in her ears continued and fingers began kneading her legs, stomach, scalp . . . Soon the sweet aroma of angelica root filled the room. The ointment was being rubbed onto her forehead, under her nose and chin, on the bottoms of her feet. It felt warm.

The shaman's motives were alien to any she knew. "Whatever is dreamed will happen," he whispered. "Heh, heh . . ."

The room evaporated and rainbow colors swirled and moving pictures assembled behind her eyelids. Picture: Daisy with Leon, both radiant, in a lush forest near a rushing river. Picture: baby being born. Picture: a toddler with saucer eyes and pouting lips. Picture: Gabriel's adolescent face. Picture: a stranger with a knife. Picture: Kate fighting with the stranger. Her eyes bolted open. Kneeling above her was Nopah, spittle dribbling out of the corners of his mouth, his breathing labored. He was clutching his chest.

"You eat too much sugar," he said in a gravelly voice. "To protect the boy, you must be strong. Eat healthy food, lots of vegetables. Forget candy. Do you understand?"

No matter how relaxed and mellow she felt, Kate stifled the desire to lash out. She waited before she rubbed her eyes, sat up and demanded answers: "You're asking me to fight someone? Physically fight the man Gabriel loves and believes is his father? If the boy is really your grandson, why don't you go to war? Why don't you find Gabriel and tell him what you want? This has nothing to do with me."

"It was your dream and your fate," he said. "I am only a teacher, but I can ease the path. I will sing for you."

Without another word, Kate stood up, brushed herself off and walked out carrying her shoes. She nearly knocked Mary over. "I'm leaving now. What do I owe you for the reading?"

"Nopah's medicine is free," his daughter said. "You're a nonbeliever, aren't you? This must be difficult for you. Here, take my card. You look dehydrated. Drink a lot of water. You should feel better by morning. If not, call me. I can probably come up with something." Kate shoved the card in her pocket and asked to buy a bundle of sage. Mary handed her one and turned away when the barefoot woman tried to pay.

When Kate approached Edward, he was stroking the cat. She motioned him to leave and the cat jumped at the sound of her scratchy voice. He looked alarmed. "Are you all right? You want something to eat or drink? You look pale."

"I'm fine." She avoided his gaze and pushed open the front door. "Please take me back to the hotel. I need time to think. I've got work to do." The ride back was silent. Kate questioned everything she knew about Daisy and the choices she'd made during her life. Why did she marry Harlan Sandoval? If she was pregnant, why not marry Leon Blue? *O child of noble family, what have you gotten me into?*

Thirty minutes later, Edward stopped the truck and affectionately touched his index finger to Kate's cheek. They were in the hotel parking lot, where lightning illuminated the mountaintops and fat raindrops bounced off the windshield.

"Pretty rough night, huh? Medicine men can be hard. They have no choice," he said. "Nopah means well. You need to understand what it is to be a shaman. They don't choose the life. It's their fate. If they refuse the call, they die. If they accept, chances are some angry family member will kill them because they failed to heal someone. Medicine men must think with their hearts. We call it heart thinking."

"Yeah, I've heard that somewhere," she said, pecking his cheek before opening the truck's creaky door. "Thanks for taking me. I'm the one who asked for it. My problem is that Nopah told me I have a fate and I don't like the idea of being fated to do anything. It's against everything I believe. Listen, I'll talk to you tomorrow morning. We're going back to work on Rainbow House—and I'm going to burn this sage for protection in every room. I'll be damned if I'm going to let Harlan Sandoval destroy what's left of my family."

Stepping outside, Kate put her hand out and caught a few raindrops. Then she remembered the papers left in the yard at Rainbow House. By now, they would be oatmeal mush. There was nothing she could do. Filthy, greasy, disillusioned, she returned to the hotel. The television screen was flickering. She clicked it off and crawled into bed with her clothes on. She hugged Terry with everything she had left. Half asleep, he mumbled, "You stink."

ROUSED FROM THE DEAD, Kate jumped at the sound of ringing. She could still smell the angelica as she rolled over on her stomach, banged the alarm and tried to go back to sleep. It had been a fitful night full of phantoms and meetings with long-dead relatives. Ghost dreams, she called them. The ringing stopped— and moments later began anew. She could hear Terry in the shower. She finally picked up the phone and mumbled a greeting.

"Sorry to wake you," Marlene said. "I have bad news."

Kate sat up and crossed her legs on the bed. "No problem. Time to get up anyway. What's the news?"

"Pastor Williams is dead."

"Cancer?"

"No, the tribal police were here." Marlene said. "They just left. They may be coming to talk to you."

"I barely knew the man. Why would they want to talk to me?"

"They asked me not to say anything. Sorry."

The line went dead. Kate scratched her head, dragged herself out of bed, pretended she hadn't heard Marlene's message and knocked on the bathroom door. "Terry, can I come in?"

"Sure," he yelled back. "Love the company."

There's nothing like hot water, soap and a naked hunk in the shower to put life into perspective. Terry lathered her up, scrubbed away the grime and grease and washed her hair. "You're incredible," she said. "Can I keep you?" Then Kate's smile dissolved into a faraway gaze.

"Is something wrong?" Terry asked.

"I had a bad night last night."

"Told you to watch out for that quack." Terry pulled her close and looked into her eyes. "What the hell did Nopah do to you?"

"We can talk about it later," she said. "I'm famished. I forgot to eat dinner."

When they got out and toweled off, Terry left to order breakfast. The steamy warmth of the small room comforted her—and the familiar buzzing of the hair dryer overpowered all other sounds and introduced a sense of normalcy. Brushing her teeth, Kate struggled to find logic in the drama that was fast becoming her life. Everything Elias had ever said to her drifted through her mind. Then there was the way the minister stood up to Harlan and his family at Daisy's funeral. And how the sweet old man looked padding around the empty church in those worn navy-blue slippers.

If the tribal police were involved, something unnatural had to have happened. The first person she thought of was Harlan. After all, an innocent dog's throat had been slit to send a message. He'd destroyed his children's toys. But why would Harlan hurt a dying man? It was pathetic. "Terry, let's get the heck out of here," she said.

"Breakfast hasn't arrived yet."

"I know. But Marlene called earlier. She said Elias Williams is dead and the police may be coming over here to talk to me."

"What? He was old and very sick. Why would the police want to talk to you? Doesn't make a lick of sense," he said. "We're just visitors passing through this hellhole. Is there something you're not telling me?"

"Give me a minute." She pulled a black, long-sleeved T-shirt over her head and began picking through a pile of dirty clothes to find a reasonably clean pair of underwear. She needed to do laundry again. Her jeans were rank but would have to do. Where she was going, cleanliness wasn't an issue. "Marlene didn't explain. I don't have a clue. All I know is that we need to get out of here."

"Not so fast. Ah, here's the breakfast." When he had laid the food out on the bed, he continued, "It's only seven on a Sunday morning, we have time to eat. Was the preacher murdered?"

"I told you I don't know," she said, pacing back and forth across the room. "Whatever happened, Elias was one of Daisy's dearest friends. Maybe the police want to ask us about Harlan. If I was a cop, I'd put him at the top of the list for everything that goes wrong around here."

"Calm down," Terry said. "Look at the situation logically. You're in a town where everyone is a suspect. If the police show up, don't volunteer information. Answer their questions—and that's it."

"Are you pretending to be a lawyer?"

"If you need one, I'll be one." Terry grabbed her, threw her down on the bed and smothered her stomach with kisses. "Eat fast, woman, and then we'll get out of here. You still smell awful. What did that quack do to you?"

"Relax, Big Guy." Kate realized the angelica must be coming out of her pores. She smelled like a skunk. "It was a bizarre experience I hope never to repeat." She sat upright, scanned the food and pointed her fork at his plate. "Do you want your tomatoes?"

Terry lowered his eyes. "You don't like tomatoes."

"I've decided to eat more vegetables," she said. "They're healthy."

"Take my potatoes too then," he said, his voice dropping an octave as he scooped a pile of country fries onto her plate. "If you don't mind, I'll take your eggs and toast in trade. What about the Snickers bar?"

"You can have it."

Terry looked at her with concern. "What has happened to you? Have you lost your mind?"

They cross-jabbed forks, shoved food in their mouths, drank a pot of coffee and a pitcher of orange juice. "Before I forget," he said, "Allen Redmond called last night. Said he's the editor of a blog called *Mesquite Musings*. He sounded freaked out. Wants you to call him back. The number is on the table."

"Wasn't he at Daisy's funeral?"

"You got me," Terry said, taking the wrapper off the Snickers bar. "You sure you don't want this? How about we share it?"

"Don't tempt me. I'm trying to gain strength. By the way, how did Redmond know we were staying at this hotel?" Kate slapped her forehead with her hand. "Almost forgot: this is a small town. Everyone knows everything. I'll call him once we get to Daisy's. We need to stop for sodas and water too."

He looked at her strangely. "Are you ill?"

Kate's nostrils flared and she jabbed him in the ribs. "No. I'm hoping the rain last night didn't destroy the papers in the yard," she said, wiping her mouth on her shirt. "I want to get over there as fast as we can. I don't want to be sitting here answering police questions when we could be finding answers."

Terry looked at her. "It rained last night?"

"You missed it?"

"Guess I was tired. Oh, George called to check up on us. I told him we were in Tombstone waiting for Wyatt Earp to arrive—and that you were having a private powwow with a medicine man. He said to give you a big hug. I fell asleep early watching a *Law and Order* rerun."

"How's George doing?"

"Not bad. He's going back to work tomorrow."

"Can't keep a good man down," she said. "You didn't hear the thunder?"

"Heard nothing until this smelly creature crawled into my bed and began fondling me. Oh, I did dream I was at the Bluebird and that waitress with the funny-colored hair was serving me uncooked eggs and coffee grounds. God, I need to get out of here. You sure you don't want to go back to Paris with me?"

"I do, but we need to finish this," she said. "Until I know the kids are safe, all bets are off. Then I want to be with you because . . . ," her voice dropped off. It was the first time she'd almost said the words.

THE SCENE WAS CHAOTIC. A fire truck lingered and a lone fireman was dousing piles of smoking rubble with a hose. Two squad cars and an ambulance were blocking the street and a handful of neighbors had gathered in the shade of a pepper tree outside the yellow police tape. Rainbow House's roof and porch were caved in; boards that had been affixed to the windows just the day before looked like slabs of charcoal; the palm trees had gone up like torches; but, ironically, the "No Trespassing" signs were still firmly affixed to the undamaged fence posts.

Without a word, Kate and Terry got out of the rental car, slowly approached the ruins and were immediately stopped by a uniformed officer with the tribal police. "Stay outside the tape," he ordered. "This is a crime scene."

"This is my niece's home. I'm the executor of her estate." Kate pulled out her court appointment and driver's license and handed the documents over. "We were just here yesterday cleaning up. We came back this morning to continue. Do you know what caused the fire?"

"Just a moment," he said. "Don't move." Without explanation, the officer took Kate's identification to another official, a scruffy-looking guy with a beefy belly and a limp who then approached them with a notepad in hand.

"So you're Kathleen Thorsen?" She asked him to call her Kate. "Well, Kate, I've heard a lot about you lately. You've ruffled feathers around here. I'm Sergeant Rudy Garcia with the tribal police. Got some questions for you. As I'm sure you're aware, this is tribal property." She nodded. "Let's go where we can talk." Garcia pointed to Terry, who raised his arms in a helpless gesture, and ordered him to stay put. Garcia lifted the police tape and ushered Kate toward the house.

"I understand you were out at Pete Linthicum's place the other day searching a vehicle. You took some things. And I understand you and your friends have been causing trouble for the Sandoval family. Is that right?"

"You've got it backward. We haven't caused trouble for anyone," she said. "As far as the vehicle goes, Mr. Linthicum gave us his permission to search my niece's car. I was looking for documents for a court case."

"We'll get to that in a minute. But two of my people were at the casino hotel this morning looking for you. Obviously you weren't there. Where were you?"

The conversation was taking a bizarre turn. "Rudy, may I call you Rudy?" Garcia didn't object. "We stopped for sodas and water in Parker before we drove here. Listen, the only reason I'm on the reservation is because my niece, Daisy Sandoval, died recently. I'm trying to settle her affairs. As the court-appointed executor of the estate, I have a responsibility to protect assets for her two minor children. I'm sure you know what an executor does. We have to inventory property, find creditors, pay bills, safeguard property and on and on . . . The boring stuff that no one likes to do, but has to be done."

"I get that," Garcia said. "But what, specifically, have you been doing at this house? It's my understanding there's some dispute over who holds the title on the home—or what's left of it. Why were the windows boarded up? Who gave you authority to post 'No Trespassing' signs on tribal land? And, by the way, did you leave flammable material inside the home?"

Kate was bewildered. Was she being accused of something? "I had the windows boarded over yesterday because they were broken. I had a locksmith change the locks too. As far as I know, the only flammable materials inside were ordinary cleaning supplies. We hadn't looked in the garage yet."

"Why were you so concerned?"

"The house has been repeatedly vandalized since my niece's death. Neighbors told me members of the Sandoval family, specifically my niece's ex-husband, were responsible. I felt the 'No Trespassing' signs might keep them and anyone else off the property until I could secure it. It never occurred to me the tribe would care that I was trying to save a home."

Garcia continued writing in his notepad. Another officer came to whisper in his ear. The sergeant said he'd be over in a minute. Kate looked helplessly at Terry, standing in the blazing sun, and then returned her attention to the house. It was completely destroyed. The fireman was rolling up his hose and she could see paramedics carrying a large black bag toward the ambulance. "Rudy," she said. "Please . . . Tell me what happened? Did someone die in the fire?"

He deflected the question. "We're not sure what went down. Who did you say has been helping you?"

"Terry Ryan, the man standing over there. Let me explain. I write for *National Geographic* and Terry, who lives in Paris, often works as my translator. I'd be happy to give you my editor's number in D.C., if you want to check it out. Anyway, Terry's here as a friend. He wanted to help out after he learned what happened to my niece."

"No one else has been helping you?"

This was a sticky question, one she was smart enough to know needed some wiggle room. "Not really," she said. "I mean, I've talked to neighbors in Mesquite trying to find out more about what happened to Daisy. Her death was a complete shock and, frankly, I'm worried about her children. I haven't seen them since the funeral. Why do you ask?"

Garcia licked his lips and carefully chose his words. "We found a body. The fire inspectors will be here soon, but it looks like this was arson. That makes it a homicide investigation. We're bringing Parker P.D. in to help. We don't have the resources. I'm sure they'll want to talk to you. Right now, I need a minute with your friend."

Kate's heart sank. "Did you identify the body?"

"Can't discuss that yet."

Garcia turned from her and walked toward Terry. Another officer joined them. After a brief discussion, she watched her best friend being handcuffed and frisked. They took a screwdriver from Terry's pocket before they pushed him into the back of a patrol car that sped away. An incredulous Kate marched up to Garcia and demanded answers. "What do you think you're doing? Terry hasn't done anything. He doesn't even live here. This is a mistake." Her protests fell on deaf ears.

"We have some questions for your friend," he said. "Don't leave town. We may have some for you too."

Kate's first instinct was to call George before realizing it was unfair to burden a man recovering from a heart attack with news that one of his closest friends had just been handcuffed and taken into custody during a murder investigation. So she got into the rental car filled with cleaning supplies and took to the road, driving aimlessly around Mesquite's few paved streets. She needed to calm herself, catch her bearings. The questions multiplied: Why did Garcia mention Pete Linthicum? The "No Trespassing" signs? Why would Harlan set the fire if he could conceivably profit from the sale of Rainbow House?

Marlene appeared to be her only option. The former showgirl had called early that morning to tell her Elias Williams was dead, but Garcia refused to disclose who was packed into the black body bag. On her way to Marlene's, she cruised past the Sandoval home. The front gate was closed, the curtains drawn, and Mama Lou's Cadillac wasn't in the carport. It looked like no one was home.

Kate continued on toward the river until she reached the ice-cube house. There was a white tow truck in the driveway. She parked her car in the street and walked warily toward the house. Before she could knock on the door, it opened. Pete Linthicum invited her in. This was an unexpected twist. Why would someone working for the Sandoval family be visiting Marlene? Her friend was standing at the open door in an embroidered silk kimono with, obviously, nothing underneath.

"Honey, what's wrong?" she said. "You look like you could chew through nails."

"Nice threads," Kate said, wondering if she'd come to the wrong place. "We need to talk." Marlene signaled Pete to leave, saying she'd see him later. "The police just took Terry into custody. When you called this morning to say Elias was dead, you said the police wanted to talk to me. What's this about?"

"Come inside," Marlene said. "I'll tell you what I've heard. But I swear I didn't call you this morning. You must have dreamed it."

This was weird and Kate decided not to react. Less than ten minutes passed before she was back in the rental car heading for the Bluebird. She hoped to find Edward, but Shirley said he hadn't arrived yet—and it wasn't like him to be late. As Kate waited for coffee, she nervously rummaged through her purse and came upon last night's phone message in Terry's scrawled writing. She placed the call.

THE PREVIOUS EVENING'S unusual cloudburst had done little more than to cause the National Weather Service to issue periodic flash-flood warnings on the radio. No big deal for veteran desert dwellers. The red Cadillac was closing in on the outskirts of Phoenix and Carlos Santana was examining his relationship with a certain black magic woman. Harlan, half his face still bandaged, smiled and tapped his fingers. The pain pills may have dulled his senses, but they made his belly ache.

Mama looked radiant in her red sundress and matching high heels. "What a beautiful day," she said, pulling out a stick of Spearmint gum. "You boys want a piece? Makes your breath smell nice." Andrew took one, but Harlan shook his head. He didn't give a damn what his breath smelled like.

The plan was to take Mama to Cousin Cherry's house while they dropped off a load of crystal meth to the skateboard punks at Grant Park. After payday, the brothers would pick up Gabriel and Dora at Aunt Ida and Uncle Clarence's. Then they would all go to Cherry's for a big family dinner. Meanwhile, Michael and Ronald had driven to Bullhead City for a meeting with their Mexican suppliers from Nogales. Even in a recession, business was booming.

It had been a while since Mesquite was without its first family for more than a day. Harlan was looking forward to the break. Despite everything, he'd actually missed his children. He hadn't seen them for a month and planned to take them to a toy store at the mall. It would be good to be with his blood kin again without Auntie Kate and Fatso Ryan bothering him. By now, Auntie and her boyfriend were probably being visited by the uniforms. Maybe they were behind bars. Before Harlan left Mesquite, he'd called a buddy with the tribal police and lodged a formal complaint. Kate Thorsen, he said, had been harassing and stalking him and his children after the tragic death of his wife. He threw in that Thorsen and her boyfriend had had the audacity to show up uninvited at his mother's home.

"I'd just been released from the hospital. Nearly lost an eye. I was recuperating," he said. "They barged in and this broad threatened me. Terry Ryan tried to physically assault me with a screwdriver. They've been telling lies about me and spreading them around town."

When asked if there'd been any witnesses to the threats, Harlan replied: "Hell, yeah. My mother and my brothers Andrew and Michael. Danny Revere, my cousin, was there too. You know Danny. He works for Parker P.D. Oh, and Marlene Stone, the ex-hooker with the glass house on the riverfront. She was there. You should talk to her."

"No problem," his friend said. "We'll look into it."

Harlan wasn't through. "Listen, this Thorsen bitch has really gotten my kids upset. They don't want to see her or have anything to do with her. I had to send them away to stay with family in Phoenix. That's where I am now," he lied. "I'm picking the kids up and bringing them home. It would be a big help if I didn't have to run into that broad or her boyfriend again."

"Do you know where they're staying?"

"At the casino hotel," Harlan said. "But they've been trespassing at my house in Mesquite. Yeah, it's mine. I've been fixing it up to sell it. My kids deserve better than living in that dump."

ALLEN REDMOND PICKED UP on the first ring. Kate had never spoken with a "blogger" before. The word itself sounded like gibberish. As a print journalist, she thought writing for cyberspace had to be one of the lowest rungs of hell.

Kate was a paper person, yet lately the articles she wrote for mainstream magazines were regularly turning up on the Internet without her permission and without additional compensation. When she complained to her editors, she was told selling electronic rights was the new standard for publishing. When she contacted journalist groups, all she received were raised eyebrows and sympathetic offerings. These days, a writer's copyright meant next to nothing.

While in myriad ways the Internet was changing the world for the better, it was also erasing the integrity of independent journalism. The publishing business was dying—and, from what she'd seen, bloggers were the bottom feeders. Most were amateurs posing as "citizen journalists," spewing out partisan rhetoric and gossip. Kate didn't care what other people did for a living. She just didn't want to be part of it.

"I'd like to talk to you," Redmond said. "I knew Daisy and understand you've been named executor of the estate. Do you have a minute?"

Kate had a sinking feeling that whatever she said to Redmond would be misinterpreted, be taken out of context, and cause more problems than it was worth. "I'm at the Bluebird," she said. "I doubt there's anything I can help you with. The reason I called you back is because something happened this morning at my niece's home."

There was a pause on the other end of the line. "I heard. Listen, I live just a few minutes from the café. I'll be right there."

While she waited, she wondered if Terry was sweating under hot lights in a cramped interrogation room. Poor guy, and for what? It was crazy. Not enough time had elapsed to raise objections with Sergeant Garcia, and shopping for a criminal attorney seemed a little premature. After talking to Marlene, she no longer knew whom to trust.

With only minutes to spare, Kate pulled out her laptop and set it on the Formica table. She did a quick Google search on Redmond and found out he was a former *Los Angeles Times* reporter who'd won a number of awards while covering county government, specifically for his investigative stories on child deaths in foster care. At the same time the veteran reporter was picking up kudos for journalistic excellence, the newspaper's ownership had changed and there was the proverbial management shakeup, which led to massive cost cutting and the usual rounds of staff layoffs.

It looked like Redmond had taken an early-retirement buyout and moved to the outback. For about a year, he'd worked as a reporter and editor at the *Parker Pioneer,* the local print weekly, before launching *Mesquite Musings.* From what she could glean from the site, the blog contained the usual small-town stuff: sports reporting, birth announcements, obituaries, gossip and a police blotter, but Redmond was also doing daily breaking news and occasional investigative features. Kate was intrigued by a special report on an influx of drugs on the reservation. It gave her hope.

When he walked into the Bluebird, she spotted him immediately. Allen Redmond looked and acted like a reporter. There was nothing unique about him. Put him in a suit and tie and he could pass for a deputy district attorney. Dress him in jeans and a T-shirt and he was just another regular at the American Legion Hall. With his cropped hair and Buddy Holly spectacles, Redmond easily blended into whatever surroundings he came in contact with—until he opened his mouth. "You must be Kate. I'm Allen. I hear you write for *National Geographic*," he said. "It must be fun to work soft news." She blanched. "I'm a hard-news reporter. You do understand the distinction, right?"

They both ordered black coffee. "*National Geographic* is one of my clients," she said. "I get what you're saying, but you're wrong. I started out in newspapers and still do what you call 'hard' news. Unfortunately, the only thing I know about you is that you write a local blog with sports scores and obituaries."

Sparring wasn't getting them anywhere. "Guess that sounded rude," Redmond said. "I apologize."

"Apology accepted. I think we have more important things to discuss. What do you know about the fire at Daisy's house?"

"I picked it up on the scanner last night. My sources tell me it was arson. They found a body burned beyond recognition. They don't know if it was the arsonist or a homicide. They think a homeless person might have been squatting at the place."

Kate rolled her eyes. If this was the best she was going to get, she might as well finish her coffee and get back to the hotel. "There was no squatter. I was at the house all day yesterday with contractors. I had the garage and windows boarded up and the locks changed. The house was secure and posted with 'No Trespassing' signs. The police were supposed to be patrolling. I don't see how anyone could have gotten in."

Redmond sipped his coffee. "There was a security problem?"

"That's putting it mildly. The house had been repeatedly vandalized and we're pretty sure we know who did it."

"Do you mind if I take a few notes?"

"I thought we were just trading information."

"We are, but I'm better if I can jot down what I hear. You're a reporter. You know how it is."

Kate reached in her handbag and pulled out a notepad and pen. "Then we'll both be jotting. Did you hear anything about Pastor Elias Williams going missing?"

"What? No, I didn't. I heard he'd been sick. Elias is a pillar of the community. Any idea how long he's been missing or who reported it?" Kate shook her head. "You don't think he's . . ."

"I don't know. Early this morning, I received a phone call telling me Elias was dead and the police were investigating. Then we went to the house and I saw the body bag. I'm having trouble putting the pieces together. It seems too coincidental. Elias was one of my niece's closest friends."

"Who's we?"

"My friend, Terry Ryan. He's a linguist and a colleague at *National Geographic*. He's been helping me get through this mess. When we got to the house this morning to continue cleaning, a tribal police officer talked to me and, the next thing I knew, Terry was taken into custody. They wouldn't tell me what was going on."

"I don't get it," Redmond said. "What are you going to do?"

"I guess I need to find a good criminal attorney. Terry's the most decent guy you'd ever want to meet. He doesn't know anything about the house burning down or a body. He'd never even met Daisy."

"There's exactly one attorney in Mesquite I trust, Larry Nash. He's a retired deputy district attorney from Los Angeles County. He's a good guy with an excellent reputation. He might be able to help you." Allen jotted down a number and handed it to her. "Who do you suspect vandalized Daisy's home? I assume it was pretty bad if you had to board it up and change the locks."

"It was beyond anything I've ever encountered. It looked like a tornado went through it. The windows were broken and the garage door removed. The locks on the doors were splintered. Anything of value was stolen and everything else was trashed and thrown in the back yard."

"Who did it?"

"You want to know who? Only one candidate: Harlan Sandoval, Daisy's ex-husband. I think he had help from other members of his family. Two days ago, Terry and I went to Harlan's mother's house and confronted him. I saw some of Daisy's belongings inside. The guy is a nightmare."

Redmond scratched his head. "Nice crowd. I work hard to stay away from that family. Did you contact the tribal police?"

"I'd been warned repeatedly that Harlan is connected to the police. I thought it wise to continue investigating myself. My job as probate executor is to protect the children's assets—and you know the saddest part? I can't even find the children. Harlan's taken them somewhere. I haven't seen Gabriel and Dora since the funeral."

"Okay," he said. "You call Larry Nash and see if he can get Terry released. I'm going to check around. Not everyone in law enforcement is Harlan's friend. Did you get the name of the officer with the tribal police?"

"Rudy Garcia."

"Okay, I know Rudy. Call me at five. If I don't hear from you, I'll find you. Is there anyone you trust around here?"

"One person," she said. "And he didn't show up for work this morning."

GABRIEL TOSSED HIS PILLOW and knocked *The Wizard of Oz* out of Dora's hands. "Hey, I'm trying to read." She looked at him as if he was beyond hope as she picked the book up off the floor. "Just leave me alone."

There were days the eight-year-old loved her brother and lately days when she didn't. It was the kind of summer Dora hoped she could forget. After her mother's death, things were changing fast, too fast. There were dark circles around Gabriel's eyes, he didn't talk much anymore, and he was getting meaner. At night, she heard him babbling in his sleep like the church ladies speaking their stupid tongues. Dora just wanted to go home.

They'd been in this run-down house that smelled like dirty rugs and cat poop for nearly a month. Uncle Clarence used Copenhagen snuff and Dora thought it was the nastiest habit she'd ever heard of. Aunt Ida was okay. At least she smelled like baby powder. Dora, who thought she might become a beautician someday, liked to watch Aunt Ida put makeup on. It was about the only thing she found interesting. The hardest part about staying in this stinky house was that there was nothing to do and no one to talk to. All they did was sit around playing cards or Monopoly, and that was hard because the board game was missing half the parts. The old boxes of jigsaw puzzles were all mixed together, making it impossible to do anything. To make matters worse, it was clear that Uncle Clarence didn't like Gabriel and Dora, probably because they were always asking to go outside. For some reason, going outside wasn't allowed.

Before Dora's parents divorced, they were a real family. Mommy smiled all the time and Daddy didn't drink beer. Everyone had fun, especially on Christmas and Easter, but they never celebrated Halloween because of the church's devil rules. She loved family camping trips and when they went to Disneyland on her fifth birthday. The fairytale castle and Small World were her favorite parts, while Gabriel preferred the Haunted House and Pirates of the Caribbean. Boys always got worked up about creepy stuff. Dora remembered how she used to imagine how it would be to take care of her parents when their hair turned white, their teeth fell out, and they got skinny and had to use canes to walk. Old people mostly just sat around in rocking chairs telling kids stories from the golden days. She thought their blubbery tongues were interesting. They weren't all grouchy, like that Mr. Wilson in *Dennis the Menace*.

Dora especially enjoyed imagining how Rainbow House would look when she grew up. It was going to be a real ranch with ponies and goats and lots of dogs. She didn't like cats because they ate birds. Rainbow House would be painted pink with purple, red and blue stripes around the windows—and there would be talking parrots in cages on a screened-in porch with purple and red flowers blooming between the pretty colored rocks that Grandma Celeste collected for them before she went to Heaven. Because Dora didn't like getting stuck, she would hire someone to pick needles off the cactus. If she had enough money, she might even pay one of the neighborhood children to walk the dogs when she didn't feel like it.

Oh, Rainbow House was going to be an amazing place with a mountain and a waterfall and walkways lit by twinkling lights. Dora would get Gabriel to help her plant a forest of shady trees. They would also have a miniature train, with enough seats for all the kids in the neighborhood to ride for free. Everyone in Mesquite would say Rainbow House was just like having your own Disneyland. Dora also planned to become a great cook, just like Mommy, and everyone in America would be impressed by the cookbook she was going to write filled with her mother's recipes. She'd been collecting Mommy's recipes since she learned to write. And she'd always hoped that Gabriel would become a carpenter, so he could make furniture and bookshelves like Grandpa Philip, who went to Heaven a long time ago. The way things were going lately, though, she was in desperate need of good thoughts and memories. "Think good thoughts," that's what her mother used to say. But Mommy was gone and now Daddy had disappeared from their lives."Why can't you respect my personal space?" Dora said, glaring at Gabriel. "It's not like we have a lot of room to spare. I was right in the middle of a chapter and you knocked out my bookmark. Now I've lost my place."

"I thought you knew that book by heart. You must have read it ten times already. Sorry, I didn't mean to knock it down. I was just trying to get your attention. Uncle Clarence said we need to pack our stuff," he said, rolling his eyes. "He's being nice for a change."

Dora's heart sank. "Are they sending us to foster care?"

"Nope," Gabriel beamed. "We're going home. Uncle Clarence said Dad and Grandma are on their way."

Dora heaved a sigh of relief. "Good. I don't want to stay in this place anymore. I'm sick of it. No friends, no phone, no TV, no school, no puppies, nothing. Are we really going home?"

"Hope so."

"Did Dad move into our house yet? Is his eye still wrecked?"

"Why are you asking me dumb questions? All I know is we're supposed to pack our shit because we're leaving. We'll find out what's going on when Dad and Grandma get here."

"You're not supposed to use cusswords."

"Why not? Shit's not a major cussword."

"Mommy wouldn't like it, that's why," she said.

Gabriel began kicking the bed as hard as he could. "Well, she's gone and she's not coming back," he said. "You keep making it sound like she's standing right here in this room. She's dead! And Dad doesn't care if I swear, so fuck it."

"You're being mean to me." Dora's eyes were tearing up. She threw her book at Gabriel's head and missed. "You tell lies. Just cut it out. I'm going to get my things ready to go home. You do the same and don't forget to pack your toothbrush. Are they going to let us take these comic books?"

"Just take them. I can't imagine either of those old people reading comic books or anything else. I doubt they know how to read. The only things Clarence and Ida care about are game shows and soap operas. Mom would have had a cow if she knew Dad brought us here. God, I can't wait to get home and see my friends. I want to ride my bike and eat tacos and take Fred on a walk."

Dora lowered her head and clasped her hands together. "With everything else going on, I didn't want to tell you," she said, lifting her head and looking into her brother's eyes. "I thought it would hurt more than help."

Gabriel's eyes widened. "What? What is it?"

"Fred and Mitzi are dead," Dora said. "I saw them together in a dream."

Dora's dreams were always right. She'd been able to predict things since she learned to talk. Gabriel made a sucking sound as if all the air in his lungs had collapsed. He wobbled when he sat down on the bed and put his hands over his eyes. Dora knew he was crying and didn't want her to see.

"When does this nightmare end?" he said. "There's got to be something we can do. Where's Aunt Kate's card? It had her cell phone number on the back. I'll tell Uncle Clarence that I need to call Dad. It's the only way he'll let me use the phone."

Uncle Clarence hovered over Gabriel's shoulder while Aunt Ida helped Dora comb her hair. "Hello, Dad. This is Gabriel. Dora wanted me to tell you that we're looking forward to going home to

Mesquite today. Going home is what we want to do. We want to see our friends and Aunt Kate. That's about it. If Uncle Clarence lets me have our cell phone back, I'll call you again and leave the number. Love you."

It took the children ten minutes to stuff their book bags before they sat down on the twin beds to wait for their father. Two hours passed. Finally Aunt Ida peeked in to ask if they were hungry. She brought them milk and bologna sandwiches. Then she kissed them goodnight and closed the bedroom door. When they finally heard their aunt and uncle go to bed, Gabriel turned to Dora. "Let's go home," he said. "We'll sneak out the front door."

IT WAS AN ACT born of desperation. Still, Kate felt optimistic when she listened to Gabriel's coded cry for help. Obviously he was being monitored. But hearing his voice was a relief. The prefix indicated he'd called from Phoenix. The children wanted to see her. They were begging their father to bring them home.

Jizo swung from his new perch on the rental car's rearview mirror.

Thank you, Jizo, now if we can just get Big Guy out of the slammer.

Good news is a powerful motivator. Kate immediately placed a call to the lawyer Redmond had recommended. Larry Nash invited her to stop by his home office. The barefoot and deeply tanned man who answered the door seemed decent enough. Nash listened patiently as she recounted the events leading up to Terry's being taken into custody. By the time she finished, Nash said it was doubtful that her friend had been charged with a crime.

"It's more likely the police were fishing. But I don't understand why the tribal police would take the lead. If it's a homicide investigation, the Parker police would have stepped in," Nash explained.

"Then why the handcuffs? Why was I ordered not to leave town?"

"That's where I come in," Nash said. "I'll contact law enforcement and find out what's up and get back to you. Then we'll figure out the next step. Before I forget, is Terry Ryan a U.S. citizen?"

"No, he's a British citizen who lives and works in Paris. Dr. Ryan is an associate professor of linguistics at the University of Paris and works with the United Nations on issues dealing with racial discrimination, particularly against the Romany people. He's a delegate to the Romany Congress. I've known him for five years because of my work with *National Geographic*. Terry is one of the few translators with a command of several dialects of Romany. After he heard Daisy died, he came out on his own initiative to help me sort things through. He's been a dear, dear friend."

Nash looked at her as if she was concealing something. "Sorry, I have to ask this: Terry's not on any terrorist watch list, is he?"

"God, no," she said with alarm.

"Was he with you yesterday?"

"Most of the day. We were working at Daisy's house, trying to salvage items for the children. Because of the probate case, I have to make an inventory of all of Daisy's belongings. Unfortunately, her ex-husband, Harlan Sandoval, got there before we did."

"What do you mean?"

"Harlan took anything of value and destroyed the rest. In the late afternoon, I had an appointment with Nopah Round, the Mohave healer, and Terry went with Marlene Stone, you may know her, to visit the tribal cemetery. He wanted to pay his respects to his former professor. George Devereux is buried there. Then he returned to the Blue Water where we're staying and waited for me."

"I've heard of Devereux. He's a legendary figure to the Mohave tribe." Nash scratched his forehead. "I may need to talk to Marlene to verify Terry's whereabouts while you were gone. What time did you get back to the hotel?"

"Around midnight. It was raining and I wasn't paying much attention to the time. Terry was already asleep," she said. "Believe me, we've nothing to hide."

"I'll see what I can do."

AFTER LEAVING NASH'S OFFICE, Kate felt clammy. She was flat-out exhausted, but returning to the hotel to rest would only reinforce the void that Terry's absence had created. If she hadn't gone to see Nopah, perhaps none of this would have happened. She slowly cruised past the charred skeleton of Rainbow

House. It looked worse than it had earlier. Black rubble had been pushed into piles and the yellow crime-scene tape still blocked the entrance and perimeter.

Crows were scavenging in the debris and an owl was perched on the fence. It seemed a curious place for a nocturnal bird. Kate hurt inside. It hurt to see what had been lost, though material things could always be replaced. Terry and the children, however, could not. Dwelling on the death that had occurred inside was pointless because Kate couldn't change what had happened any more than she could breathe Daisy back to life.

There were so many questions. She forced herself to think about what she could do and tried to let go of everything else. The market, which doubled as the neighborhood post office, was across the field. The proprietors, who had been so friendly to Terry, averted their eyes when she walked in to pick up Daisy's mail. She rifled through the envelopes: medical bills from the hospital stay, credit card bills, and a statement from the Bank of Mesquite indicating her account had been closed several days after the funeral. Someone had withdrawn the entire balance of $588.

Livid, Kate went to the bank. She walked in, demanded to see the manager, and was ushered into a glass office where May Peony, a dark-haired woman in a charcoal pants suit, sat behind a large walnut desk eating a Reese's Fast Break bar. "What seems to be the problem?" Peony said, in a way that conveyed she had no time to waste on foolishness.

"I'll tell you what the problem is. I just received this bank statement in the mail. I'm executor of my niece's estate and it's my role, under court supervision, to secure her assets." She pulled out the probate court documents. "Who closed Daisy Sandoval's checking account after her death? I want to know why the funds were released and who they were released to."

Peony took another chunk of the Fast Break and chewed slowly. "If I may, I'd like to make copies of these documents. It'll just take a moment. I'll check with my staff. Please sit down."

A good ten minutes passed before Peony returned with a smudge of chocolate at the corner of her mouth. "I'm sorry, Ms. Thorsen, we had no idea there was a probate case. After Mrs. Sandoval's death, we talked to her husband and released the funds to him."

Kate pulled her chair closer to Peony's desk until her knees were touching. "Why? Harlan Sandoval was no longer her husband. They were divorced. That fact is clearly noted on Daisy's death certificate."

"Yes, I noticed that," Peony said. "But they had children together."

"I don't understand what the children have to do with this." Kate tried hard not to sneer. "This wasn't a joint checking account. Daisy was the only authorized signer. You gave her money to Harlan Sandoval? Daisy's only legal heirs are her two minor children. By the way, you have some chocolate on your face."

Peony licked the chocolate off. "Because you're from out of town, I don't think you understand how things work around here. You see, we know this family. Daisy Sandoval was a longtime customer of our bank. At one time, so was her husband. When he presented us with a copy of Mrs. Sandoval's death certificate, it was our assumption he had a legal right to the funds. While Mr. Sandoval was here, he signed a notarized affidavit stating there was no probate case and the decedent's estate did not exceed fifty thousand dollars."

Peony handed Kate a copy of the one-page affidavit, signed by Harlan and notarized by the woman sitting across from her. "You must be kidding me," she said. "This is an outright lie. It's fraud."

"No, I'm not kidding. This is normal procedure. Mr. Sandoval claimed he was entitled to all Mrs. Sandoval's property."

Adrenalin pumping, Kate began drumming her fingers on Peony's desk. "You mean to tell me that your bank just hands over money to anyone who comes in with a death certificate? I must be in the wrong business."

"That's unfair," Peony shot back. "My advice for you is to contact the police."

"How lovely . . . Are you seriously trying to tell me the Bank of Mesquite has no legal responsibility to my niece's estate for this mistake?"

"That's what I'm saying. In Arizona, the law states anyone

known to the staff may present a death certificate to withdraw funds and close an account. It's common practice. Because Mrs. Sandoval's estate is worth less than fifty thousand dollars, the bank isn't liable for its actions."

"Sorry, I'm a little confused here. How do you know Daisy Sandoval's estate is worth less than fifty thousand dollars? Explain that to me. I'm in the process of taking inventory for the probate court and I haven't ascertained the total worth of the estate. Do you know something I should know?"

Peony blushed. "Because she was poor."

"She was *what?*"

"I can't discuss this further . . . I have other appointments waiting. I'm sorry for your loss and wish you the best of luck. Good day."

Kate felt she'd been sucker-punched, but only for a moment. "Don't worry, May," she said. "I'm sure we'll be seeing each other again."

OUTSIDE, IN THE BANK'S parking lot, Kate kicked her tire and then called Allen Redmond. He told her the tribal police had received an anonymous tip that a man, matching Terry's description, had been seen near Daisy's house shortly before the fire broke out. The police had also received a recent complaint from Harlan Sandoval alleging that Terry, carrying a weapon, had trespassed at his mother's home and threatened him.

"I'm sorry," Redmond said. "It looks like they're going to hold your friend."

"These allegations are bullshit," she said. "I'll be back in touch. Thanks for directing me to Nash."

After they hung up, Kate began sneezing uncontrollably. Once she regained composure, she called Nopah's daughter, Mary. "I need the help you offered," she said. "I feel sick."

"I know. Don't worry," she said. "My father wants to tell you about the house fire. We'll meet you at the Bluebird in about an hour. I'll bring more sage."

With time to kill, Kate stopped at the preschool to pick up Daisy's things. She'd finally met Candy Estrada, her niece's boss, at the funeral—and Candy had invited her to stop by anytime. Before she went inside, however, she stood at the wire fence watching the children playing hopscotch and four square. On the other side of the playground, three dark-haired girls were on the swings and two boys were in the sandbox, filling plastic buckets with sand in a futile attempt to create mountains. These were the little people Daisy had written about, the ones who so touched her she felt compelled to chronicle their stories in long e-mails that her homesick aunt hungrily read over and over again and saved.

Kate would never forget the story of Iris, a four-year-old Latina struggling to learn English. Daisy said the little girl was stubborn and sweet with dark eyebrows that she scrunched together when making a joke. Iris had the face of an imp and a flapper's bob hairdo and wore a tiny plastic barrette to hold her bangs back. She liked to paint and make messes with glue and wear pink girly clothes. Iris said "thank you" and "goodnight" and "where's Mommy?" One morning she said, "I'm so tired. I miss Daddy."

"The other night her face appeared in my dream," Daisy wrote. "I don't know why. The meaning of the dream had something to do with children, that the children needed me to do something for them and were counting on me. Many of these kids come from violent homes. It's heartbreaking. Yesterday, Iris's mother, who looked nervous and afraid, came to the school early. She said they were returning to Mexico. I knew it meant she was going back to the husband who beat her. All the kids at school were sad. We didn't get a chance to really say goodbye. Sometimes I just feel inadequate."

At the time, Kate didn't understand why Daisy, an earth mother if there ever was one, would feel inadequate. How could she? Kate was proud of Daisy for raising great kids, working full-time and finishing college. She was proud that Daisy had had the courage to dump Harlan, and proud she'd successfully handled her own divorce. What Kate didn't know was that her niece was stretched thin from fighting an unending battle with her abuser. In the last e-mail Daisy wrote, she said: "If we do what we know to be right, then everything will be okay."

Inside the schoolhouse, Kate saw Daisy's boss standing near the window.

"You look tired," Candy said. "You've been here for a while. How are you holding up?"

"Okay, I guess," Kate replied. "Hope you don't mind, I stopped by to pick up Daisy's things." Candy frowned and Kate wondered if she'd misunderstood. "You did say Daisy had personal belongings here, didn't you? I'm trying to pull everything together for her children."

"Yes, I did say that. Unfortunately, I said it before we gave her things to the family."

Kate didn't want to hear the answer, but asked the question anyway: "What family?"

"Harlan stopped by after the funeral and took everything."

"He's no longer part of the family," Kate said. "They were divorced."

"I know," Candy said. "Harlan wanted Daisy's last paycheck. I told him it was automatically deposited into her checking account. He looked angry. Gabriel and Dora were with him. They asked to see their mom's desk. We had all her things packed in boxes. I'm sorry . . . It seemed the right thing to do."

Feeling outmaneuvered, Kate fought back tears.

"We heard about the fire," Candy said. "What happened?"

"I don't know. The police said it was arson. Everything's gone."

After a long hug and another quick look at the playground, Kate returned to the hotel. She needed to freshen up before meeting the shaman. The room had been cleaned and Terry's clothes were hanging in the closet. She wanted him to be with her, holding her safe. *How much more could she take?* Everything was working against her—and Harlan, as usual, was two steps ahead.

THEY WAITED until they could hear Uncle Clarence snoring in the other bedroom before they began feeling their way through obstacles in the darkened living room. "Ouch," Dora said as she stubbed her toe on the foot of the couch. Gabriel shushed her. When they opened the front door a crack, a streetlight briefly illuminated the room and they noticed their cell phone and a bag of Mother's chocolate chip cookies on the hall table. Aunt Ida was looking out for them.

Gabriel and Dora had run away once before when their parents were arguing, but they'd only gotten as far as Marlene's house. She'd let them sleep on her couch and drove them home early the next morning. Luckily, their father was gone or they would have faced the belt. Their mother cried when she saw them and put them on restriction for a week. This time was different. They weren't running away from home; they were running *to* home. After an hour of waiting for their father, they'd both known he wasn't coming. He'd let them down again.

At first, they weren't sure which direction to go until they saw a white light in the sky and followed it. They ran several blocks before the spotlight directed them to a major thoroughfare. They saw a shopping center called Buckeye Plaza and an Arco station on the corner with a little mini-mart. "Let's go to the gas station," Gabriel said. "We'll pretend we're supposed to be meeting Dad at the entrance to Interstate 10 because our mother's in the hospital. I'll do the talking. We can probably hitch a ride home."

"We're not supposed to hitchhike. You know that." Dora was twisting her hair, something she started doing when she finally stopped sucking her thumb. "Why can't we just use our phone to call Aunt Kate to come and get us?"

"Act your age," Gabriel said with irritation. "Let's get as far from here as we can before we call her."

"Okay," Dora replied, her mouth covered with crumbs and saliva. "Do you want a cookie? They're really good."

"No thanks. But we better buy some water in case we get stuck in the middle of the desert. How much money do we have?"

Dora was glad her brother trusted her to hold the money. She sat down on the sidewalk, checked her change purse and counted out each coin. "Exactly five dollars and twenty-seven cents."

"Way to go! We're on our way home."

The clerk behind the counter at the Arco station's mini-mart was wearing a white turban and spoke with an accent. Dora thought he looked like a genie and wanted to ask him if he granted wishes, but Gabriel flared his nostrils to warn her away. The clerk sold them two bottles of water and said the freeway entrance was half a mile down the road. He warned them to be careful and walk on the side where the streetlights were.

"Do you kids want me to call your father to pick you up here? I don't think you should be out alone in the dark. This is not a nice neighborhood."

Gabriel said he understood that, but their father trusted them and had given a direct order about where to meet. "Our father is a policeman. He will be at the on-ramp waiting for us in his squad car." The clerk looked sad and Dora could see he didn't believe Gabriel's lie. She wished she'd been allowed to ask the clerk if he could grant her one wish. It was a big one: She wanted her mother back.

They headed toward the on-ramp, skipping and shooing away gnats buzzing around their heads. "What do you think happened to Dad? Why didn't he pick us up?"

"He probably forgot," Gabriel said. "Maybe he got drunk or met a new girlfriend. I think he means well. He just can't . . ."

"I know, I know. Mommy always used to say Dad was 'commitment adverse.' I wasn't sure what she meant, but I think it had something to do with not finishing the things you promise to do."

"We'll be fine on our own. Don't worry. All we have to do is get to Mesquite. Aunt Kate always comes through for us. If we can't find her right away, we'll go to Marlene's. She always treated us like her kids anyway. Maybe she'd let us live on Don's boat in the garage. That would be fun. We wouldn't have to change schools or anything and we could go to our house every day and start fixing it up the way you always talked about."

Two small figures stood illuminated at the freeway on-ramp with their thumbs stuck out. Cars sped past and a few slowed down, but no one stopped until a bald man in a rusted pink Thunderbird pulled onto the easement and rolled down his window. "You kids need a ride? Where're you going this time of night?"

Gabriel moved toward the vehicle and stopped short, shocked at what he saw. The man's hand was moving up and down on his crotch. Gabriel turned toward Dora and began backing away. "No, that's okay," the boy said. "We're waiting for our father and grandmother. They should be here any second now."

The bald man started to open his door. "Then why'd you have those thumbs out? Looks like you were hitching to me. Come over here!"

"Run!" Gabriel yelled at his sister. They could hear the man swearing as they scurried into the bushes. The Thunderbird sped away. "Phew, that was close."

"It was creepy. You sure you don't want to call Aunt Kate?"

"Five more minutes and we'll call," Gabriel said, heading back to the on-ramp with his sister behind him.

The next car to stop was driven by a woman that Dora thought looked like a kindly grandmother because she wore wire-rimmed spectacles and had short white hair. She was so small she could barely see over the steering wheel. "What on earth are you kids doing out here this time of night?"

"We're trying to get home," Gabriel said. "We were kidnapped and a robber took our money."

The driver looked hard at them. "Oh, my . . . That's quite a story." Dora thought Gabriel should stop telling lies because he wasn't any good at it. "My name is Mrs. Teubler. You can call me Trudy if you like. Where do you kids live?"

Gabriel told her Mesquite, near Parker. Mrs. Teubler said she knew it well, her son and grandchildren lived there. "If you're interested, I can drive you as far as Quartzsite," she said. "That's where I live. I'll call my boy when we get there. Maybe he can get hold of your family to come and get you."

Before she got into Mrs. Teubler's car, Dora offered her a cookie. The woman smiled and took it, thanked her and ate the whole thing. So this grandma couldn't be a bad person. A bad person wouldn't eat someone else's cookie because it might be poisoned. Dora never forgot about her Uncle Zack, the one who died at a party in Yuma after drinking a can of beer laced with Drano. In her eyes, Mrs. Teubler was probably a good person.

THEY'D JUST LEFT Grant Park and were flush with the skateboarders' green.

Harlan was smitten as soon as he saw the redhead in the black Lycra dress and thigh-high boots standing in front of the fleabag hotel. Her hair was cut stylishly short like one of those New York models. She smiled at him, one of those inviting smiles that told him she was a hooker. But she was the prettiest little thing he'd seen in a long time, at least with one eye. He told Andrew to drop him off at the corner, said he'd take a cab to Cherry's house.

"Well hello there, sweet thing," Harlan said, being as charming as he could be under the circumstances. "You look like a ray of sunshine."

"What happened to your eye?"

"Walked into a door. No big deal. I thought you might be interested in going to a party. Are you a working woman?"

"You bet, sugar," she purred. "What kind of party?"

"The works," he said. "Do you have a place nearby? I'm from out of town."

"Sure do, sugar. Right behind me," she replied, pointing to the hotel.

They went up to a second-floor room. The redhead danced a little, showed him she had the right moves. He told her what he wanted and money was exchanged. Then the closet door opened. And that's how Harlan ended up getting busted by an undercover police officer and her partner. He spent the night in a holding cell until Mama Lou and Andrew bailed him out the next morning. Mama was furious, but Andrew just called him a fool.

It wasn't until they were nearing Cousin Cherry's house that Harlan remembered he'd forgotten all about picking up Gabriel and Dora. When he called Uncle Clarence, he learned they'd run away.

"Well, Gabriel called you, said he wanted to go home and see his friends and Aunt Kate. Then you didn't show," his uncle said. "What the hell did you expect them to do?"

"My son didn't call me." Harlan was puzzled. It took him a moment to figure it out. The children couldn't have gotten away by themselves. They were way too young—and there was only one other person they would have called for help.

BACK AT THE HOTEL, Kate was a wreck, filled with nervous anticipation until Larry Nash called to say Terry would be, in all likelihood, released in the morning. There was no evidence, the lawyer said, linking Terry to the Rainbow House fire, other than an anonymous tip from a female caller. "I'll keep you posted," he said.

After they hung up, Kate began sneezing again and then fell asleep sitting in a chair by the window. She dreamed dead people were trying to force her to eat their food: pudding, nuts, fish, melons . . . The more she refused their offerings, the more aggressively the phantoms pursued until they were throwing steaming plates and bowls.

She awoke with a start. The clock indicated she'd been asleep only a few minutes. Nopah and Mary would be waiting, so she quickly splashed her face with cold water, ran a brush through her hair, gargled, and then walked briskly through the hotel. The dim casino was filled with elderly people, computer sounds and flashing lights. It was ironic that she and Terry were staying at a destination resort where everyone came to gamble. She had always likened gambling to driving down the street throwing money out the window.

It was a relief to walk into the Bluebird, humming with customers, and see Edward sitting with Nopah and Mary. With the exception of the shaman, who ate nothing, they were finishing dinner and laughing. The two children Kate had seen earlier at the hospital in Phoenix were playing video games near the back door. It seemed normal, a quiet family dinner. "I'm sorry to be late," she said. "I fell asleep."

Nopah observed her caustically. "You didn't eat their food, did you? If you ate the food of the dead, you will go insane."

Oh, god . . . Best to ignore him or he'll start spitting again. How could he possibly know about her dream? Kate rolled her eyes and sat down just as Shirley arrived to ask what she wanted for dinner. "I'm not sure." Kate scanned the menu. "What's good tonight?"

"We have a nice turkey pot pie, but you look like you need a warm tuna melt with fries and plenty of ketchup. And how about iced raspberry tea to wash it down?"

Nopah frowned and tapped his index finger on the table while Kate considered her options. "Sounds luscious, but tonight I'll have the vegetable plate and unsweetened raspberry tea. I need to build up my strength. Never know when you're going to need it."

"Um . . . The white woman is all right," Nopah said. "She knows something. Tell us what has changed."

"We thought you were sick," Mary said, handing her another bundle of sage. "You're glowing in the twilight of evening."

"I was sick," she said stuffing the sage in her purse with the other bunch. "It was crazy. I felt awful and couldn't stop sneezing."

Nopah insisted ghosts were approaching her. "*Weylak nevethi.* Expect pain in your anus."

Then Mary stepped in. "It may not be that serious, Father. Did you bless yourself each time you sneezed?" Kate looked at the woman and shook her head. "Well, begin now. It's just a precaution. It might be ghosts. But you're probably sniffing things out, struggling to express new feelings. Or you could be allergic to angelica. A long arrowweed bath would do the trick. You can buy it at any drug or health food store. They may even have it in the spa at the hotel."

"Thank you both for your advice. This has been a difficult day in a succession of difficult days. I've had some good news too. I'm happy to see you're all here. Edward, I was worried about you— afraid you'd been hurt or worse." She reached across the table and squeezed his hand; he squeezed back. They communicated without speaking. "I've heard from the children."

"Oh . . ." Nopah leaned forward in rapt attention. "What is the news?"

"They're trying to get home."

At that moment, Shirley set down a steaming plate of squash, onions, potatoes, green beans and tomatoes. Kate swore she'd never smelled food so heavenly and attacked it with her fork. After several bites, she asked the shaman to tell her about the fire. "I need to know what happened."

"The land itself has long been haunted ground," he said. "And the house was possessed by an angry ghost. The fire helped purify some of it. I doubt everything was driven away. More will need to be done."

"Who died there?"

"The preacher," Nopah said. "He was bewitched and met a violent death. At first, he was slow-witched. A shaman shot power into him and then visited his dreams causing him to waste away."

"You're talking about Pastor Williams and his cancer?"

Nopah's piercing eyes looked heavenward and then he glared directly at her. "No names. I told you no names." Kate mouthed a sorry. "So, when he didn't die soon enough, the shaman became greedy and fast-witched him with fire."

"Who is this other shaman?"

"A rival. We cannot speak the name or we will draw the witch to us." He spat on the floor, an action Kate found disgusting, especially in a restaurant, but better than the behavior of a reporter she knew in Washington who always blew his nose on the linen napkins in fancy restaurants. "I can direct you to look for what form the witch's poison takes."

Kate was confused. More than one shaman was involved? One was a witch? Nopah had already said he wasn't a witch. She believed him. Okay, who was it? If it was a Mohave, she knew it could be either a man or a woman. In the old days, if the victim's family members or tribal warriors caught a witch, he or she would be stoned to death and cremated. But this was the 21st century. Surely such things didn't happen any longer. Or did they?

"We must be careful, take slow steps. I may be able to kidnap the souls the witch is holding," Nopah said. "My power is strong."

"Father, don't sacrifice yourself," Edward said. "You are old. I'll look for the signs. Big Nose will come too. We're warriors."

Nopah shook his head.

Determined to treat this as a normal, everyday conversation, Kate stepped in. "Obviously, I'm not from your tribe and don't know what you're talking about," she said. "But I saw crows and an owl at the ruins of the house today. I thought their appearance strange. What do you think?"

"Hum . . . You are a manly woman." Nopah seemed to be reappraising, looking at her with fresh eyes.

Although she knew the Mohave treated homosexuals with reverence, she was fairly sure her sexual identity hadn't shifted—and, if it had, her relationship with Terry negated Nopah's compliment. "Guess I should have had my mustache waxed," she quipped.

"You misunderstand my words. I see you're determined to save the children, and you have a connection to the house." He turned to Edward. "We won't need Big Nose tonight. We will bring Manly Woman with us."

Kate flexed her sagging arm muscles while Edward stifled a giggle by placing his hand over his mouth. Just then, Mary's children approached the table begging for more quarters for video games—and were shooed away. The scene was so wildly out of context that Kate compulsively started in on the vegetables again, savoring every morsel. Why did she suddenly crave buttered vegetables when she was a tuna-melt-with-fries freak? The plate was nearly empty when she drained the last of the tea. She felt the urge to scoop up the butter from the plate when Nopah abruptly commanded her attention by snapping his fingers.

"You have eaten enough. We have serious business to discuss," he said, rubbing his palms together. "I want to tell you that the owl is a free soul. The owl you saw today may be the guardian of the house. Or it is a messenger from the dead. It would explain the anger I see in my dreams and why I believe your niece has not been set free. She is a restless spirit.

"The crows are the familiars of the witch. They must be driven out. This other shaman bewitches the souls of humans and keeps them for his pleasure. These souls are trapped and cannot go to the place of the dead. When this shaman dies, he will take the trapped souls with him to the next world. It is a horrible fate."

"Sounds like the Mormon version of paradise," Kate said. "I've always believed the dead could take care of themselves. My niece wasn't a Mohave. She had her own belief system. Did I miss something? I thought we were trying to protect the living."

"Trust me. There are more colors in the rainbow than you can see," Nopah replied. "If we can persuade the owl to reveal his identity, we have taken the first step. If the bird is a messenger, he will guide us. So, we go to the house tonight and use sage to purify the area. But I warn you, this will be tricky and it is not without danger. Manly Woman and I will travel together. Daughter, you take the children home. Edward will bring me back before the sun rises."

"Are you sure?" Mary looked worried. "Father, I don't want to leave you."

"Don't question," he replied. "You know this is my burden. I did not choose it. Go to the car and bring me my medicine bag. I will have need of it."

NIGHT ENVELOPED the landscape. Kate had never seen quite so many sparkling stars. It was eerily quiet when they reached the ruins of Rainbow House. When she shined a flashlight on the skeleton of the home, police tape fluttered and glowed like yellow fingers beckoning her forward.

Edward took the two bundles of sage and slipped into the darkness, leaving her alone with Nopah. Since explaining their mission, Nopah had become a puzzle within a puzzle. The shaman, whose lips were dry and parched, hadn't spoken a word since he'd disappeared into the Bluebird's restroom only to return with his hair in braids tied with red yarn. Black paint and burgundy lipstick were smeared on his face. He had returned to the old ways. As they walked out of the café, Shirley said, "Ya'll going on the warpath?"

Now, sitting in the passenger seat, Nopah looked dead, an uncomfortable reminder of Kate's vigil at Daisy's bedside. Frustrated, Kate jerked open the passenger door and commanded the shaman to get out of the car. When he didn't, she prodded him with the flashlight. "Come on, time to wake up!" No movement. So she slugged his bony arm as hard as she could. Finally his eyes opened to a slit and a jerky hand moved toward his shirt pocket. Drooling from the sides of his mouth, Nopah took out an American Spirit and lit the fag. He inhaled, then blew a stream of blue smoke through the open door and into the warm night air.

"Manly Woman has good muscles for an old lady," he said.

"Thanks a lot."

From the field, Kate heard Edward singing and smelled sage burning. In an ancient custom common to many cultures, she knew her friend was in the process of walking around the perimeter of the property—protecting and purifying the ground inside the boundary. Edward was doing what she and Terry would have done had they not encountered fire trucks and police with handcuffs earlier in the day.

Tonight, she didn't feel comfortable with Nopah. He wasn't himself. In her mind's eye, she pictured him as a coyote and couldn't shake the feeling. Fueling her frustration was the fact that she missed Terry. She always felt safe with him. The Big Guy was the best guide through the vagaries of religious and mystical practices she'd ever encountered. He was always there and now he wasn't.

A shrill sound caught her off guard and made her jump. She whirled around and trained the flashlight on the source before she realized it was Nopah. He was behind her, sitting in the car with his head bowed, beating a little drum with one hand and rattling a gourd with the other. He was screeching like an injured animal. But how had he projected his voice to make it sound as if it were coming from another direction?

"Jesus, you almost scared me to death," she said to him. "Don't do that again!"

Ignoring her, the shaman leaped out of the rental car and danced toward the burnt-out house, shaking the gourd. It was then that she thought she saw barely discernible multicolored shadows moving toward her in the dim light. She stood frozen as the shadows joined together, assembling in a unit as a blue ball. The ball resembled an illuminated butterfly bouncing up and down through the air. She thought of the butterfly dream she'd had when Daisy was dying. Was it Daisy? Kate stood her ground until the blue ball disappeared.

Then she noticed Nopah, his body bent, creeping toward a fence post where the owl with golden eyes sat vigilant. The crows were gone—or at least not visible. Nopah stood up straight and, without coaxing, the owl hopped onto his shoulder like a trained parakeet. She watched the shaman reach up and pluck four feathers, two from each of the bird's wings. Then he stuck the feathers into his scraggly braids before he waved his arm and pointed an index finger skyward. The bird hopped into the air and flew away.

As if on cue, Edward emerged from the darkness and took long objects from the bed of his truck. Without a word, the two men left her and began placing wooden stakes at the farthest four corners of the property. She could hear the drum beating and the men chanting. She watched as they tied a plucked owl feather to each pole with red yarn. Then they walked the perimeter of the property burning the second bundle of sage. The night air smelled sweet. When they reached the last corner, Kate heard howling, an explosion of sound. It was a Mohave bird song—words remembered, treasured and passed on to each new generation.

Out of nowhere, Kate's phone rang. The caller was Dora, saying she and Gabriel had run away and were waiting for her at a rock store in Quartzsite. "Please, please, please hurry . . . Come and get us." The girl sounded desperate. Kate knew exactly which rock store. She owed the proprietor a dollar.

When Nopah and Edward returned from the field, she told them about the children. "I'm going to bring the children home," she said.

Nopah smiled and Edward strode to his truck, took something out of the glove compartment and handed it to her as if it were his greatest treasure. It was a homemade CD of powwow songs from a gathering of tribes he'd attended in New Mexico. "To smooth the way, listen to the drums," he said. "It's the most powerful of medicines."

Kate's flashlight illuminated her companions. The shaman's appearance was shocking. His hair was jumbled and clung in long strands to his sweat- and tear-streaked face. Nopah looked exhausted, as if ready to fall down, and his voice was a nearly inaudible rasp. "Big problem," he said. "Before you go, I want you to know the other shaman's witchcraft is stronger than I thought. We will need to return. I must rest now and consider this problem."

LISTENING TO THE THROBBING of the drums, Kate turned up the volume and felt invigorated as she confidently navigated the roadway to Quartzsite. As she felt the throbbing grow stronger, she refused to be rushed or distracted by passing motorists bent on outpacing her. As a newly forged "manly woman" on a rescue mission, she pictured relieved children's faces and big hugs greeting her at the end of the journey. Confidence is often an illusion.

What Kate didn't know was that, after Dora called for help, Mrs. Teubler contacted her son. Gordie Teubler was a motorcycle mechanic in Mesquite who occasionally did work for the entrepreneurial Harlan Sandoval. Mrs. Teubler told Gordie about the two children she'd found hitchhiking on a freeway on-ramp near Phoenix. She also told him that they'd used her land line to call an aunt to come get them.

"I don't like the idea of turning these little ones over to a stranger without any bona fides," she said. "Do you know these people?"

"Sure do," he said. "Ma, don't let them go with that woman. She's bad news. Fact is, the cops are looking for her, something about burning down a house."

"Burning down a house?"

"Yeah . . . And I heard there was a body there."

"Oh, my . . ."

"Don't worry, I know the kids' dad. He's a buddy of mine," Gordie said. "I'll call Harlan Sandoval right now and tell him where to pick up his kids. Don't let them out of your sight, you hear? If that woman shows up, use Pa's shotgun if you have to. I'll call you back after I make the connection. If I can't get hold of Harlan, I'll come out there and bring them back myself."

"Did you say Sandoval? Are these children Mexican? Should I call the militia? They're always on the lookout for illegal aliens."

"No, no, Ma . . . Not that kind of Mexican. The kids aren't illegal aliens; they're homegrown American citizens. No need to worry."

"Well, that makes it easier, doesn't it?"

So Mrs. Teubler, a widow who found nothing unusual about displaying a Nazi flag outside her mobile home, was glad she had called Gordie. She could always count on him. But what was she going to do with this aunt? Just imagine . . . A wanted criminal was on her way to the Teubler home. Gabriel and Dora hadn't told her the truth about anything. For heaven's sake, she certainly didn't believe one word of their silly stories about being kidnapped and robbed. These kids hadn't been raised right, that was for sure. And it was a good thing she and her late husband had gone through survivalist training. Mrs. Teubler was an excellent shot.

When Kate arrived at the rock shop, she didn't see Gabriel or Dora. All she saw when she turned to approach the mobile home was the face of a little white-haired grandmother wielding a big shotgun. "Right this way," the woman said, as she used the gun to nudge Kate into a small wooden shed at the outskirts of the property.

The shed had no windows and only one entry point. Her captor bolted the door. It was pitch-black inside. At first, Kate pushed on boards looking for an escape route. Finding nothing loose, she realized there was no escape. Frustrated, she didn't bother to struggle and sat down on the dirt floor waiting for dawn to replace the dark. That's when awareness encompassed thought and capacities were distorted. She again thought she was surrounded by multicolored lights. When she looked closer, the illusions became the faces of children. Was her sanity slipping away? At the same time, Edward's drums reverberated in her mind and she could hear Nopah singing, lulling her into a dreamless sleep.

HARLAN'S HEAD HURT and the scar near his right eye was burning. "Step on it, fool!"

"Look who's calling *who* a fool," Andrew angrily shot back. "Only you would mistake an undercover cop for a hooker. This time I'm not loaning you money to pay the fine. You can go to prison for all I care. I hear they make you wear pink underwear."

"Boys, boys . . . Stop! You're giving me a bellyache with all this bickering." Mama was fit to be tied. She was in the backseat sitting next to a box filled with Cousin Cherry's homemade fried chicken. Cherry was a fine cook, didn't need recipes or anything.

Mama had planned a grand day in the city. She wanted to visit old friends and go shopping. She had an appointment to get her nails manicured, her bunions shaved and her eyebrows plucked. She was even contemplating one of those new orange-peel facials and maybe, just maybe, a bikini wax. Personal grooming was important for a woman's sense of confidence, Oprah said, and Mama knew it to be true. She believed in the Gospel of Oprah, especially the part about living your own best life.

Now two ill-mannered grandchildren had ruined her plans.

"What's your hurry, Harlan?" Mama was angry. "Don't you know that things will fall into place? They always do. Have you lost your faith? We'll get those kids and take them to Danny's house for the time being. His wife just sits around on her fat ass all day anyway. She won't even notice."

It wasn't a bad idea, at least until Daisy's Social Security money started coming in. "Sorry, Mama," he said. "My faith is intact. And I want you to know that I didn't even touch that woman cop. It was a sting operation and I was framed. But I'm not sure Danny's house is the best place for my children. It's a nuthouse. Danny's still working graveyard at Parker P.D., and Gabriel and Dora were spoiled rotten by their mother. They need a structured environment."

"That's obvious," Mama said with glum despair. "Otherwise we wouldn't need to be rushing to Quartzsite to get those little scamps. I want you to know I had my whole day planned out before this nonsense happened. I had to cancel important appointments. If you ask me, what those kids need is a good beating—and I've a mind to do it myself."

Harlan was afraid his children wouldn't survive the kind of beating his mother could dish out. "I'll handle the discipline, Mama. Listen, why don't we take them straight over to one of the family houses? The way those kids have been behaving, it's time to put them to work, introduce them to the real world."

"I need to stop by my place first," she said. "Then we'll figure out how to handle this situation."

Harlan could see Quartzsite on the horizon and knew the Teubler rock shop was next door to the service station. Been there a million times, but never bought anything. Couldn't figure out why anyone would pay good money for rocks when they were all over the ground for nothing. Not that he would ever pick one up, unless it was gold or silver, you know, worth something. The Mohave thought rocks were dangerous and had cantankerous personalities that could bring you good luck one day and bad the next. And he could never figure out why Daisy's wacko mother collected them.

Andrew rubbed his nose. "Hey, I think I see Auntie Kate's rental car. Wonder if she's got Fatso with her? This could be fun."

"I know for a fact that Fatso is currently sitting in a jail cell, just where he oughta be," Harlan said. "But we could have a little fun with Auntie Kate."

They pulled the Cadillac into a parking lot filled with loose gravel. "Mama, you come with me. Mrs. Teubler's not going to say no to another grandmother. Andrew, why don't you take care of Auntie's car while we're gone? Do your specialty."

Andrew grinned and pulled out his pocketknife. Some kids like popping bubble wrap; but, since he was a kid, Andrew had enjoyed deflating tires. It gave him a sense of power and control. It was a rush. "My pleasure," he said.

"Daddy! Daddy!" Gabriel and Dora were all over Harlan before he knew it. "We were waiting for you! Where have you been? We were worried."

It was quite a homecoming. Mrs. Teubler came out behind the children, said there was a little trouble with another visitor until she locked her up. Harlan thanked her, said he'd take care of everything, and introduced the rock shop proprietor to his mother.

"It was mighty nice of you to watch out for our children," Mama Lou said. "Their mother died a while back and they've not been acting like themselves. They've never run away before. I can't believe they made it all the way to Phoenix. Who knows what could have happened if you hadn't come along? Praise the Lord! We were so worried. All right kids, let's go home. Grandma's got some nice fried chicken in the car. We'll get sodas at the service station."

Gabriel and Dora obediently climbed into the backseat of the Cadillac to wait for their father and grandmother. They watched their father waving his arms at Mrs. Teubler. He was shouting. It looked like he was angry with her, but Dora still thought she was a nice lady. A few minutes later, Grandma Lou squeezed her bulky frame into the backseat.

"Where's Auntie Kate?" Dora whispered before Gabriel pinched her arm.

Mama's ears perked up. "What did you say, child?"

"I said this smells like good chicken," Dora said. "Can I get a Fanta to go with it? Gabe likes Dad's Root Beer."

"You bet, sweetheart," Mama Lou said. "Anything you want. Hope you two enjoyed your vacation. It'll be a while before you have another one."

BEAMS OF SUNLIGHT filtered through tiny cracks in the shed's walls and sheets of dust filtered down. A rooster crowed and tinkling chimes swayed in the slight morning breeze. Groggy, Kate wiped the sleep out of her eyes and was horrified to see red ants swarming out of a sand pile on the dirt floor. They were near her feet. She'd already been attacked by ants once and didn't like the prospect of a second match. Moving to the other side of the shed, she felt her stomach rumbling and realized she was hungry.

Outside, she could hear what sounded like Harlan arguing with an older woman, probably the grandma with the shotgun. "Don't let that bitch out until we're gone," he said, "or we'll come back and take care of you."

Heart racing, Kate crouched low to the ground and waited until the angry voices stopped. Then she stood up and brushed dirt off her clothes and spotted a small board to use as a weapon. She braced herself behind the door and heard a car speed away. An eternity seemed to pass before the rickety door opened. It was Shotgun Grandma without the shotgun, saying the children were gone and she was free to go. Kate dropped the board and reached into her wallet, coldly handed the puzzled woman a dollar bill and ran out of the shed as fast as she could.

When Kate got to the rental car, she screamed, "Shit, shit, shit!" when she saw the tires had been slashed. She immediately headed for the service station next door to use the restroom before she burst a gut. Afterward, she scrubbed her hands and face with powdered soap and rinsed off. The hand blower was broken and there were no paper towels, so she let herself air dry. Why was it that public toilets were always a disaster?

Then she went inside the mini-market and approached the manager for help. The name embroidered on his grease-stained blue shirt said "Clyde." Unfortunately, Clyde explained that he didn't sell tires—new or used—and advised her to have the vehicle towed to Phoenix for servicing. Phoenix was hours away. In desperation she called the only person she wanted to talk to—and he answered in his sleepy, bedroom voice.

"Where are you? Did they let you out?" she asked.

"Yeah, they freed me," Terry, his breathing labored, said. "Lovely place, I must say. My jailers claimed I ate too many bologna sandwiches and they couldn't afford to keep me. Larry Nash brought me back to the hotel last night. Thanks for finding him. The police didn't press charges. There wasn't any evidence, just some anonymous tip, and the hotel checked their surveillance cameras and verified I never left my room the night of the fire."

"It's great to hear your voice," she said. "I've missed you."

"Same here . . . Where the hell are you? Edward says he hasn't seen you since last night when you left Daisy's place in a rush. He said you went to find the kids. What's going on?"

"I'm stuck in the middle of nowhere," she replied. "I'm at the service station in Quartzsite, next to the rock shop, the one I told you about. Gabriel and Dora called me last night to come get them. They sounded scared. Things turned upside down when I got here."

"Are you in danger?"

"Not at the moment," she said, nervously looking in all directions as she spoke. "I'm trying to figure out how the children got here, but they did. Someone must have notified Harlan, who arranged to have me locked in a filthy shed all night."

"Oh, God, darling . . . Did I hear you right?"

"You heard right. This morning Harlan slashed my tires and snatched the kids. Any chance you could come to rescue me? I know you don't have a car, but I think it's dangerous to stick around here—and if I have to have the rental car towed to a place where they sell tires, it's going to take all day. I need to get back."

She could practically hear his concern through the phone line. "Sure, I'll be there in about an hour. Sit tight. Lock yourself in the car if you have to. Don't speak to strangers."

While waiting for Terry, Kate called and arranged for Hertz to pick up the damaged Toyota Camry. The rental car company promised to deliver another vehicle to the casino hotel in Parker later that day. She also called the Arizona Highway Patrol and reported the vandalism. She put Jizo in her purse.

When the AHP Chevy Tahoe SUV arrived, she told Officer Kevin Jones, an elegant hunk in a neatly pressed uniform, that Harlan Sandoval was responsible for slashing the Camry's tires. Jones was passive, betraying nothing: "Did you witness the vehicle being damaged?"

Kate shook her head. "No, I was locked in that shed over there. But I heard him."

"Why were you locked in the shed?"

"I arrived around ten last night to pick up my grandnephew and grandniece. They'd called me for help and sounded frantic. They're little kids, ten and eight. Their mother, my niece, died recently and I'm the executor of her estate. I've been trying to get custody of the children. But their father, Harlan Sandoval, who has a history of domestic violence and was divorced from my niece, took the children this morning."

Jones seemed interested. "Go on."

"When I got here, an elderly woman I'd never seen before came out of that mobile home." Kate pointed to the trailer with the Nazi flag and then took a few deep breaths to calm herself. "She had a gun and forced me into the shed and locked the door. For some reason, my cell phone wouldn't work in the shed. I couldn't do anything but wait."

After five years with the AHP, Jones was normally skeptical of stories involving custody disputes, but the woman seemed genuinely upset. "Why don't you calm down, take a deep breath, and tell me about yourself?"

"Okay. My name is Kate Thorsen. I'm a freelance journalist and live in New York. If you need someone to vouch for me, I can give you the number of my editor with *National Geographic*. I'm in Arizona because my niece died and I'm worried about the safety of her kids."

Jones wrote down George Small's number and continued his questioning. "What happened after you were locked in the shed?"

"It was dark in there and I didn't know what was going on," she said. "I made it through the night. This morning, the old woman with the gun let me out. She said Harlan took the children and left. That's when I saw what he did to my car and called you."

Jones continued writing until they heard a door slam. He automatically put his hand on his revolver and spun around to face the direction of the noise. Kate marveled at how quick and seamless the officer's reactions were. From the shadows, a tiny woman approached them in a baby-blue bathrobe and worn bedroom slippers. Her hands were empty.

"This is my fault, officer," she said. "My fault, my fault . . . I thought this lady was a criminal. Whoops, forgot my manners . . . I'm Trudy Teubler. This is my rock shop. I saw the man who vandalized the car. He was in a red Cadillac, late model. Didn't get the license number . . . Sorry about that."

"We've met before, Mrs. Teubler," Jones said. "I was at the Neighborhood Watch meeting last April after that series of break-ins in your community. Do you remember that night?" He was treating her tenderly, as if she was daft, and he spoke in a soft, fluid voice. It was mesmerizing.

The tiny woman looked up before removing her glasses and wiping them on the sash of her coffee-stained bathrobe. Then Mrs. Teubler put the spectacles back on and stared hard at Jones's clean-cut face and cropped hair with her twitching blue eyes. "No disrespect, son, but at my age all you youngsters look alike. People tell me I have a remarkable memory—and I don't recall ever meeting you," she said, extending a bony hand in greeting.

Jones smiled at her but didn't proffer his hand.

"Anyway, to get back to the man who did this terrible, awful thing . . . He was big with dark hair. I didn't get his name. He arrived with Harlan Sandoval, the children's father. I think he may have been a brother because they looked just alike. Same bone structure. You know, one of those half-breeds, didn't favor the mother at all. She was white as chalk. I can spot half-breeds right off."

With a condescending look, Jones again began taking notes. "Mrs. Teubler, do you own a gun?"

"Of course I do. Who in their right mind would be out in the desert without protection, what with all these drug addicts and illegal aliens crawling around? Son, this is the United States of America. I have a right to bear arms—and don't you forget it."

Jones gave her a closed-mouth smile. "Ma'am, if you don't mind me asking, if this is the United States of America, why are you flying a Nazi flag on your mobile?"

Mrs. Teubler jerked her head back, as if standing at attention. "A woman alone can't be too careful. The flag scares the riffraff off," she said. "They figure we're white supremacists and stay the heck away. My son was the one who came up with the idea. Pretty smart of him, if you don't mind me saying so."

Jones let out a belly laugh. "I hear you. Okay, tell me about your gun."

She looked at him as if he were stupid. "Well, it's a shotgun . . . Nothing much to say about it. The gun belonged to Charley Teubler, my late husband. I'm a crack shot though. I spent a week at one of those survivalist camps in '86. Never know when that kind of training will come in handy."

"If I understand correctly, Ma'am, last night you pointed your shotgun at Ms. Thorsen here and locked her in your shed," he said. "Is that right?"

Mrs. Teubler flushed. "Well, yes, but I had good reason."

"What was that reason?"

Before she replied, the old woman shuffled one slipper in the gravel covering the parking area and continued doing so until she'd created a small trench. "Mr. Sandoval and his mother, I didn't catch her name, came by this morning to collect his children from my house. My son, who operates a motorcycle shop in Mesquite, told me the Sandovals live near him. He said they're a respectable family.

"But let me tell you, I'm not so sure about that, given what I saw today—and those kids, well, they were odd. But they sure were happy enough to see their father and grandmother. I was relieved to see the pack of them leave. Good riddance, as far as I'm concerned."

The officer stopped writing. "Ma'am, I'm afraid I don't understand."

"What don't you understand?"

"Why were the children at your home? What does Ms. Thorsen's vehicle have to do with this? And, most important, why did you use a weapon to hold Ms. Thorsen against her will?"

"When you say it that way, it makes me sound awful." Mrs. Teubler's eyes watered and she looked as if she were about to cry. "I thought I was doing a good deed. I'd picked up those two little ones hitchhiking on the freeway in Phoenix. Can you imagine? Just kids they were. They could have been killed. I brought them home with me so they could call their family. The little girl called her aunt, this one here."

"What happened then?"

"I called my son and he told me the aunt was a criminal and the police were looking for her. My boy called the children's father, but the aunt got here before he did. So I locked her up to protect the children. Did I do the wrong thing?"

"Ma'am, I don't know. I'm going to step back to my car for a moment to check out a few things. You ladies stay put."

The Tibetans believe that life is an illusion, that each person creates his or her own reality. Kate wondered why she was creating this peculiar nightmare. Since Daisy's death, she'd not experienced one really good day. And, with the exception of her relationship with Terry, life was moving downhill fast. When Officer Jones returned, he asked if she wanted to file charges against Mrs. Teubler.

Kate shook her head. "It was an honest mistake," she said. "What would be the point?" Jones told her she was free to leave, but he'd be in touch.

But Mrs. Teubler wasn't finished talking—and Kate, who had nowhere to go, didn't budge. "I saw the other man get out of the Cadillac they'd all come in," the old woman said. "He had dead eyes and a hard look on his face. From my kitchen window, I saw him take a pocket knife out and cut this lady's tires." Then she turned to Kate. "I'm real sorry for the trouble I caused you. I thought I was doing the right thing."

"Don't worry, Mrs. Teubler," she replied. "We all make mistakes. A month ago, I took a marble from your shop. That's what the dollar bill was for. I felt guilty about it. Looks like we were destined to meet again."

"A marble? Now I'm confused," Jones said. "You ladies work this out. I've got another call."

As the highway patrolman drove away, Terry arrived in the black Mercedes with Marlene in the passenger seat. "Jesus, Kate," he asked. "Are you in trouble with the law too?"

Mrs. Teubler looked at the Mercedes and its occupants, blushed and began walking back to her mobile home. "It was a misunderstanding," Kate replied, as she watched the Chevy Tahoe SUV become a speck on the highway. "Let's get out of here. Hertz is coming to take care of the car and I don't need to be here for that. They told me to leave the keys inside. How was jail?"

Terry grinned. "They grilled me real hard, baby, but they couldn't break me. I was as cool as Bogart in *High Sierra*. They didn't make me shower—and they kept me in a holding cell with a bunch of passed-out drunks and townies. Besides, I would have threatened to put a Gypsy curse on anyone who came near my prized bottom."

For the first time in days, Kate laughed and Marlene blew a raspberry. "You fool," Marlene said. "Don't you know anything? They don't mess with big boys, just the little ones."

"Ma, you shudda warned me," he quipped. "I wouldn't have grown so tall."

Then Marlene turned her attention to Kate. "Honey, you look like you've been dragged through the mud. What on earth did that old hag do to you? I've always thought this truck stop was full of fruitcakes and crooks."

DANNY WAS WAITING on the porch when the Sandovals arrived home with Gabriel and Dora in tow. Although Harlan wanted to discuss business, he needed to put the fear of God into his kids first. He'd decided to teach them a lesson. Dora was, after all, a little thing and he would go easy on her. Gabriel, on the other hand, he wouldn't go so easy on. The boy needed to learn the meaning of respect.

Harlan was pulling off his belt when Mama intervened. "Son, send the little ones to the guest bedroom," she said. "We need to talk in private."

Gabriel and Dora were sullen as he marched them to the back of the house. Their father told them to think about what they'd done. "You disrespected your Uncle Clarence and Aunt Ida. You brought dishonor to our family and should be ashamed," he said. "You're both going to get a licking when I come back. Don't move an inch or make a sound."

When he returned to the living room, Mama had slipped off her high heels and was picking through what was left of Cousin Cherry's chicken. "Yum, this is good. Try some." She licked her fingers and sat down on the couch and put her feet up on the coffee table. "Come sit by me," she said, patting the cushions. Harlan did as he was told.

"Son, I'm afraid we lost a lot of cash money with that house burning down. I want to know who gave Danny permission to do that. I understand Pete was with him. Now I told you to personally take care of things. I didn't ask you to delegate the job."

Harlan hadn't expected Mama to call him out on his business methods, especially since the preacher, per Mama's instructions, was no longer around. Even so, he never knew what her reaction would be to any given situation. He chose his words carefully.

"As a former minister," he said, "I decided that I was too well-known around these parts to walk into that church and do the job myself. It would have drawn attention. My concern was protecting the reputation of our family. Besides, Danny's so flaky no one pays attention to him. Heck, half the time I don't know if his kids know who he is. As far as I'm concerned, he's as necessary to us as a disposable razor."

Mama smacked her lips and licked her fingers. "I love it when you talk smart. You want some lemonade?"

In the end, Harlan's mother always came around. Besides, he'd made sure their tracks were covered every which way when they'd had Danny tell Diane to report that she'd seen Fat Boy at Rainbow House—and it was Mama's idea for Harlan to call the cops to let them know he was hours away in Phoenix when everything came down. No one could tie the Sandoval Clan to anything.

"Tell Andrew to get his butt in here and invite Danny in," Mama said. "I want my gun back."

Andrew, expressionless, took a seat in the new EZ chair. Danny walked in behind him like he owned the place, puffed up like a peacock. "Howdy, family members," he said. "Just stopped by to see if my paycheck is ready . . ."

Mama glared at her nephew. "Daniel, where's my gun?"

"Got it right here in my pocket," he said. "Didn't even waste a bullet."

"I'll take that," she said, snatching the gun. "It has sentimental value. Been in our family so long it's an heirloom. Why don't you tell me what happened over at that house we were about to sell for cash money before it was burnt to the ground?"

With excitement dancing in his eyes, Danny proceeded to tell a story about taking Pastor Williams from the church and driving him to Rainbow House. "You won't believe how screwy it was. He didn't fight, just came along, kinda like he was expecting me. He was jabbering and going on about how much he missed his family. He talked about Daisy too, said he didn't believe her death was natural. It was irritating. After a while, I just wanted to take him inside the house and plug him, shut him up for good."

"Why didn't you?" Mama asked.

"I wasn't expecting the place to be boarded up like a fucking fort. The doors were locked and I couldn't get in. So I took him out back by the trees. Nobody could see us. Then he started rambling on about wanting a 'three-fold death.' Shit, I didn't know what he was talking about."

Uncomfortable, Harlan felt a chill pass through him. As a former theologian, he knew the definition of a three-fold death. Three-fold deaths were for martyrs and saints. It was a ritual. Did Williams think he was a holy man? If he did, it put a different light on things—and Harlan didn't like the notion that the preacher had been questioning the cause of Daisy's death in front of his dimwit cousin. Danny had definitely become a liability.

"Daniel, I thought you were a professional," Mama said. "Why didn't you just shoot the preacher and get it over with?"

"You have to understand. It was a difficult situation," he replied. "The man said he forgave my sins and asked me to accept Jesus as my Savior. It was upsetting when you consider that my mother, rest her soul, used to take me to Pastor Williams's church every Sunday when I was a kid. I needed moral support, so I called Pete over at Marlene's and explained the situation. He came right away and brought a can of gasoline."

Mama drummed her red fingernails on the coffee table. "Was Pete wearing gloves?"

Danny scratched his head. "As a matter of fact, I believe he was. Yep, his tan leather ones . . . Real nice pair . . . Pete's classy that way. I think he bought them in Vegas one weekend. Don't worry, Auntie Lou. We didn't leave any fingerprints, if that's what you mean. You can take my word on that."

"Lord, save me from imbeciles," Mama said, waving her hands dramatically through the air. "Danny, since when did you start thinking you were running the show around here? We gave you a simple job to do—and you blew it."

"No disrespect, Auntie Lou, but the man was begging to die. How did I know that he would grab the can out of Pete's hand and pour gasoline on himself?"

Mama nearly choked on her lemonade. "Are you saying Elias Williams committed suicide? That's a mortal sin! A man of the church? My God, I just can't believe he'd risk his soul that way. Harlan, you knew him better than any of us, did you hear what your cousin just said?"

"Yeah, I did."

"Not exactly suicide," Danny interjected. "I was the one who provided the lighter to help him along. It was amazing. He didn't scream or anything. He burnt up right in front of us, like one of those Buddhist monks in Vietnam. I've seen documentaries on the History Channel, but I'd never seen anything up close like that. Man, his flesh was bubbling like fried chicken. You could smell it."

Gently, Mama pushed Cousin Cherry's empty box of chicken away with her bare foot. "Watch your mouth, boy! That's disgusting. Didn't you mother teach you any manners?"

But Mama's words were deceiving; Harlan noticed her neck was flush and quickly concluded she was enjoying herself. "Excuse me . . . ," she said. "Got me one of those darned hot flashes . . . I need the ice pack. Will you get it for me, Andrew? Good . . . What happened next? Did you and Pete just stand back to watch or did you sprinkle more gasoline around?"

By this time, Danny was pacing the room. "No, we didn't have to do a damn thing. It was raining. Big, slow drops . . . The only reason the house caught fire was because of the shit Harlan scattered around the yard. There was garbage right up to the house. Everything started going up like a bale of hay. So we ran like hell and got out of there before anyone saw us. We went over to the Legion for a few beers, just in case we needed alibis. Diane was there. We danced a bit. Pretty soon we heard the fire engines."

Andrew hadn't said a word during the entire exchange.

"You're still paying me, right?" Danny said.

"Of course, we're going to pay you," Mama said. "But we'll need to get the money from our suppliers. We don't keep cash at the house. Andrew will take you in his truck—or, better yet, why don't you follow him? That's probably best. Harlan and I will stay here to look after my grandkids."

When Harlan entered the back bedroom, Gabriel and Dora were cuddled up like kittens in one of the twin beds. He woke them up. Dora's lower lip trembled and Gabriel quickly sat up straight with his back to the wall. "Don't worry, I'm not going to punish you," their father said gently. "Go brush your teeth and comb your hair. Grandma and I are going to take you to your favorite restaurant for dinner."

THE FUNERAL OF Pastor Elias Williams was to be held the next morning. The Bluebird was crowded and smelled of burnt toast. Children, who had earlier in the day participated in a tribal dance competition, were wearing colorful native costumes and noisily having dinner with proud parents and grandparents.

In a corner booth, Nopah and daughter Mary quietly shared a bowl of vegetable soup—and Myra, who'd left her daughter in charge of the motel, sat alone drinking cup after cup of black coffee at the counter. She was hoping to hook up with the long-haul trucker with the salt-and-pepper beard passing through on his way to Phoenix.

Meanwhile, Edward, hands flying, was scrambling to control chaos in the kitchen because the assistant cook had called in sick and the busboy kept burning the toast. Shirley, her hair a new shade of hot pink, was taking orders and rushing around delivering steaming plates to her customers.

All heads turned and conversation stopped when the Sandoval family—Mama Lou, Harlan, Gabriel and Dora—entered the restaurant and sat down at the last empty table in the center of the room. No one in the community had seen or heard from the children since their mother's funeral. Shirley put on a big smile and went to the Sandoval table, hugged Gabriel and Dora and told them how much she'd missed them. "It's good to have you kids back home," she said.

Without acknowledging the server's words, Harlan ordered for the entire family: medium-rare porterhouse steaks, baked potatoes with sour cream and chives, and milk to drink. The steaks were the most expensive item on the menu. When Shirley delivered the meals to the Sandovals, Mama, Harlan, Gabriel and Dora all bowed their heads and prayed together for God's blessing and deliverance. When the prayer ended, the Bluebird became noisy again. That's when Dora noticed friends from school and waved, but Gabriel kept his head down and ate quickly.

After the family finished their dinners, Harlan rubbed his belly and pronounced it an excellent meal, perfectly cooked, and ordered desserts of hot fudge sundaes all around. Mama, a big fan of vanilla ice cream, practically licked her bowl. The children giggled. Then Shirley brought the check and Harlan profusely thanked her. He paid in cash and left a fifty-dollar bill, the biggest tip Shirley had ever received, because he wanted the waitress (and everyone else) to know he was back, back in a big way.

As the Sandoval family filed out of the restaurant, Nopah

nudged his daughter. "The snake is shedding his skin," he whispered. "But he's still a snake."

The next day Mama took Dora to the beauty parlor, where they had their hair and nails done. Then they shopped for new clothes and shoes. While the girls were busy beautifying themselves, Harlan took Gabriel to the nearest dealership to look at Cadillacs in the showroom. Harlan was taken by the Escalades, as was his son. They laughed and called themselves "car guys." The family later met up at Burger King for burgers and fries before they went to Walmart's toy department, where the children were allowed to choose any three items they wanted, regardless of cost. Gabriel chose a remote-control helicopter, a skateboard and a blue bicycle. Dora selected a Barbie doll, a pink bicycle and a jewelry-making kit. Both children said it was just like Christmas. Mama Lou smiled and said nothing was too good for her little prince and princess.

Harlan, chuckling at his cleverness, felt himself a king. For a certain type of personality, abuse is always interspersed with kindness. Mental health practitioners call it the "honeymoon period" before depravity resumes anew. But the abuser's victims often hope for the best. They have to. That night the children, wearing new pajamas, talked quietly in the back bedroom about the miraculous changes they'd witnessed in their father since returning to the community where they'd been raised. Of course, they were unaware of any of the events that had transpired in Mesquite since their mother's funeral.

"I think Dad's changed," Gabriel said. "Maybe he stopped drinking."

"Yeah," Dora agreed. "He's acting like his old self, like he did before he and Mommy started fighting. We should give him another chance."

Gabriel nodded. "Maybe Pastor Williams will let him come back to the church. Dad was happy when he was a preacher. He was good at it. Tomorrow, let's ride our bikes home and see how it looks."

"And then we'll go to Mommy's grave at the cemetery and ask her how she's doing," Dora said. "I miss her so much. I'm going to pray and tell her Daddy's better now and we're doing okay."

THOUGH SHE'D BEEN UP most of the night cowering in a shed, Kate asked Terry to stop at Diane's house before they returned to the hotel. He ignored her. "*Ma chère,* why don't we check and see if the rental car company came through? We need to give our friend her wheels back."

"Oh, I don't mind riding along," Marlene said. "But what does Diane have to do with anything?"

Kate nervously ran her fingers through her greasy hair. "Allen Redmond mentioned that the police received a tip from an anonymous caller, a woman, saying Terry was at the house around the time the fire started. We know he wasn't. Diane was Daisy's friend, right? Since she lives right across the street, she may know who that mystery caller was. I'm curious. It's a good place to start."

"Of course, she was Daisy's friend," Marlene said. "Diane wouldn't make a false police report. She's not a monster."

"I didn't say she was."

"Well, I can't imagine she had anything to do with it. This sounds more like the work of the Sandoval family. I think you're pointed in the wrong direction."

Marlene was being defensive and Kate snapped back. "What direction do you mean?"

"The *wrong* one."

The ball was back in Kate's court and she swung wild. "Well, I'd like to talk to Diane. Plus, I'm worried about the children. I did a purification ceremony with Nopah at Rainbow House and he said another shaman, a witch, was blocking him. Do you have any idea what he's talking about?"

"How interesting," Marlene said. "So the great Nopah thinks he's got some competition?"

"Come on . . . I need to understand."

"I don't think you do," Marlene said, raising her eyebrows. "It's way above your pay grade."

"You can insult me if you want. I'm getting used to it. First you tell me one thing and then you tell me another. I'm confused about why you said Pete Linthicum works for the Sandovals—and then I see him at your house the morning after the fire. Can you help me out here?"

"Ladies, ladies," Terry, becoming agitated, said. "Come on . . ."

Marlene's response was curt. "It's none of your business, but Pete's a longtime gentleman caller of mine. I told you earlier that I've known him since we were kids. What are you getting at? Are you accusing me of something? If you are, you have a lot of nerve. I've done nothing but try to help since you arrived."

Kate had hit a nerve. "Yes, you've been very kind to me, to us. However, we both know that I didn't imagine you calling me to say Pastor Williams was dead. Why did you later insist you didn't make the call? Who told you to lie? Was it Pete?"

The snarl that came back was a shock; the woman in the backseat was seething. "No one, and I mean no one, would dare to tell me to do anything. Don't you know who I am? You're right about not understanding this community. It's dangerous to get involved in other people's business. You're in over your head. If I were you, I'd take that new rental car to the airport and go home."

Ever the diplomat, Terry tried to defuse the situation. "Let's calm down. I think we're all tired. Why don't we stop for lunch?"

But Marlene brushed him off, saying she wasn't interested in socializing. Then she lobbed a boulder at Kate. "Don't you get it? It's not safe for you here any longer. Trust me. The children will be fine as soon as you're gone. They'll be looked after. No one's going to touch them as long as the money's coming in."

"Money? What money?"

"There's always money connected to underage children," Marlene said. "Never mind . . . I thought you knew that. You're supposed to be the reporter. If you're so desperate to talk to someone, why don't you take it up with Harlan Sandoval?"

Terry drove straight to the hotel and winked when he handed Marlene the car keys. "Thanks for letting me drive. Sorry about the misunderstanding. You're an amazing woman. If you don't mind, I'm going to put my girl to bed now. She's had a rough night."

Once in a while, Terry did something that blew Kate's mind. Steaming mad, she stood in the parking lot using every cussword she could think of—and was stunned when he yanked her by the arm and pulled her toward the hotel as Marlene sped off in the Mercedes.

"Do you mind telling me what's going on?"

"Just buying time," he said. "We need to talk."

While Kate showered and dressed, Terry ordered a room-service lunch of fresh salmon with asparagus and a bottle of Chardonnay. For good measure, he slipped a Kenny G disc into the music system and lit a white candle. When she came out of the bathroom towel-drying her hair and wearing the yellow sundress she'd purchased before Daisy's funeral, he appraised her as she sank into the easy chair.

"You've got some explaining to do," she said.

"Nice frock and you smell good too." He sat on the bed and patted it, motioning for her to sit beside him. When she did, he brushed his hands through her damp hair and then wrapped his arm around her waist. "Let's dance. One final dance before I share information that will change everything."

Now she was worried some long-buried sin was about to be revealed with disastrous consequences. She looked at him with questioning eyes, but stood and allowed him to lead her around the room.

"My time in the slammer wasn't wasted."

She took a deep breath. "You enjoyed yourself?"

"Wouldn't say that . . ." He twirled her around. "But I met a couple of guys, anti-uranium-mining demonstrators, made some new friends."

"Should I be jealous?"

Terry pulled her closer. She could feel he was aroused. "Were they arrested for demonstrating?"

"Yeah," he said. "They were on private property."

"What's this have to do with us?"

"Remember when you told me Marlene's late husband was a retired utility executive?"

"Yes," she said, as he twirled her around.

"Well, he may have been more than that. He was connected, probably how they met in the first place. After he died, Marlene apparently stepped up to run the other family business, the scrap business. My new friends said she owns salvage yards all over the desert."

"Are you kidding me?"

"I'm only telling you what I heard," Terry said. "But these guys were locals. They said Pete Linthicum acts as Marlene's business manager. The scrap business is a great front for moving things—exports and imports."

The dance ended when the music stopped. "You have got my complete attention," Kate said. "I can't believe this."

Terry looked at the floor, feeling at a loss for words. "It gets worse. I heard Marlene is a business associate—sort of a sub-contractor—for the Sandoval family's enterprises," he said. "And it was in their interest to have her keep an eye on Daisy. Your niece may have known too much. It could explain what happened to her."

Kate tried to absorb what she was hearing. How or why Daisy died was still a mystery. It was time to get back to work, to put all the pieces together. "Okay, let's get this over with. Did your friend manage to patch together Daisy's last phone calls?"

"I've been meaning to talk to you about that. He did, but there wasn't much there. On the day of the accident, she called her boss at the preschool. We know about that. There were also repeated calls in the days leading up to the accident to a military base outside Phoenix. Could have been calls to a friend, maybe a boyfriend, but you mentioned you heard she was carrying around documentation about the Sandoval drug business. She may have been in contact with federal drug agents. I can do more checking, but as a foreign national here on a tourist visa, I don't expect to make much headway."

Kate was frustrated. "It's a dead end then?"

"There's not a lot more I can do to help you," he said. "I'm sorry."

The phone rang. It was Allen Redmond asking Kate to meet him. "I don't want to talk over the phone," he said. "I'm at the Bluebird."

THE SHADOW WOLVES, a group of American Indian trackers employed by the federal government, were scouting with Colorado River Indian Tribes police when they discovered a 1971 gray

Chevy sedan on a remote fire road. The vehicle had chrome rims and elaborate pinstriping. There was a body inside. The victim, a white male of about thirty with blond hair, had been shot in the head execution-style. The vehicle's tires had been slashed.

At the time, the trackers, formidable counter-narcotics agents, were hunting for drug smugglers trespassing on CRIT land. The Shadow Wolves weren't surprised to find a body in the hills. They'd come across four in the last month. Identification found on the victim indicated the deceased was Daniel Revere, twenty-six, a resident of Mesquite who worked part-time as a dispatcher for the Parker Police Department. Less than an ounce of marijuana was found in a plastic bag in Revere's pocket. There was no money in his wallet, but they discovered a driver's license, a Parker Police identification badge and a coupon for a free meal at Taco Bell.

To the Shadow Wolves, it initially looked like a drug deal gone sour. The car's trunk was strewn with pieces of burlap, the material smugglers use to carry marijuana in bags across the desert, and a tool kit in the backseat contained a variety of prescription bottles containing barbiturates (none of them prescribed for Revere). Footprints and a second set of tire tracks were found at the scene, but the Shadow Wolves couldn't figure out why the killer would slash the dead man's tires.

It was a mystery until one old-timer with the CRIT tribal police recalled a boy in Mesquite who was arrested after puncturing tires in a church parking lot during a Sunday service. "It turned out the kid had a tire fetish, liked watching the air go out," Sergeant Rudy Garcia said. "Darndest thing I ever heard of . . . What was his name? Andy something . . . He'd be in his late twenties by now."

After the vehicle was dusted for prints, a towing service was called to transport it for storage at a salvage yard. When the tow truck arrived, the driver instantly recognized the car and was able to positively identify the victim. Pete Linthicum, the tow truck operator, said the deceased was Danny Revere, a casual friend who lived in Mesquite. "We had a couple of beers at the Legion the other night," he said. "This is awful. Danny was a great kid."

Working with other law enforcement agencies, CRIT police learned of an incident reported by the Arizona Highway Patrol in nearby Quartzsite. Once again, a vehicle's tires had been slashed. And that incident had happened the same day Daniel Revere was murdered. They spoke to the Arizona highway patrolman who took the report and quickly zeroed in on the Sandoval family in Mesquite.

High drama was Mama Lou's specialty. When tribal police confronted her and Harlan at their home and told them Danny was dead, a great wailing began. It was a wailing so piercing that Dora and Gabriel came rushing out of their room to comfort their grandmother, who was holding her hands over her heart and looked on the verge of collapse. "This can't be, this can't be . . . ," Mama sobbed. "No, not Danny! First Daisy and now Danny . . . God, grant mercy on our family 'cause somebody done put a curse on us."

Disturbed at the mention of her mother, Dora became protective. "It'll be okay, Grandma, it'll be okay," she said in a soft voice. "We're here for you." Pouting, Gabriel wiped tears from his eyes. He liked Uncle Danny, liked him a lot. The boy slammed his fist on the back of the couch before he stomped out of the room and then returned with his hands in his pockets.

Once Mama calmed down enough to speak, Sergeant Rudy Garcia asked if she had other children besides Harlan. Mama said her son Andrew had gone to Mexico on a camping trip. "Was your son ever called Andy?" Mama dismissed Garcia's question and stared daggers at him. She quickly added that her two youngest boys, Michael and Ronald, were working on a construction site in Laughlin, Nevada, and would be home that weekend. She said she hadn't seen Danny since he'd stopped by her house two days earlier to say hello to Gabriel and Dora.

"My grandchildren had been staying with our family in Phoenix for the summer," she said. "Their mother died recently. They'd just come home. It's just been one awful thing after another."

Garcia avoided any mention of Elias Williams's death or the fire at Rainbow House. However, he did ask if Danny had seemed nervous or upset when she saw him.

"Oh, no, no . . . He talked about going fishing. It must have been the day he went missing," Mama said, again breaking into loud sobs that elicited more comforting hugs and kisses from her grandchildren. "We had a nice visit. He was just the sweetest boy . . . Danny was my late sister's only child, an angel from the day he was born. I practically raised him after my sister died. Who in the world would have wanted to hurt that boy?"

Garcia shrugged his shoulders.

When asked if her nephew was involved with the drug trade, Mama Lou became indignant. She clenched her jaw, lowered her voice into a growl and essentially told Garcia he was an idiot. "Danny was a devout family man and avid churchgoer. I'm amazed you would even bring up such a thing in my home."

"I'm sorry, Mrs. Sandoval," Garcia said. "To solve these kinds of crimes, we often have to ask unpleasant questions."

"My God, how dare you! Danny would never have become involved with illegal substances," Mama said. "That boy was like Jesus walking the Earth on the straight path. Never did a wrong thing in his life."

After thanking Lou Sandoval for her cooperation, Garcia asked Harlan to step outside. Separated from his mother and children, Harlan wiped his eyes and wrung his hands before essentially recounting the same story his mother had told about their last visit with Cousin Danny. In a whisper, he added that he was embarrassed to mention it, but he'd heard rumors that the father of five gambled a bit and had a girlfriend on the side.

"A few months ago, after my wife died in a car accident, Danny told me he was thinking of taking off, going someplace new. I thought it was idle talk. Maybe his girlfriend, if he had one, had a jealous husband. It could explain things, right? Did you guys consider that angle?"

But the tribal police had already located a credible witness who'd seen Danny and Elias Williams getting into Danny's car the day the preacher died. Even before his body was discovered, Danny Revere was a person of interest in both Williams's death and the house fire in Mesquite. Recent events gave rise to new questions. What was the motive? Was Danny killed to keep him quiet? But then why was Williams killed? Harlan and his mother had solid alibis for everything. Too solid, Garcia thought.

Trouble surfaced quickly. Kate and Terry walked into the Bluebird and saw Allen Redmond, cell phone glued to his ear, oblivious to everything going on around him as he simultaneously talked on his phone and typed on his laptop.

"Hey, this is Allen. I understand your suspect in the Williams death was found dead yesterday . . . Yes . . . I heard a rumor you suspect foul play? What do you mean you can't you talk about it? Why? What jurisdiction? I don't understand . . . Okay . . . Call me when you get confirmation."

They sat down at Redmond's table. "Big news day?" Kate asked.

"You know how it goes," he replied. "It's all or nothing. Thanks for coming over. Give me a moment." Redmond continued typing.

Terry said nothing, but it was clear to Kate that he was sizing up Redmond and finding him deficient. Just then, Shirley arrived with a pitcher of iced tea, three tuna sandwiches and a plate of raw carrots. "Compliments of the house," she said.

"Lord Almighty, woman, you are a saint," Terry said, kissing Shirley's hand as he simultaneously reached for a tuna sandwich. Edward waved from the kitchen and Kate blew him a kiss.

"Finish your work," she said to Redmond, her mouth full of carrot sticks. When she finished chewing, she asked: "Who died?"

"Danny Revere."

"Who?"

"Harlan's cousin, the one with shaggy blond hair, always wore a baseball cap."

"Didn't he work for Parker P.D.?"

Redmond nodded.

"What happened?"

"I don't have confirmation, but I hear they found him up in the mountains with a bullet in his forehead."

"Suicide?"

"Not likely—and my police sources tell me Danny was a suspect in Pastor Williams's death and the house fire. This is all confidential, of course. Nothing leaves this table. You both understand?"

"We hear you," Kate said, turning to face Terry. She noticed he had a dismissive smirk on his face.

"One could say that after this summer of discontent, the bad guys are now offing each other," Terry said. "What a delightful turn. Could it be that our dear friend Harlan Sandoval is involved in these recent dark deeds?"

Redmond pondered the question. "I don't know Harlan all that well, but he doesn't strike me as someone who would kill a relative or his former boss. The Sandovals are a tight-knit family. Loyalty is all they know. Besides, they practically ran that church, although it was strange that they didn't attend the pastor's funeral. People around here notice things like that. But what would be their motive for murder? It doesn't make sense to me."

"Nothing makes sense," Kate said. "But when you look at what that man did to his children's home and their personal belongings, why would you think him incapable of killing someone? I wouldn't put anything past him."

Redmond surveyed the room for potential eavesdroppers. Once he was satisfied, he said, "This is a little off the wall. But the last time I talked to Harlan, he told me the house and everything in it was haunted."

The conversation had taken a strange turn.

"Do you believe in haunted houses?" Kate's eyes widened. "I never saw any evidence of unusual phenomena at Rainbow House—and I spent a lot of time there over the years. My older sister bought the house after her husband died."

Redmond looked confused, as if he'd underestimated Kate. "Sorry, I forgot about your personal connection. I was thinking of you as a professional colleague." He lifted half of a tuna sandwich from the plate and gulped it down in two bites. After he swallowed, he began talking again.

"You know, I knew Daisy pretty well, a lot better than I knew Harlan," he said. "And she talked to me about ghosts. She thought there was at least one in the house. She said she heard noises and things banging around at night. She was frightened—and it crossed my mind that maybe, just maybe, Harlan was slinking around throwing pebbles at the windows to scare her. Did you know she asked Nopah Round to come over and do a ceremony to purify the house? He's the local shaman. Have you met him yet?"

"Nopah's a friend," she said, not wanting to share more. "We were over at what's left of the house the other night. I can't speak for him. I don't know what he thinks."

Redmond leaned in closer. "You do know that Harlan was alone in the house the day he was injured? He swears up and down that something came at him. He told the nurses at the hospital that a cloud came out of the closet and attacked him."

"I'm sure he was drinking at the time," Kate said. "If I were you, I wouldn't put too much stock in the recollections of a drunk. Allen, we're both journalists. We're supposed to be above ghosts and superstitious nonsense."

"Normally I'd agree with you," he said. "But after living here for a few years, I can tell you I've seen things that I can't explain."

"Some day you'll have to tell me your stories," she said.

The sandwich plate was empty. Terry was polishing off the last of the carrot sticks when he asked Redmond if he'd seen Gabriel or Dora Sandoval. Kate's hands were trembling as she set her tea glass down.

"Everyone in town's talking about them," Redmond replied. "The kids are back and living with Harlan at his mother's house. I hear he's been taking them out for dinner and lavishing them with gifts. New bikes, clothes, everything . . . People tell me they look happy. School starts next week. We'll see if they show up. That's all I know."

"I'm sorry to hear the children are with their father," Kate said. "I don't think Daisy would have approved."

"You were very close to Daisy?"

"I'd known her since she was born. In a way, she was like a daughter to me."

"You don't have kids of your own?"

"Didn't have time and didn't see the need," she said with an abruptness that startled her. She looked at Terry and he turned away. She knew he was angry.

"Let's go, Kate," he said. "We've got work to do."

Walking out to their car, Terry laid into her: "That guy's a bottom feeder. Can't you see he's just milking you for information that he can put in his crappy little newsletter? He's using you, Kate."

"I know that, but what am I going to do? I'm an outsider working in the dark here. I can't close any doors. I need all the information I can get. He's not that bad. After all, he's the one who recommended Larry Nash, the attorney who got you out of jail."

"Point taken, but listen to me. You're being had every which way," he said. "These people don't respect you. Consider what happened with Marlene. And while Daisy may have been a nice person, she married Harlan. What kind of woman would marry scum like that? Think about it. Look at the big picture."

Kate stared at him in disbelief.

Terry stumbled on his words. "Okay, maybe I'm wrong. Good women sometimes choose outlaws. From what you've told me, I probably would've liked Daisy. But I watched her kids at the funeral. Kate, they're Sandovals. They're going to grow up to be blood-sucking grifters. They don't want to be like you. They want to be like their daddy."

At that moment, she knew their relationship was ending.

He continued: "Plus, face the facts: you don't want children, any children. You never have. Being a journalist is the only thing you care about. Now you've gotten yourself sidetracked and you're on a holy crusade to get Harlan. You've lost your focus. My advice is to get out while you still can. I honestly don't know who you are any more."

The blood drained from her face. "I can't," she said. "It's not who I am. I thought you understood that."

"Apparently I don't. So, that's it. I have to return to Paris," Terry continued. "Summer vacation has come and gone. I have a job to get back to. If you want to go with me, we'll try to work it out because I love you. Otherwise, I'll call the airline tonight and see if I can get a reservation. I'd like to leave tomorrow. I've had enough of this place."

They returned to the hotel. Terry was able to get a reservation out of Phoenix for the next day. That night they made love like strangers, devoid of passion or caring. Turning her back to him afterward, Kate felt a sadness, an aloneness she'd never felt before.

They were no longer a team. They checked out of the hotel the next morning. She drove Terry to the airport. "I'm sorry," he mumbled, before leaving her standing in the terminal with an empty kiss.

AFTER LEARNING Uncle Danny had been killed, Gabriel and Dora desperately needed a touchstone, something to hang on to, and they believed it could only be found in one place. The next day they got up before their father and grandmother and rode their new bicycles to Rainbow House. On the corner of their street, they hit their brakes and couldn't speak. Their home had been burned down. Everything was gone, even the trees were torched. They moved in closer and got off their bikes and walked timidly toward the charred ruins.

"Whoa! What happened?" Dora asked. "Do you think it was a lightning strike?"

"Then why would there be police tape and scorched 'No Trespassing' signs?" Gabriel said. "Something really bad happened and no one told us about it."

"Let's get out of here," Dora said. "I'm sick of grownups treating us like we're not old enough to have feelings. What's wrong with this world?"

In shock, they pedaled as fast as they could to Marlene's glass riverfront home, which sparkled as it always did in the sunlight. The children dropped their bikes in the driveway when they saw their mother's best friend, wearing a loose-fitting dress and her favorite floppy sun hat, watering the flowers in her garden.

Feeling lost and alone, they screamed their lungs off: *Marlene! Marlene! Marlene!* She turned and ran toward them, leaving the hose gushing down the driveway like a waterfall. She kissed them both as a mother would. She kissed their hands, their mouths, their cheeks, their necks . . . She couldn't stop kissing—and with each embrace felt a softening in her heart, a rush of tender emotion. Here were the children she'd watched grow up, never realizing—until this moment—how much she cared. Words could never describe this reunion, one where tears mingled freely with the water rushing down the driveway and soaking their clothing.

When emotions calmed, Gabriel asked if they could sit in Don's powerboat. Marlene turned the hose off and led them to the open garage. She wanted them to see the boat hadn't been touched since they'd last played in it. It was dusty and full of their plastic toys. Gabriel and Dora climbed inside and sat on the benches in silence. Marlene joined them. "Remember when we had a picnic right here?" Dora asked. "And Mommy made us peanut-butter-and-jelly sandwiches and put potato chips inside?"

"I remember that day," Marlene, choking back memories, said. "It was right before Easter."

Gabriel hesitated before gaining the courage to speak: "Marlene, who ruined our house? Where are our dogs? Why didn't someone tell us? We would have found a way to get home. We could have stopped this."

"I'm sure your father didn't say anything because he knew you'd be upset," she replied. "Let's go inside, sweethearts. Let's get you dry. You're both soaked. Then I'll make you hot chocolate and we'll talk about it. A lot of things happened after you left. And I haven't seen you for so long. I swear you've both grown taller over the summer."

Inside the home, Dora, wrapped in a beach towel while her clothes dried in the laundry room, ran her fingers over the stuffed peacock's feathers in the living room and watched dust rise in the air. "Why did someone kill this beautiful bird?" she asked. "Did you do it?"

"No, I would never kill a bird. They're sacred to my people. The Mohave believe birds are messengers," Marlene replied. "I saved this pretty boy from a crummy antique store."

Dora was confused. "What do you mean? This bird is dead."

"Not really. Nothing ever dies. He's my companion." Marlene's lips trembled when she tried to explain the reason for the peacock. "You see, the peacock in mythology is a friend of the Roman goddess Juno. You kids will understand this one because you're both Christians. In your church, the peacock is a symbol of resurrection and immortality."

"What does that mean?" Gabriel asked.

"It means what I was saying before. Nothing ever really dies. Our souls change form, that's all. We're all connected."

Eyes glowing, Dora was intensely interested in this conversation. "Mommy always said you were a wise woman, that you knew magic. My friend said you're really a witch. If you are, do you think you could bring Mommy back to us? We have a lot of questions for her, a lot of important questions."

Marlene frowned. "No, I can't bring her back. She's in a special place now. But you can talk to her anytime. She's in your heart, both of your hearts."

"I do that all the time, but I don't get any answers." Dora sounded discouraged. "When our clothes get dry, do you think we could go to the cemetery? Daddy and Grandma Lou won't take us. They said Auntie Kate bought Mommy a cheap headstone and it's embarrassing for our family. I don't care about how much a stone cost."

"Me neither," Gabriel said.

"Let's go check the dryer," Marlene said. "We'll put your bikes in the garage."

Part VI

Myra at Motel 6 gave Kate her old room back at a re-
duced rate with laundry privileges, which meant she could wash
her clothes in Myra's comfy kitchen instead of going to the laundromat. Accustomed to being alone, Kate settled in. There would
be no tears shed for Terry. She'd grown used to solitude and had
learned to combat loneliness by moving forward. There was nothing else she knew how to do.

The day after Terry left, an orchid plant arrived. Kate had never
received an orchid before—and hadn't a clue how to care for one.
She was the original black-thumb gardener. It was from George.
Terry must have told her editor that they'd broken up before he
returned to Paris. The card attached to the plant said: "Miss you.
Come home." It was an irritating intrusion into her private life.
Still, she called George and thanked him, but said she wasn't going
anywhere. There was work to be done and the probate court was
close to ruling Daisy's estate insolvent. Thanks to Harlan, there
was no money to pay the accumulated bills. It appeared the only
thing Daisy would be able to leave for her kids' future welfare was
a small insurance policy with Kate named as the beneficiary. Life

insurance policies are excluded from the probate process. When the insurance check arrived, she planned to open a trust account for Gabriel and Dora. At least they'd have seed money for college.

Every so often, Kate fed the yellow orchid a little water. A week later, she noted that the leaves were turning brown but the flower wasn't dead yet. It was a victory of sorts. Every day she called Lou Sandoval's home and left a message, saying she wanted to see the children. Not one of her calls was returned. She kept in touch with Rudy Garcia, Edward, Nopah and Mary. The rest of the time she buried herself in paper, sorting through each scrap in the boxes and files related to Daisy's incomplete life. Had the house and its contents not been destroyed, the job would have been much easier.

Going slow and steady, she was determined to make do with what she had. One thing nagged at her. Kate found prescription receipts with Daisy's name on them for atenolol, a common drug used for treating high blood pressure. But the medical reports she'd obtained indicated Daisy had amphetamines in her system when she arrived at the Phoenix hospital. Kate had found a prescription bottle for blood-pressure medication with the other items she'd discovered on the floor of Daisy's wrecked car. There were three pills left inside.

Was it possible that someone had emptied the prescription bottle with the blood-pressure medication and replaced the pills with amphetamines of similar size and color? It could explain the headaches and sickness Daisy had been experiencing before the accident. Kate knew enough about amphetamines to realize that no one in their right mind, especially with high blood pressure, would use such powerful stimulants. From everything she understood about her niece, Daisy valued life and would never have taken such a risk. Kate made a note to contact a drug lab to have the pills analyzed. That was easy enough. The hard part would come if it turned out the pills had been deliberately replaced. There would be no way to prove who did it.

While reviewing the sale and lease documents for Rainbow House she'd obtained from the tribal real estate company, Kate hit a snag. With the house destroyed, she couldn't figure out whether the estate continued to have legal responsibility for the lease. She couldn't find Daisy's homeowner's insurance documents—and began to believe Harlan, the only likely suspect, had taken them.

Rather than hiring another attorney she couldn't afford, she needed to find out if other Mesquite homeowners had been faced with similar situations. She contacted Allen Redmond and agreed to meet him at his home office. As a local journalist, Redmond probably had access to information that could give her a sense of direction.

Redmond's house in Mesquite was nondescript, the sparse front yard covered only in red synthetic rock and a tall flagpole without a flag, but Kate was impressed by the inside of the home. One wall was covered in award plaques the journalist had received while working in Los Angeles, and photos of a younger Redmond with various dignitaries. Another wall featured floor-to-ceiling bookshelves filled with hundreds of books. While waiting for Redmond to finish a telephone interview, she perused the book collection. She pulled G. Edward White's biography of Justice Oliver Wendell Holmes off the shelf and opened it. The stamp on the inside cover read: "Property of the Los Angeles County Library." Confused, she shelved it and pulled out William Marvel's biography of Ambrose Burnside. It was marked as the property of the Palos Verdes Library District. She tried a third volume, a biography of Abraham Lincoln, and found it stamped: "Property of the San Diego County Library."

When she turned around, Redmond was standing behind her. "You like my books? I brought them with me from L.A."

"You have quite a collection," she said. "Are all these books from public libraries?" Redmond nodded. "Where did you get them? Garage sales or something?"

"To be honest, some I bagged and others I simply checked out and never returned. I need a lot of reference material for my work. You can't expect someone on a journalist's salary to afford a collection like this," he said, peering into her eyes. "Do you have a problem? Heard your boyfriend left town?"

This wasn't the kind of conversation Kate was expecting. "Terry had to go back to his job. As for your books, I'm just surprised you would steal them. That's all."

"No one cares about books anymore—except people like you and me. They'd have eventually ended up in a recycling bin. Look at it this way, I saved them for posterity. I've got a better collection than the tribal library. People around here come to see me when they have questions. I suspect that's why you're here."

"Yes, I was hoping you could help me understand something," she said, stifling her revulsion. She couldn't stop thinking about all the adults and children who used public libraries because they couldn't afford books. How they'd been denied the opportunity to read and learn from the very volumes on Redmond's shelves because this egomaniac thought himself superior to them. Terry was right. Allen Redmond was a jerk.

Pushing personal qualms aside, she pumped him for information about land leases. He said that leaders of the tribal council were patient and understanding when Mesquite residents couldn't make their payments.

"Why? Don't they need the money?"

"Sure they do," he replied. "But I've only heard of one attempted eviction of a guy who owned a boat yard near the river. He hadn't made his lease payment in years. The tribe backed down after I wrote a story saying the guy was going to sue."

"What about individual homeowners?"

"Most of them are dirt poor. No one tries to evict them when they fall behind. I think the tribal leaders figure these people have nowhere else to go. This is the end of the road. They wait until the people die or the lease expires. Then they sometimes let tribal members move into the houses, most of which are falling apart anyway. Or they rent them out cheaply to people like me. Must be a cultural thing," he said. "Oh . . . and there are a couple of real estate speculators in Mesquite. I'm not sure what their game is."

"I've run across them," Kate said. "I doubt they'd have any qualms about tossing people into the street."

ONE AFTERNOON, CRIT Tribal Police Sergeant Rudy Garcia came to Kate's motel room to talk about Danny Revere's death. He wanted to go over what she recalled from the tire-slashing incident in Quartzsite. In time, she had come to like and trust Garcia.

He seemed decent and forthcoming, so she shared her concerns about Daisy's medication, asking if he knew where she could have the pills analyzed. To her surprise, Garcia offered to take the bottle to the police lab and promised to get back to her with the results.

They also discussed drug use on the reservation. "We have a big problem," he said. "We have all this poverty, open land and isolated buildings. It's the perfect setting for criminal activity."

While Garcia didn't mention the Sandoval family, it was obvious to Kate that he was investigating more than Danny's death. "Listen, I've heard from a source here that my niece had obtained documents implicating her ex-husband and his family in drug trafficking," she said. "I was trying to find those documents when I went to Pete Linthicum's storage yard. I searched her car and didn't find anything. The person who told me about the documents had, as far as I know, no reason to lie to me."

Dark eyes glistening, Garcia looked at her carefully. "If you can tell me who told you about the documents, I'd like to talk to them. We need all the help we can get."

"It was a confidential source," she said. "I'd have to check first."

"Do that," he replied with force, before going on to explain how serious the drug problem had become. The CRIT Police Tribal Drug Unit had recently made a dozen arrests related to drug trafficking and use. It was believed that local dealers were working directly with Mexican cartels to bring drugs to the reservation before moving them through a transportation network to other parts of the country. Methamphetamine, in particular, had become the number one drug problem on the reservation.

"It's relatively cheap. They call it the poor man's cocaine," he said. "It has been responsible for a number of reservation deaths. Six months ago, a mother who was high at the time murdered her two small children. The drug causes psychosis and it's fifty times stronger than cocaine. In other words, it makes good people do crazy things."

Kate was skeptical. "Do you realistically think you can win this war?"

Garcia asked for a glass of water. He looked tired. After he'd downed a few gulps, he continued on: "Do we have a choice? I'm worried for the future of my people, especially the children. We've worked hard to regain what was taken from us in the beginning when we lost everything. Coming from a different background, you may not understand how we feel."

"I think I do," she said.

"As far as I'm concerned, the drug pushers have no soul," he said. "I'm not going to stand back and watch everything we've built up here destroyed."

• • •

After Garcia left, Kate felt emotionally sucked dry. She needed fresh air. Now that the temperatures were dropping, it felt good to be outdoors in the sun again. As she walked toward the river, she thought about calling Marlene. Would she be able to persuade her to talk to Garcia? She decided to wait. Eventually, she walked back to the Bluebird, where she asked Edward if he would take her to see Nopah. "I desperately need a dose of courage," she said. "I'm so in over my head."

"Tomorrow is my day off," he replied. "We'll leave in the morning."

Late into the night, Kate continued working on Daisy's papers. Taking small bits of information at a time, she moved slowly, sifting, looking for more clues. She took notes and made a timeline. She sorted through the mail collected from Daisy's post office box. Other than the expected utility and doctor statements, she discovered past-due bills for purchases by Harlan Sandoval using one of Daisy's credit cards. He'd bought a sound system, men's clothing, satellite equipment, and racked up restaurant tabs. Not only was he not paying child support, he'd been stealing from his ex-wife while she was working and struggling to put food on the table. Perhaps it was why he'd been shadowing the post office picking up Daisy's mail, even after her death.

O child of noble family, did he really believe he could get away with it?

THE WEATHER WAS SHIFTING. After Labor Day, the children returned to school and began the slow process of rebuilding their lives. One night while Mama Lou was ladling spaghetti sauce onto everyone's plates, she said it was time for a family meeting. "I saw how you do it on Dr. Phil," she said. "It's a democratic process."

Harlan, crescent scar glowing, rolled his eyes and sipped his beer. "Why do we have to have a meeting?"

"I can't tell you the official agenda until we begin the process," she said. "Otherwise it wouldn't be for real. Dr. Phil says we need to follow a protocol. In case you didn't know, that means rules."

"Okay, okay . . . Whatever you want," he said. "Let's get it over with."

"I'm tired of this place. It doesn't feel comfortable anymore," Mama, honest in her own way, said. "Why don't we go where the air is fresh and cool all year round? That way we wouldn't have to pay for air conditioning bills."

"Where would you like to go, Mama?"

"I've heard Washington State is a real nice place. We could start over. We've got that money coming in from Social Security. Michael and Ronald could look after this place for us. Son, you could start your own church up there and we could all pitch in and help you get it going. Wouldn't that be a dream come true?"

The children stopped eating and stared hard at their grandmother.

Mama continued: "My cousin, Charley Winters, tells me the fish jump out of the water and onto your hook up there. You can almost eat for free. What do you say, kids? You could go to a new school and make new friends. We could stay with your aunt and uncle in Spokane until we find a place. Though it pains me to do so, I'd even sell my diamond rings to get some extra cash to pay for the trip."

Gabriel asked if they could get a dog—and Mama, while Harlan squirmed in his chair, said of course they could. The children looked at one another and filled the room with toothy grins. So Mama, presiding over the family meeting at the dinner table, took a vote. She asked for a show of hands. Gabriel and Dora's hands shot up.

Harlan grumbled, said he'd think about it and give Mama his decision in the morning. Not that he ever crossed her. He just wanted to hang on to his manhood one more night. After the children went to bed, Mama put her pretty rings up for sale on eBay. They sold so quickly, she decided to sell Daisy's computer too.

EDWARD PLAYED with the longhaired gray cat. Except for the sound of a lilting Indian flute on the CD player, all was quiet inside the Angelica Trading Post. The children were at school— and Mary, wearing a denim floor-length dress, served herbal tea in the tiny room filled with golden light. Nopah, barefoot in his cowboy clothes, sat on the floor smoking cigarette after cigarette.

Inside the store, Kate again felt a sense of peace and tranquility in this nook where the old ways suspended belief in the new— and where there were no documents to dissect or other people's inadequacies to digest. After he finished smoking, the first thing Nopah told her was that he'd had a prophetic dream. "The owl showed me a feather floating on a star," he said in his raspy voice. "It was a message for you, Manly Woman. Your destiny is to take action on this message."

Kate scratched her head and grumbled. Sometimes the teachings of Nopah Round, master shaman, brought nothing but consternation and more work. Yet, as she sipped the strong herbal tea and relaxed, the first picture that came to her mind's eye was of two faces, one kind and one distorted. It was Marlene Stone, the mixed-race former showgirl whose Mohave name was Star Feather. Kate was getting better at translating messages, at least when they were as literal as "feather floating on a star." Now she knew who the other shaman was—and she owed it to Daisy to take action.

When she stood up to leave, Nopah uncharacteristically took her hand and kissed it. "Be careful," he said. "The witch is a powerful woman."

"So am I," she said with confidence.

"I will sing for you."

She put her nose to his nose. "What are you *not* telling me?"

Pushing her away, Nopah put his hand on his heart. "The owl has told me that my grandson and his sister are gone. Do not grieve for them. One day they will return to recognize and embrace you."

NATIVE AMERICAN TRIBES are not permitted by federal law to prosecute serious crime committed on Indian reservations. The cases are tried in federal court. Determined to seek justice, Sergeant Rudy Garcia, compelled to work with federal law enforcement officials, refused to back off and continued slowly building a case against Andrew Sandoval for the murder of Danny Revere.

Tired of watching a criminal element take over the reservation, Garcia met with Trudy Teubler at her home in Quartzsite and questioned Kate Thorsen at the Motel 6 in Mesquite. He interviewed Danny's widow and questioned Pete Linthicum again. It was all coming together. His gut told him Andrew had not acted alone and that other members of the Sandoval family were involved. Unfortunately, he didn't have a motive or enough evidence yet to go after them. He would focus on finding Andrew, who had a history of petty crime and an extensive juvenile record, and see if he could crack him. A federal warrant was issued for Andrew's arrest for the murder of Danny Revere on tribal land.

Garcia learned that Andrew Sandoval was in a Mexican jail after being arrested for drunk and disorderly conduct in Nogales, a municipality on the northern border of the Mexican state of Sonora on the U.S.-Mexico border. Garcia took his warrant to the feds and U.S. prosecutors attempted to have Andrew Sandoval extradited back to Phoenix to stand trial in federal court for first-degree murder. It was a potential death-penalty case. Like many nations throughout the world, Mexico does not impose the death penalty. It rebuffed the extradition request. However, the Mexican government did allow Sergeant Garcia and federal investigators to travel to Nogales to interview Sandoval at the jail. During their interrogation, a surly Andrew refused to incriminate his family members and denied killing Revere. The case was at an impasse.

Rudy Garcia returned to the reservation empty-handed and discouraged. His limp was growing more pronounced and he was occasionally feeling chest pains. Sylvia, his wife, urged him to see a doctor. "No," he said. "I may be getting old, but what's happening on our land is wrong. Drugs are killing our people. We have never needed drugs and we don't murder others because of them. This is coming from the outside—and outsiders are teaching our younger people that they're not responsible for their behavior. They make a mockery of our traditions."

"But you're growing sick trying to fight this by yourself," Sylvia said. "You should think of retiring."

"Not yet," he replied. "The ways of our ancestors have been passed down to us. We must pass on these traditions and knowledge. If we don't try to stop this craziness, it will one day take the lives of our grandchildren."

A week elapsed before Garcia was able to give the lab test results to Kate Thorsen. Her hunch had been correct. Someone had replaced Daisy Sandoval's prescription medication with a powerful street drug that had, in all likelihood, contributed to her death. Without a confession, however, proving who did it would be difficult.

After he left the Motel 6, Garcia gulped down two aspirins for his chest pain and went straight to the home of Louise Sandoval. Her sons Michael and Ronald answered the door. The rest of the family was gone. The brothers insisted their mother, older brother and his two children were on a much-needed family vacation, stopping here and there at various relatives' homes throughout the South and Southwest.

Garcia didn't believe a word of it. He returned to the tribal police offices to obtain a search warrant. The next day, CRIT Police's Tribal Drug Unit, using a drug-sniffing dog, conducted a thorough search of the home. They found thousands of dollars' worth of illegal drugs and paraphernalia hidden in a crawl space in the attic. They also found guns and burglary tools. Michael and Ronald Sandoval were arrested.

A story about the brothers' arrests appeared in *Mesquite Musings*. Phones at tribal police headquarters began to ring and tips from concerned neighbors led police to contact Ned Dickens of the Arizona Pioneer & Cemetery Research Project. Using his divining rods, Dickens discovered what he believed to be two bodies buried near a tree in the backyard of the Sandoval home. When the skeletal remains were unearthed and autopsied, Dickens's suspicions were confirmed. The bodies were of an adult male with a bullet wound in his chest and an infant female whose skull had been crushed. DNA tests would later confirm the deceased male to be Vernon Sandoval, the husband of Louise Sandoval. The infant was the unnamed daughter of the couple. There was no record of her birth.

Mad as hell, Garcia sprang into action. Federal arrest warrants were issued for Louise Sandoval and Harlan Sandoval. A fifty-thousand-dollar reward, contributed by an anonymous donor, was offered for information leading to the whereabouts of Harlan's minor children, Gabriel and Dora Sandoval. The children's pictures were also placed on a national website for missing and exploited children—and their photos appeared daily on the front page of *Mesquite Musings*, accompanied by an appeal for assistance in locating them.

Less than a week later, Kate Thorsen personally confronted Marlene Stone and persuaded her to turn herself in to the tribal police. Stone was taken into custody. Following questioning from Garcia and federal investigators, she agreed to turn over information about drug trafficking on the reservation. In addition, she agreed to testify before a federal grand jury about criminal racketeering involving the Sandoval family and others. In exchange for her cooperation, she was promised immunity from prosecution and placed in the Federal Witness Protection Program. Her assets were forfeited.

This breakthrough led to several arrests, including that of Pete Linthicum, who was charged as an accomplice to the murder of Elias Williams. After Linthicum's arrest, Andrew Sandoval was found dead in his jail cell in Nogales. Sandoval, who was still being held by Mexican authorities on a minor drunk-and-disorderly charge, had been stabbed forty-six times. Law enforcement authorities on both sides of the border suspected the thirty-year-old had been killed at the behest of a Mexican drug cartel.

After being informed of the death of Sandoval, Linthicum had a change of heart and began fully cooperating with tribal police and federal investigators. In exchange for a plea deal, he confessed to the murder of Williams and said his accomplice was Daniel Revere, since deceased. Linthicum also implicated other members of the Sandoval family in a drug trafficking operation on reservation land owned by the Colorado River Indian Tribes. As a consequence, two veteran tribal police deputies were brought in for questioning. They were later allowed to resign from the force in disgrace.

The Tibetan Book of the Dead: Forty-nine days after breathing is gone, the dead are not really dead. They linger and roam to familiar places, sometimes sitting on the roofs of their homes. They hear voices from the mortal world and see visions. Rainbows appear and sacred music plays. Teachers come and go. The dead can take action and connect with the living. But if the spirit cannot dispel negative influences, it becomes mired in delusion and the horror of its past sins intensifies. A lifeline of compassion is extended. If it is cast off, the spirit moves to a place where there is no liberation and the soul is condemned to the wheel of reincarnation, where only karma lasts. But there is a worse fate: There are those called the *delok* who return from death and refuse to leave the living. The *delok* are described as angry ghosts. It is wise not to call them to you, but to pray for their deliverance. *O child of noble family, you were a woman who did much good for your family and community. Go now and seek peace.*

• • •

It had been forty-nine days since Daisy Sandoval took her last breath. Kate awakened in the middle of the night to a dream of her niece dressed in pink, the color of success. Daisy was standing in a hot-air balloon with a group of people. The tether came undone. As the balloon rose, Daisy waved and said "Thank you." Then she was gone.

The Tibetans believe in "untying the knots" that impede. And in the Mohave belief system, important things are revealed only through dreams. There was nothing more to do. Kate hoped with all her heart that she would eventually see Gabriel and Dora again.

As for Mama Lou and Harlan, they were not her burdens to carry. Kate released them to the fates they'd created. She was free. There was no reason to remain on the reservation. She called Nopah to tell him of the dream and her intention to leave.

The Mohave shaman said he would meet her at Rainbow House at noon. "We will do a blessing of the land," he said. "You don't want to miss the meaning of your experience."

With a sense of resignation, Kate began packing and called the airline to make a one-way reservation to New York City. She would leave the next day. Then she sat back and looked out the window at the backdrop of mesquite, cottonwoods and willows framed by the majestic purple and black mountains. She watched the pigeons feeding in the parking lot below. When she was finished reflecting, she carried the still-living yellow orchid plant downstairs to Myra's office. It would be her farewell gift. Afterward, she walked to the Bluebird to thank Shirley and Edward.

Just before noon, she drove to Rainbow House and saw that the ground had been bulldozed and cleared. An awning had been erected where Celeste's rock and flower garden once flourished. Underneath the awning, Mary and her children were busy setting up folding picnic tables and plastic lawn chairs. Nopah, his face painted and hair braided, was standing in the center of the field singing a bird song. Kate ran to him and they embraced, long and hard, until she heard the sound of car doors slamming.

People were arriving, young and old, bearing containers and baskets of food and drink. The air filled with delicious smells. The baskets and containers were placed on the tables under the awning as people began forming a circle around Kate and Nopah. Though she recognized familiar faces—Edward, Mary and her children, Tommy, Shirley, Myra, Lori and little Leslie, Sister Sarah, Sister Eileen, Candy, Abby—Kate didn't recognize others. Looking beyond them, she saw the CRIT Police Department's Rudy Garcia getting out of his squad car accompanied by two uniformed deputies, young graduates of the Central Arizona Regional Officers Training Academy. Joining the circle, Rudy stood tall and grinned when he caught Kate's eye.

Stepping away from the group, Edward and Tommy, wearing

red headbands and traditional native clothing, solemnly carried old newspapers and bundles of fresh-cut wood to the center of the property. They stacked the wood close to where she and Nopah were standing. They struck matches on the papers and the bonfire caught quickly. The onlookers then joined hands and hummed, sounding like hundreds of bees swarming toward a hive.

Overhead, the bright sun was high as Nopah danced and sang bird song after bird song. Kate watched in wonder as ash from the fire clung to the air before filtering to the ground like falling snowflakes. Singing louder, Nopah passed her a rawhide-covered drum and, with hand gestures, ordered her to play it. She knew it was a great honor to be asked to play his drum—and she sat, cross-legged, in the dirt and pounded. Two hours passed before the blessing of the land ended—and people gathered around for a feast under the shade of the awning. It was a shared communion, full of talk and hope. For the first time since arriving in the desert, Kate felt accepted—and realized she'd finally stopped sweating.

CPSIA information can be obtained
at www.ICGtesting.com
Printed in the USA
BVOW08s1634270118

506475BV00002B/266/P